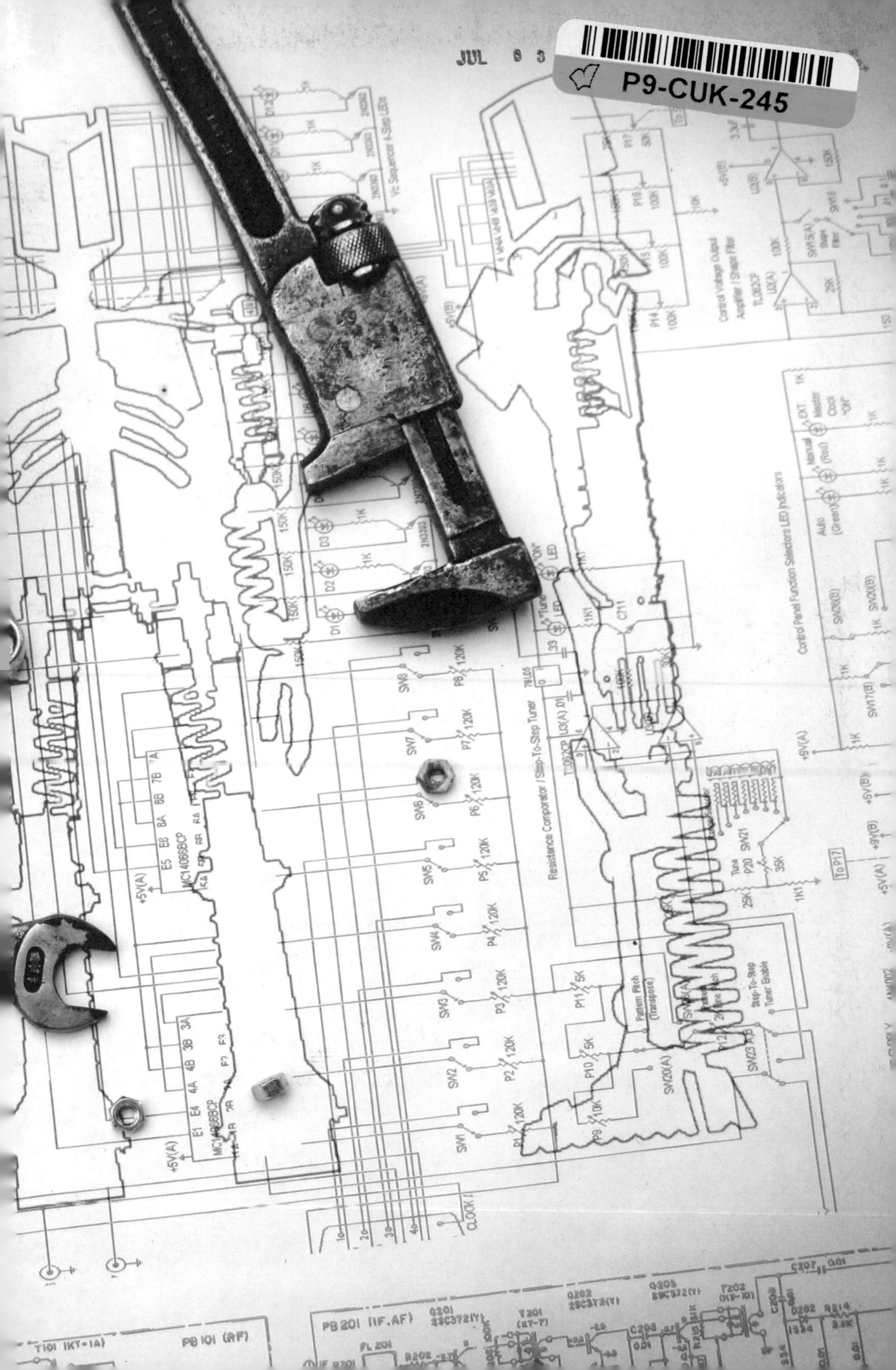
Resistence Comparator / Step-To-Step Tuner
Control Panel Function Selectors LED Indicators
Control Voltage Output Amplifier / Shape Filter
Vc Sequencer 4-Step LEDs
MC14066BCP
Pattern Pitch (Transpose)
Step-To-Step Tuner Enable
CLOCK
PB 201 (IF.AF)
PB 101 (RF)

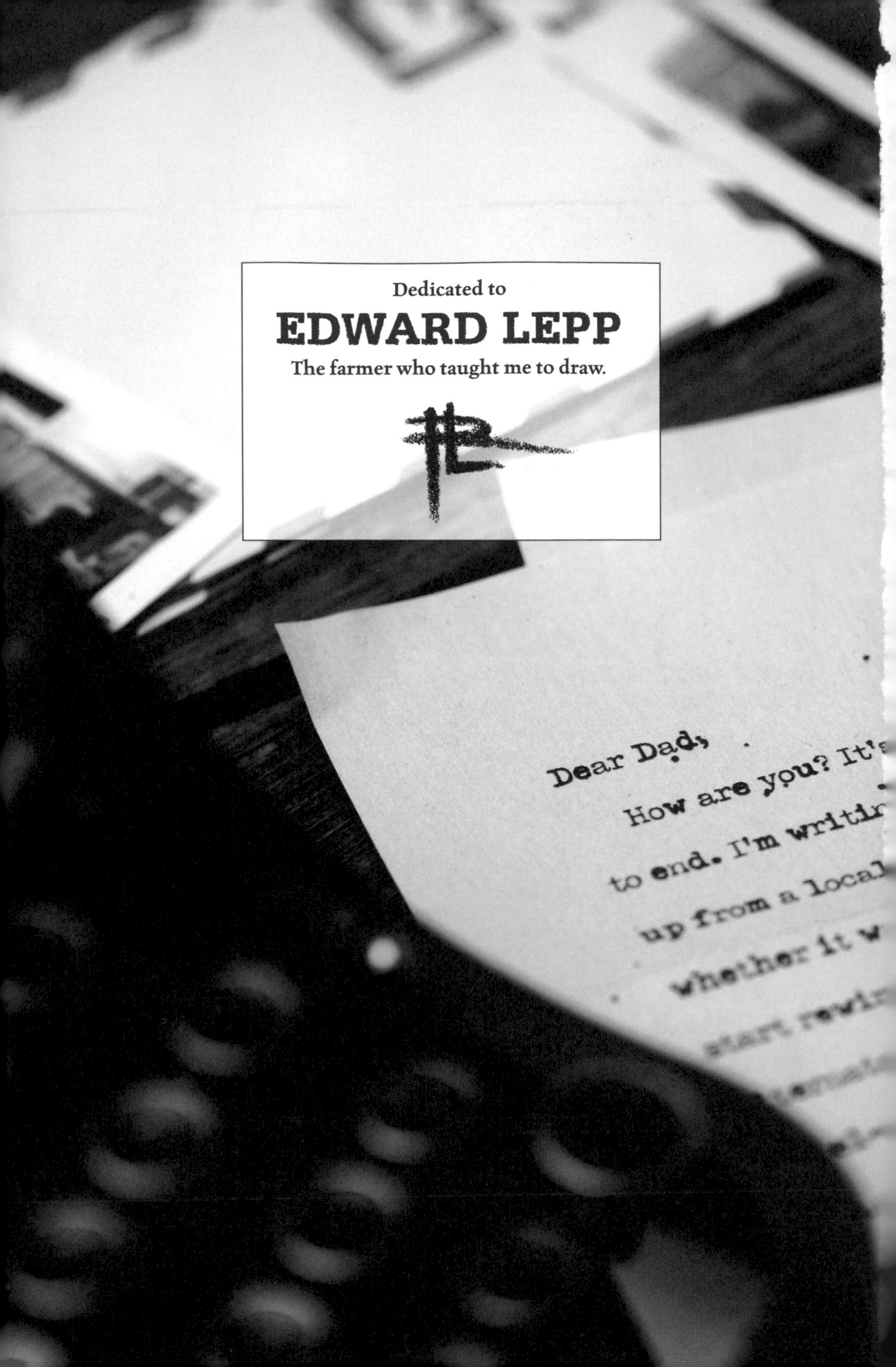
Dear Dad,

Dedicated to

EDWARD LEPP

The farmer who taught me to draw.

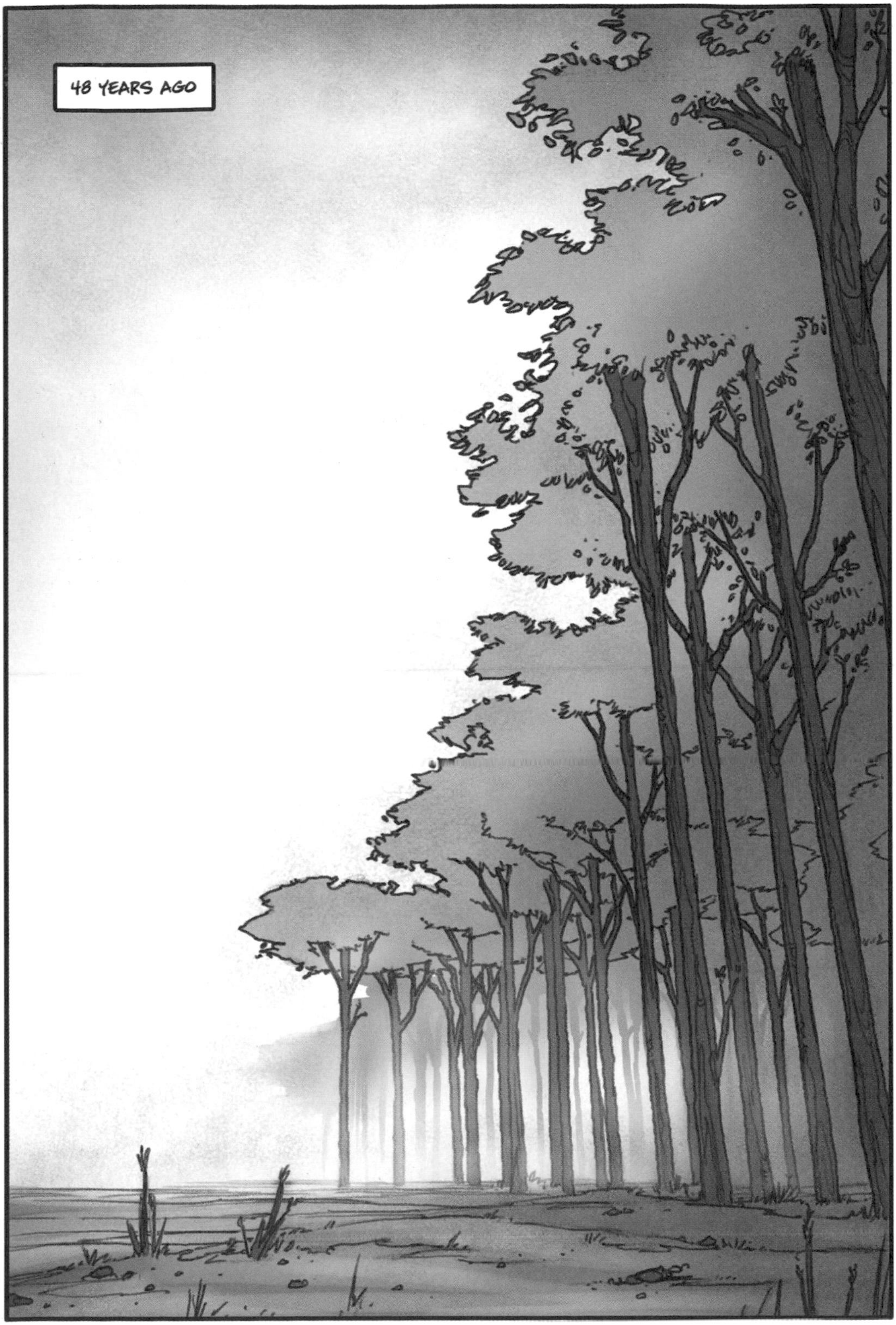
48 YEARS AGO

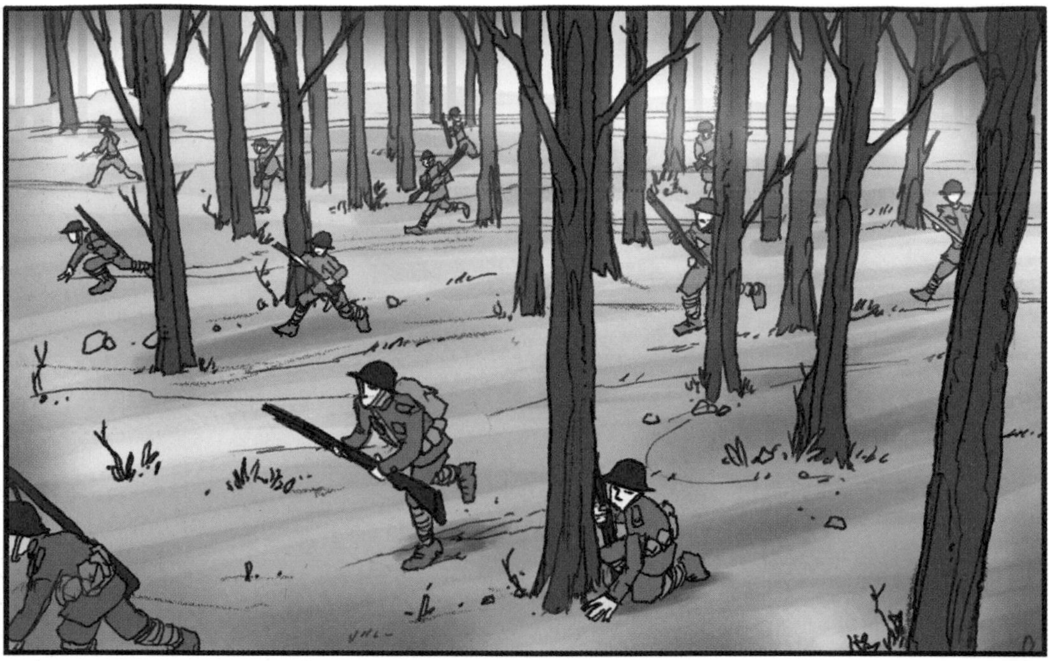

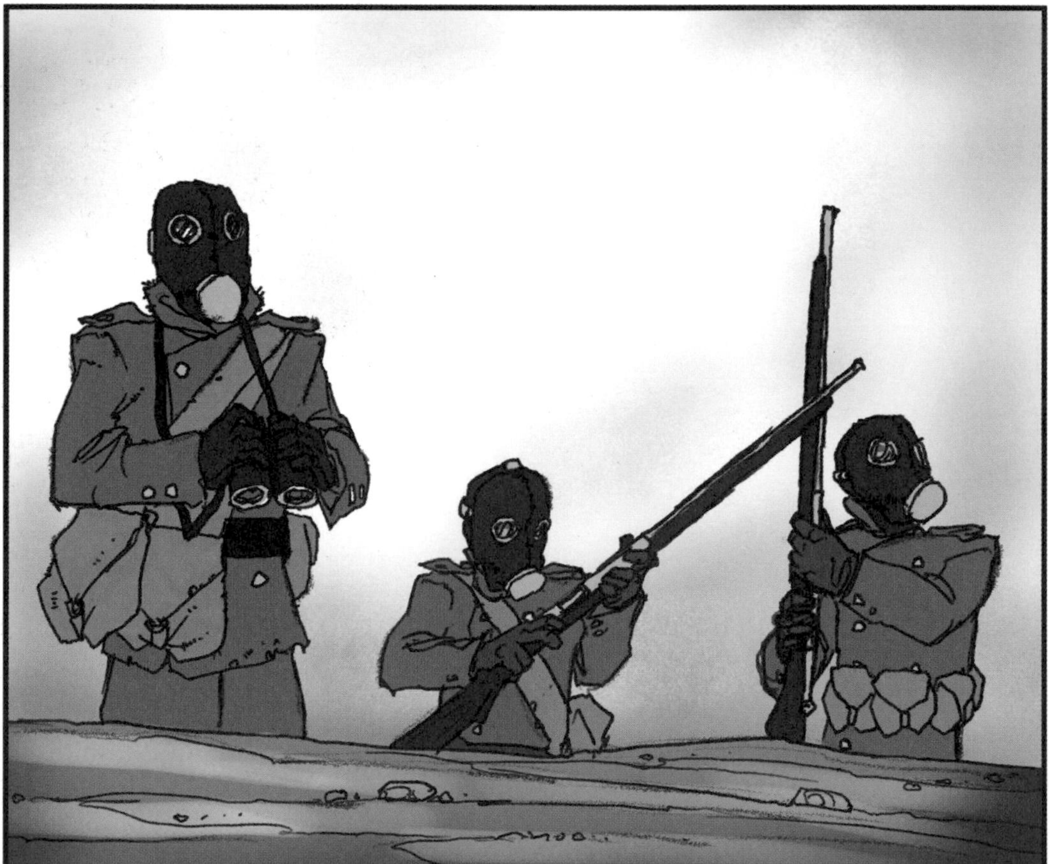

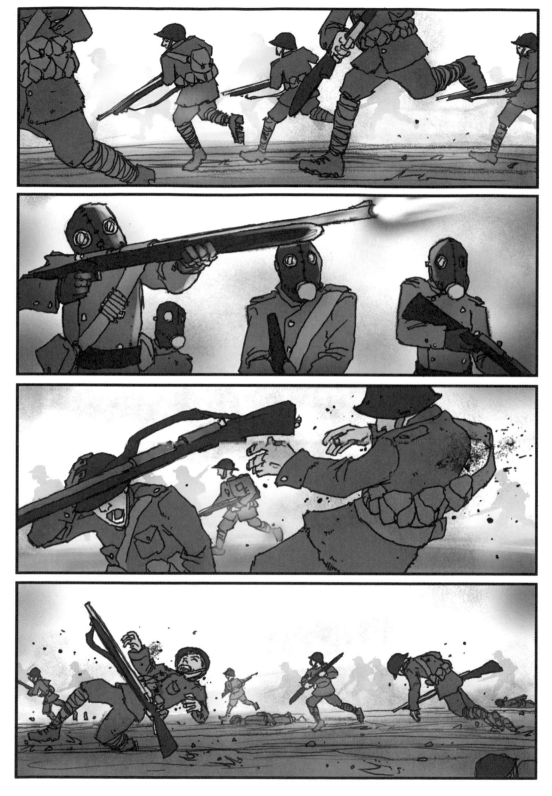

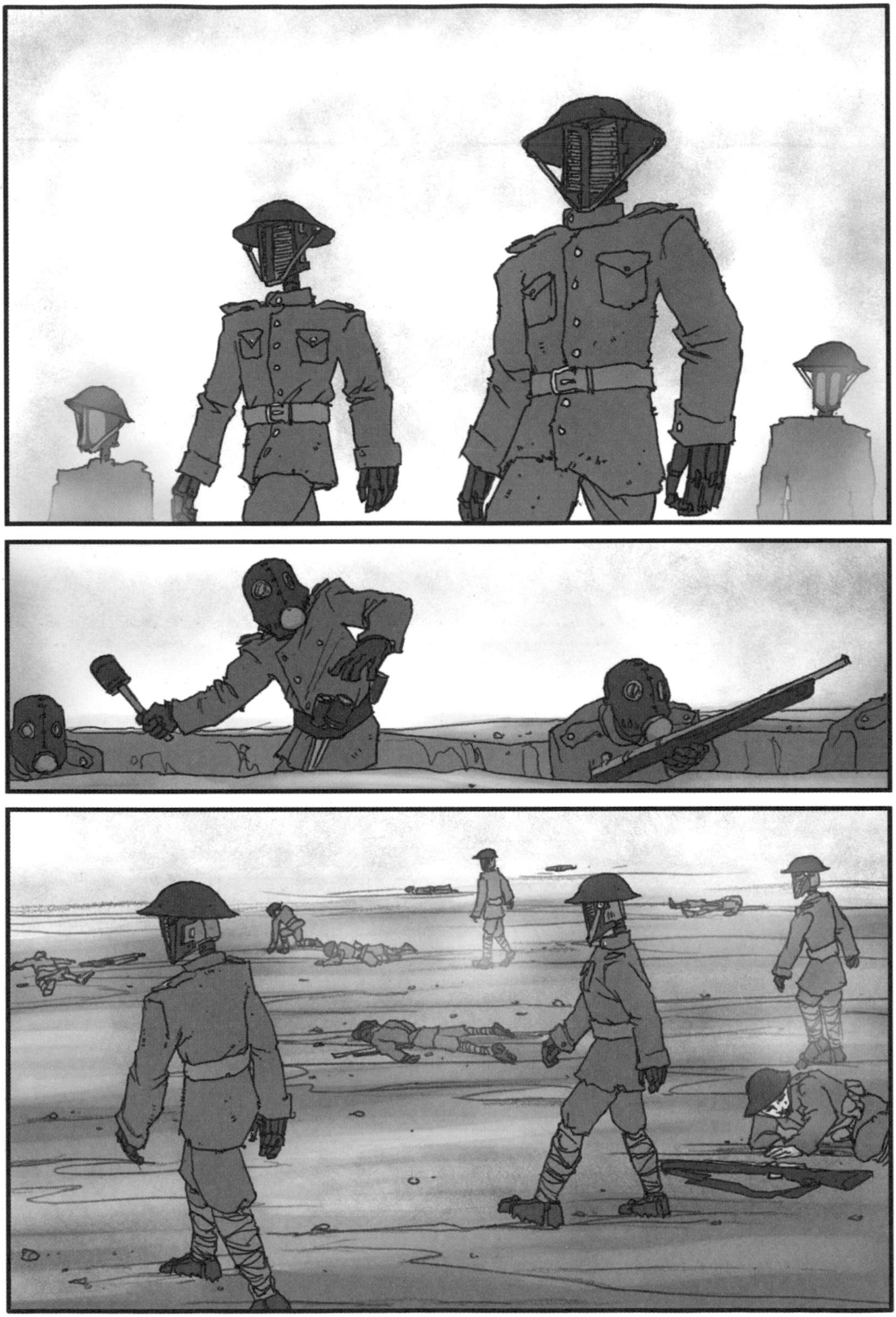

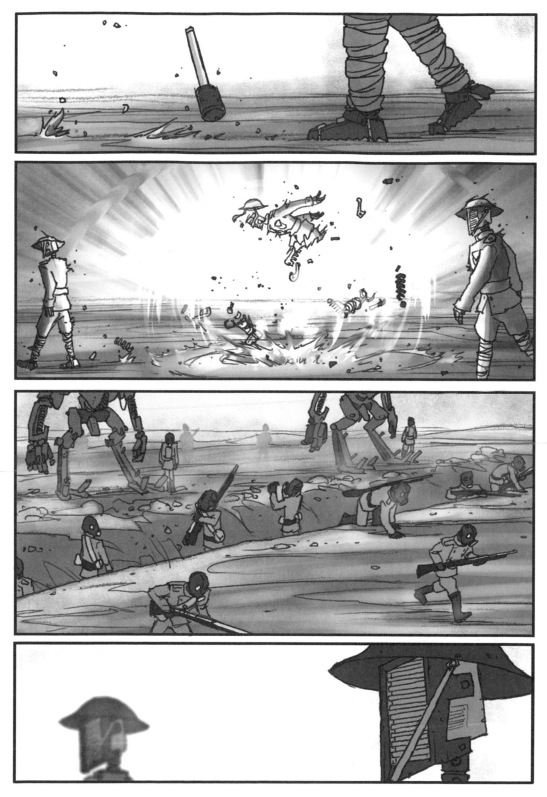

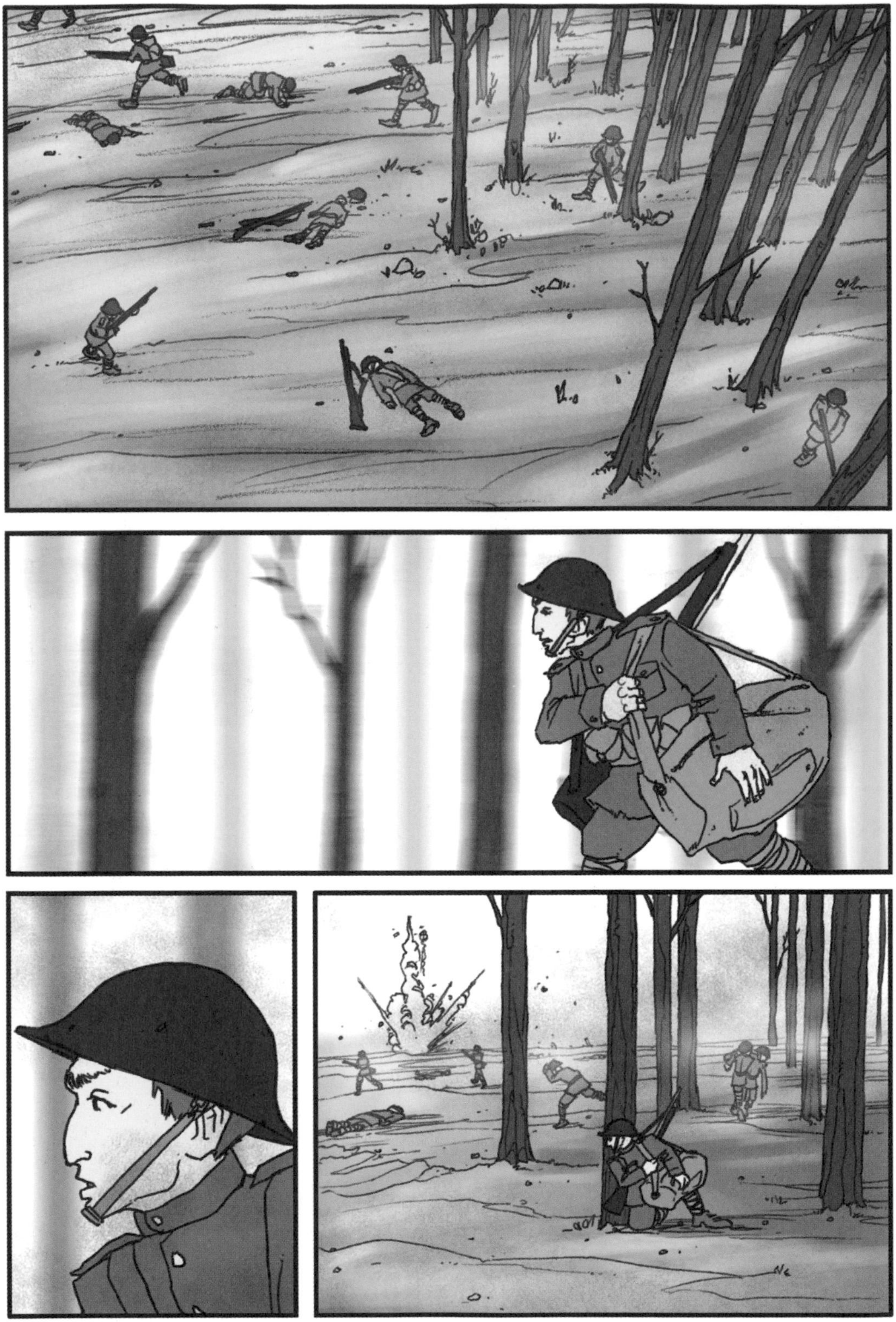

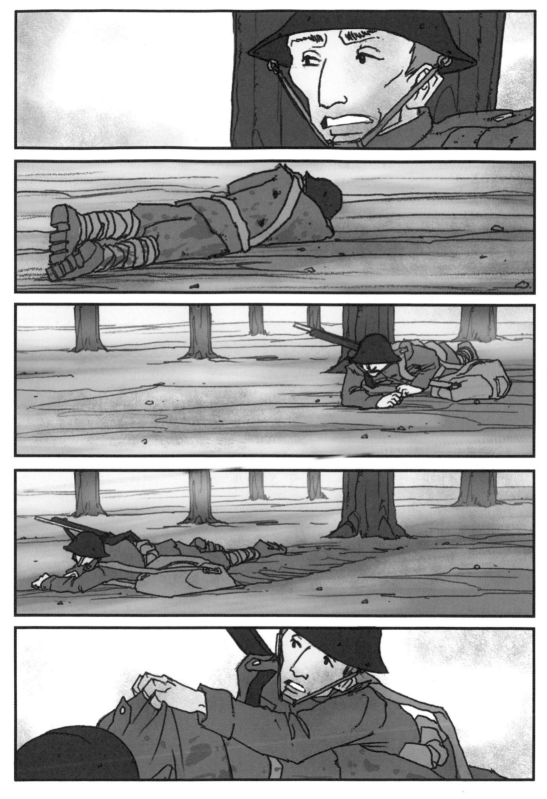

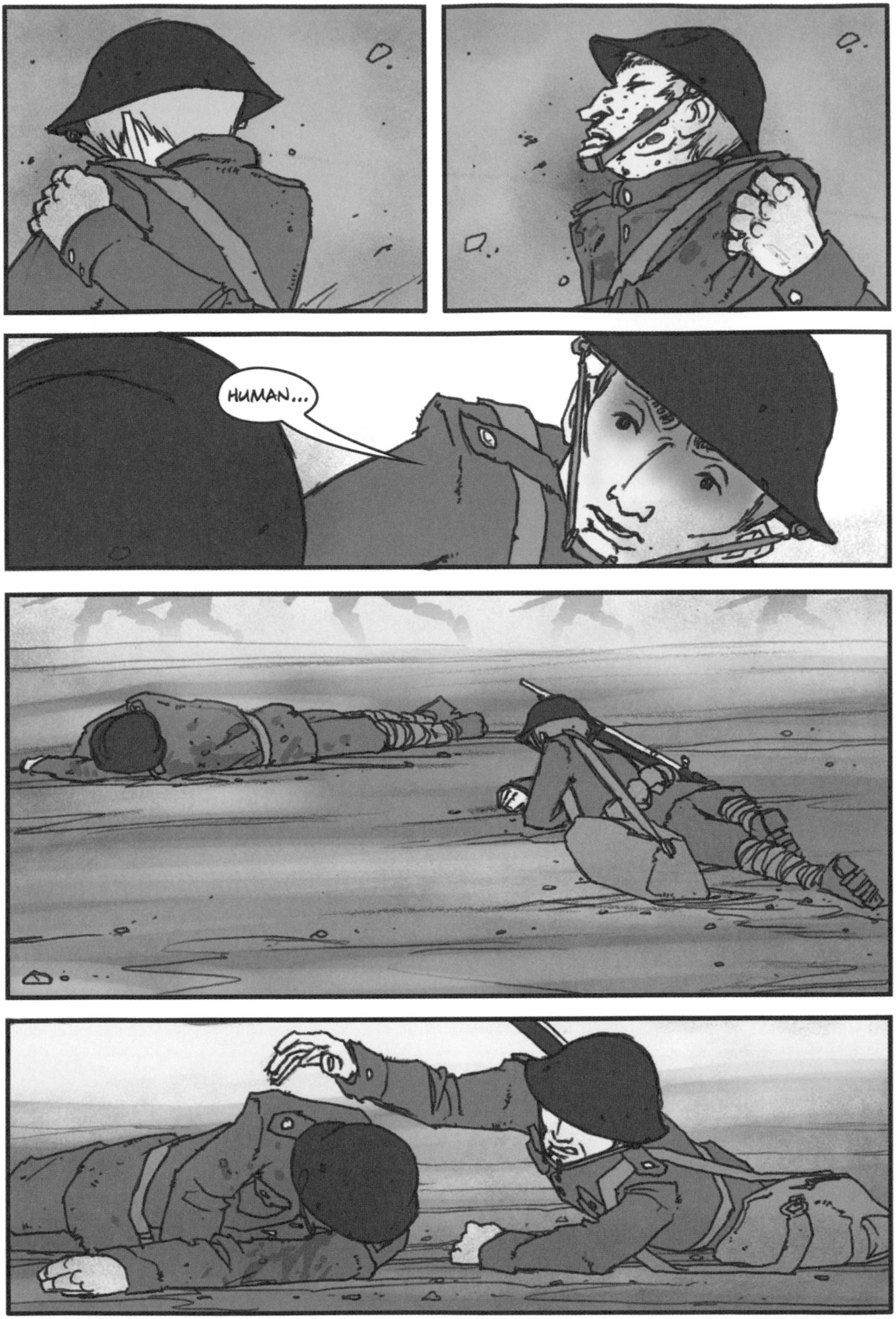
HUMAN...

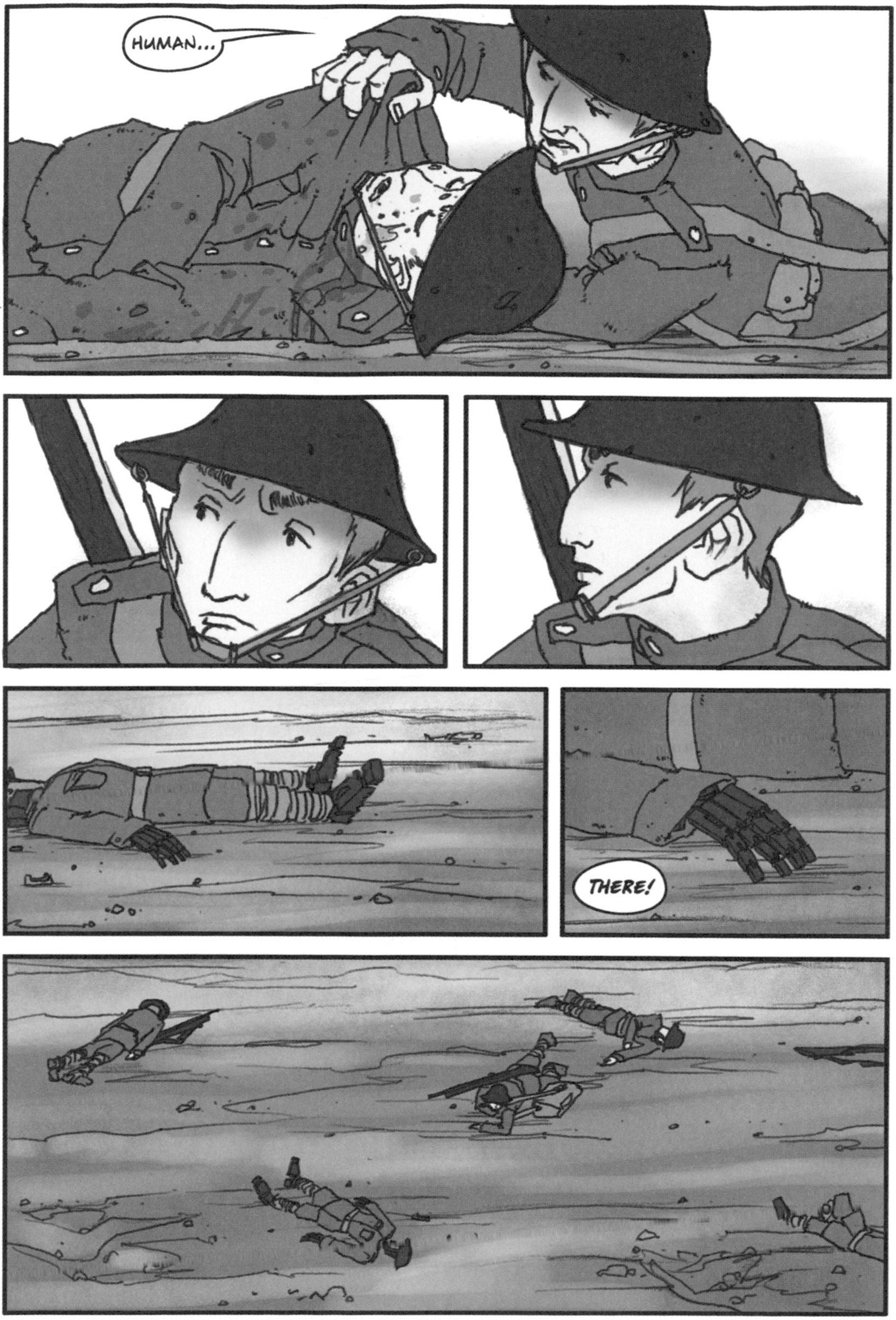
HUMAN...
THERE!

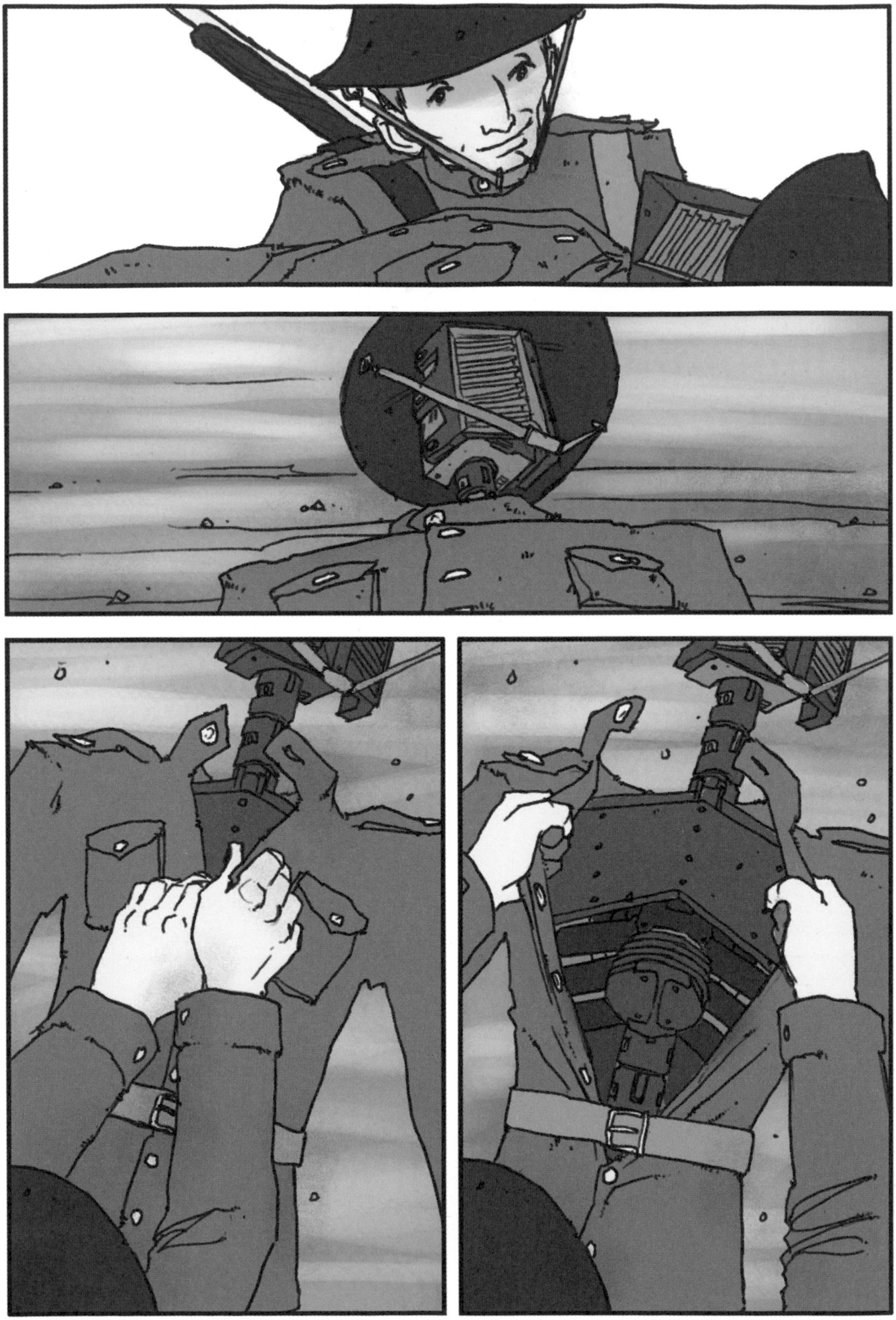

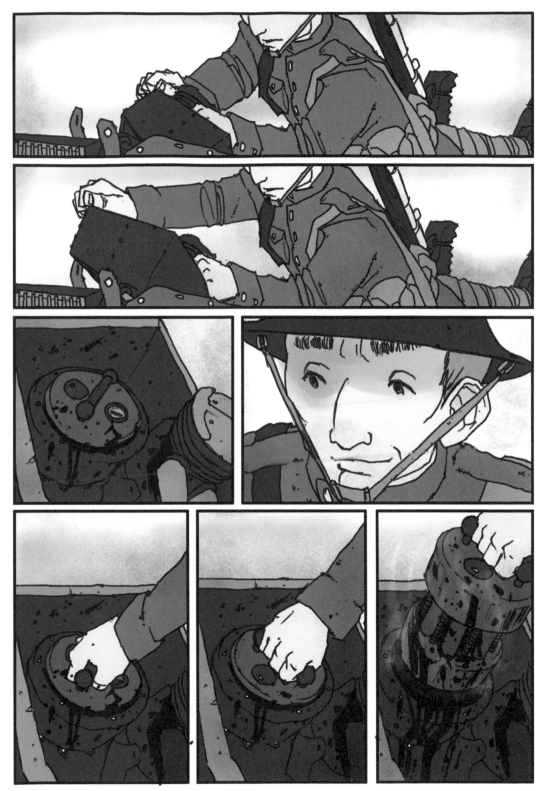

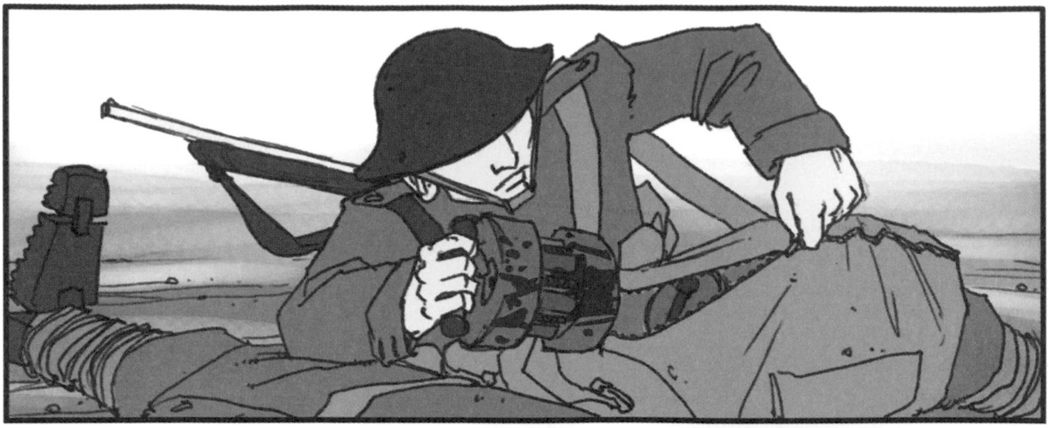

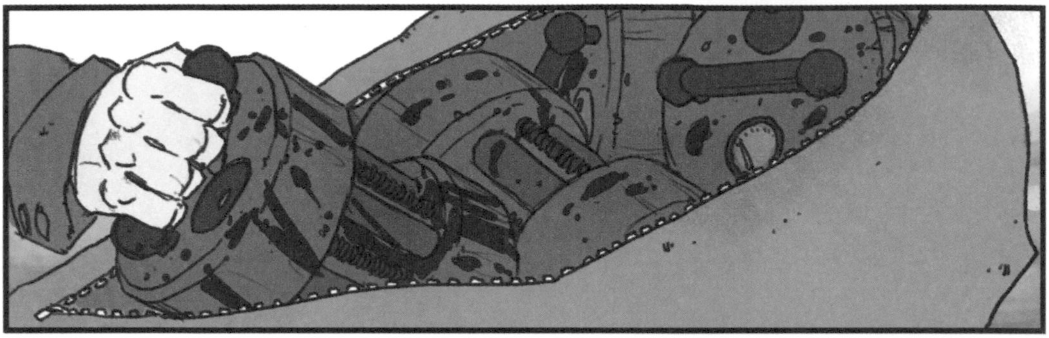

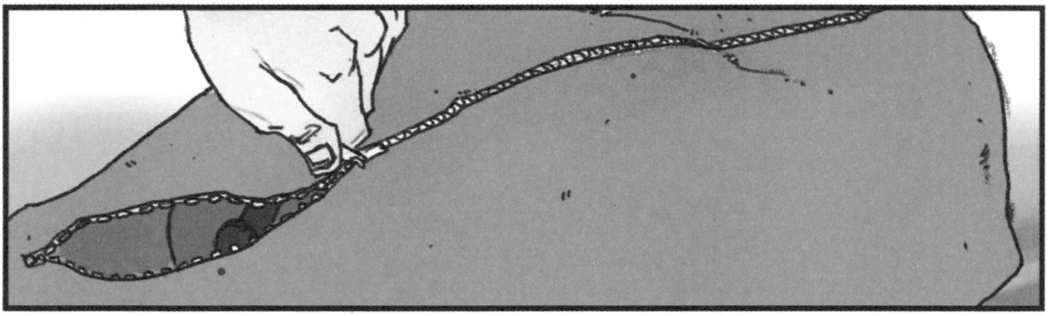

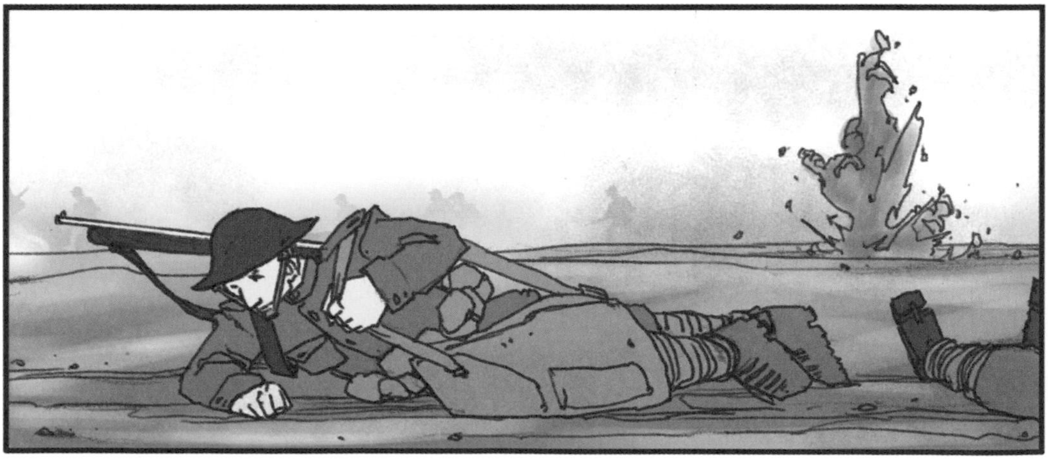

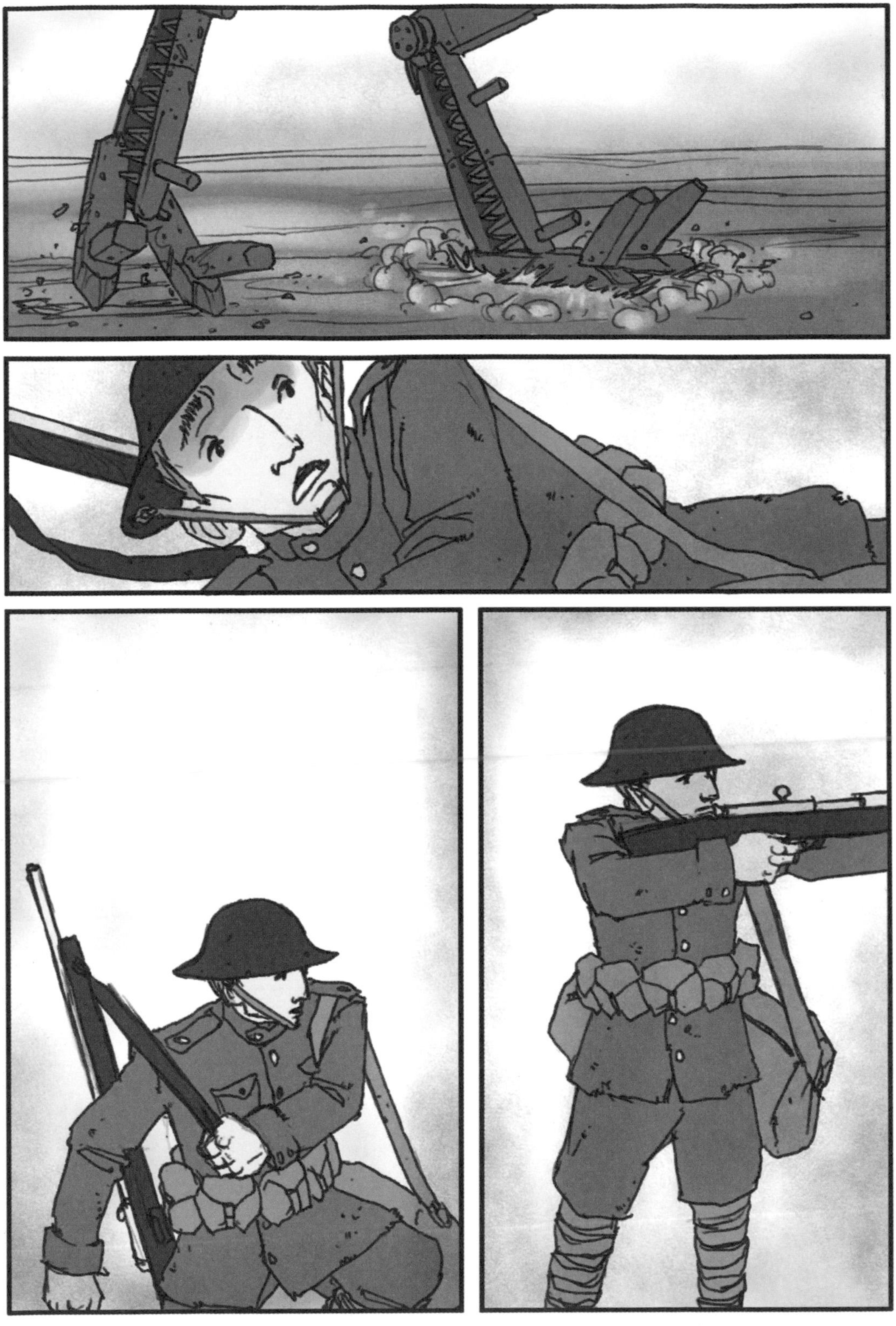

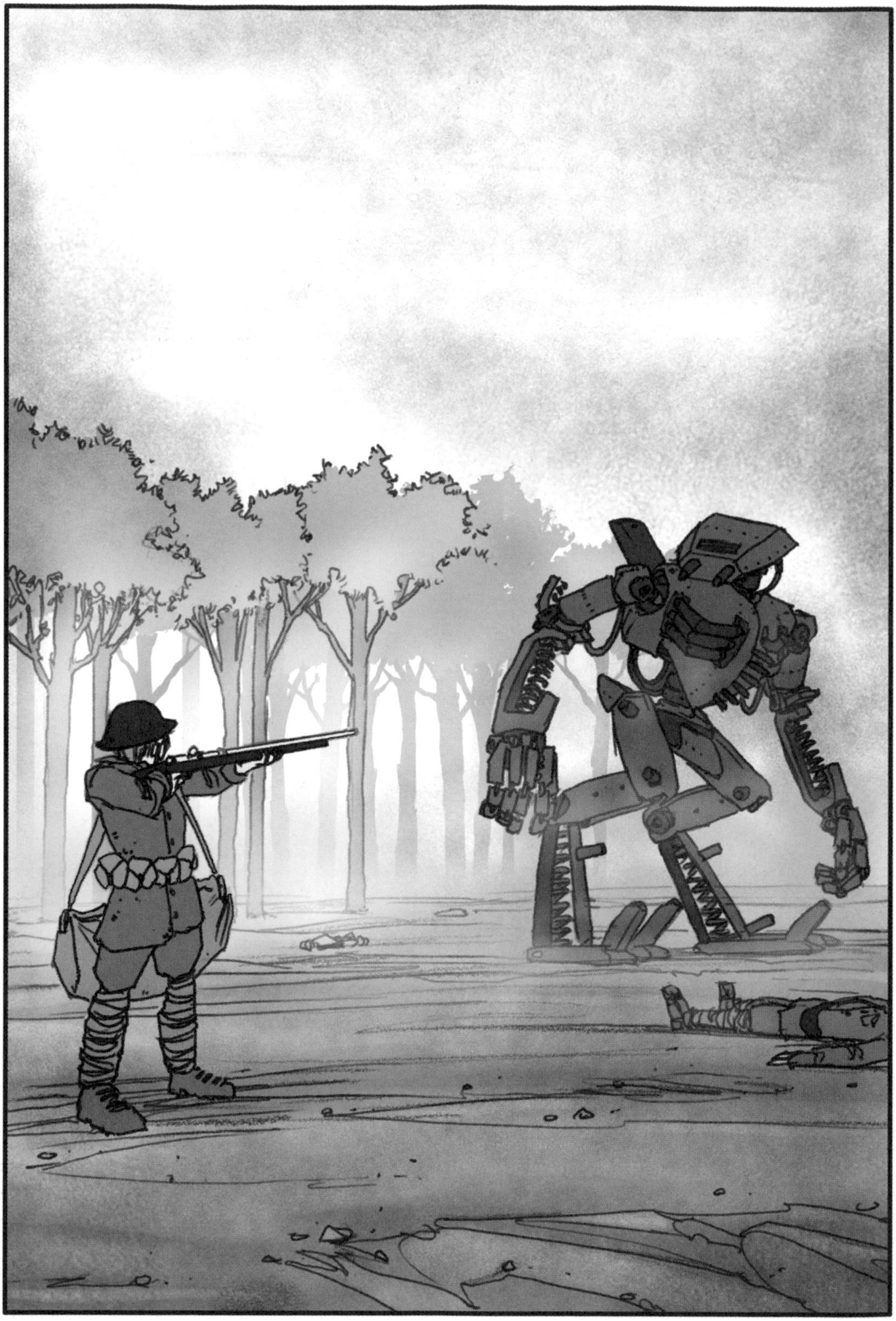

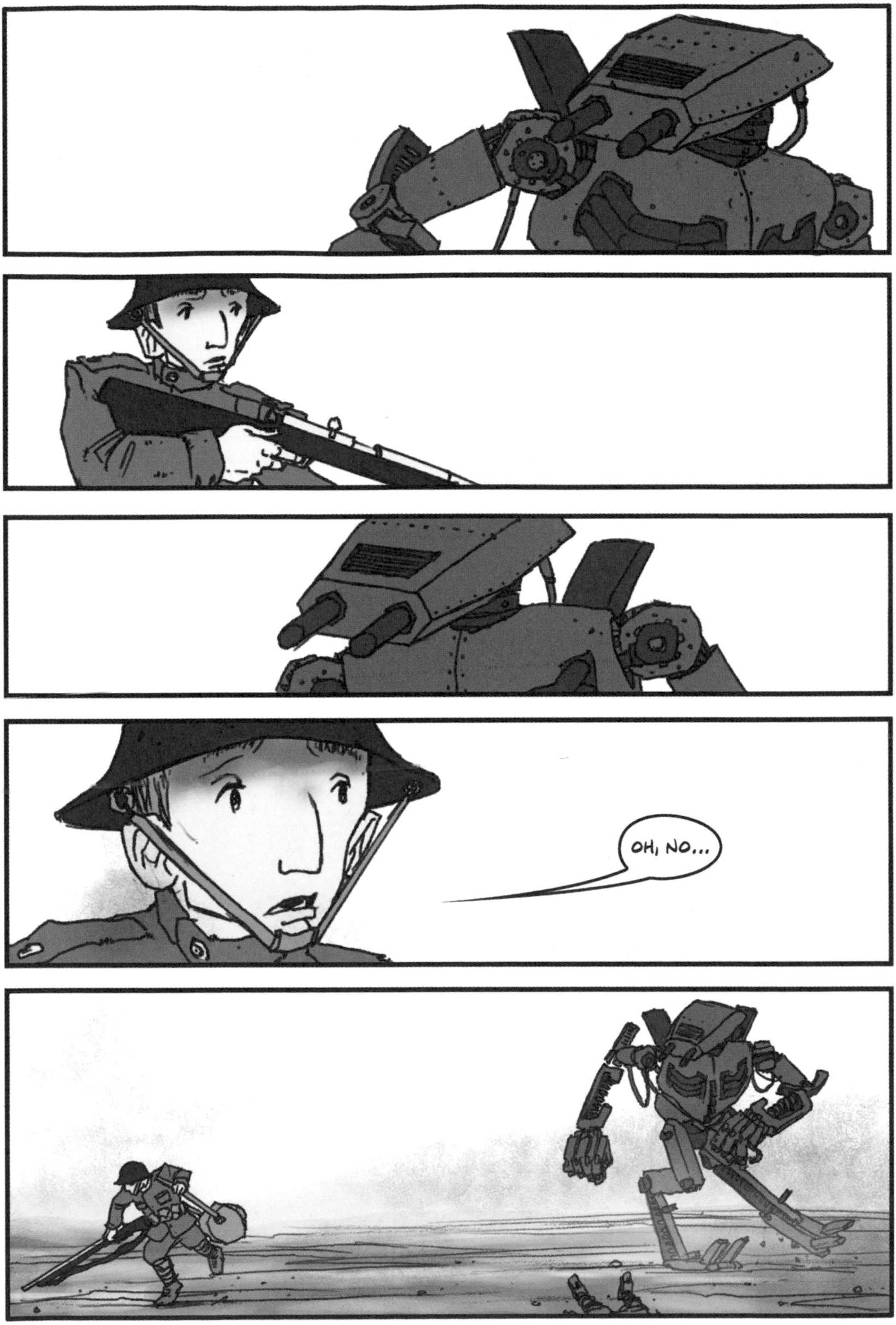
OH, NO...

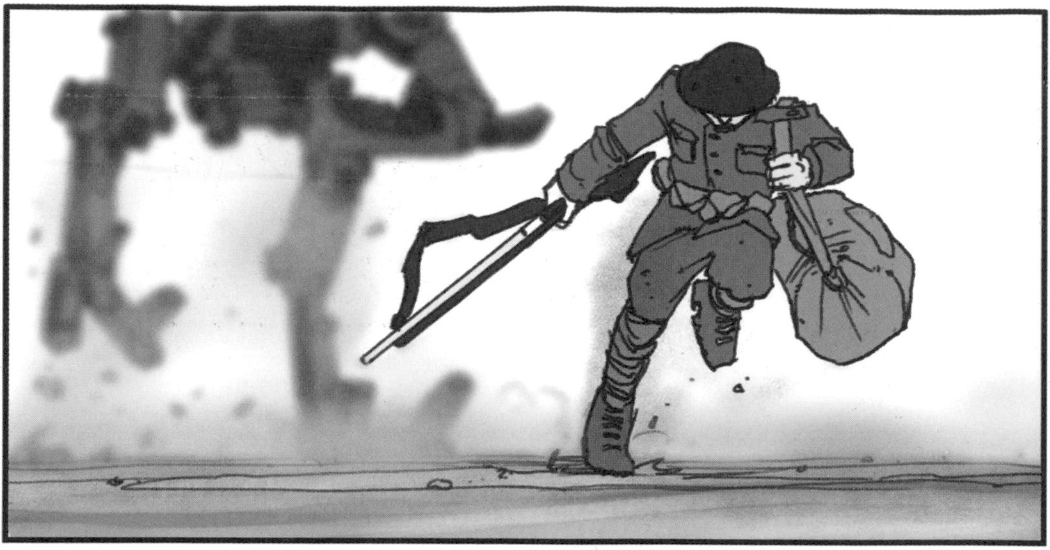

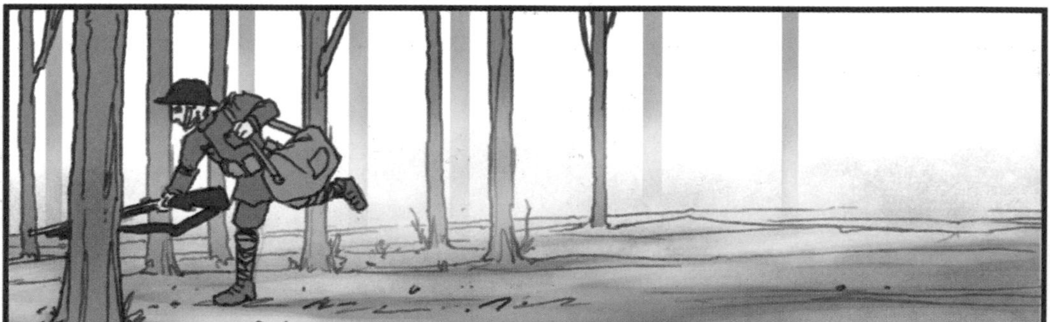

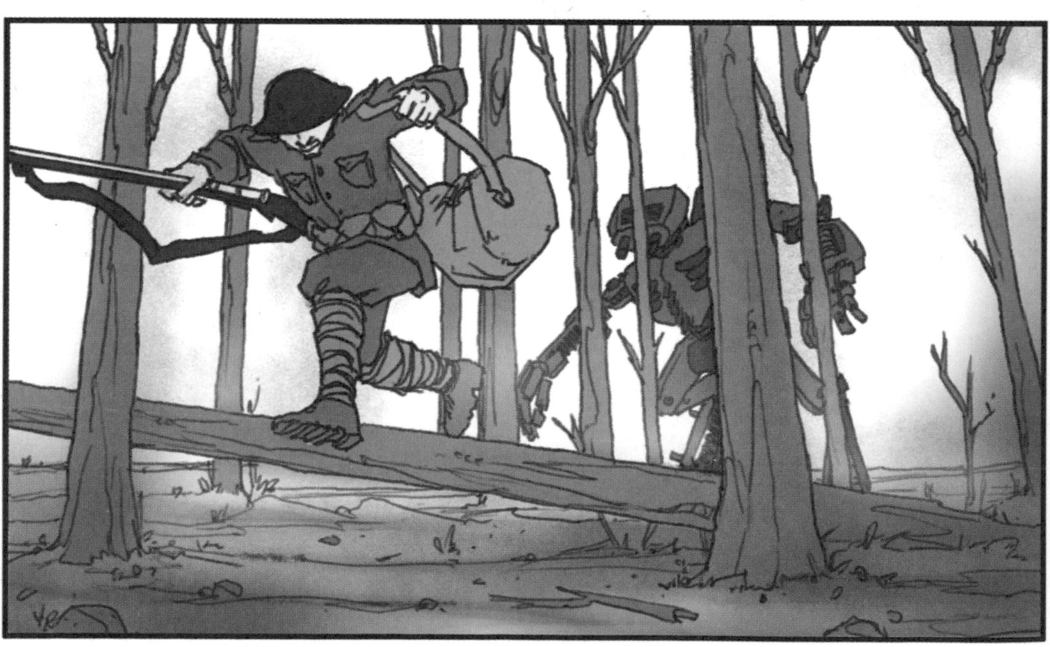

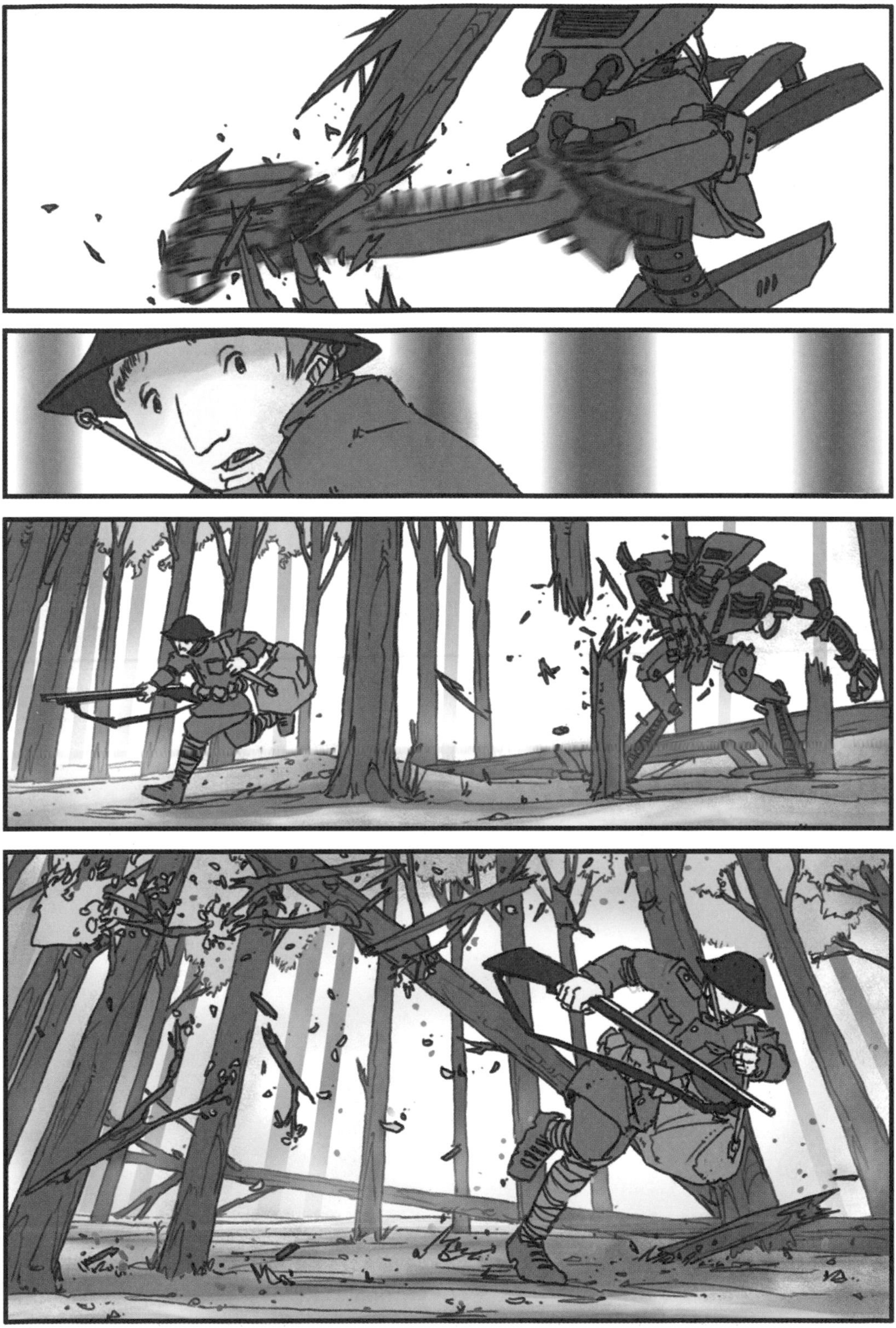

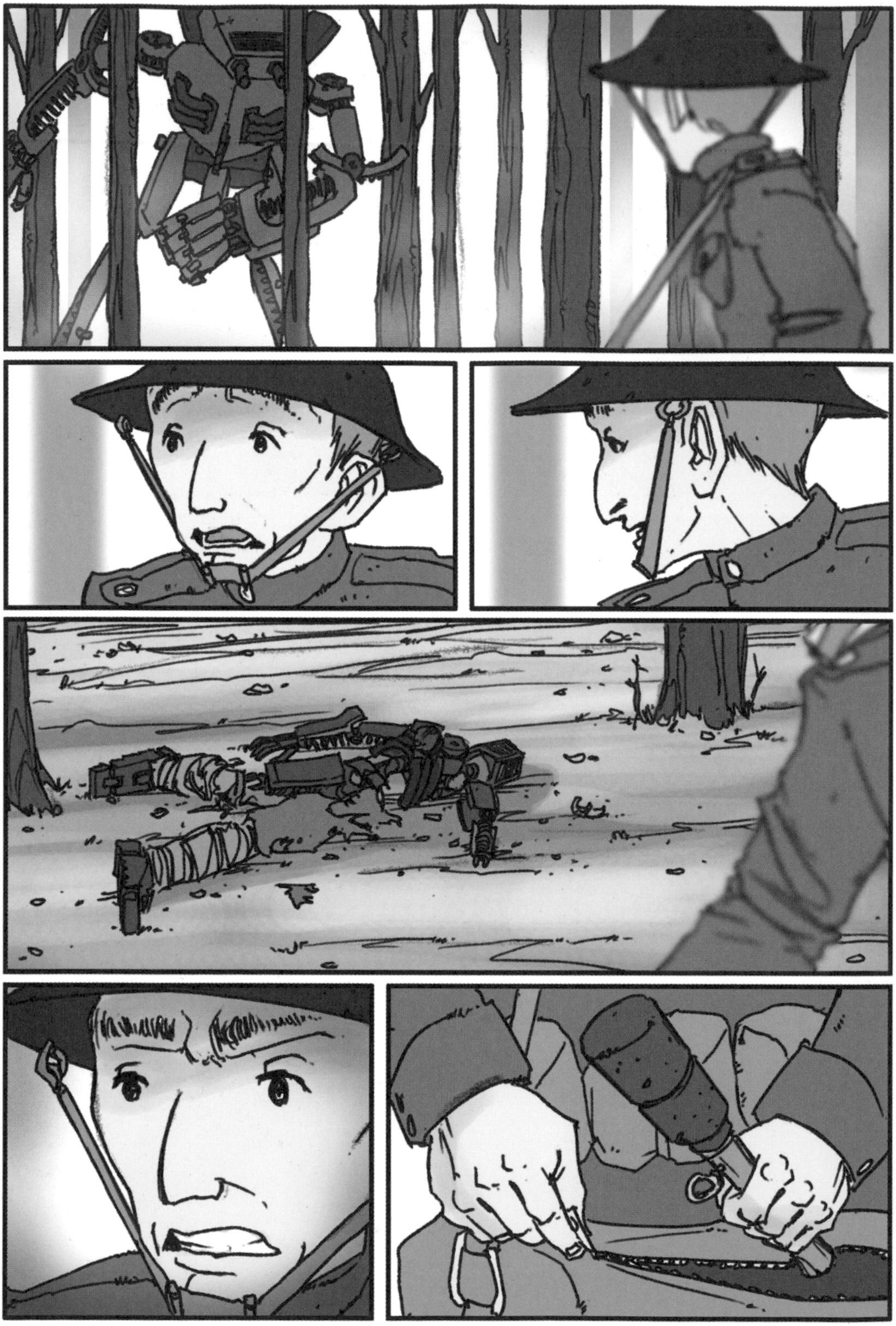

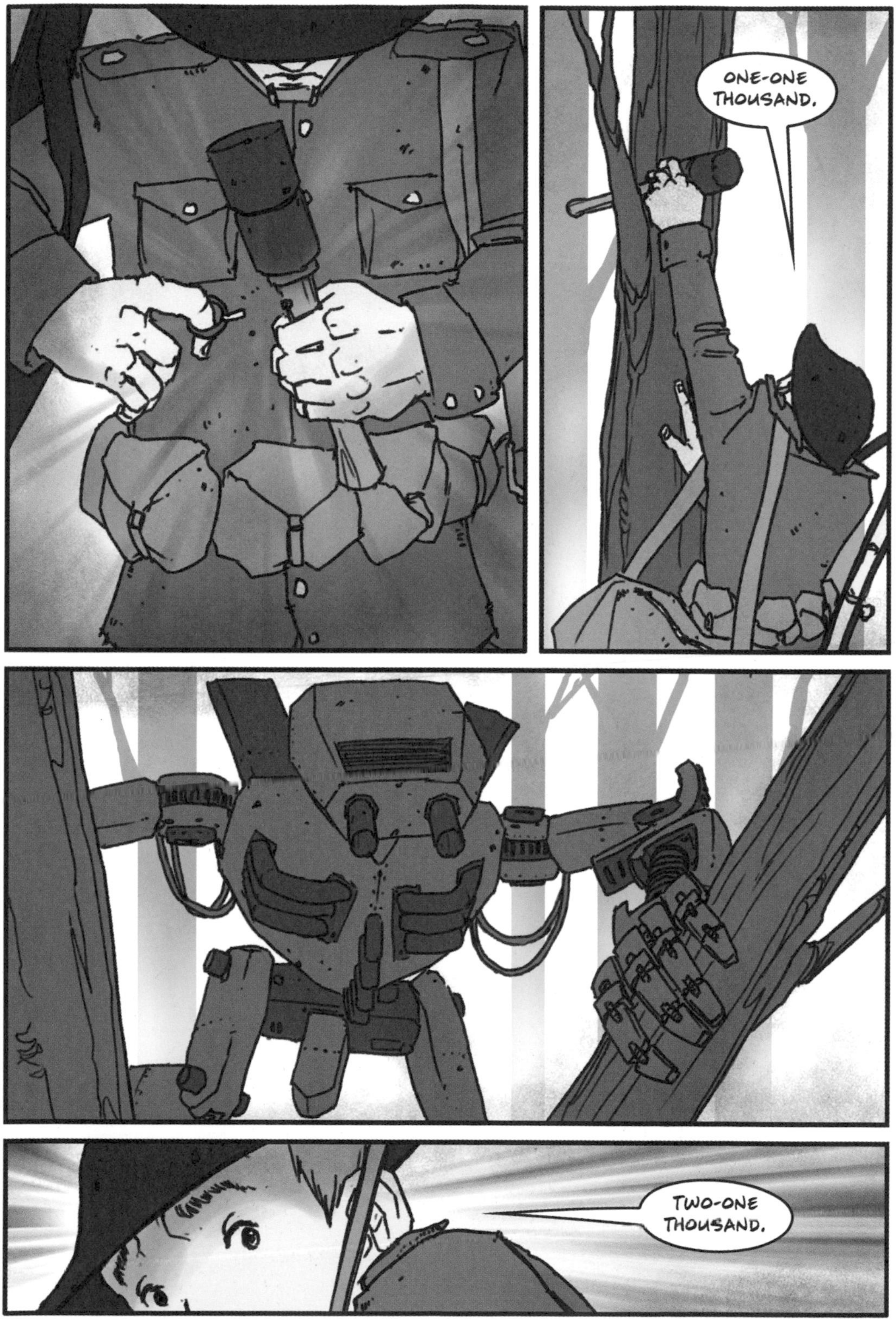
ONE-ONE THOUSAND.
TWO-ONE THOUSAND.

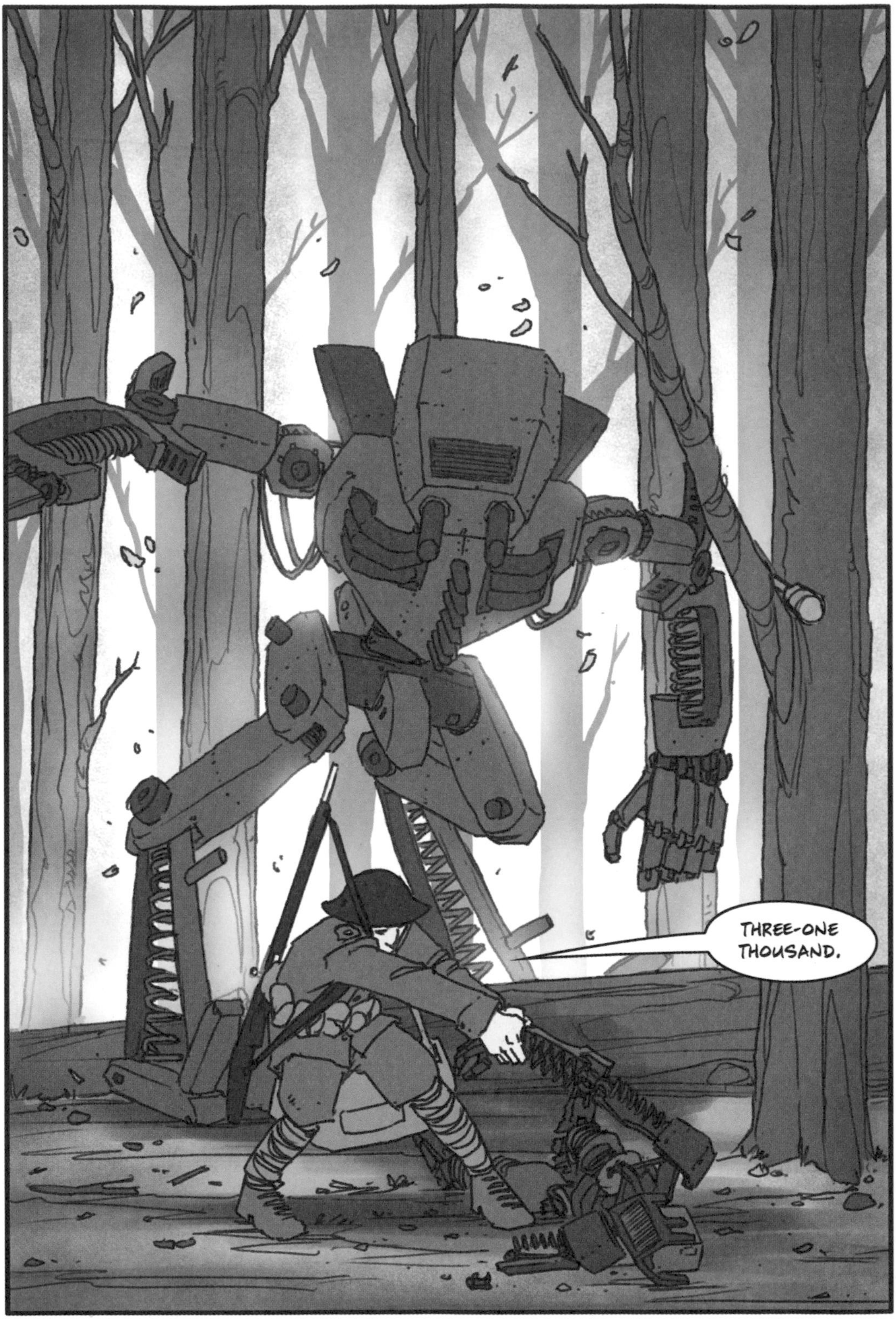
THREE-ONE THOUSAND.

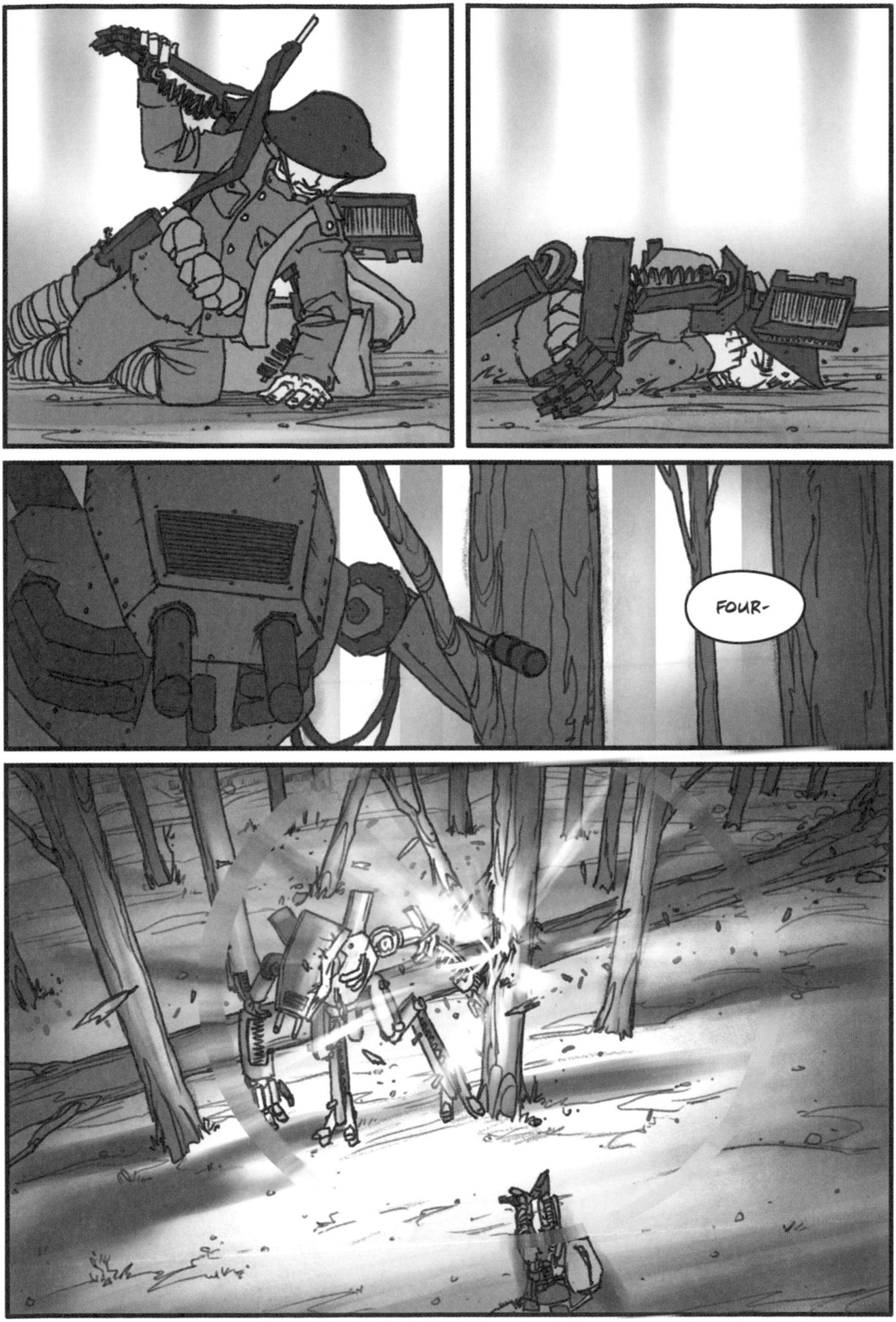
FOUR-

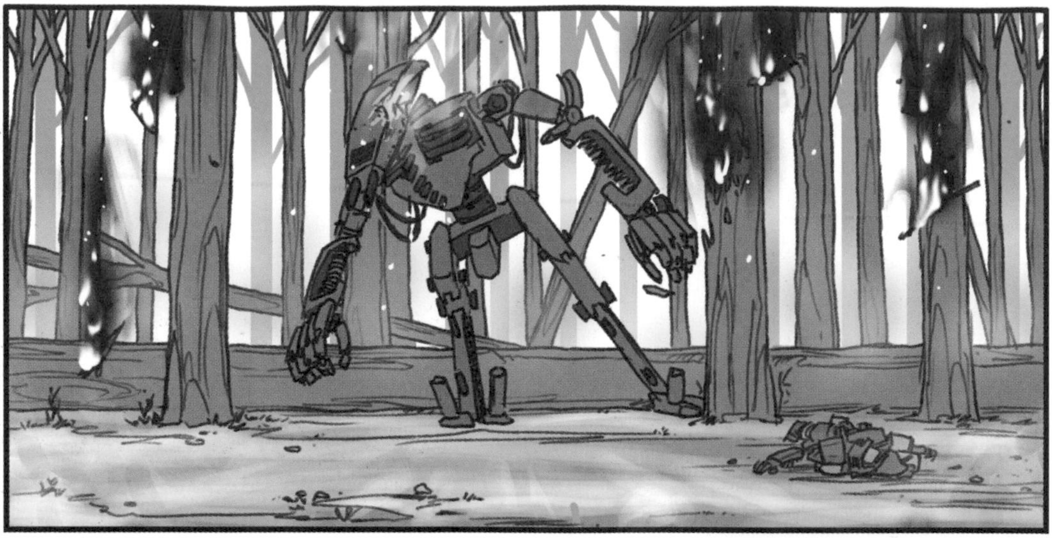

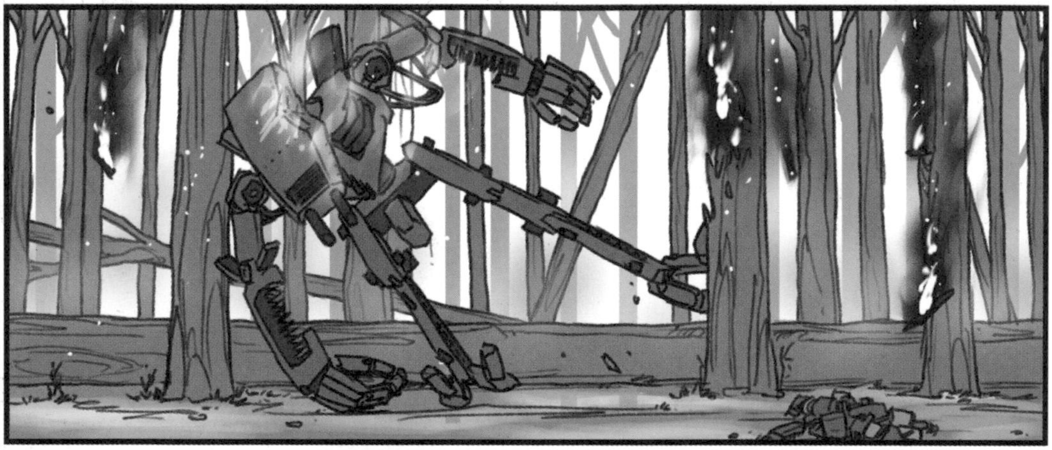

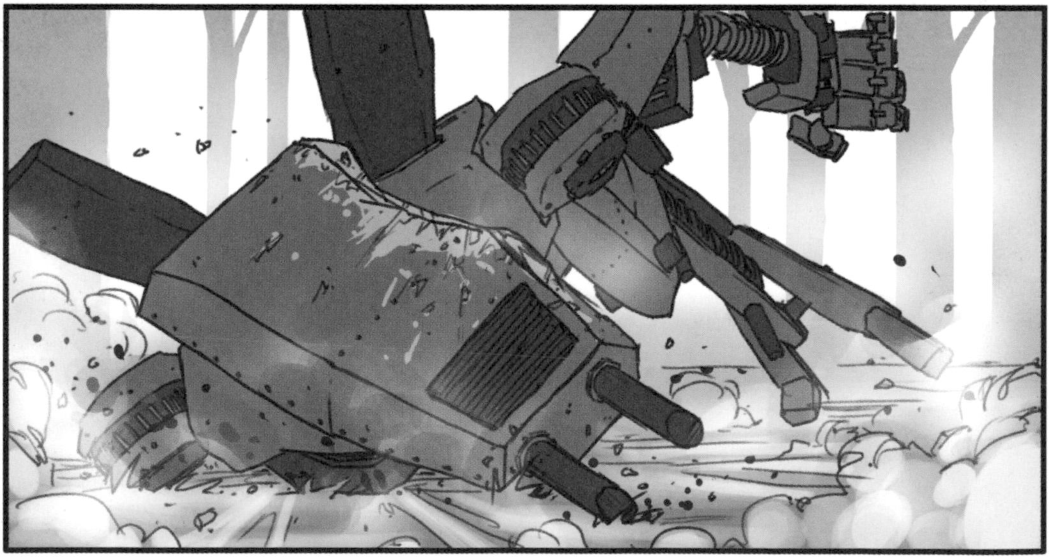

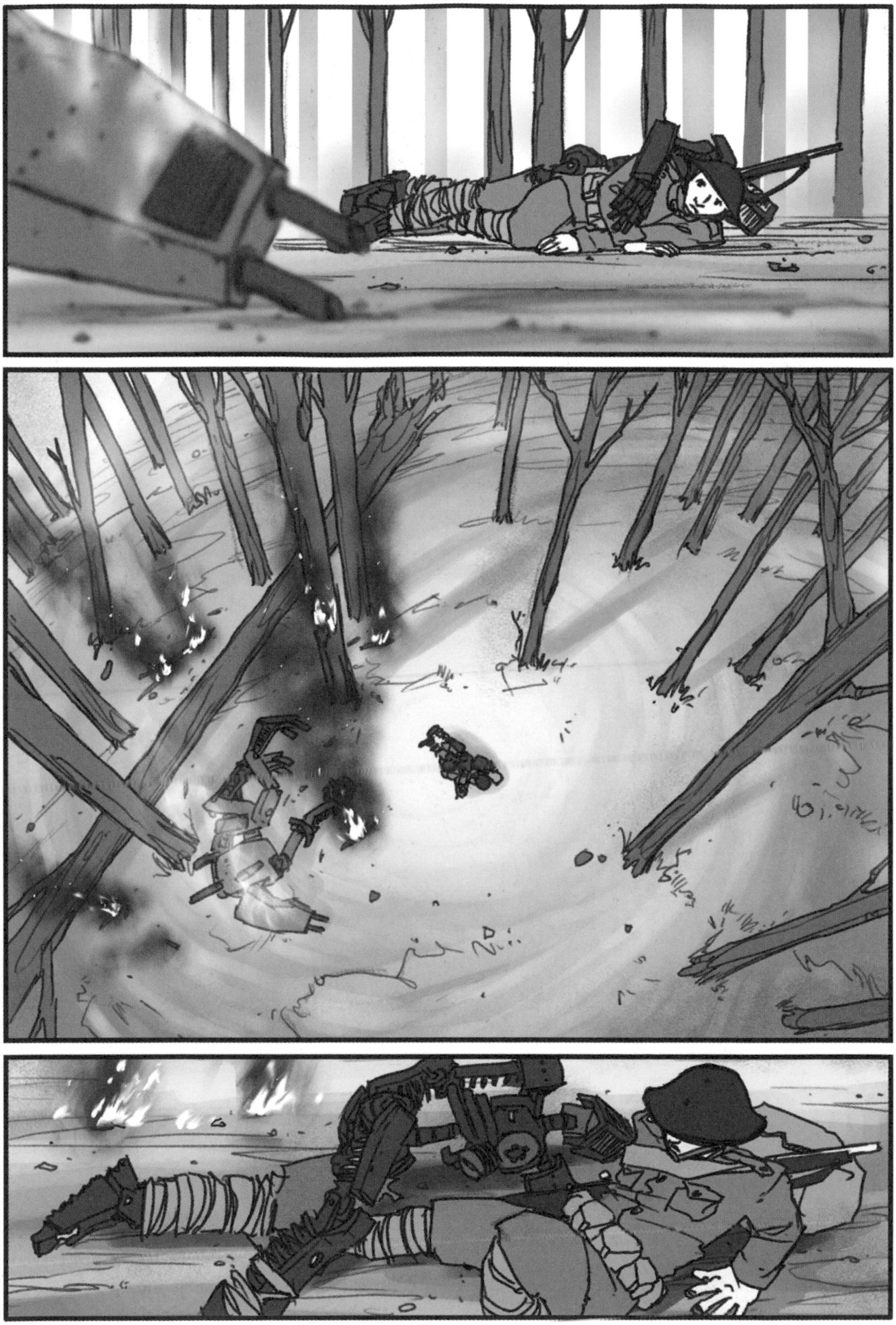

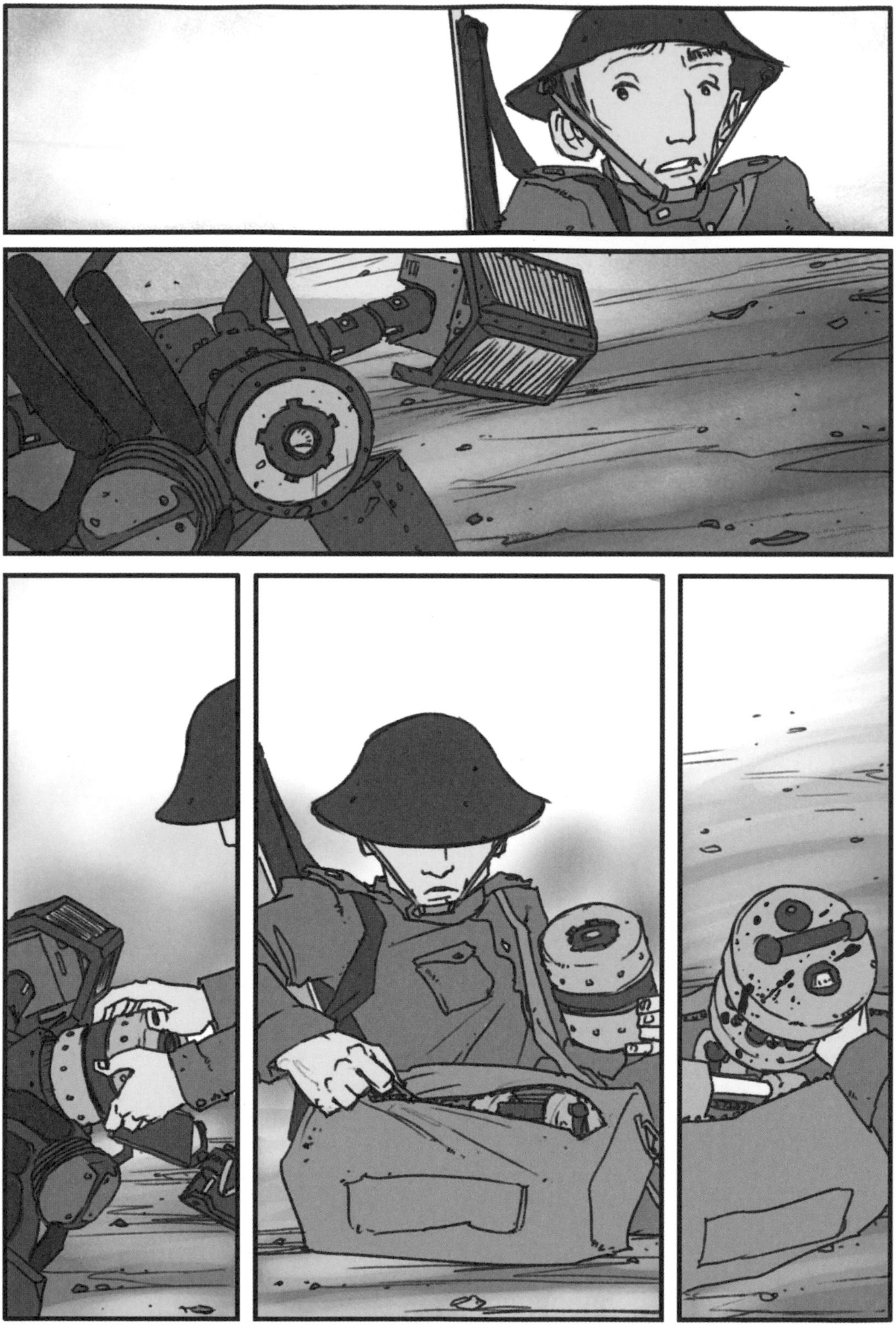

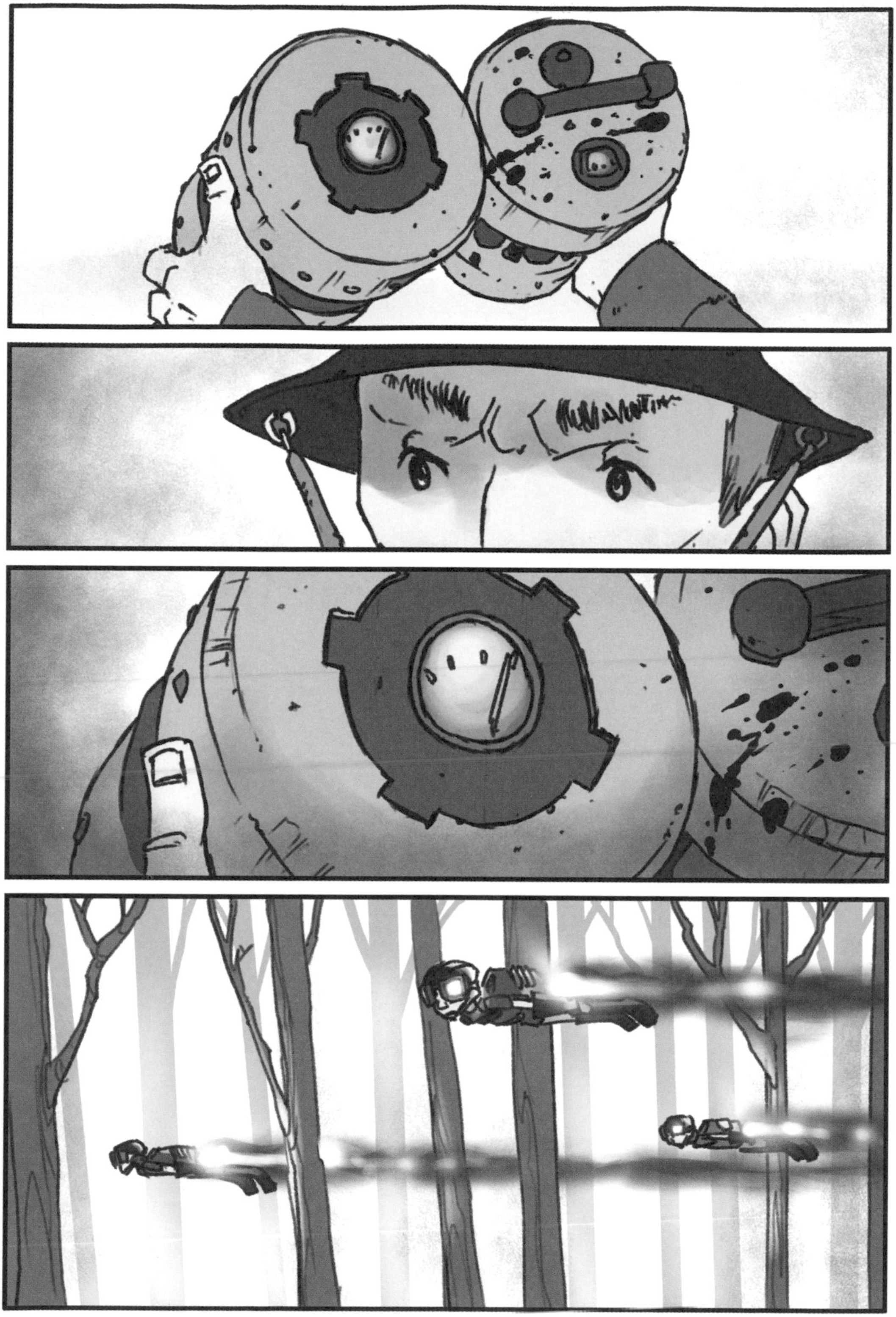

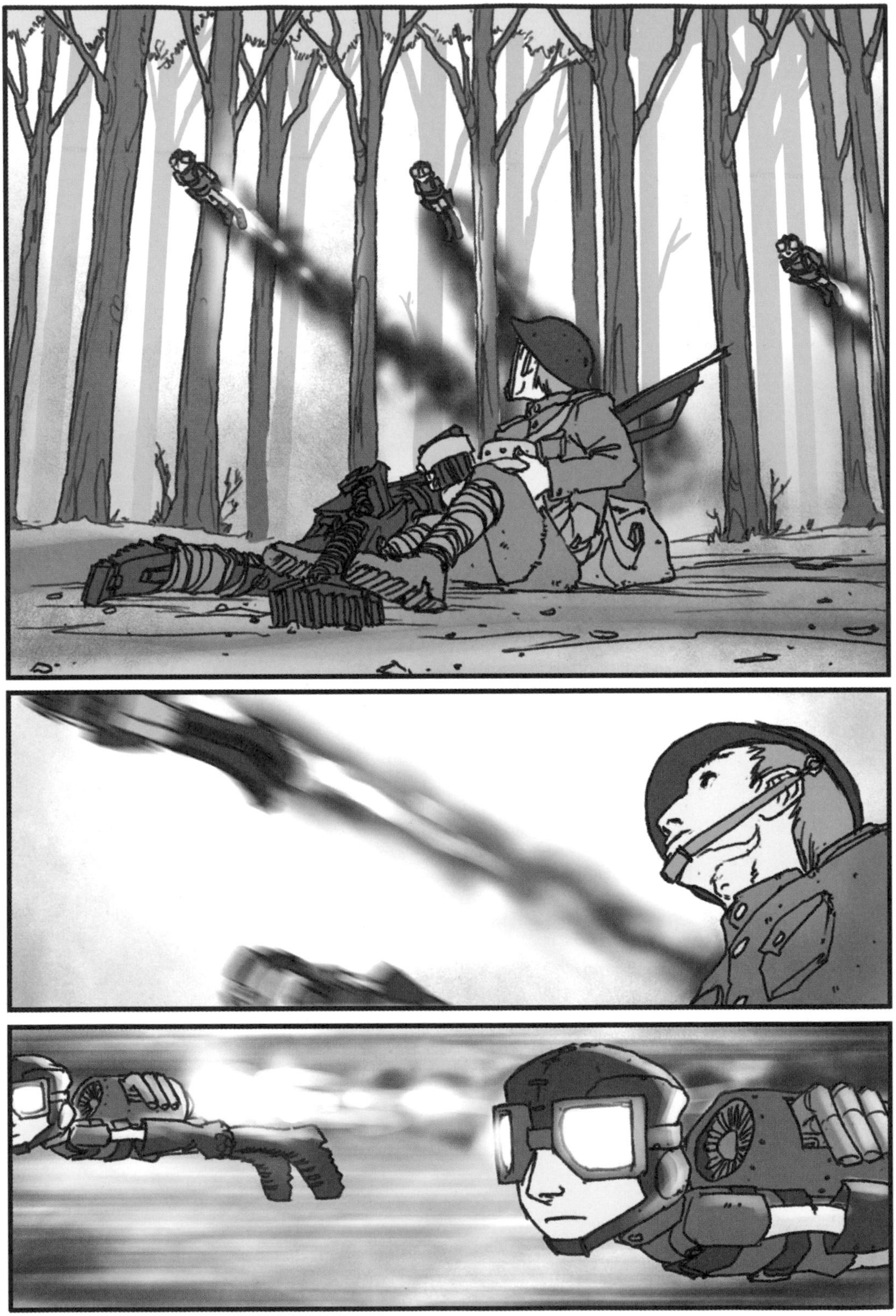

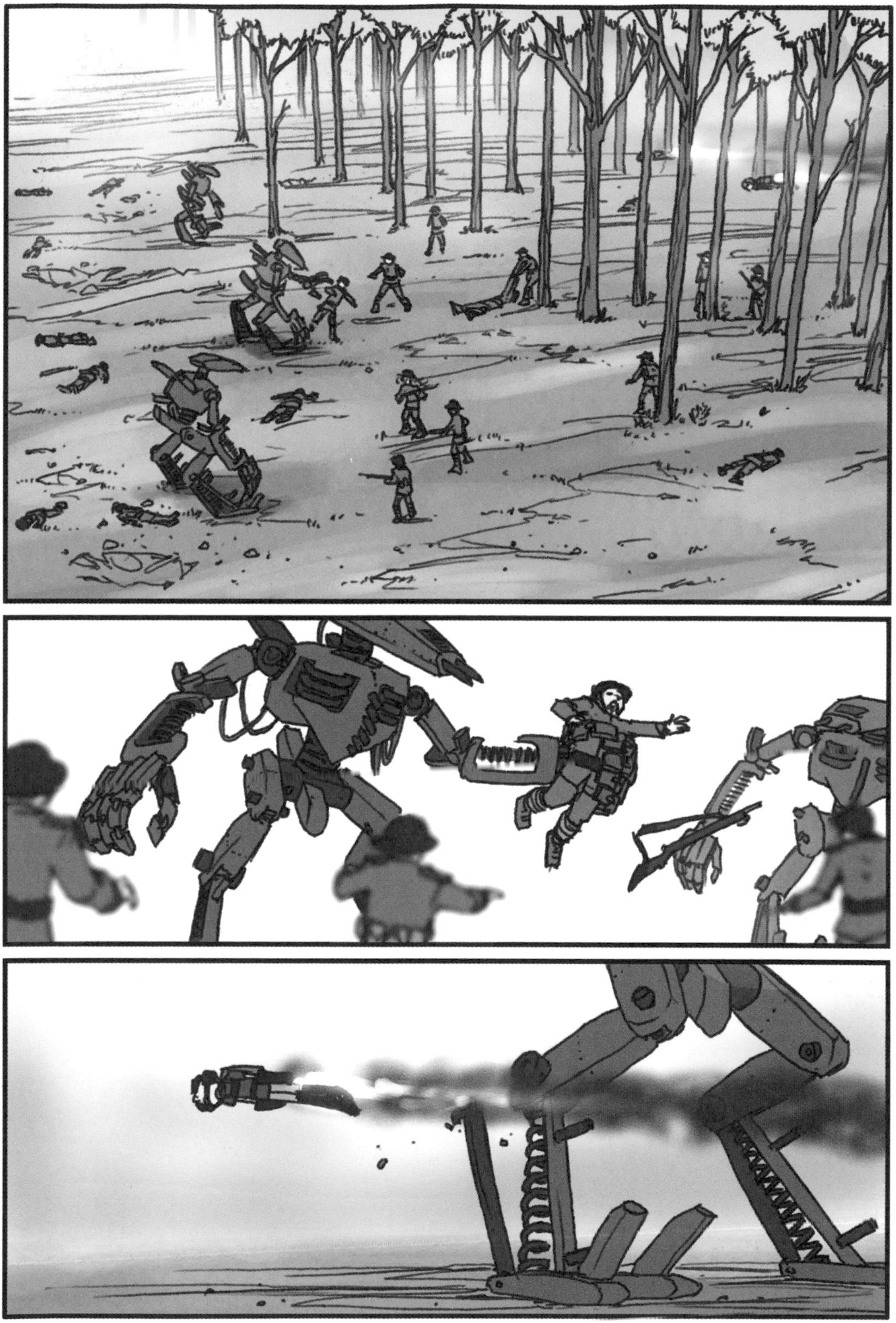

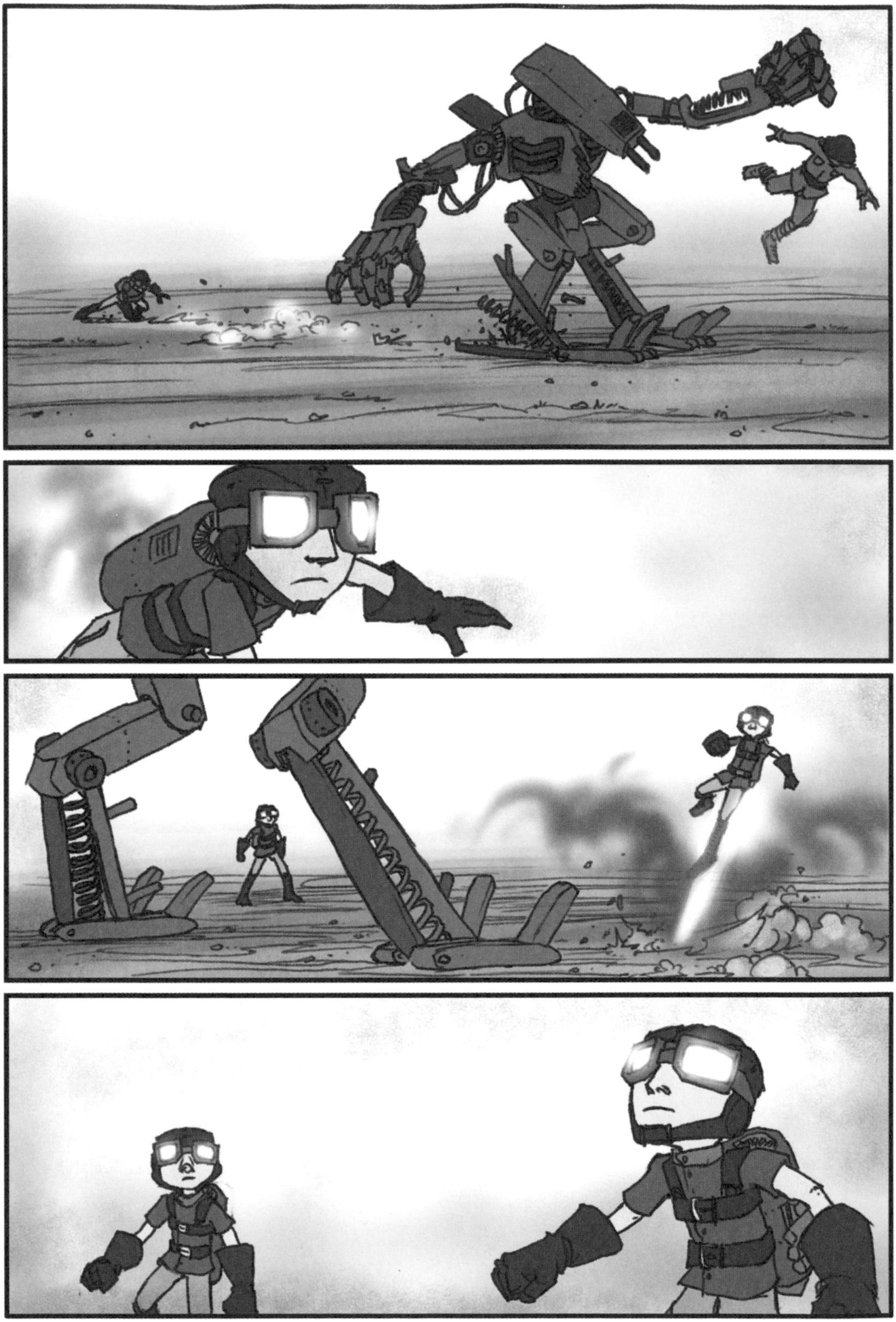

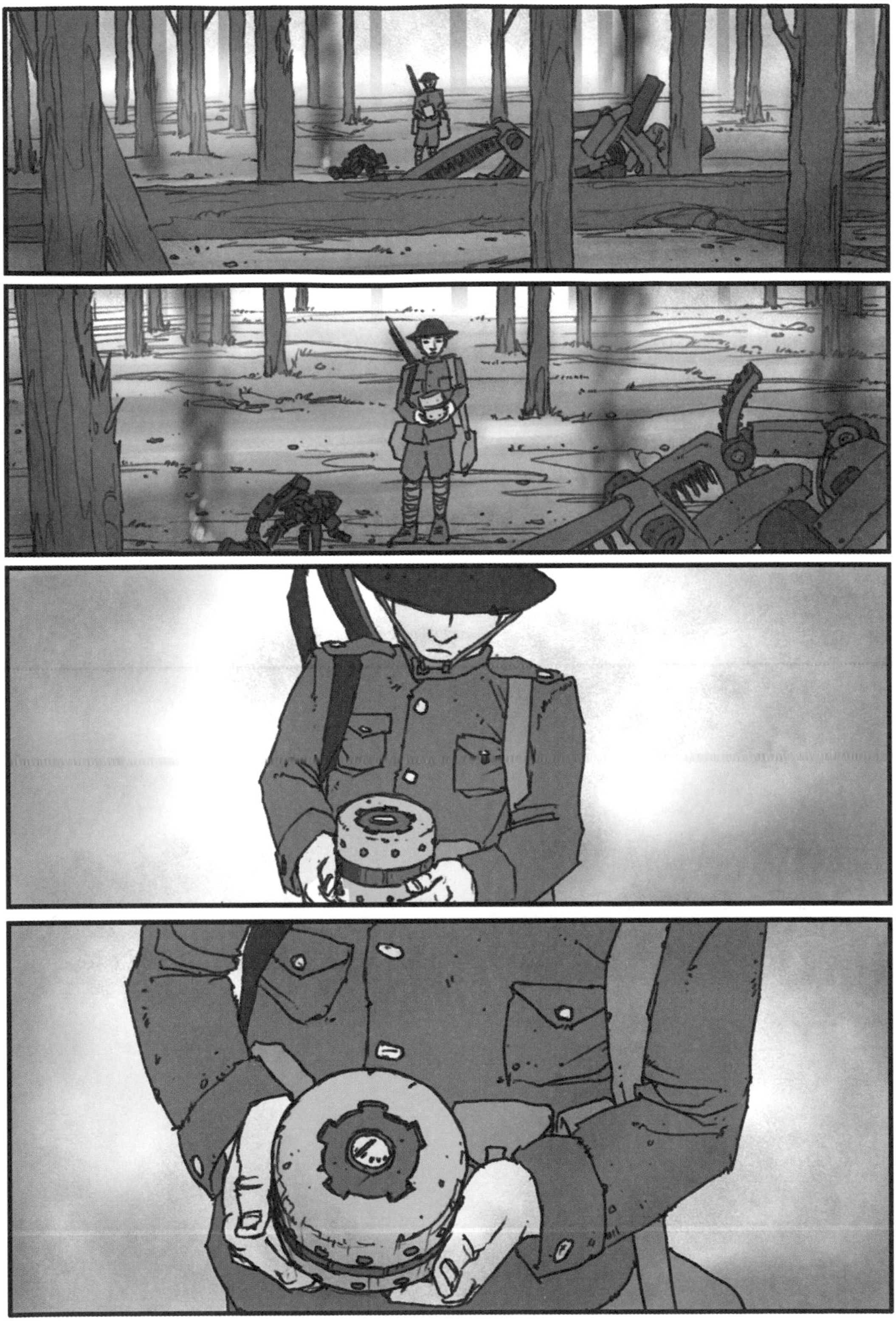

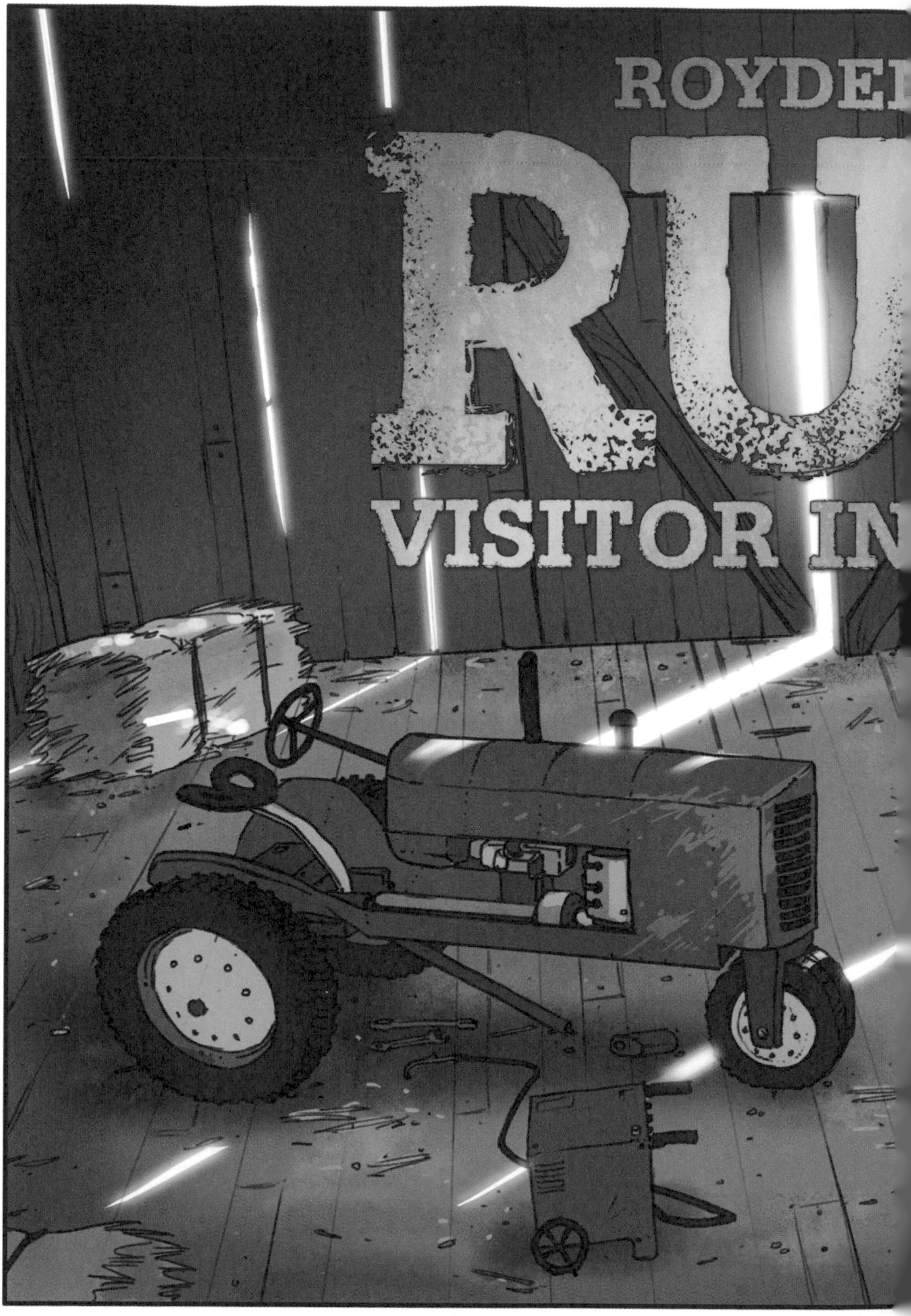
ROYDE
RU
VISITOR IN

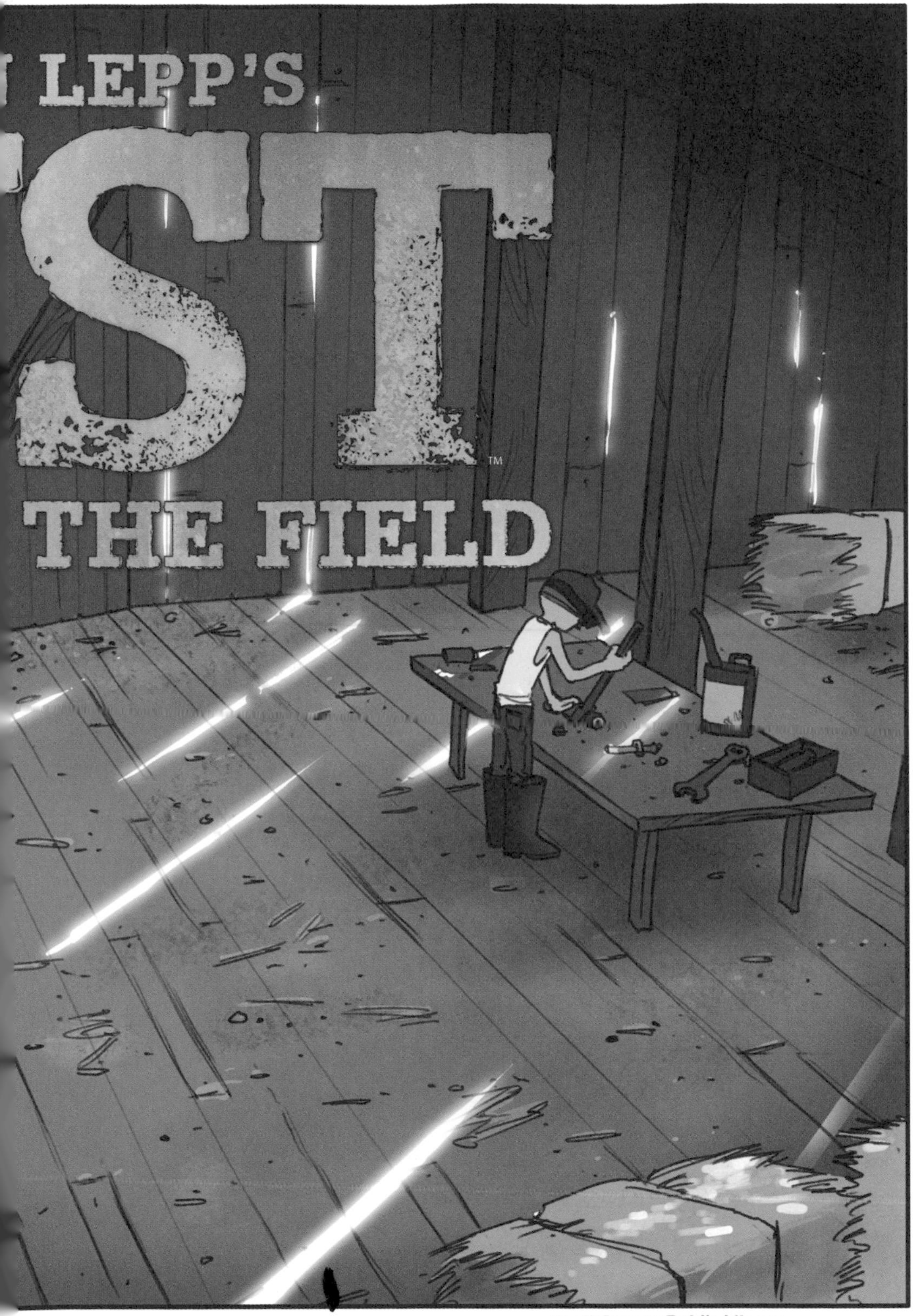
LEPP'S
ST
TM
THE FIELD

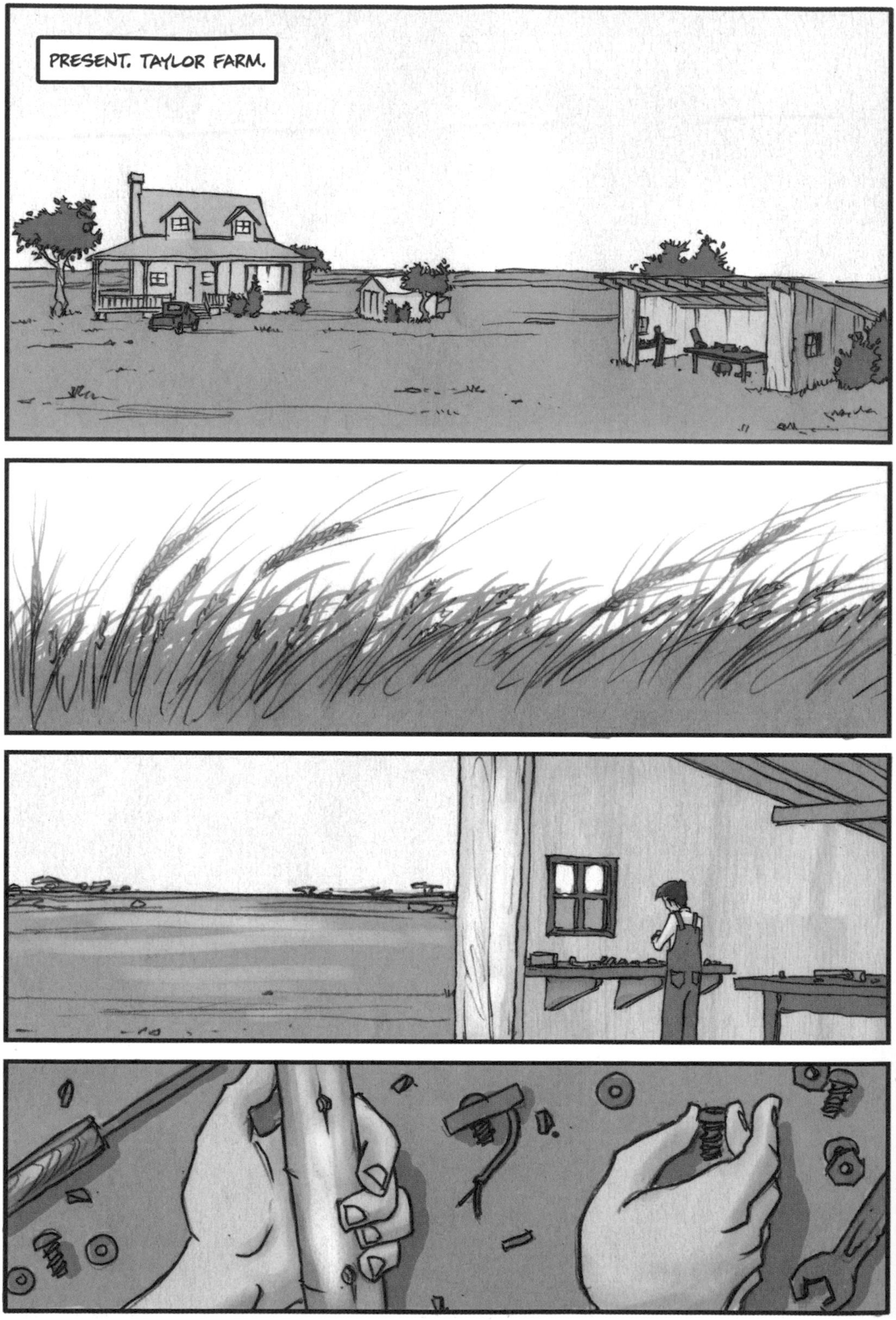
PRESENT. TAYLOR FARM.

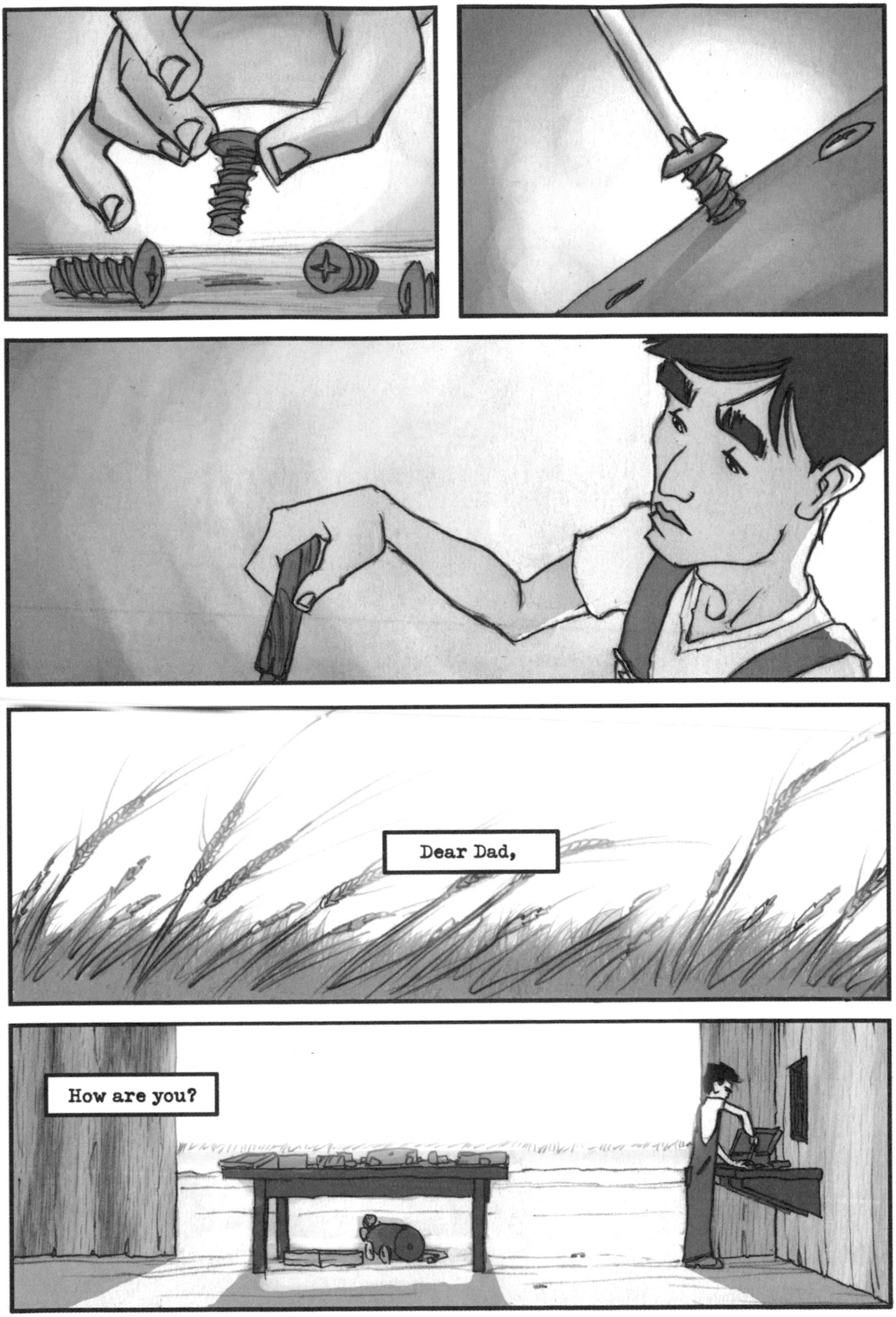
Dear Dad,
How are you?

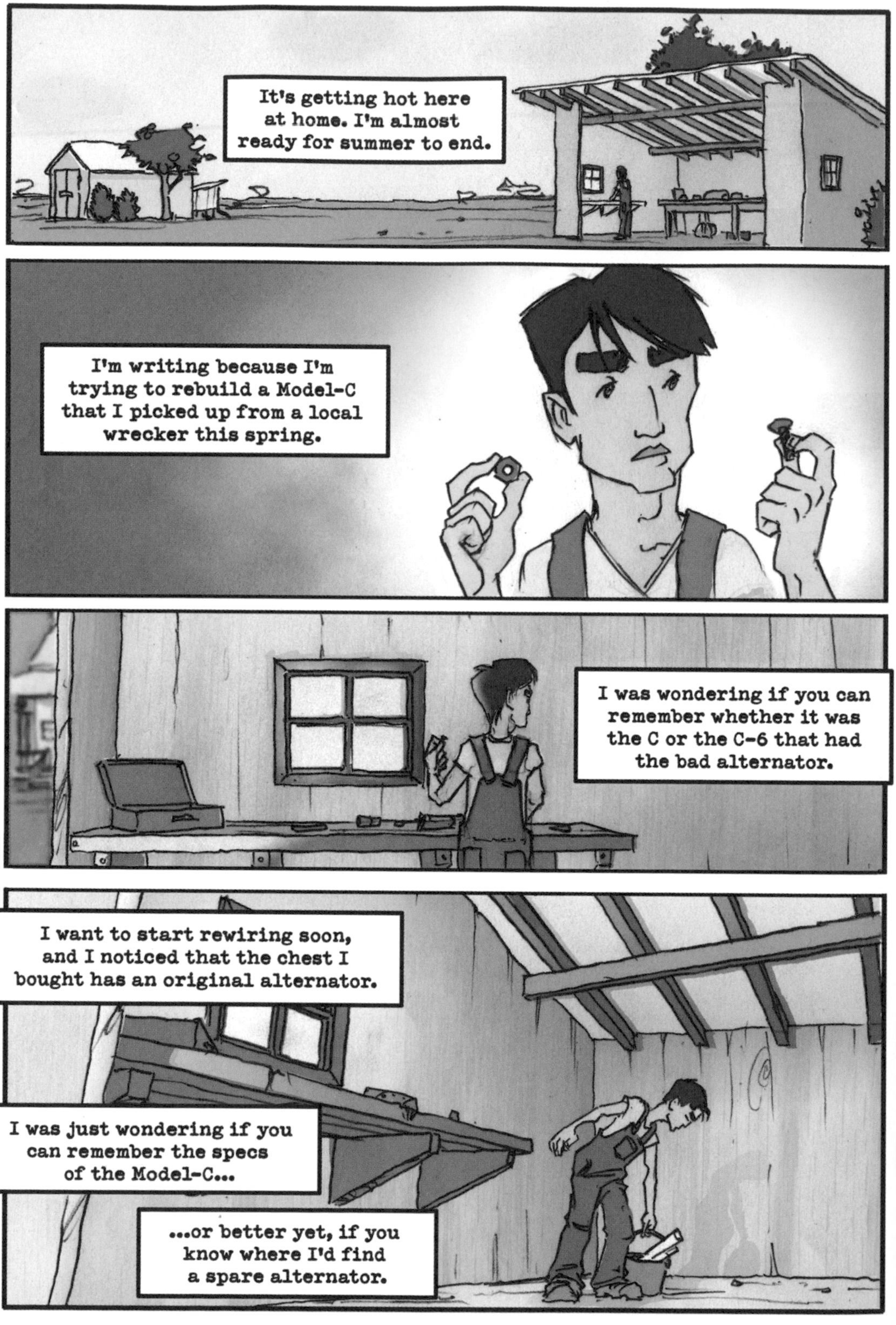
It's getting hot here at home. I'm almost ready for summer to end.
I'm writing because I'm trying to rebuild a Model-C that I picked up from a local wrecker this spring.
I was wondering if you can remember whether it was the C or the C-6 that had the bad alternator.
I want to start rewiring soon, and I noticed that the chest I bought has an original alternator.
I was just wondering if you can remember the specs of the Model-C...
...or better yet, if you know where I'd find a spare alternator.

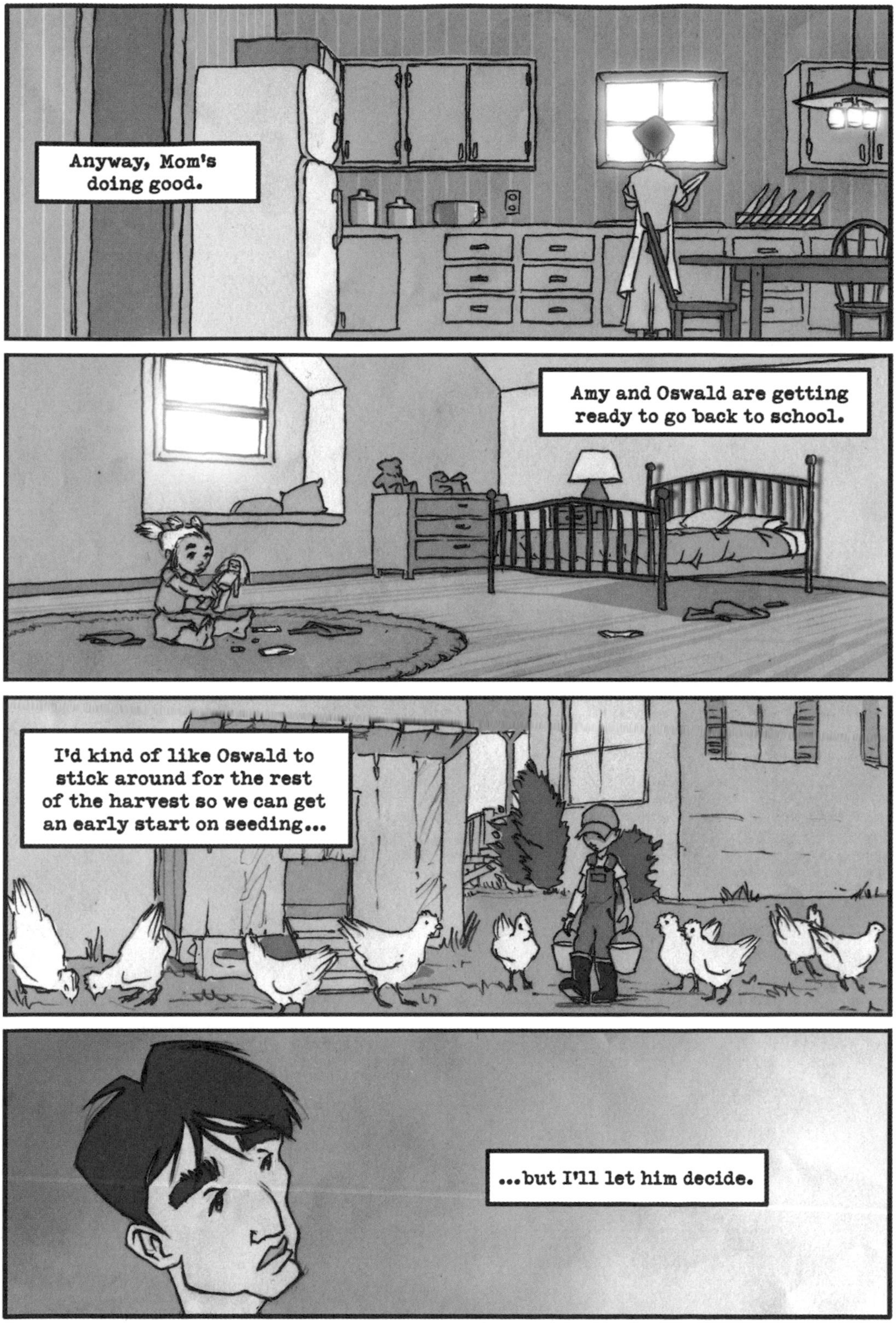
Anyway, Mom's doing good.
Amy and Oswald are getting ready to go back to school.
I'd kind of like Oswald to stick around for the rest of the harvest so we can get an early start on seeding...
...but I'll let him decide.

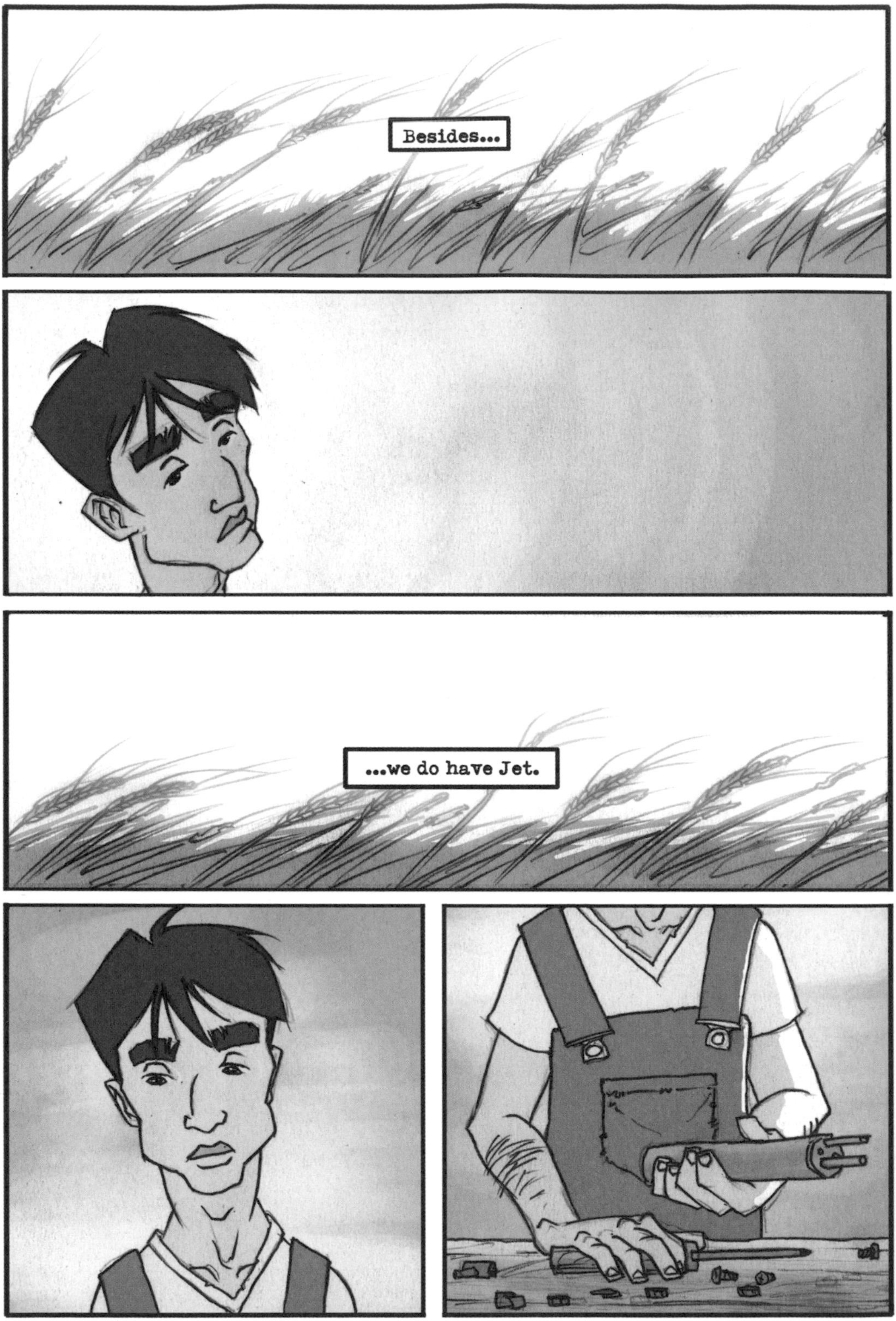
Besides...
...we do have Jet.

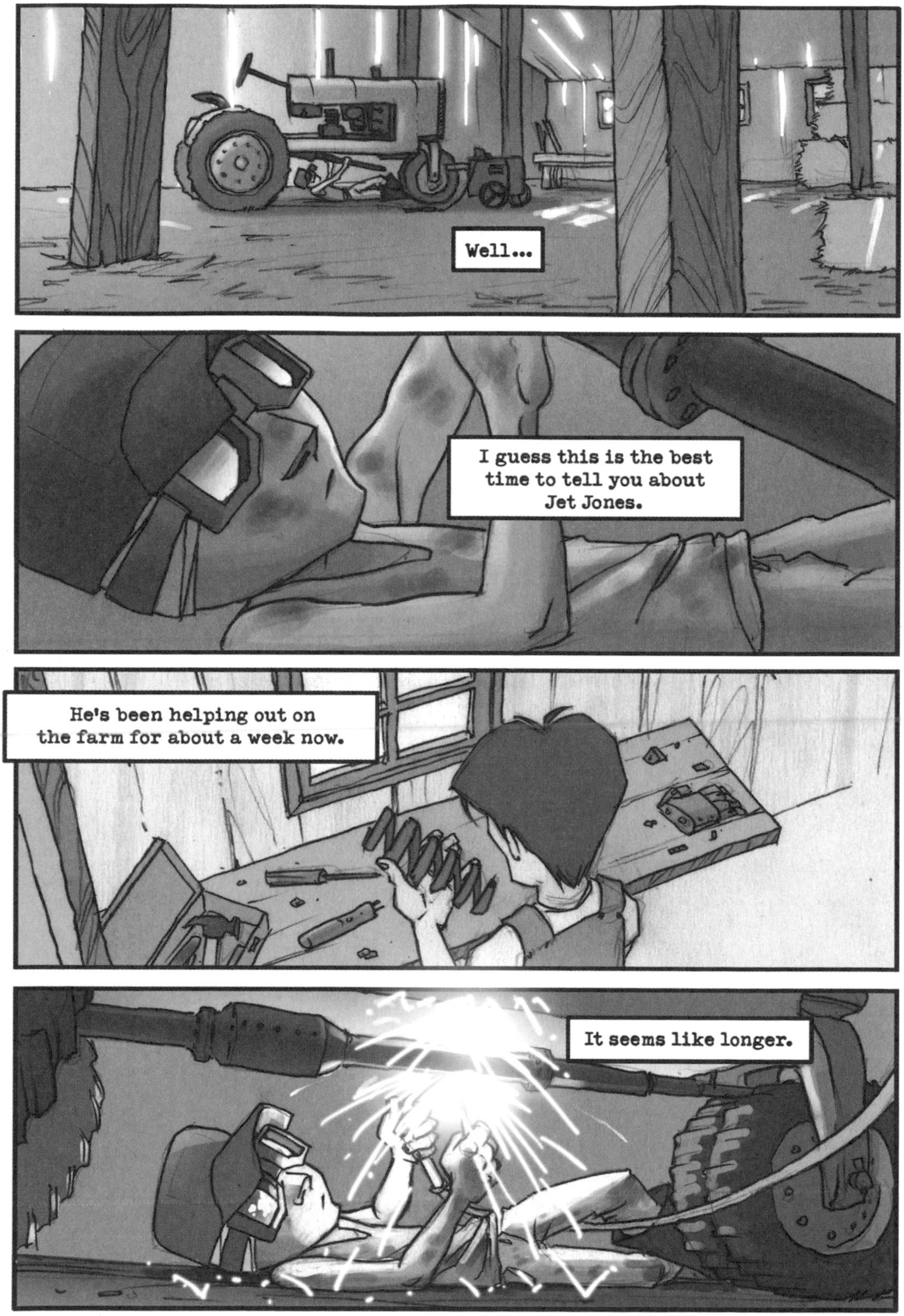
Well...
I guess this is the best time to tell you about Jet Jones.
He's been helping out on the farm for about a week now.
It seems like longer.

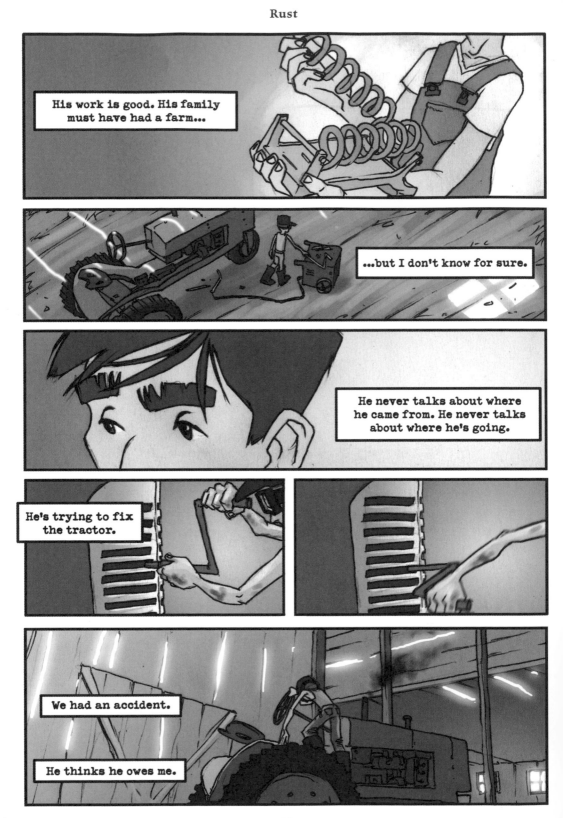

His work is good. His family must have had a farm...

...but I don't know for sure.

He never talks about where he came from. He never talks about where he's going.

He's trying to fix the tractor.

We had an accident.

He thinks he owes me.

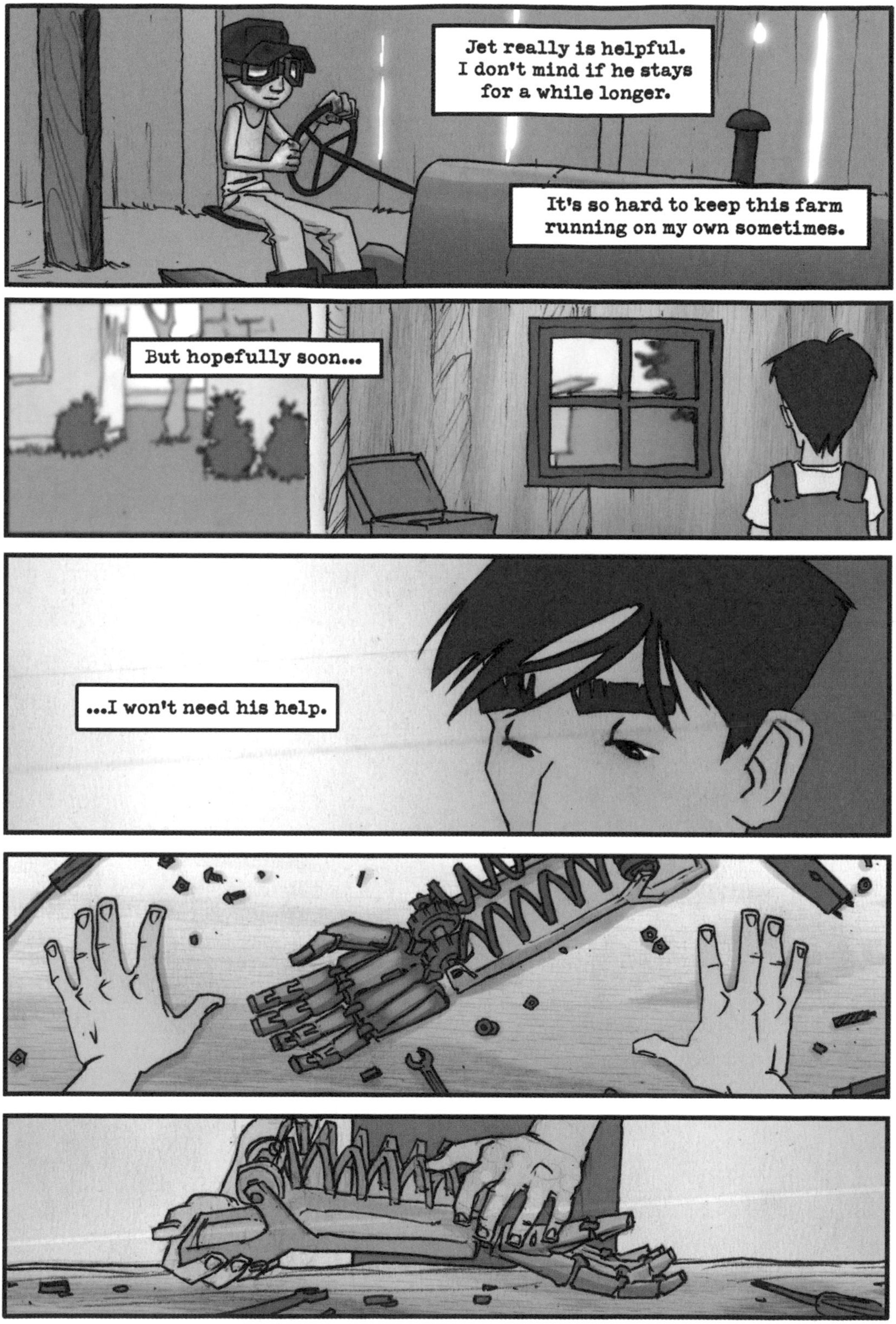
Jet really is helpful.
I don't mind if he stays
for a while longer.
It's so hard to keep this farm
running on my own sometimes.
But hopefully soon...
...I won't need his help.

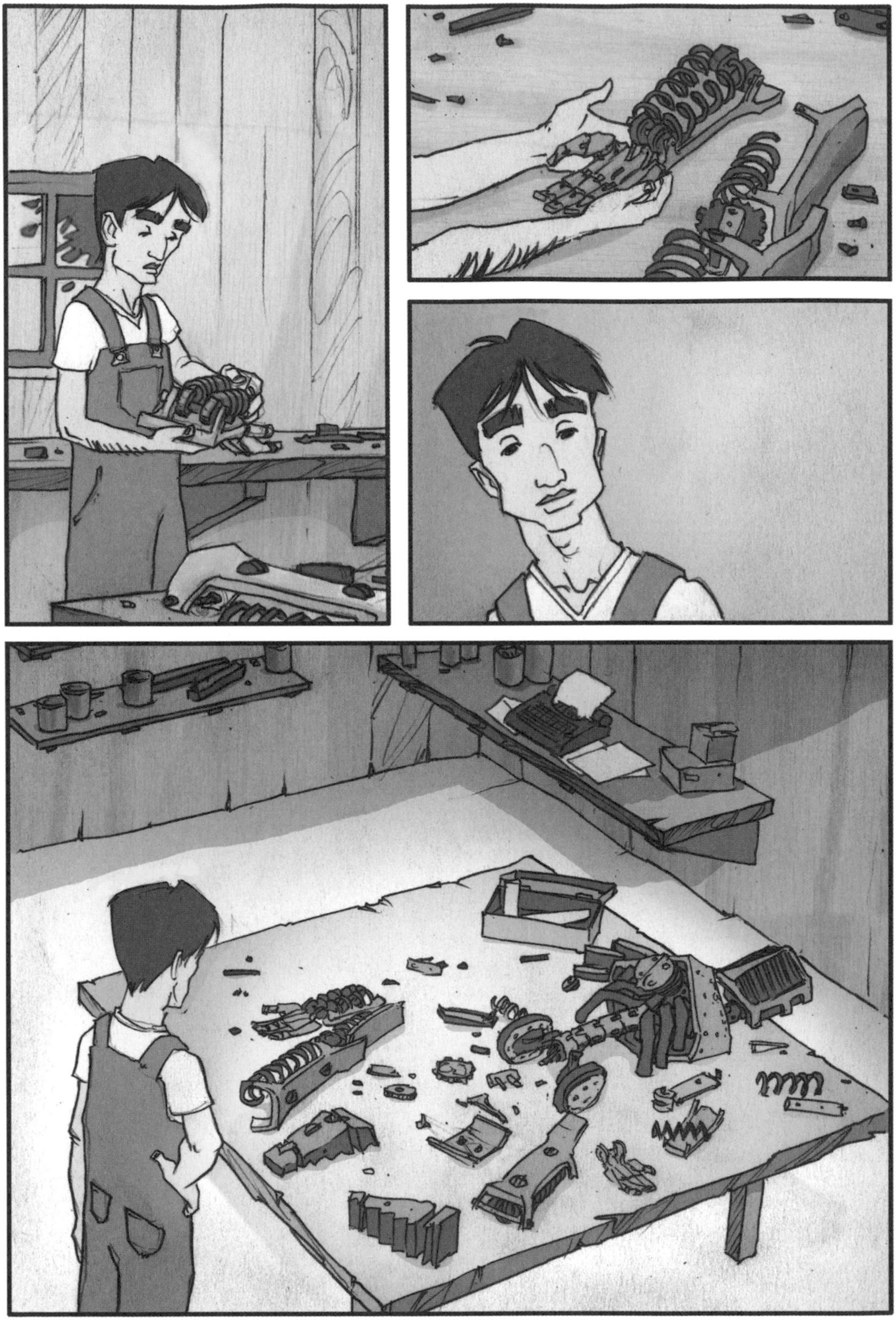

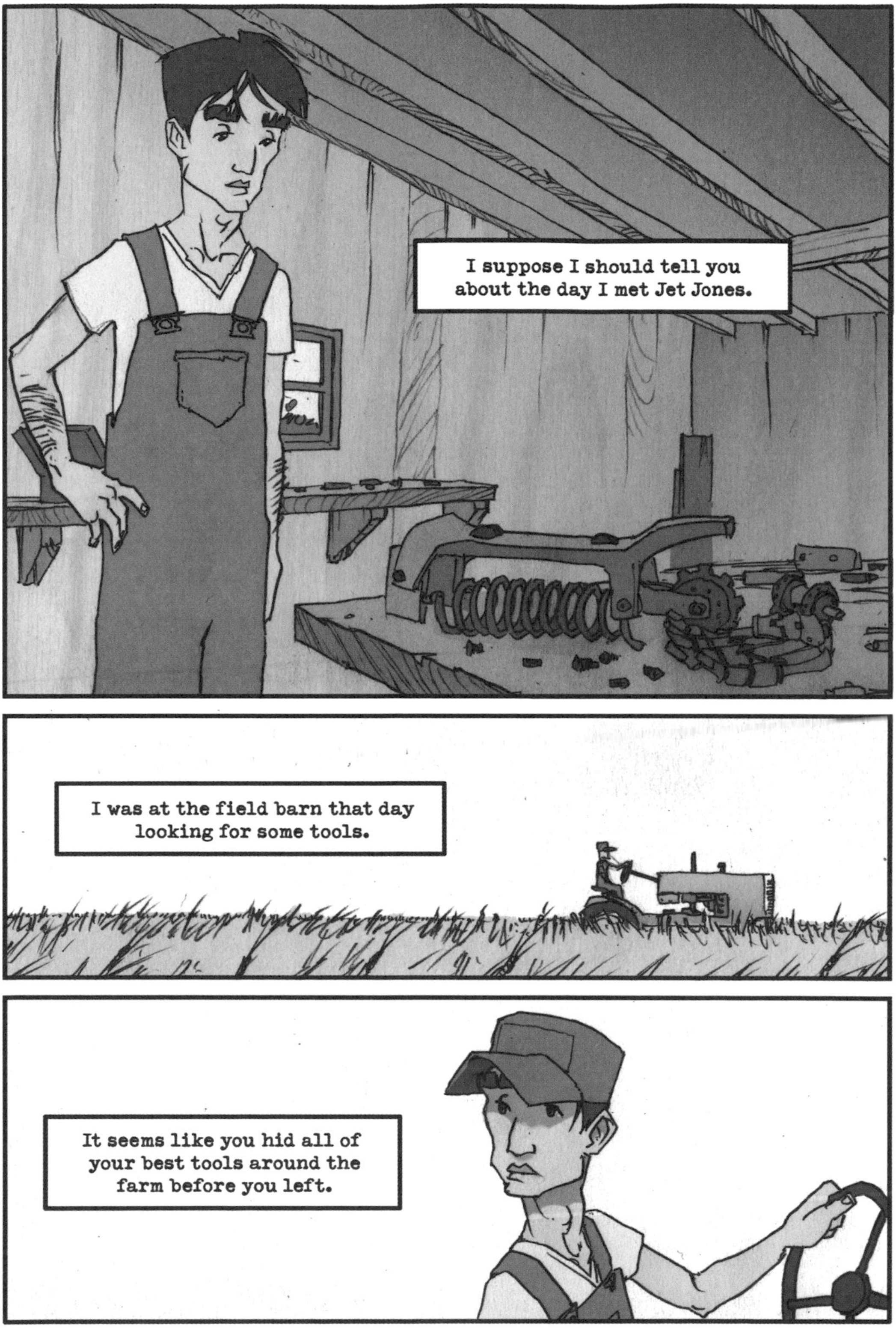
I suppose I should tell you about the day I met Jet Jones.
I was at the field barn that day looking for some tools.
It seems like you hid all of your best tools around the farm before you left.

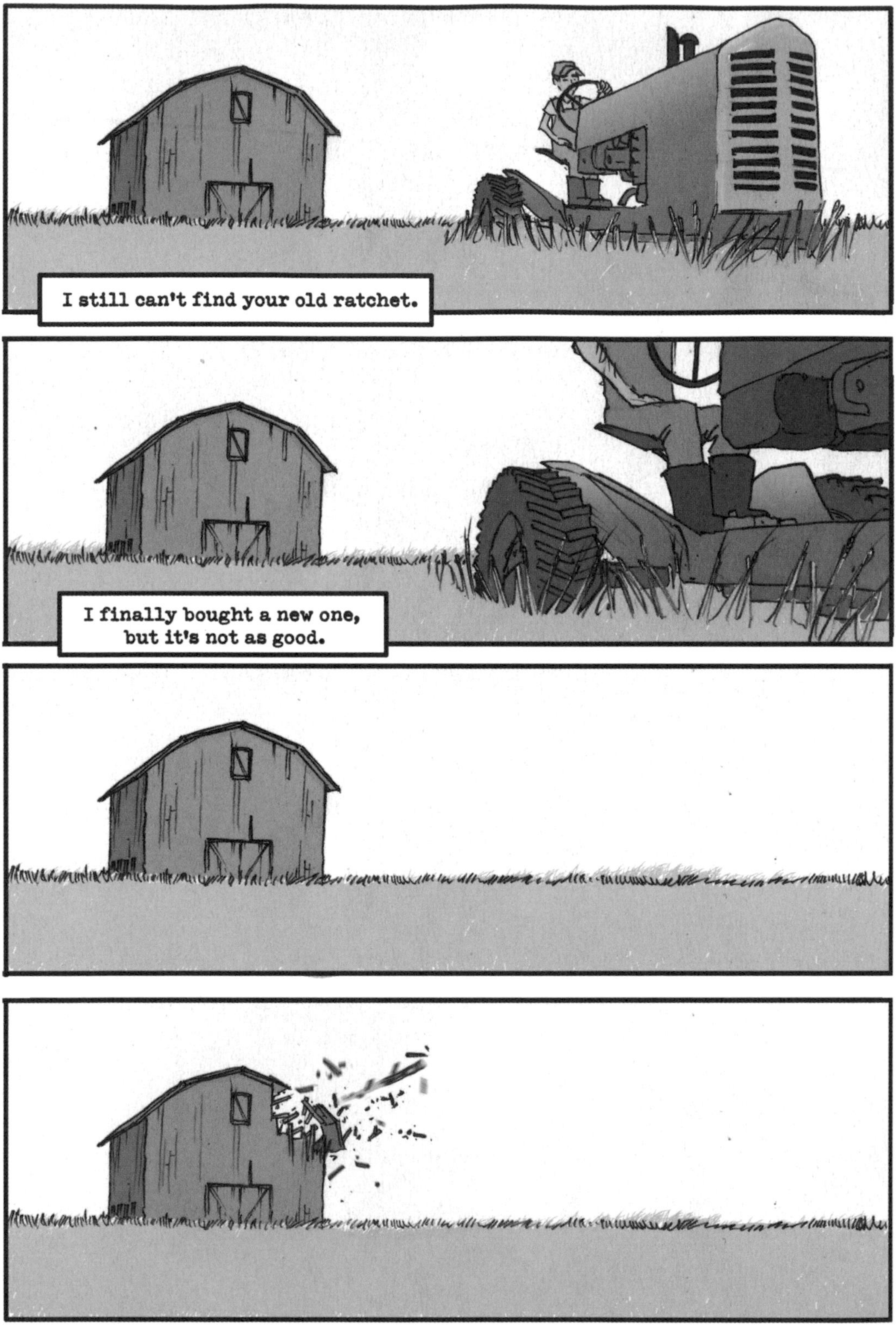
I still can't find your old ratchet.
I finally bought a new one,
but it's not as good.

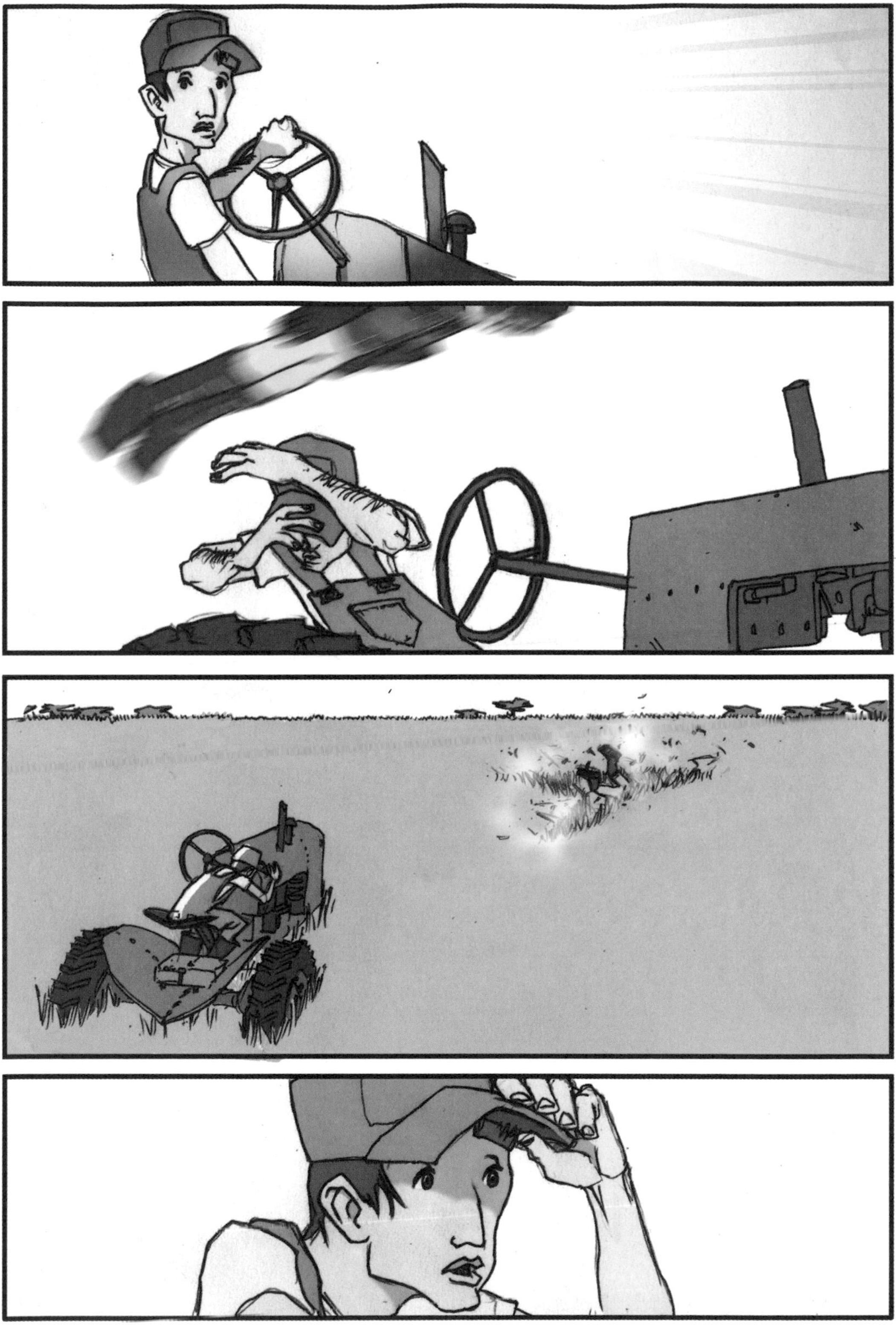

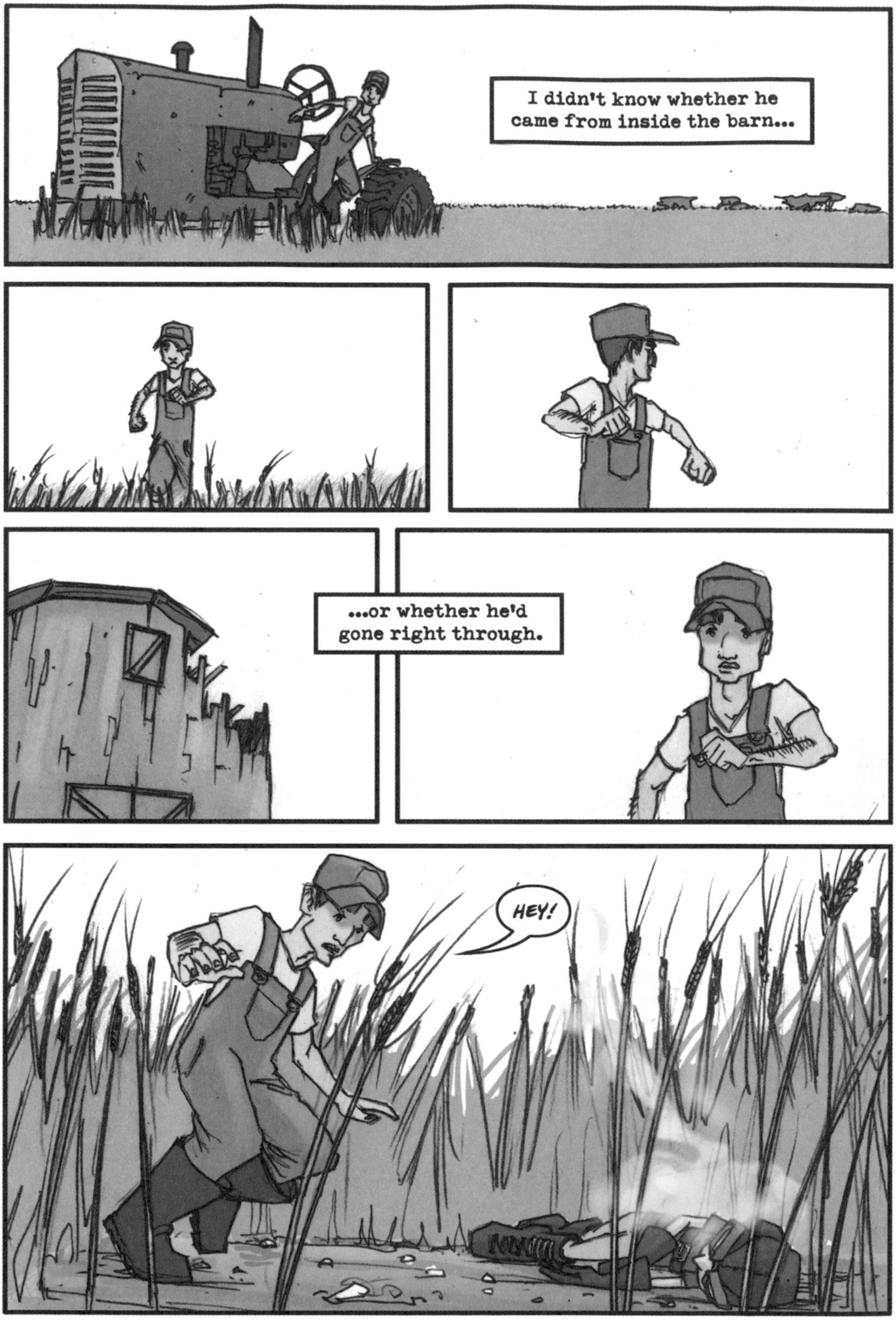
I didn't know whether he came from inside the barn...
...or whether he'd gone right through.
HEY!

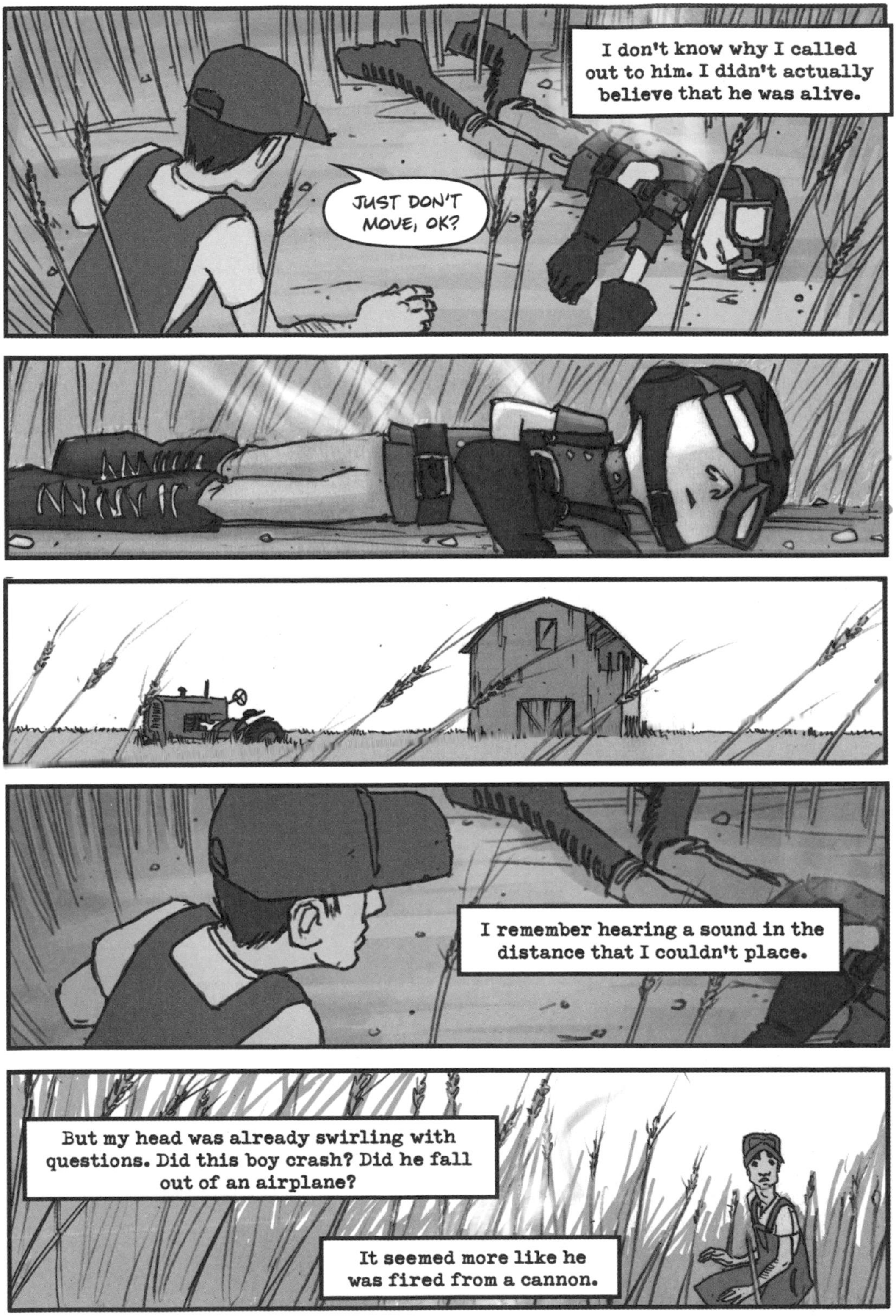
I don't know why I called out to him. I didn't actually believe that he was alive.
JUST DON'T MOVE, OK?
I remember hearing a sound in the distance that I couldn't place.
But my head was already swirling with questions. Did this boy crash? Did he fall out of an airplane?
It seemed more like he was fired from a cannon.

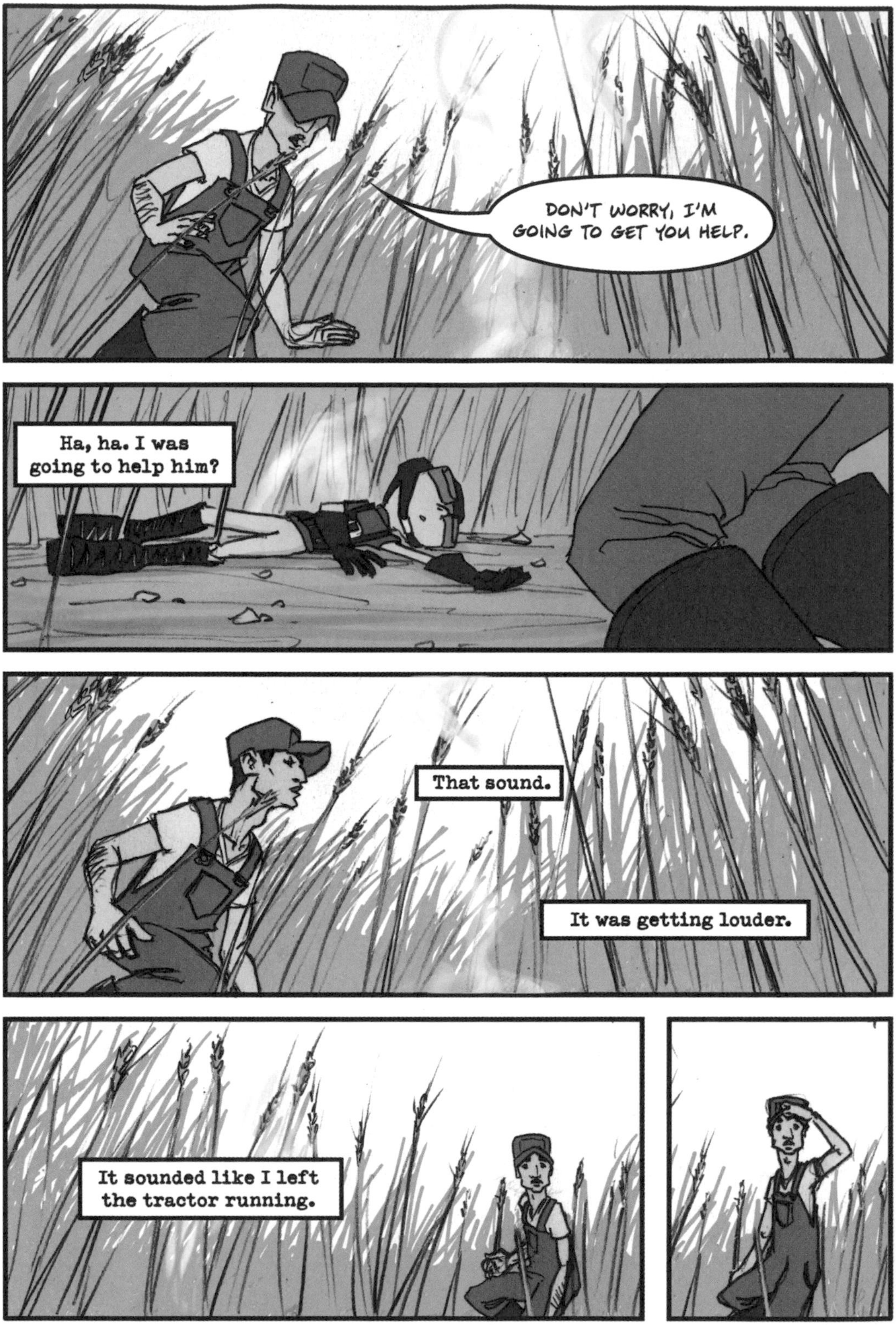
DON'T WORRY, I'M GOING TO GET YOU HELP.
Ha, ha. I was going to help him?
That sound.
It was getting louder.
It sounded like I left the tractor running.

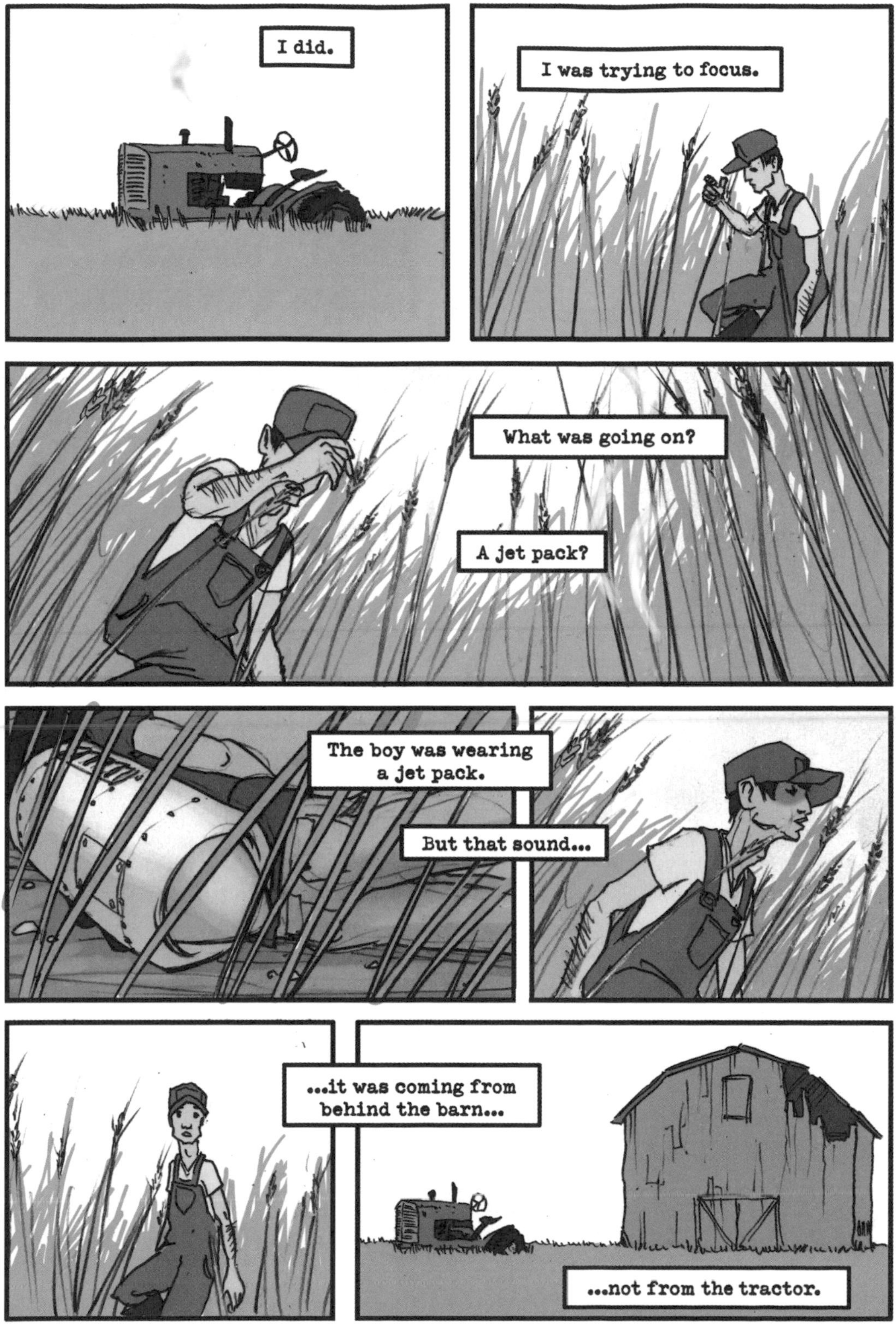
I did.
I was trying to focus.
What was going on?
A jet pack?
The boy was wearing a jet pack.
But that sound...
...it was coming from behind the barn...
...not from the tractor.

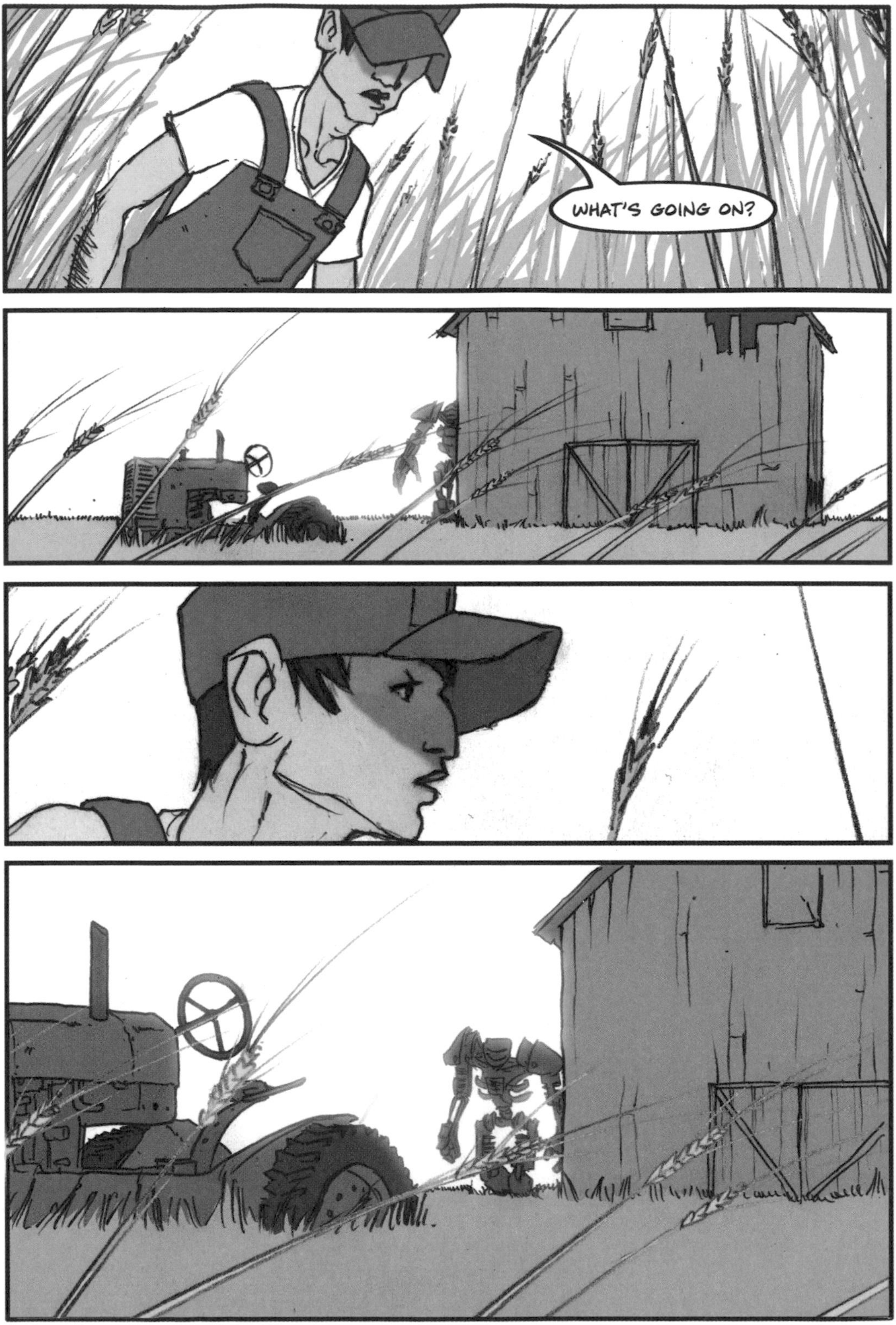
WHAT'S GOING ON?

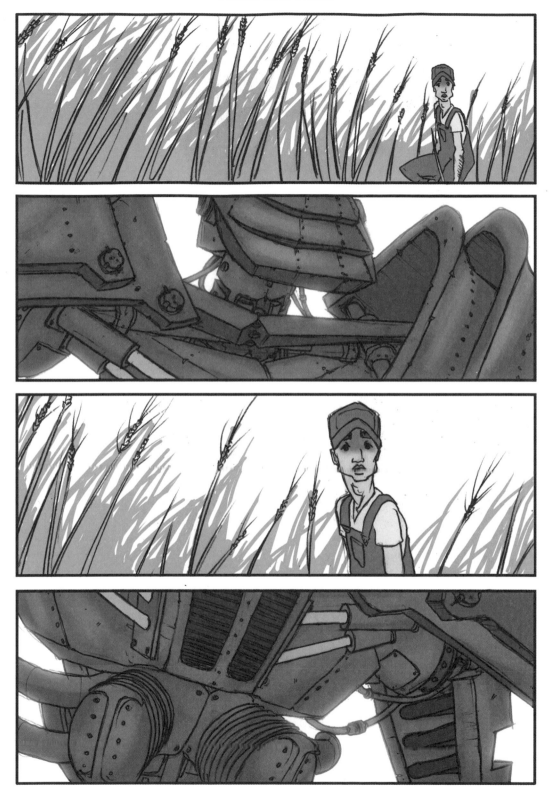

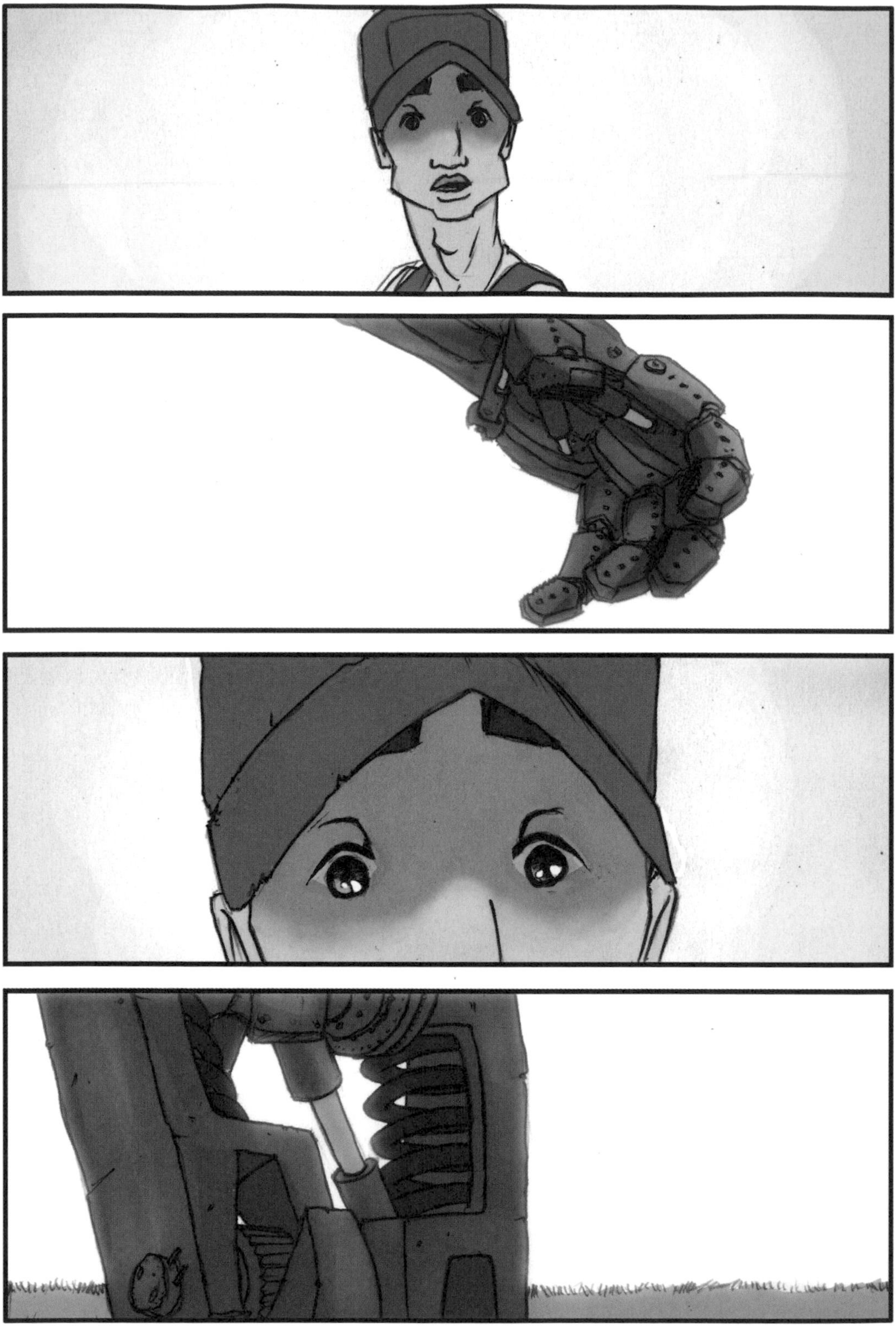

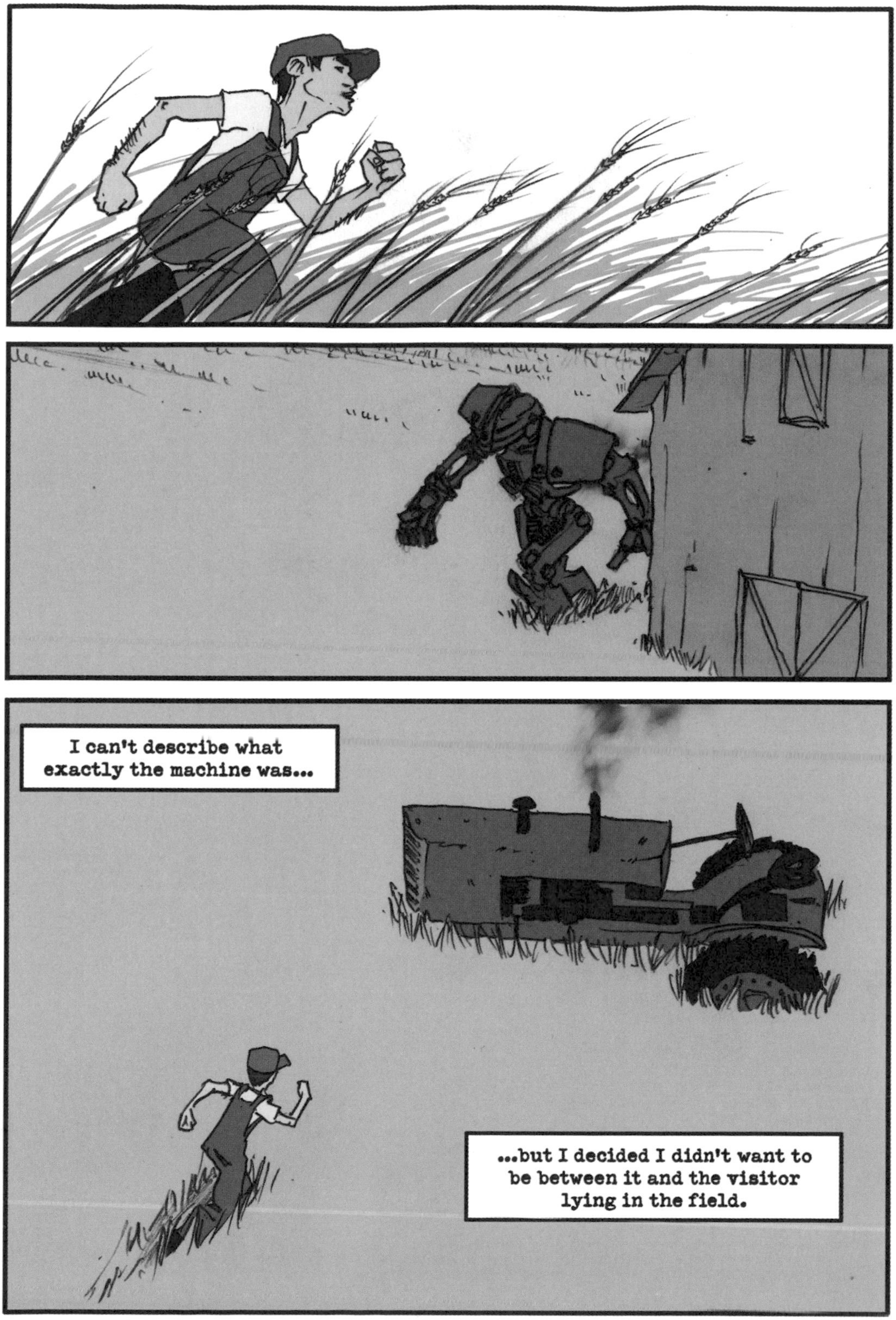
I can't describe what exactly the machine was...
...but I decided I didn't want to be between it and the visitor lying in the field.

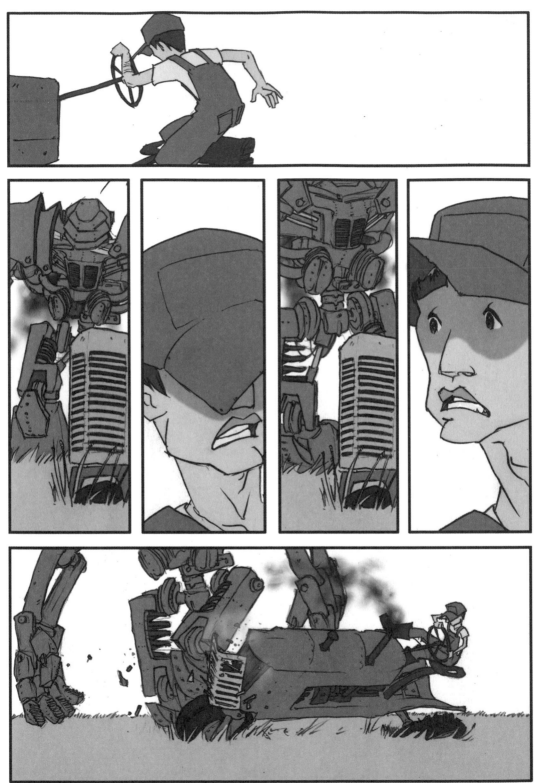

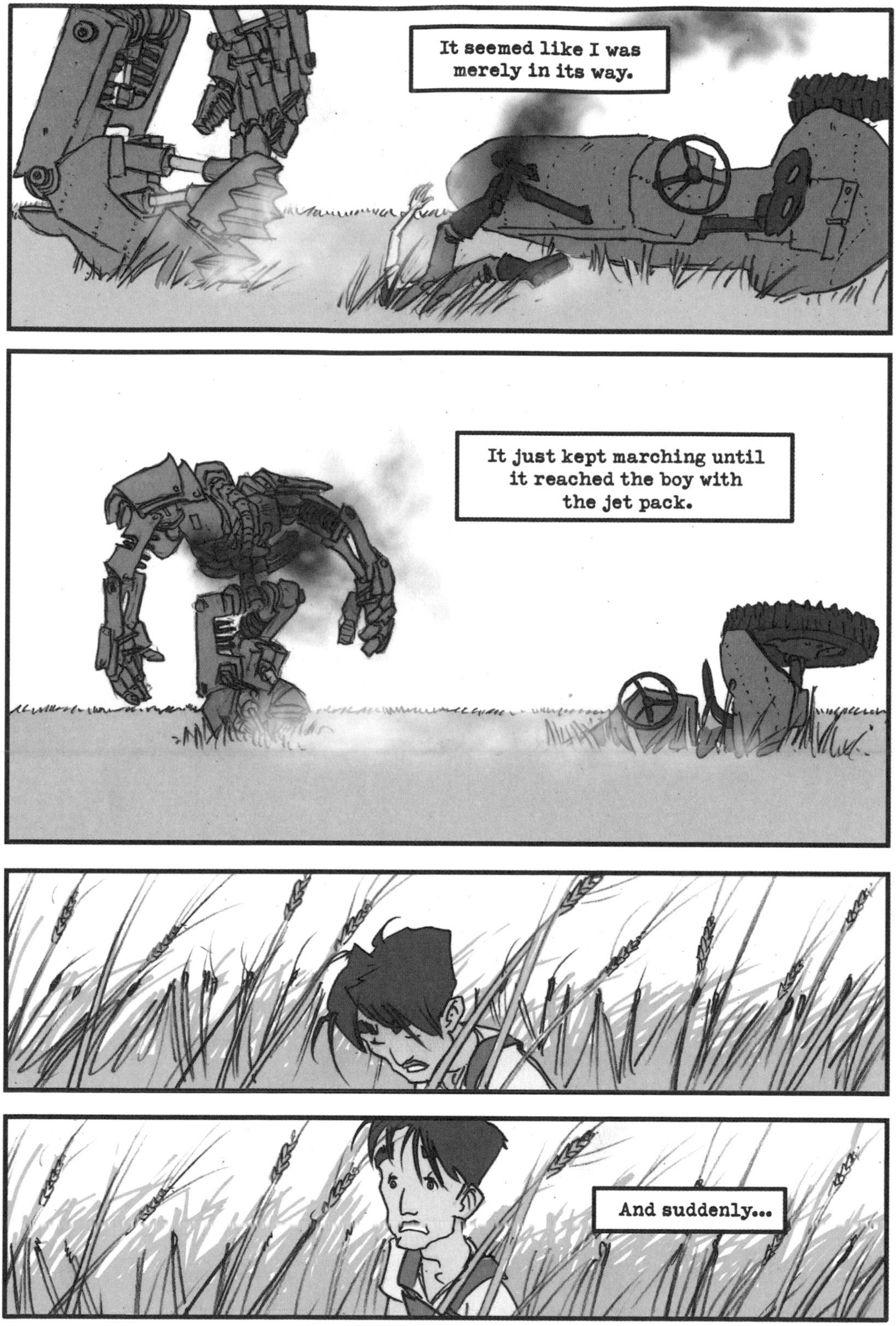
It seemed like I was merely in its way.
It just kept marching until it reached the boy with the jet pack.
And suddenly...

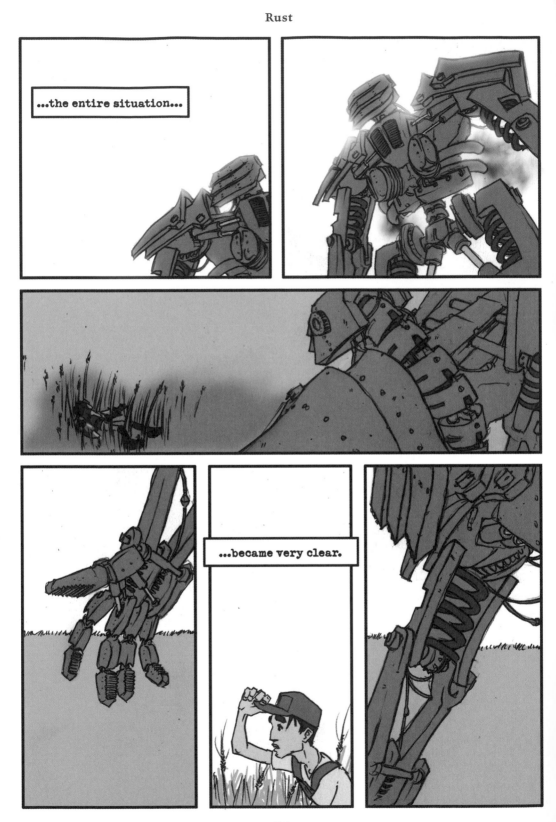

...the entire situation...

...became very clear.

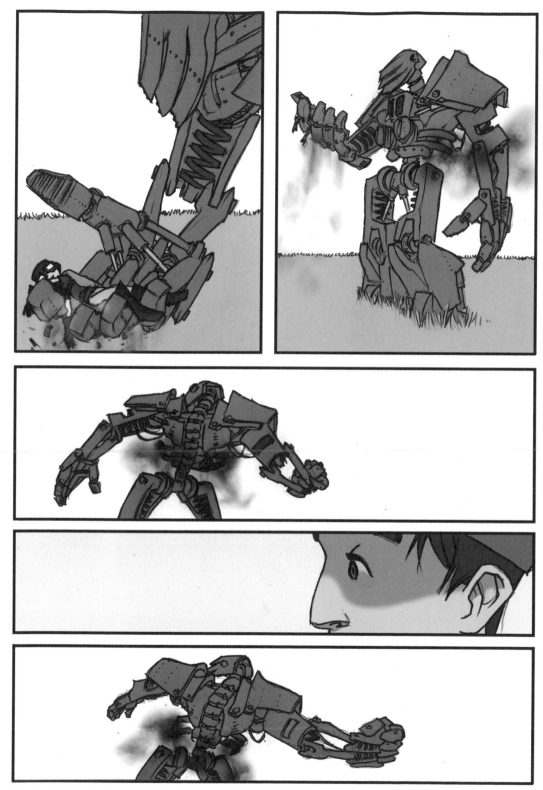

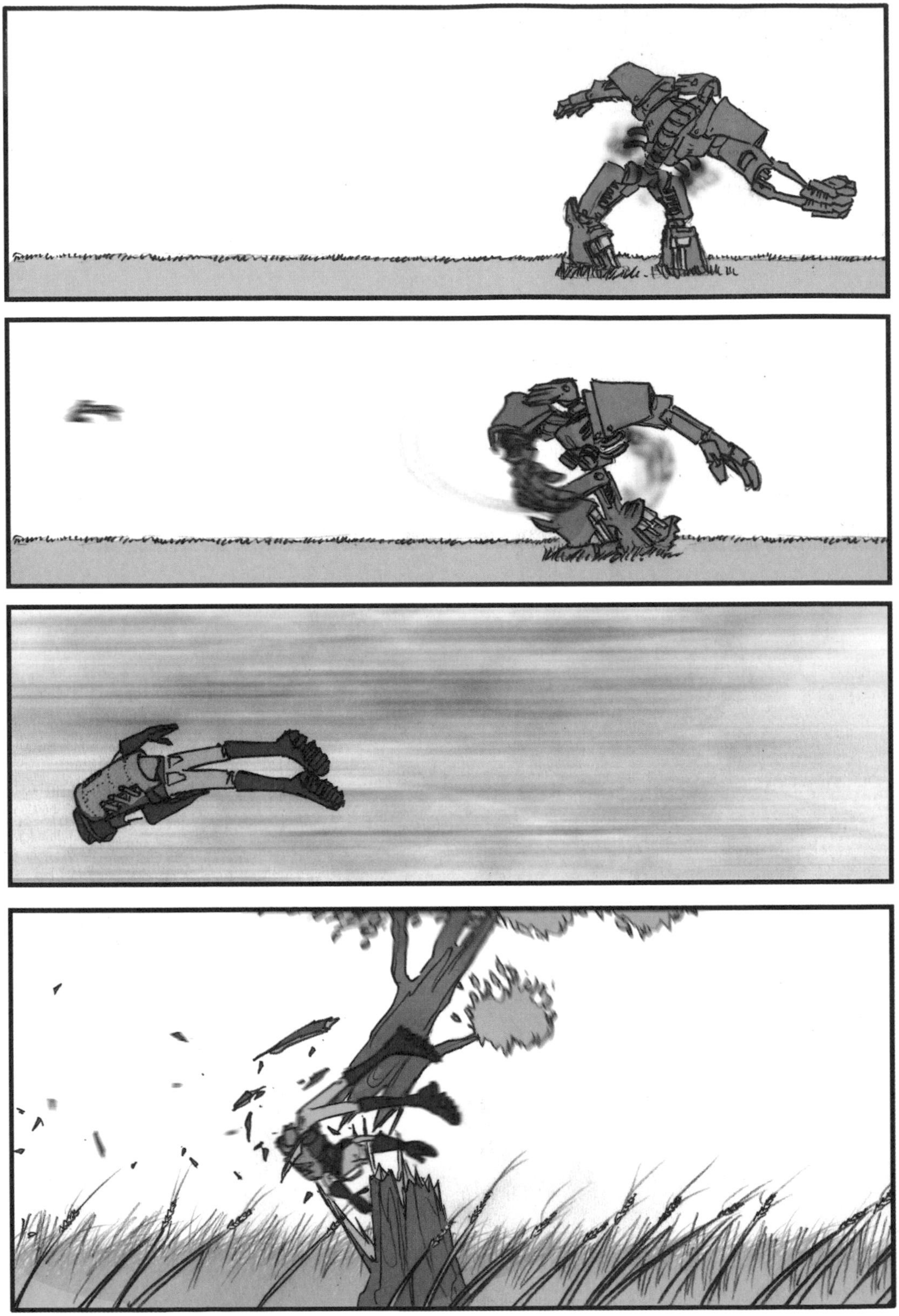

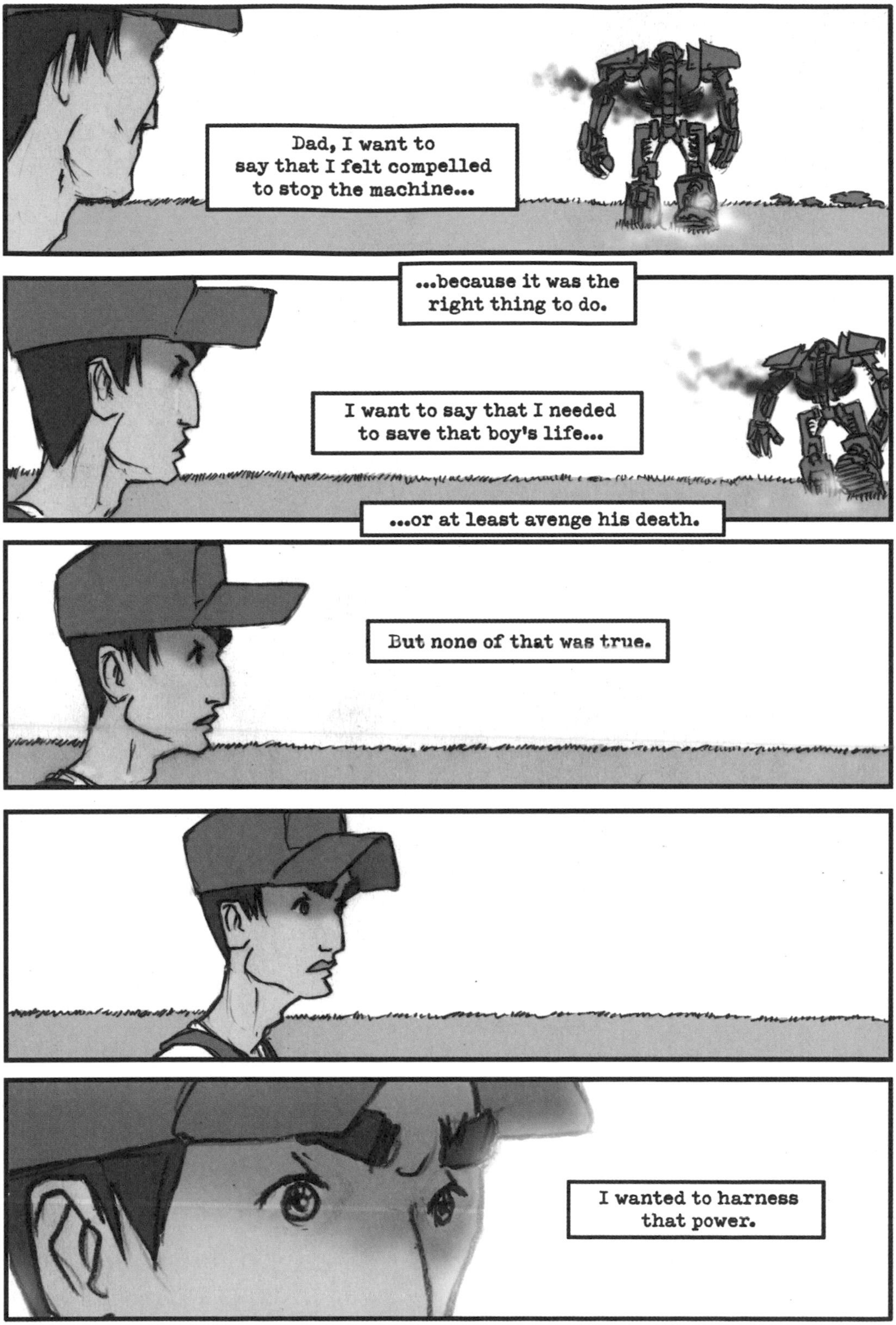
Dad, I want to say that I felt compelled to stop the machine...
...because it was the right thing to do.
I want to say that I needed to save that boy's life...
...or at least avenge his death.
But none of that was true.
I wanted to harness that power.

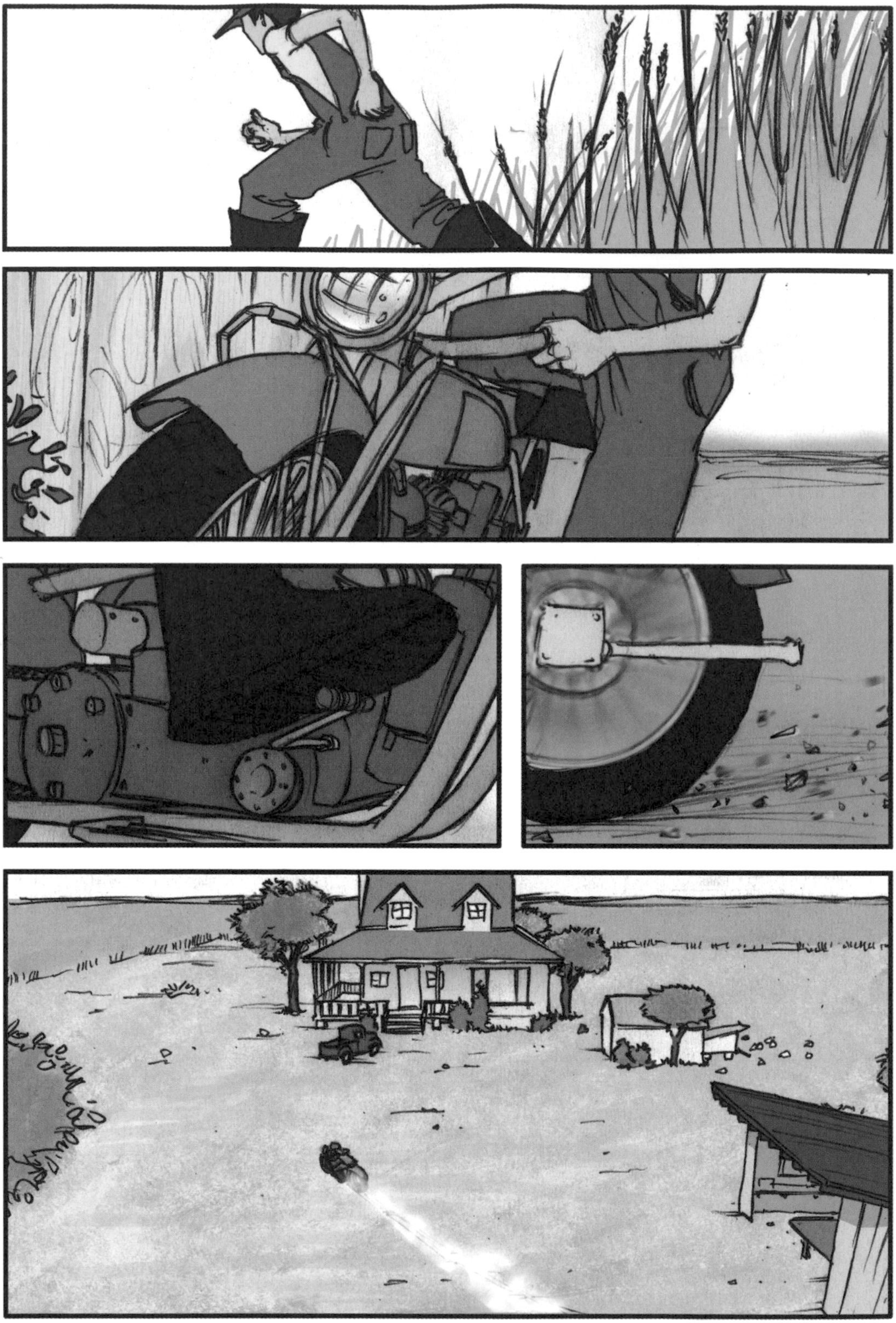

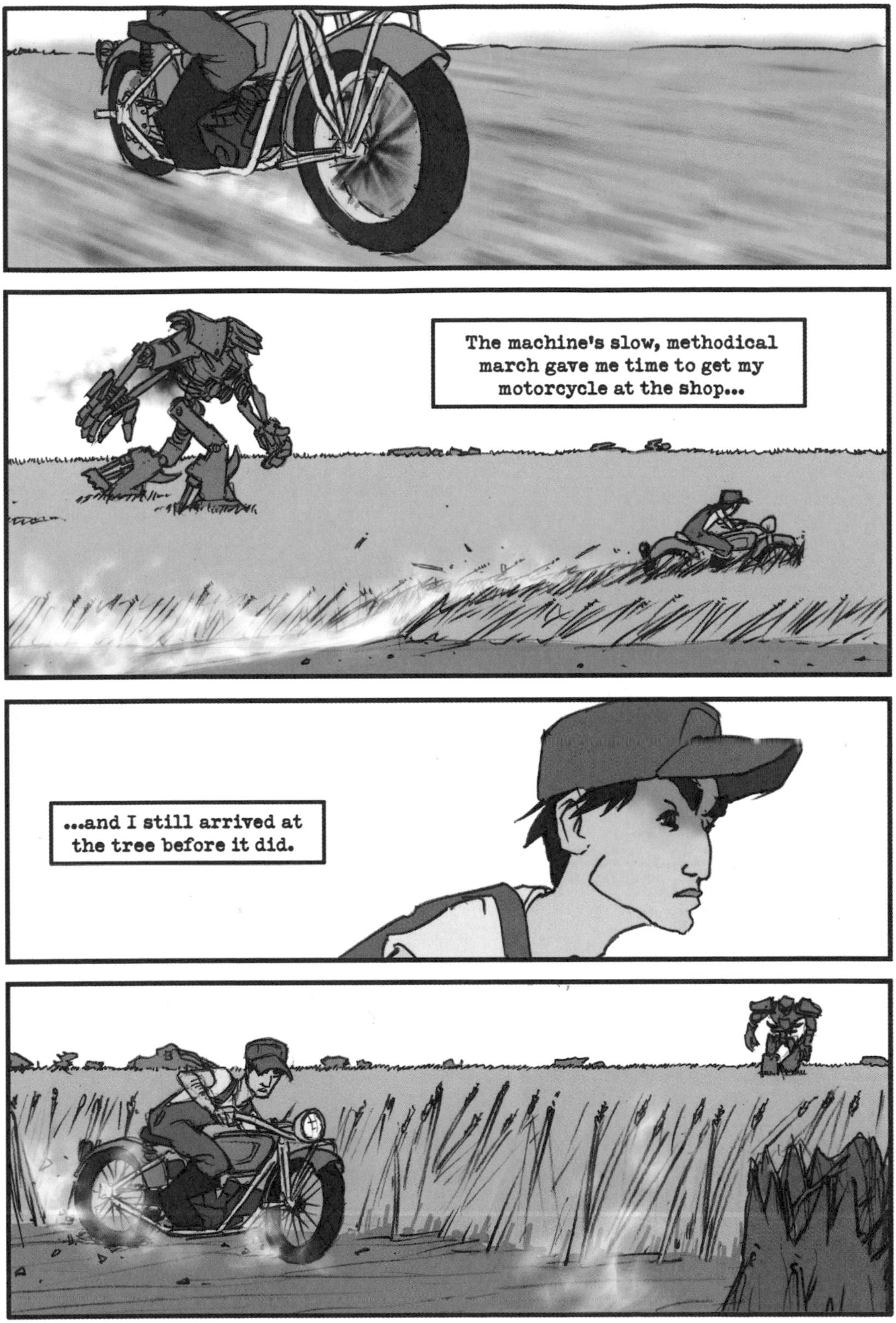
The machine's slow, methodical march gave me time to get my motorcycle at the shop...
...and I still arrived at the tree before it did.

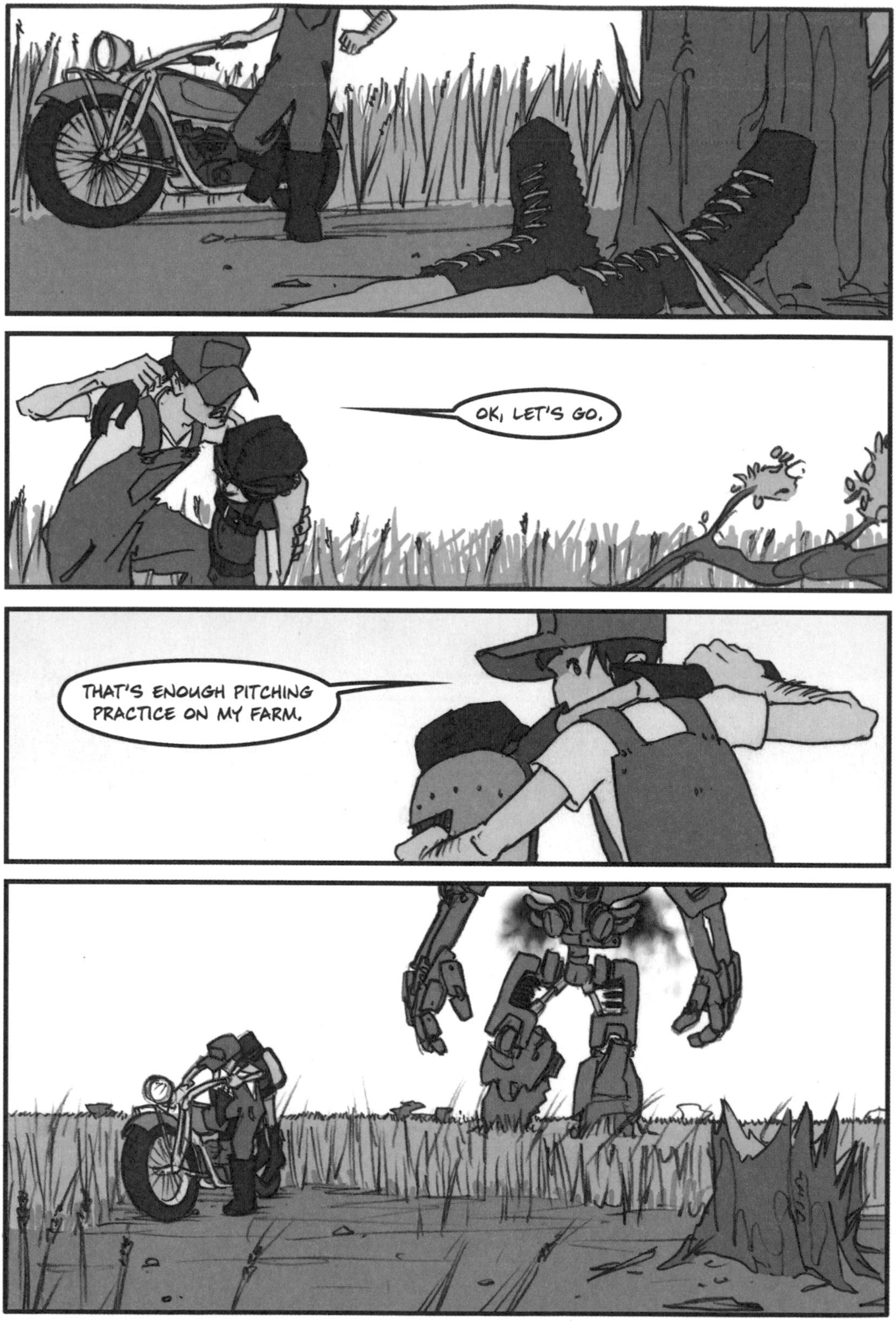
OK, LET'S GO.
THAT'S ENOUGH PITCHING PRACTICE ON MY FARM.

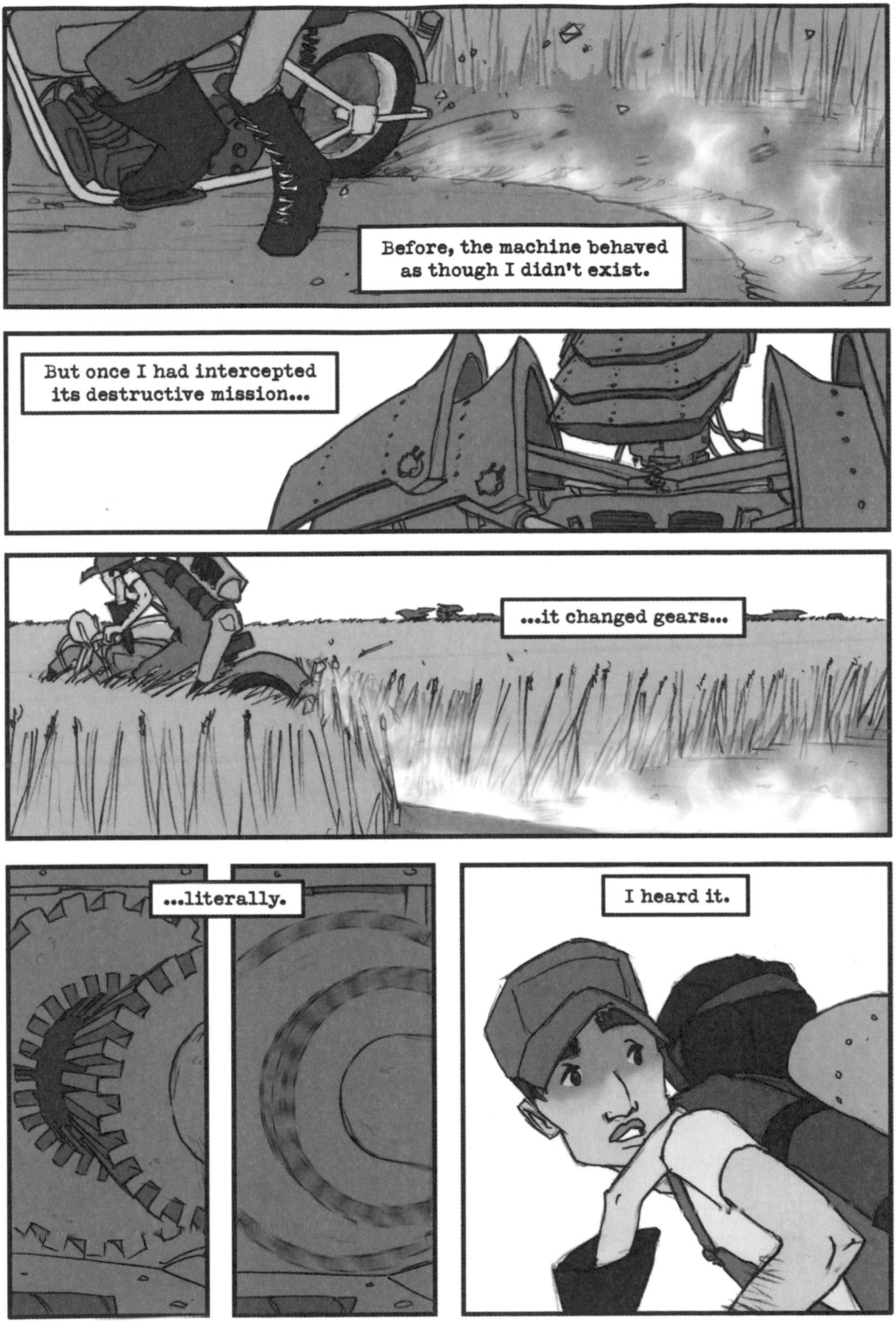
Before, the machine behaved as though I didn't exist.
But once I had intercepted its destructive mission...
...it changed gears...
...literally.
I heard it.

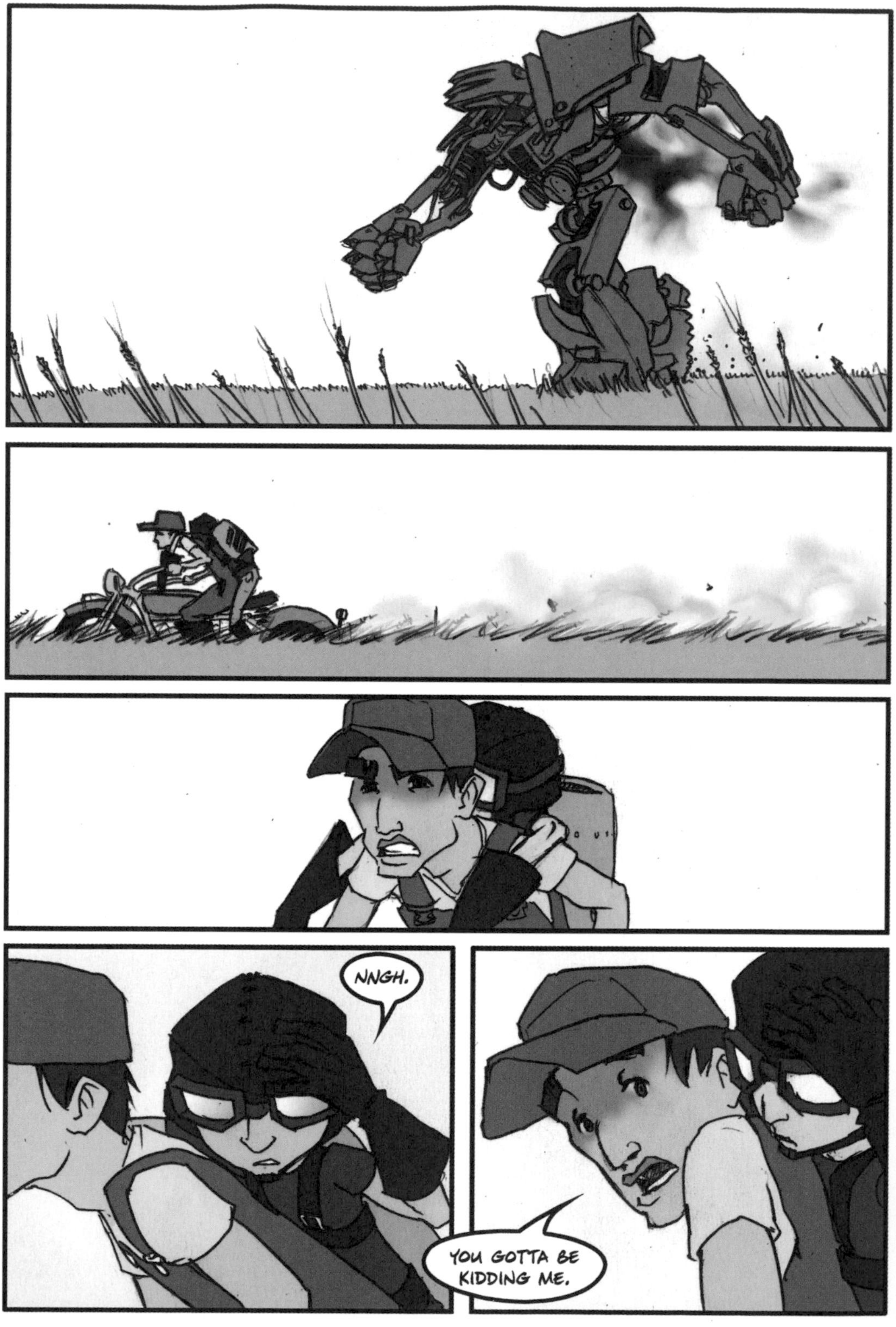
NNGH.
YOU GOTTA BE KIDDING ME.

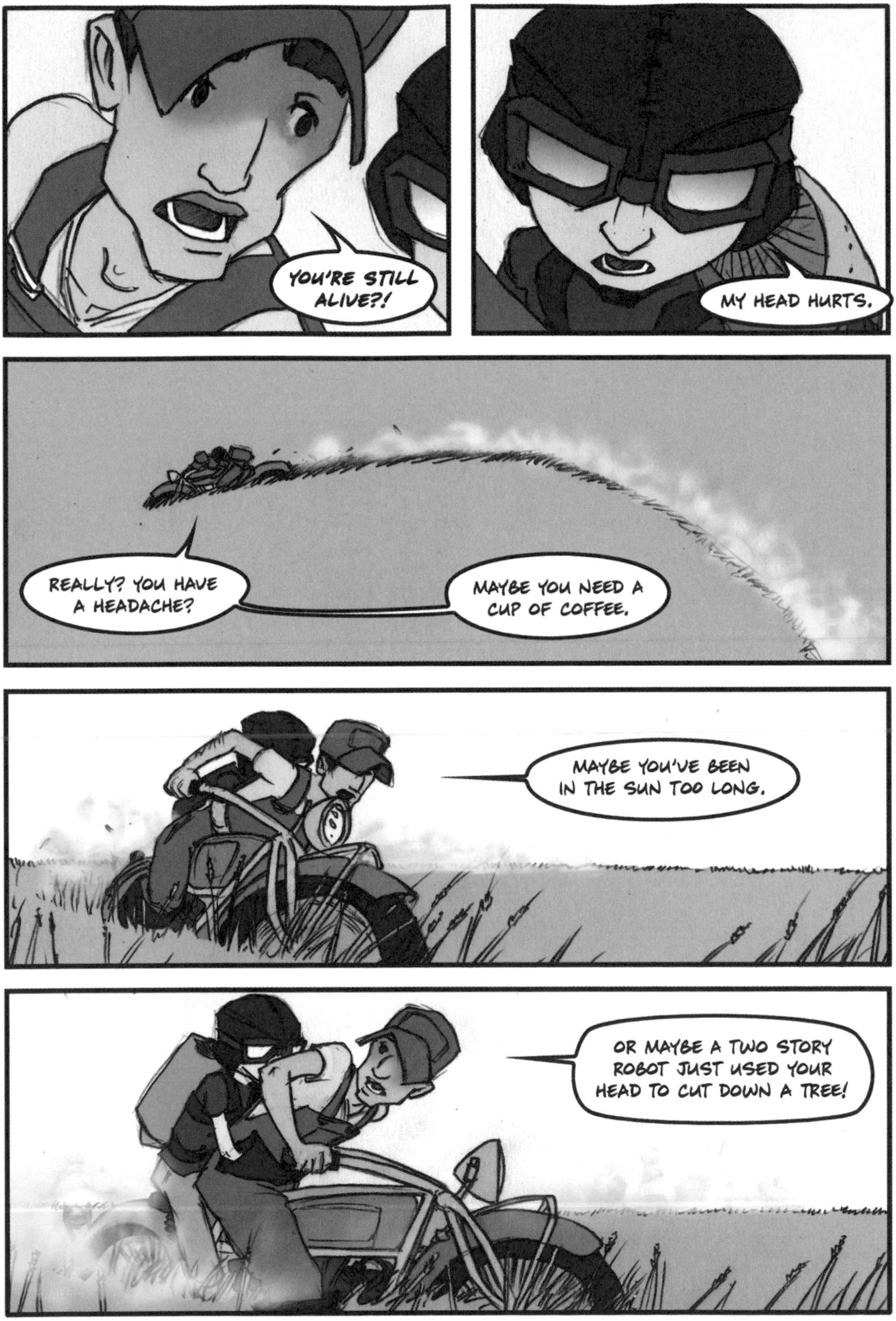
YOU'RE STILL ALIVE?!
MY HEAD HURTS.
REALLY? YOU HAVE A HEADACHE?
MAYBE YOU NEED A CUP OF COFFEE.
MAYBE YOU'VE BEEN IN THE SUN TOO LONG.
OR MAYBE A TWO STORY ROBOT JUST USED YOUR HEAD TO CUT DOWN A TREE!

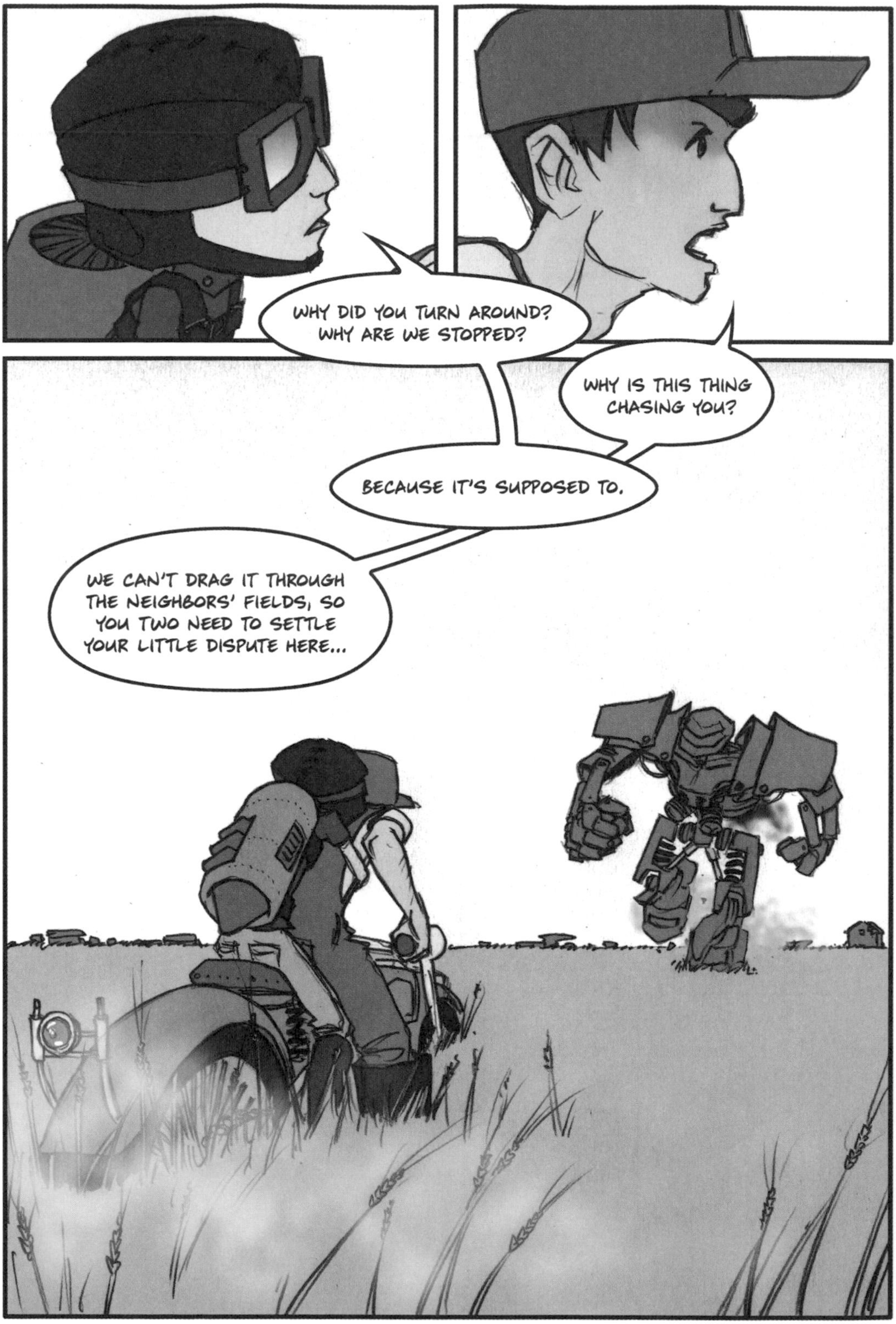
WHY DID YOU TURN AROUND? WHY ARE WE STOPPED?
WHY IS THIS THING CHASING YOU?
BECAUSE IT'S SUPPOSED TO.
WE CAN'T DRAG IT THROUGH THE NEIGHBORS' FIELDS, SO YOU TWO NEED TO SETTLE YOUR LITTLE DISPUTE HERE...

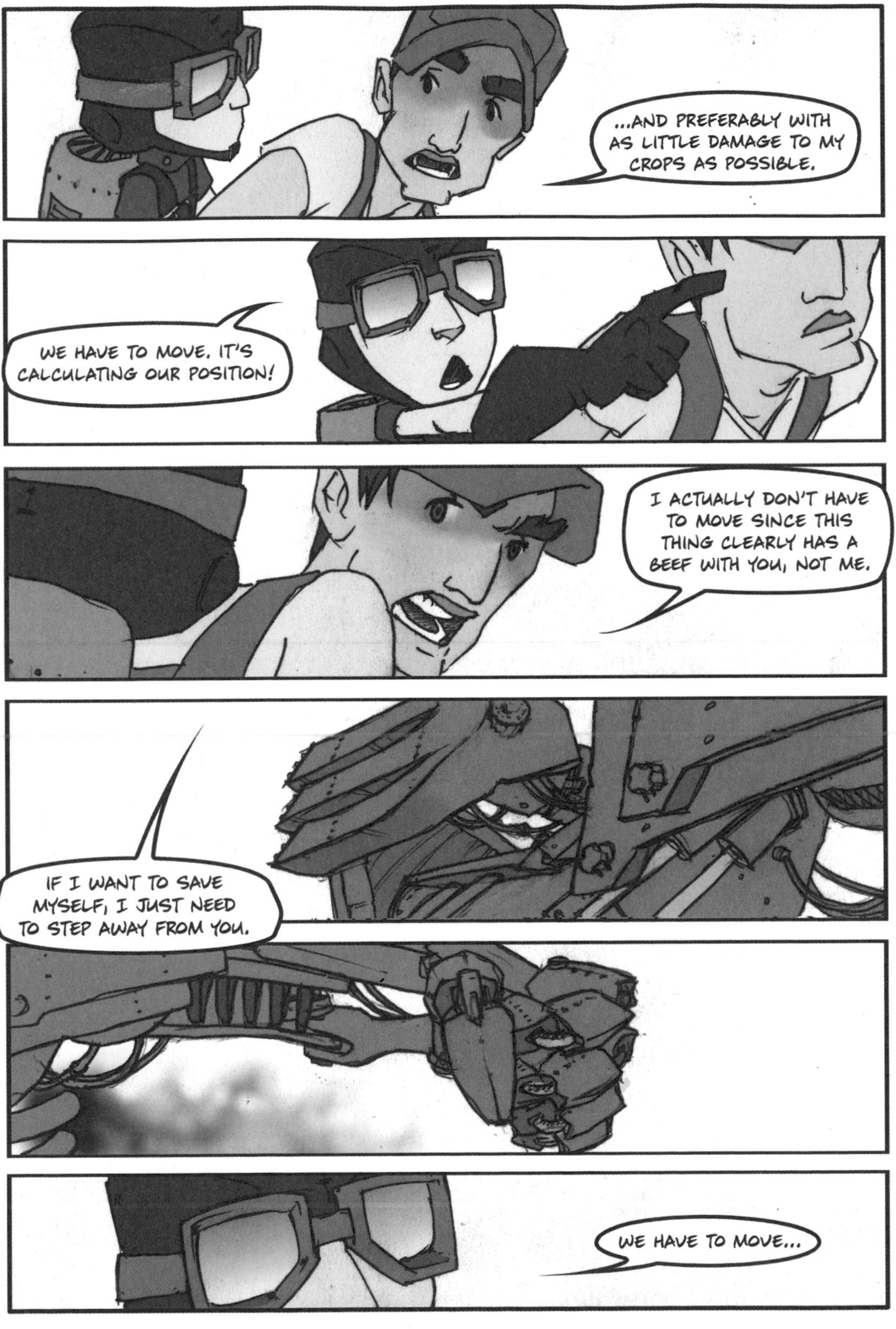
...AND PREFERABLY WITH AS LITTLE DAMAGE TO MY CROPS AS POSSIBLE.
WE HAVE TO MOVE. IT'S CALCULATING OUR POSITION!
I ACTUALLY DON'T HAVE TO MOVE SINCE THIS THING CLEARLY HAS A BEEF WITH YOU, NOT ME.
IF I WANT TO SAVE MYSELF, I JUST NEED TO STEP AWAY FROM YOU.
WE HAVE TO MOVE...

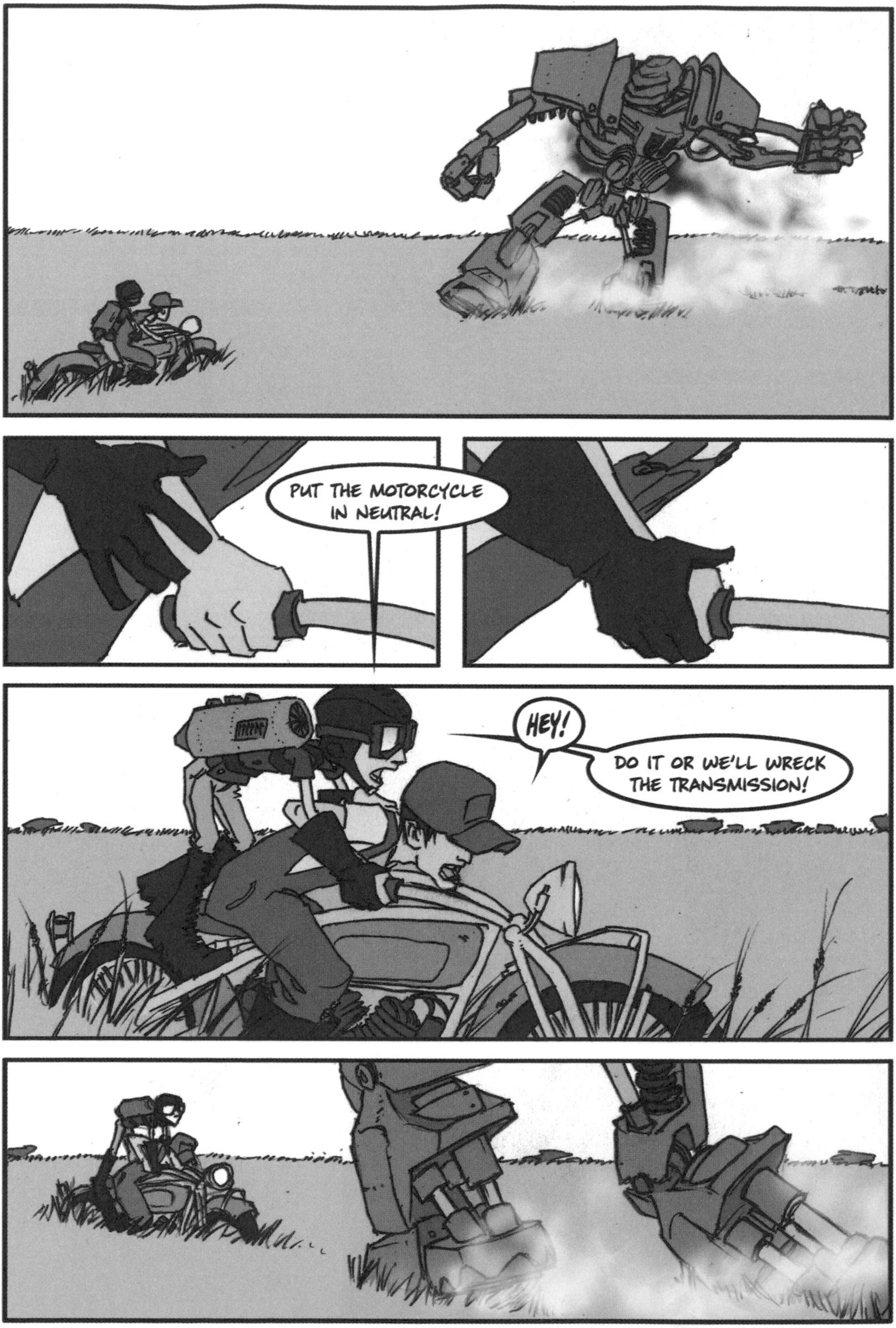
PUT THE MOTORCYCLE IN NEUTRAL!
HEY!
DO IT OR WE'LL WRECK THE TRANSMISSION!

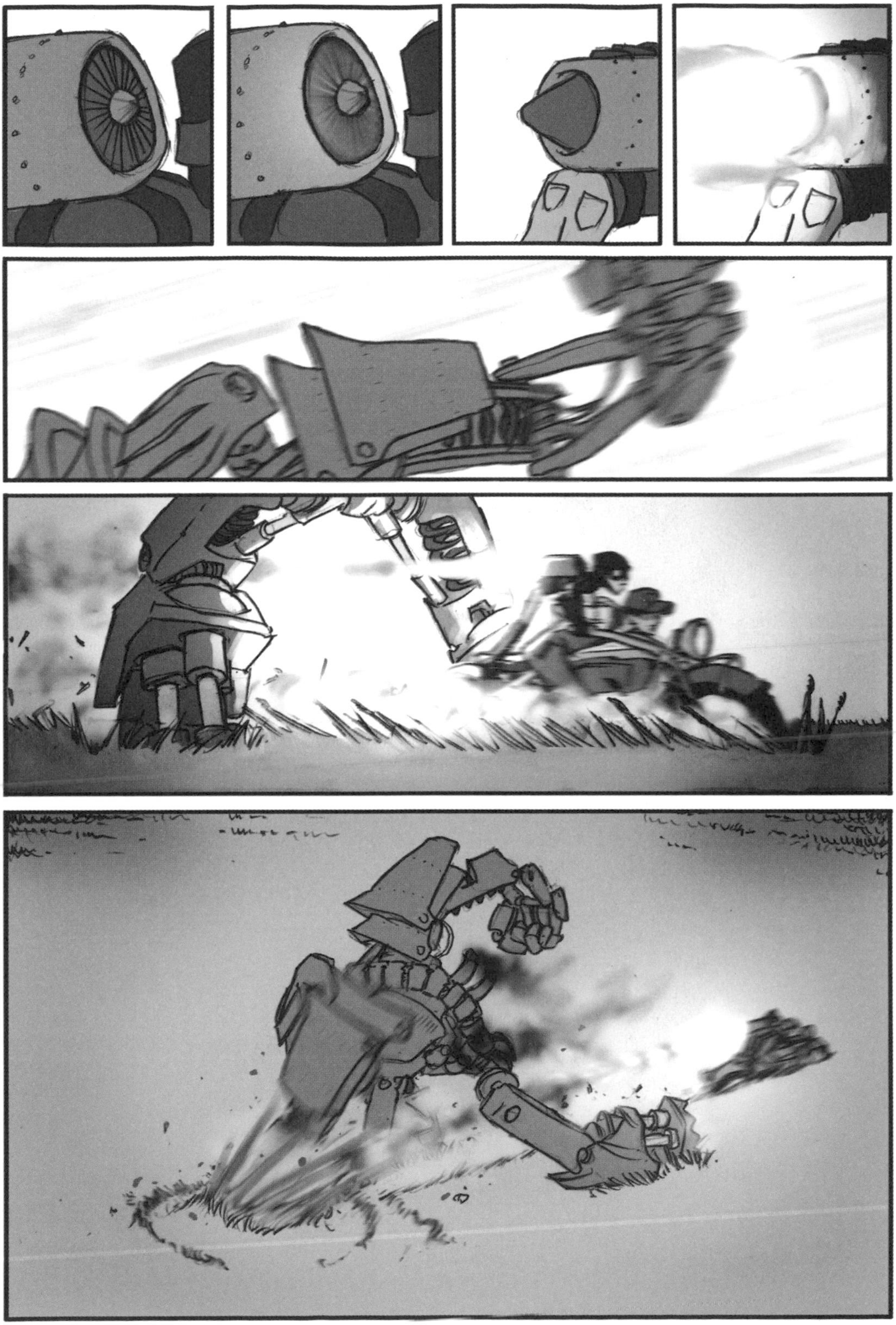
10

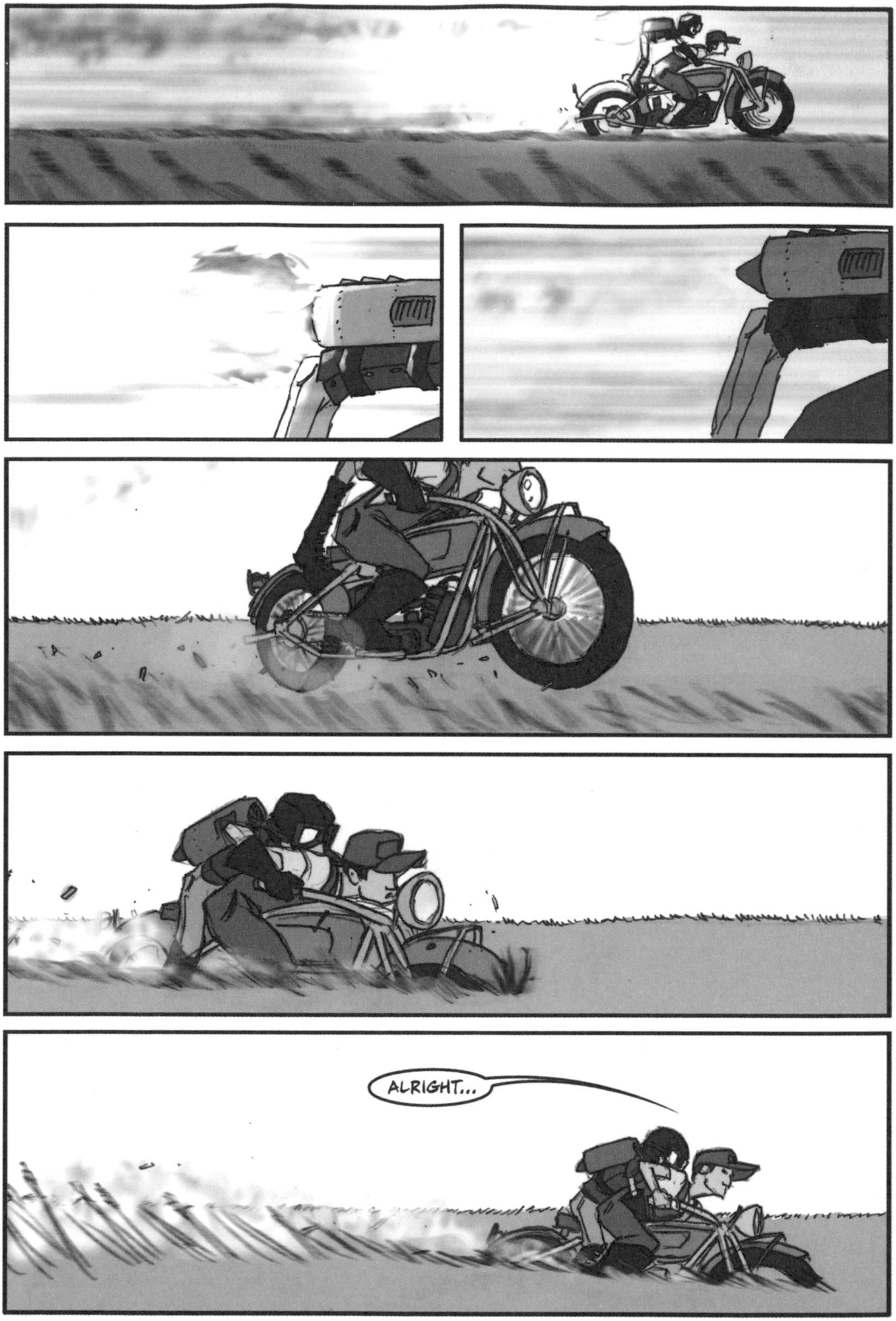
ALRIGHT...

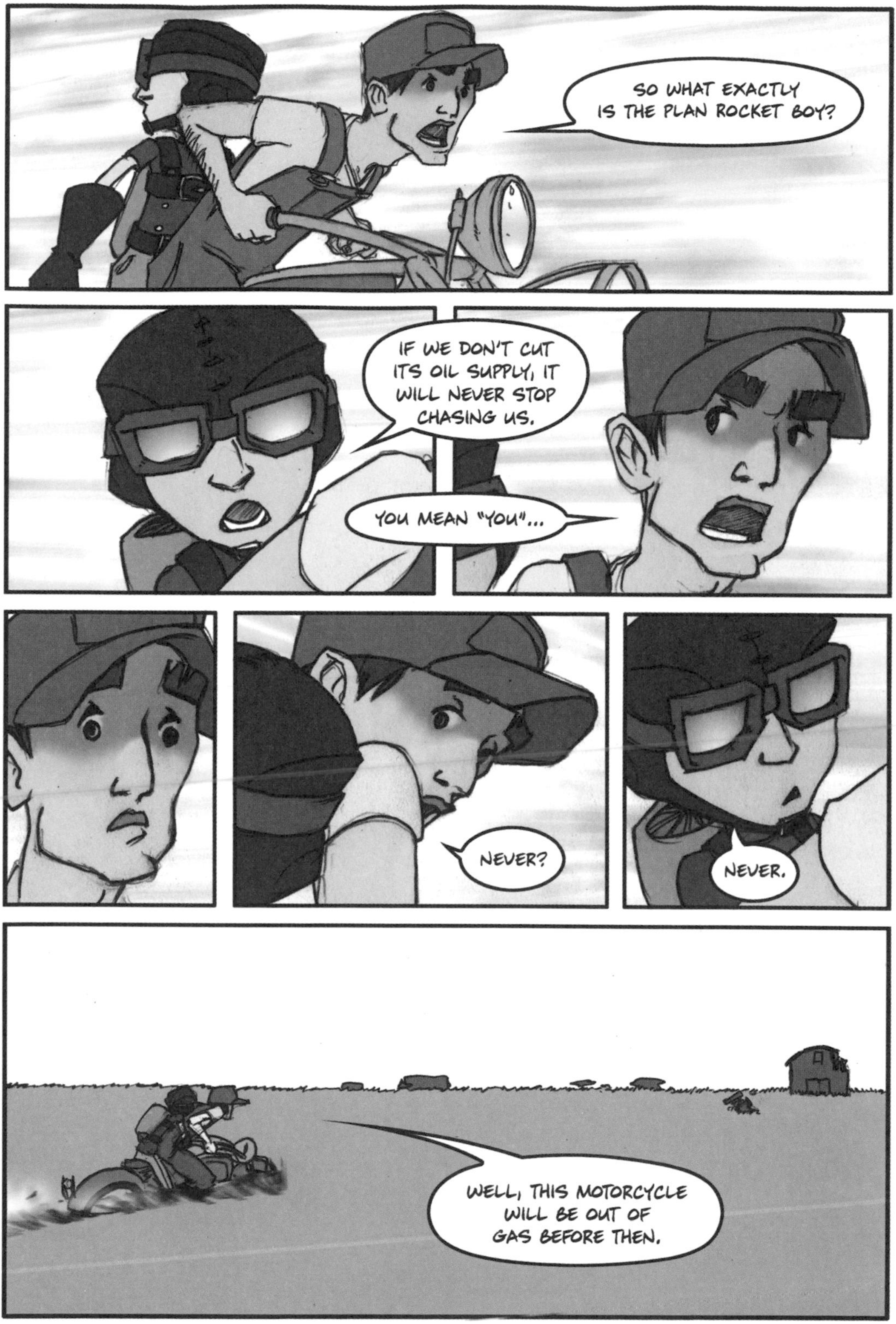
SO WHAT EXACTLY IS THE PLAN ROCKET BOY?
IF WE DON'T CUT ITS OIL SUPPLY, IT WILL NEVER STOP CHASING US.
YOU MEAN "YOU"...
NEVER?
NEVER.
WELL, THIS MOTORCYCLE WILL BE OUT OF GAS BEFORE THEN.

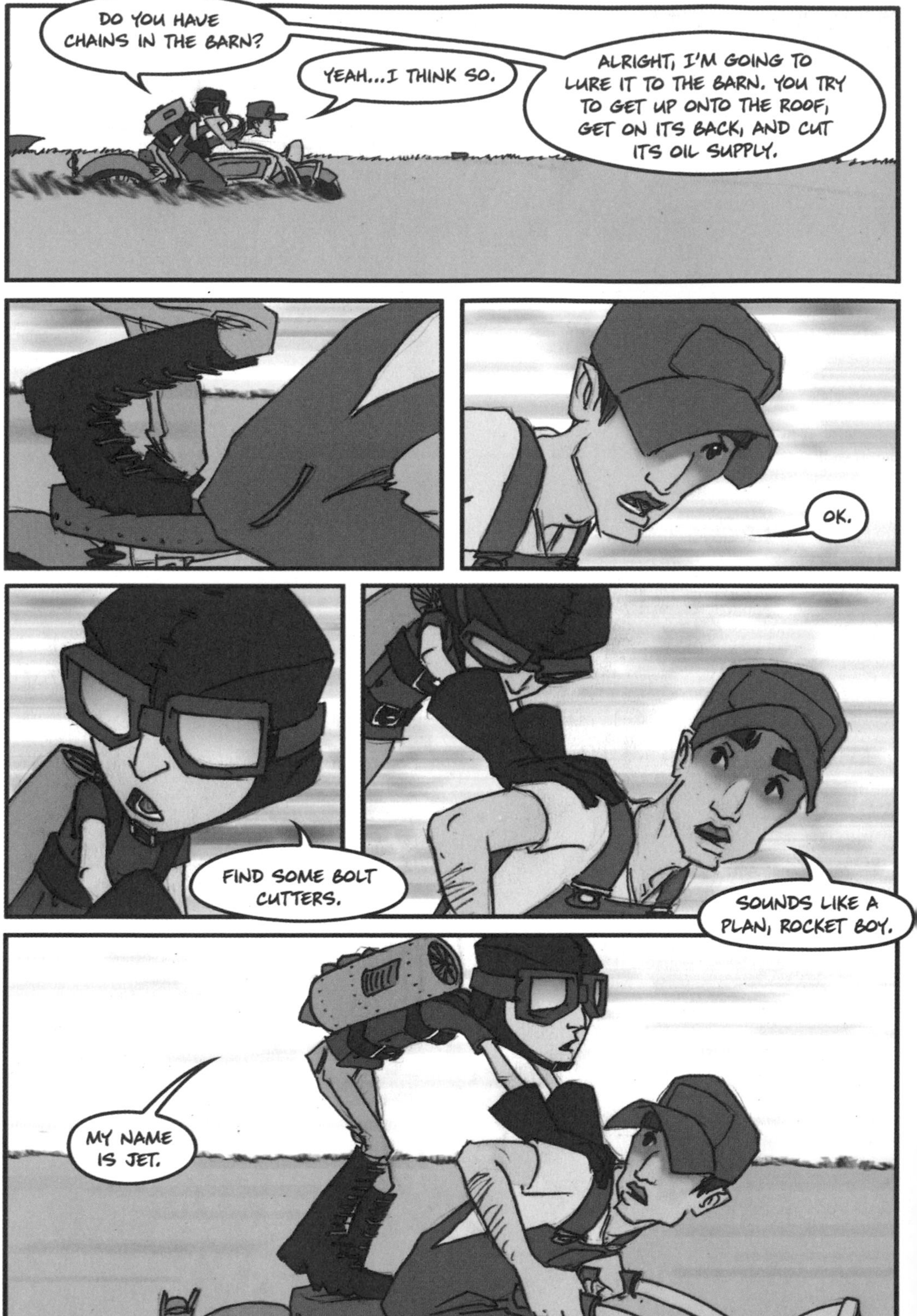
DO YOU HAVE CHAINS IN THE BARN?
YEAH...I THINK SO.
ALRIGHT, I'M GOING TO LURE IT TO THE BARN. YOU TRY TO GET UP ONTO THE ROOF, GET ON ITS BACK, AND CUT ITS OIL SUPPLY.
OK.
FIND SOME BOLT CUTTERS.
SOUNDS LIKE A PLAN, ROCKET BOY.
MY NAME IS JET.

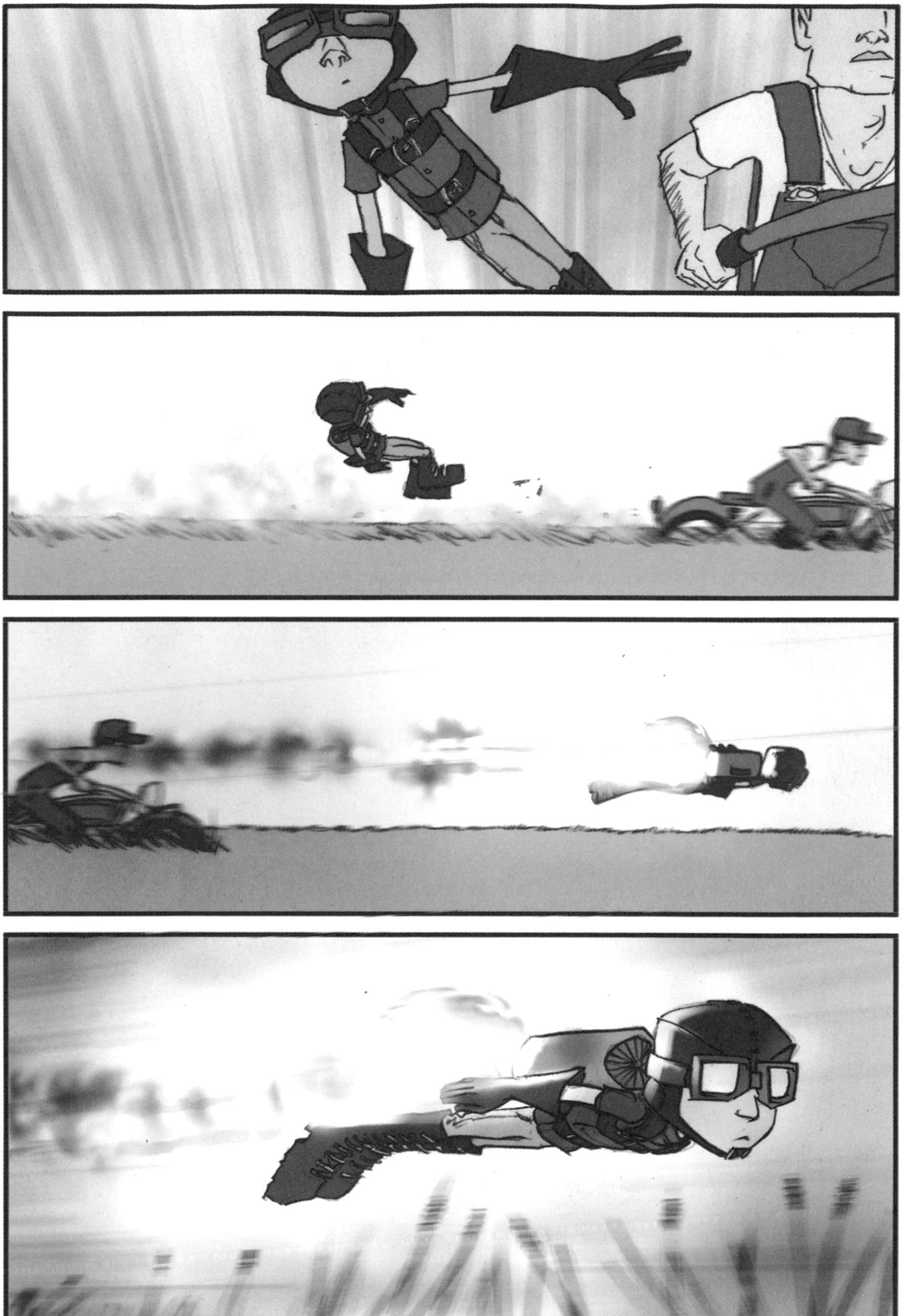

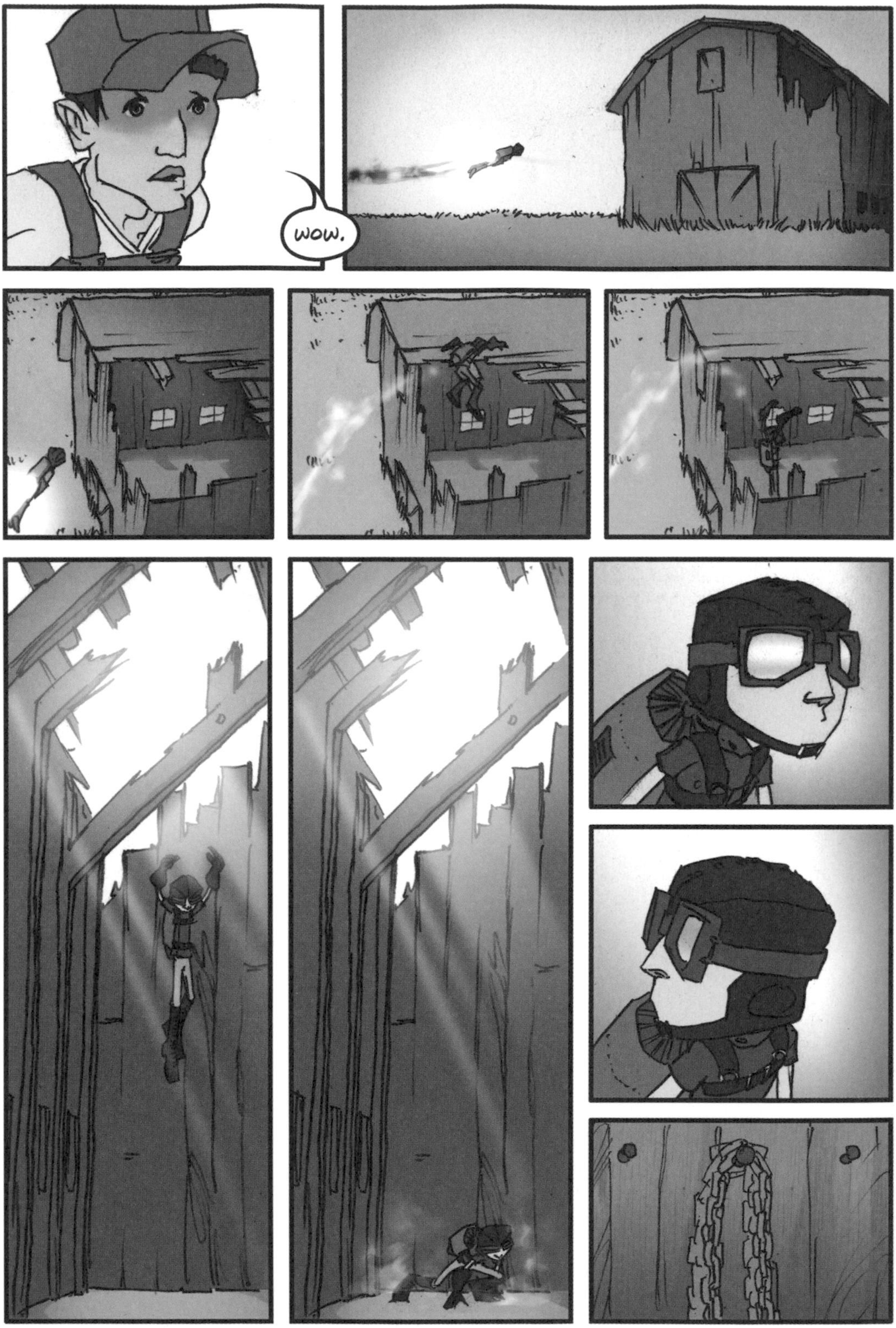
WOW.

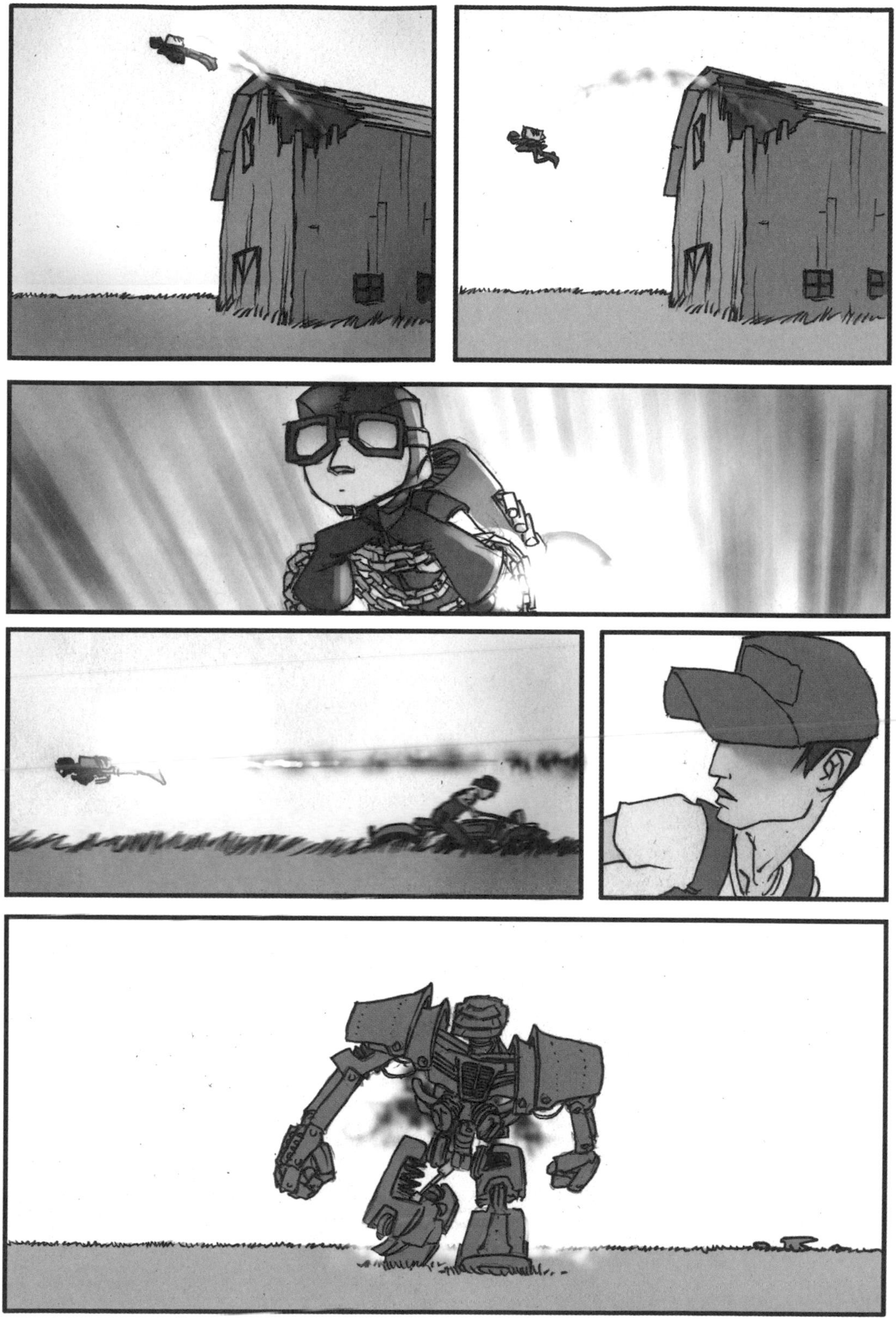

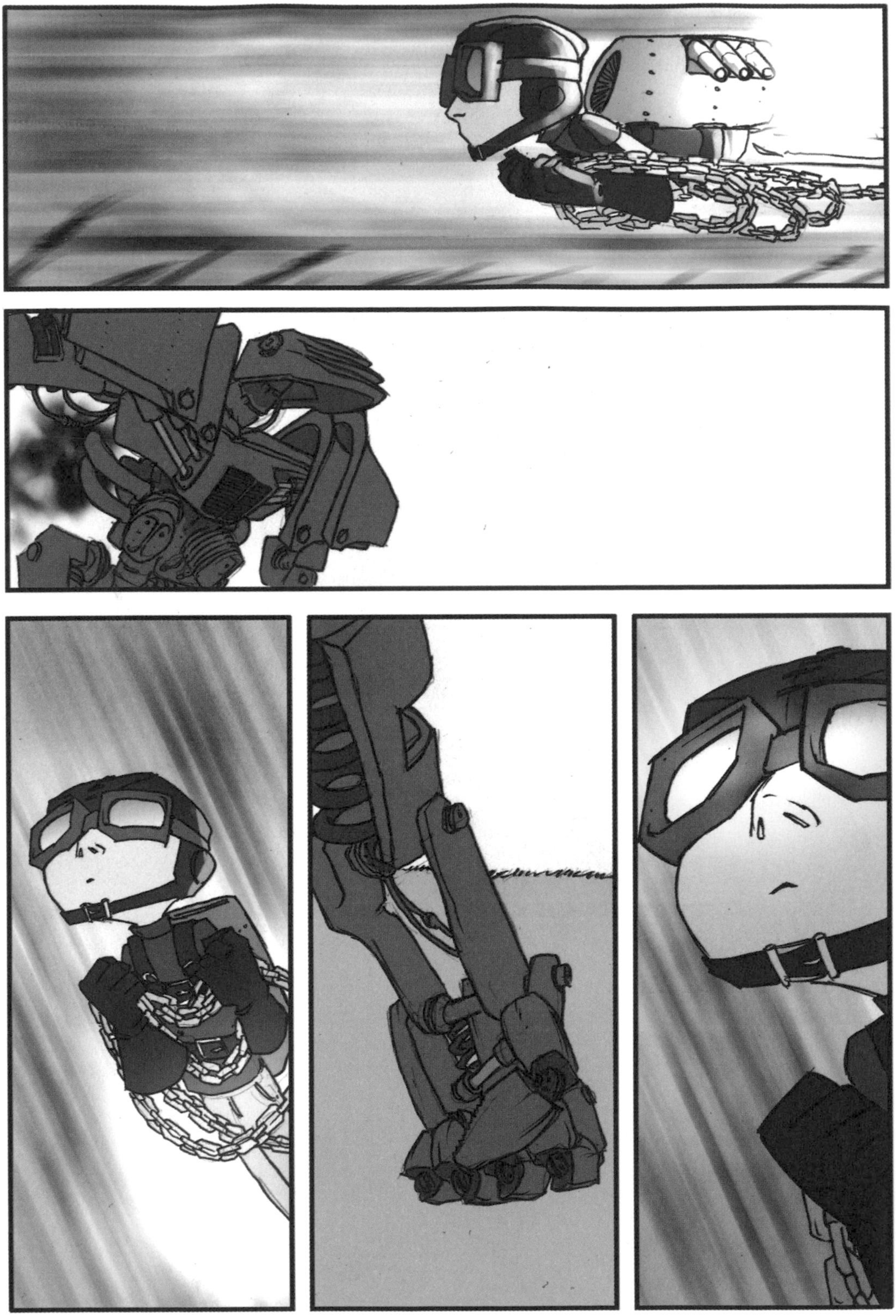

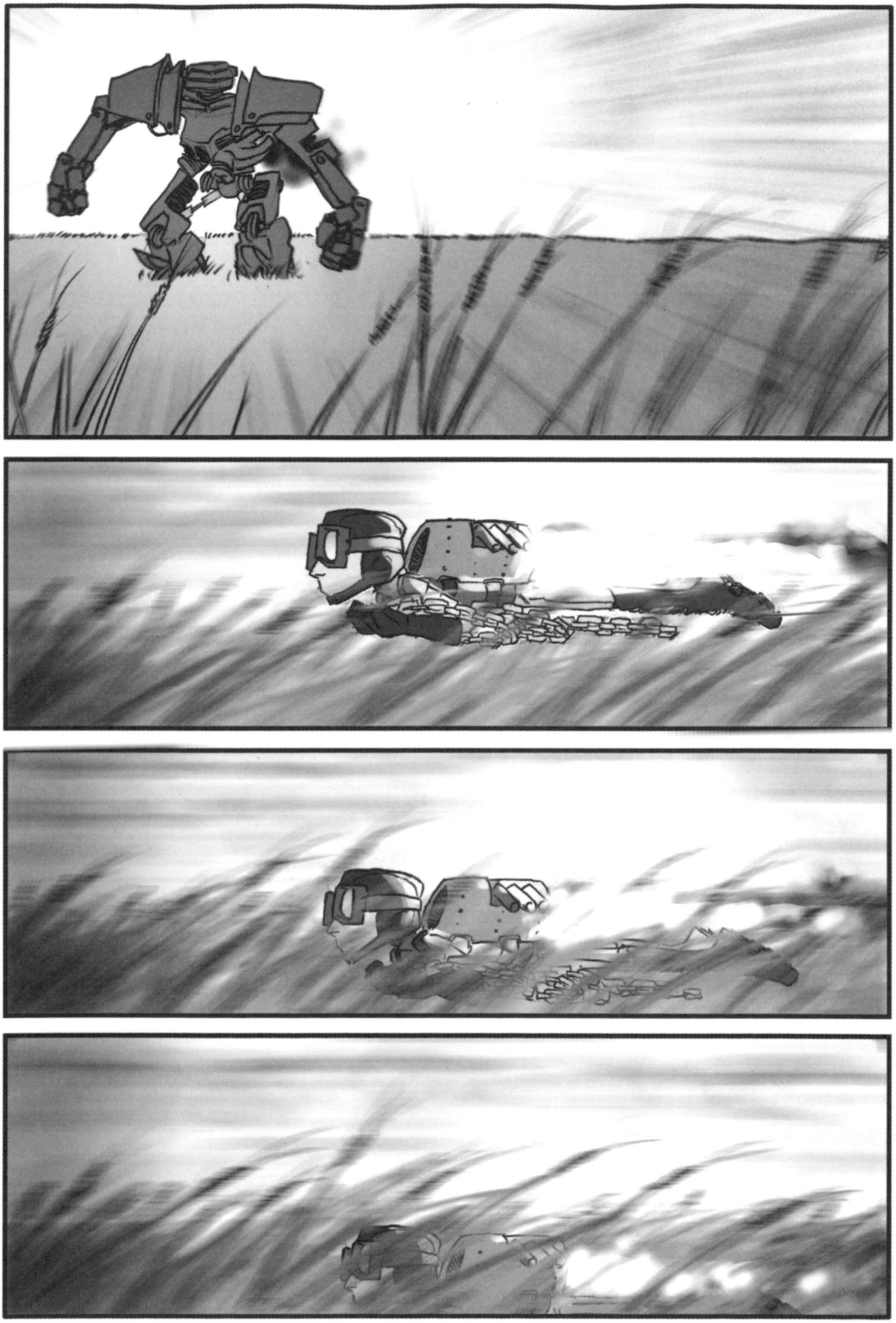

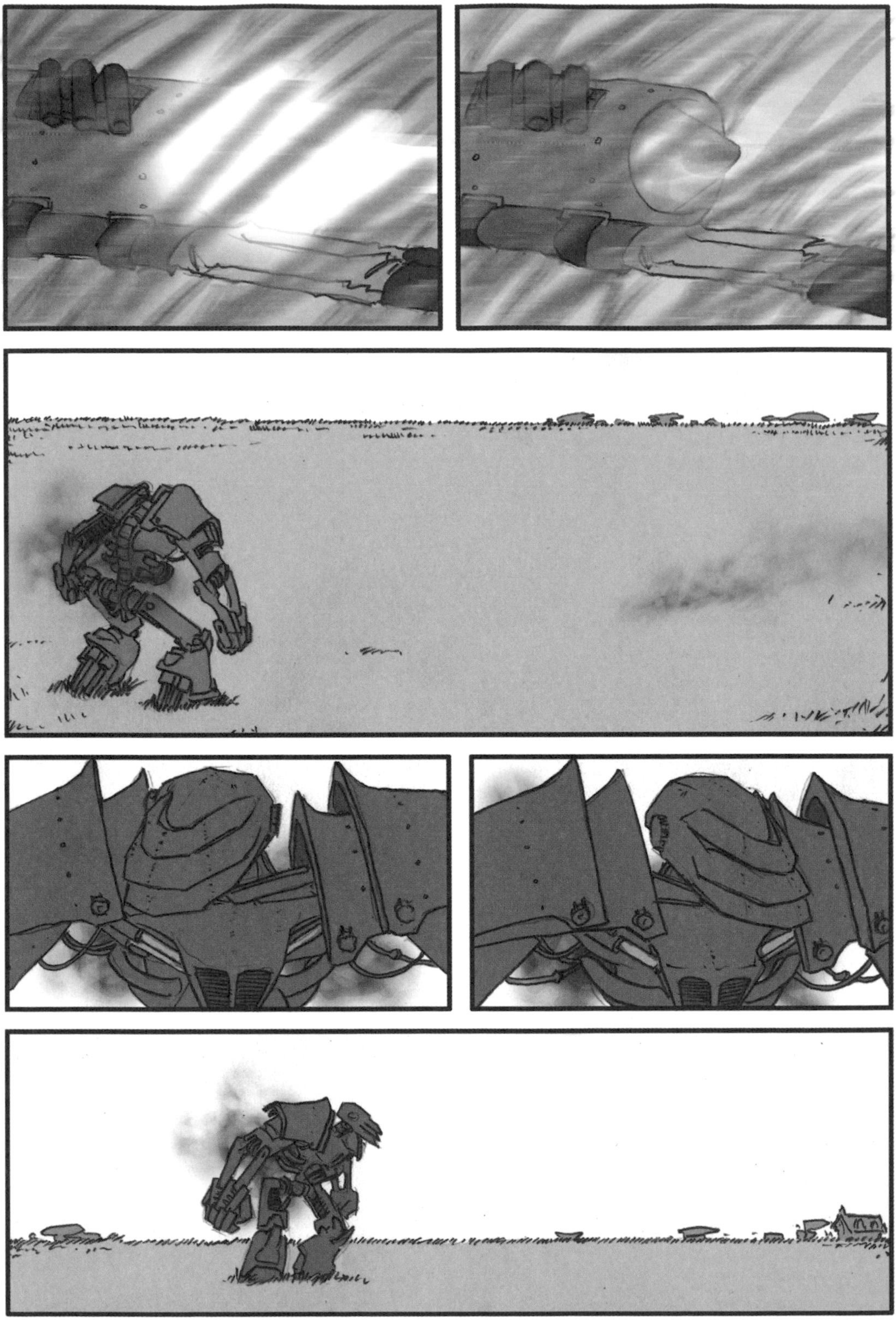

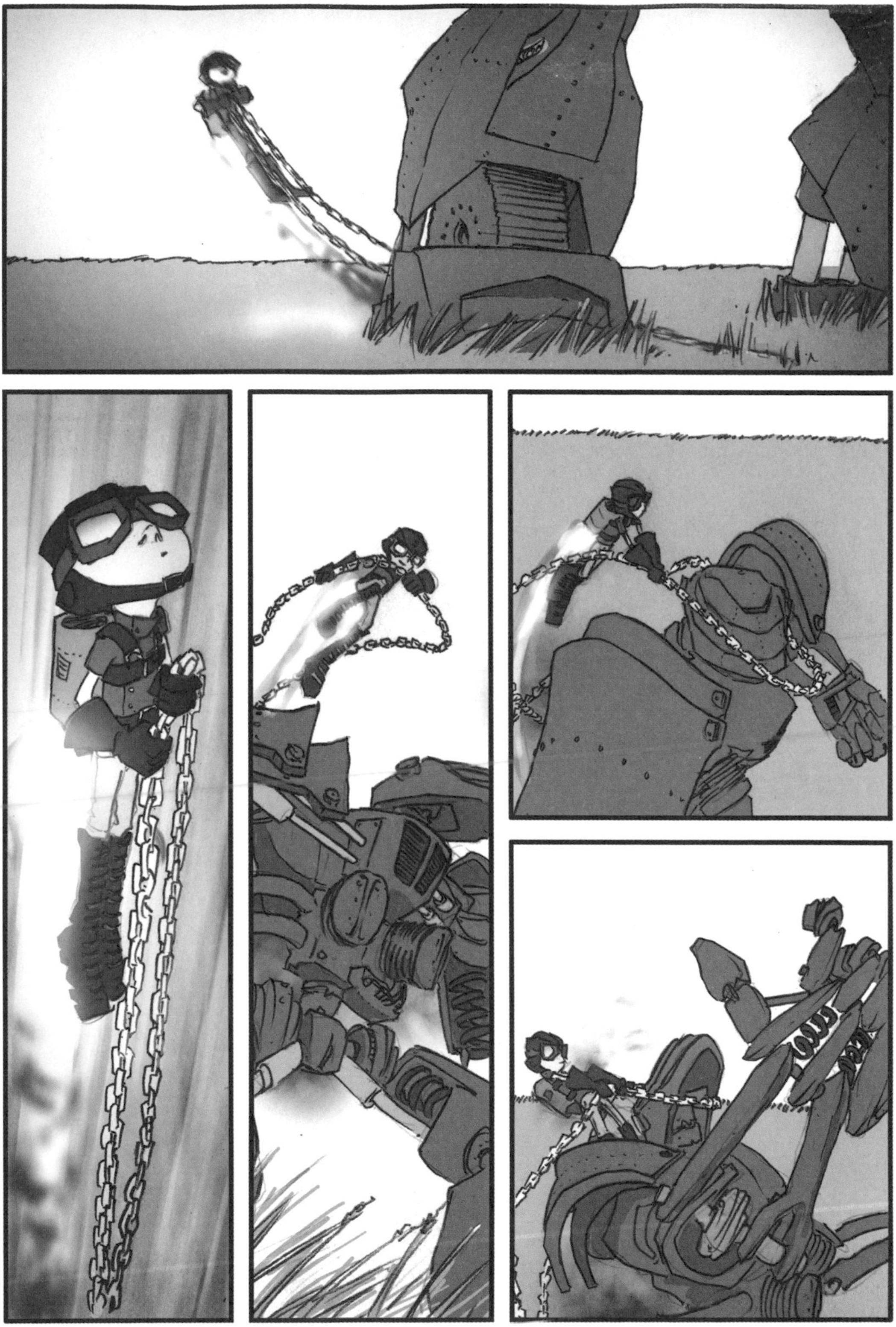

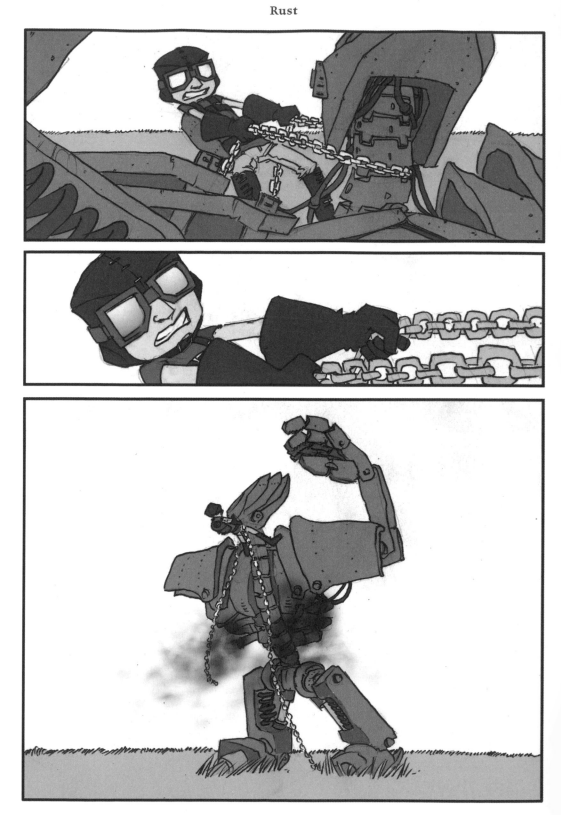

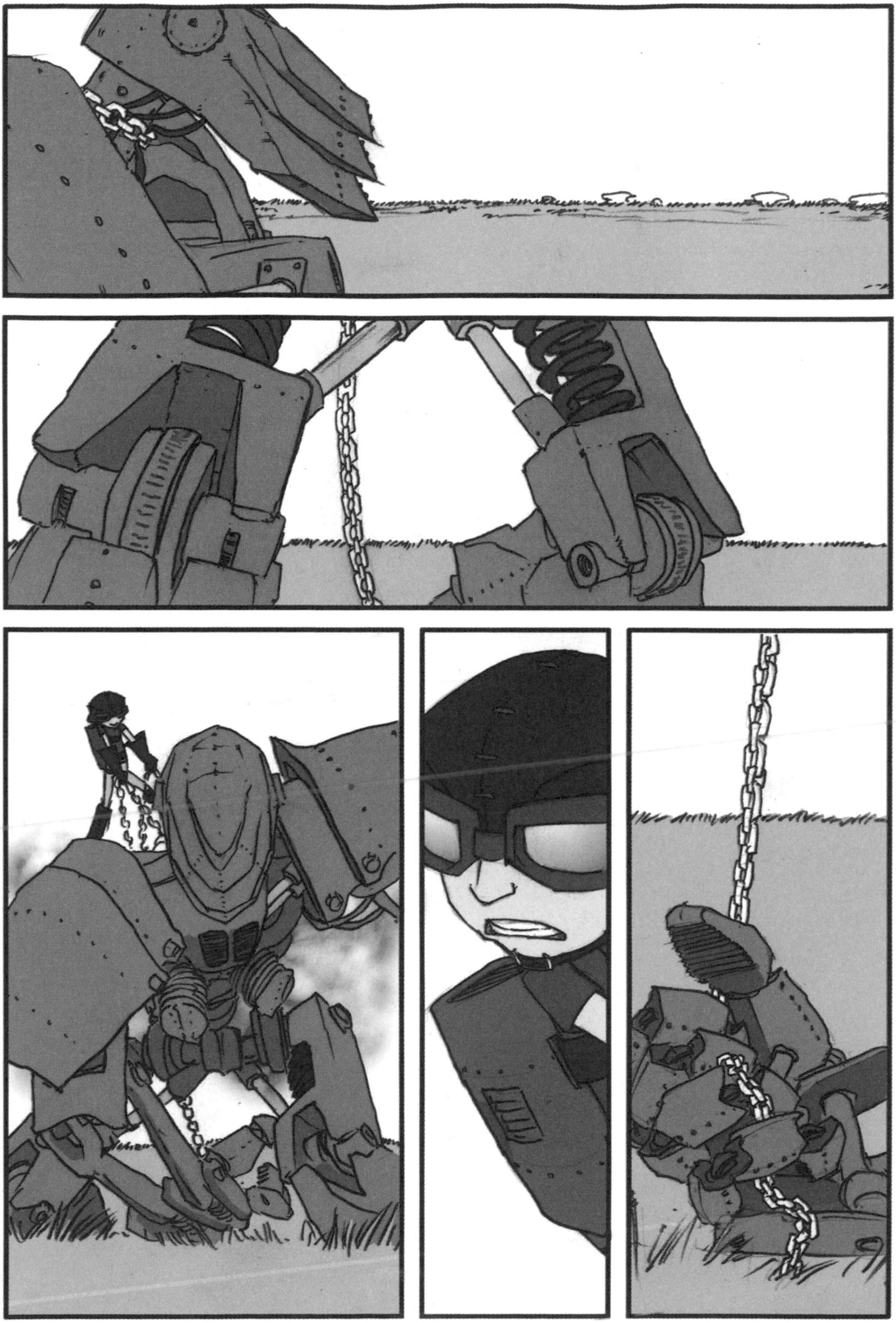

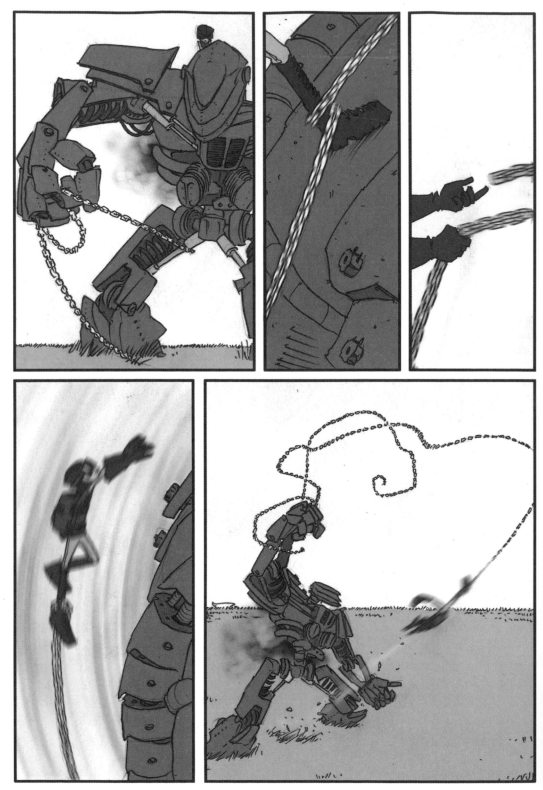

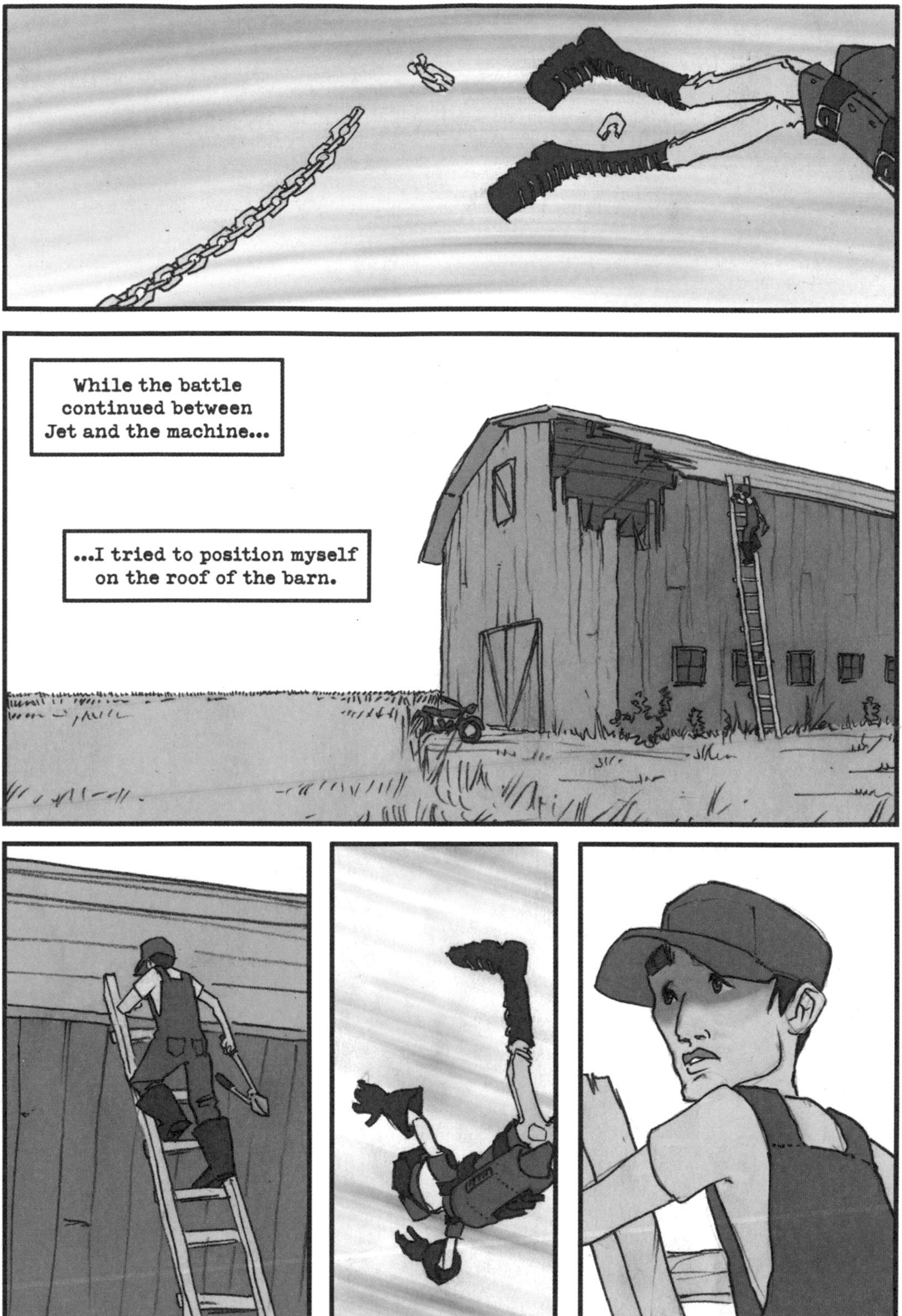
While the battle continued between Jet and the machine...
...I tried to position myself on the roof of the barn.

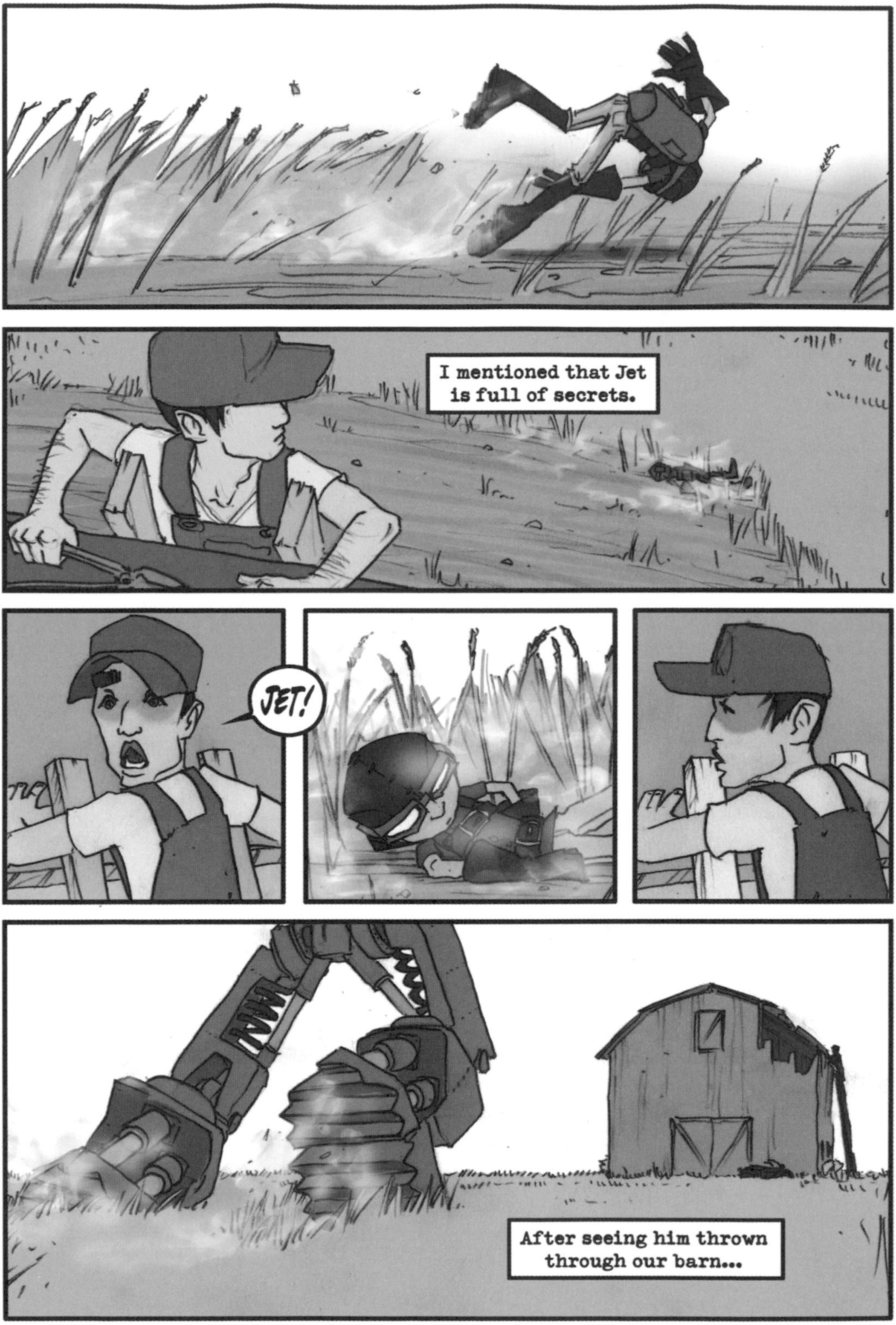
I mentioned that Jet is full of secrets.
JET!
After seeing him thrown through our barn...

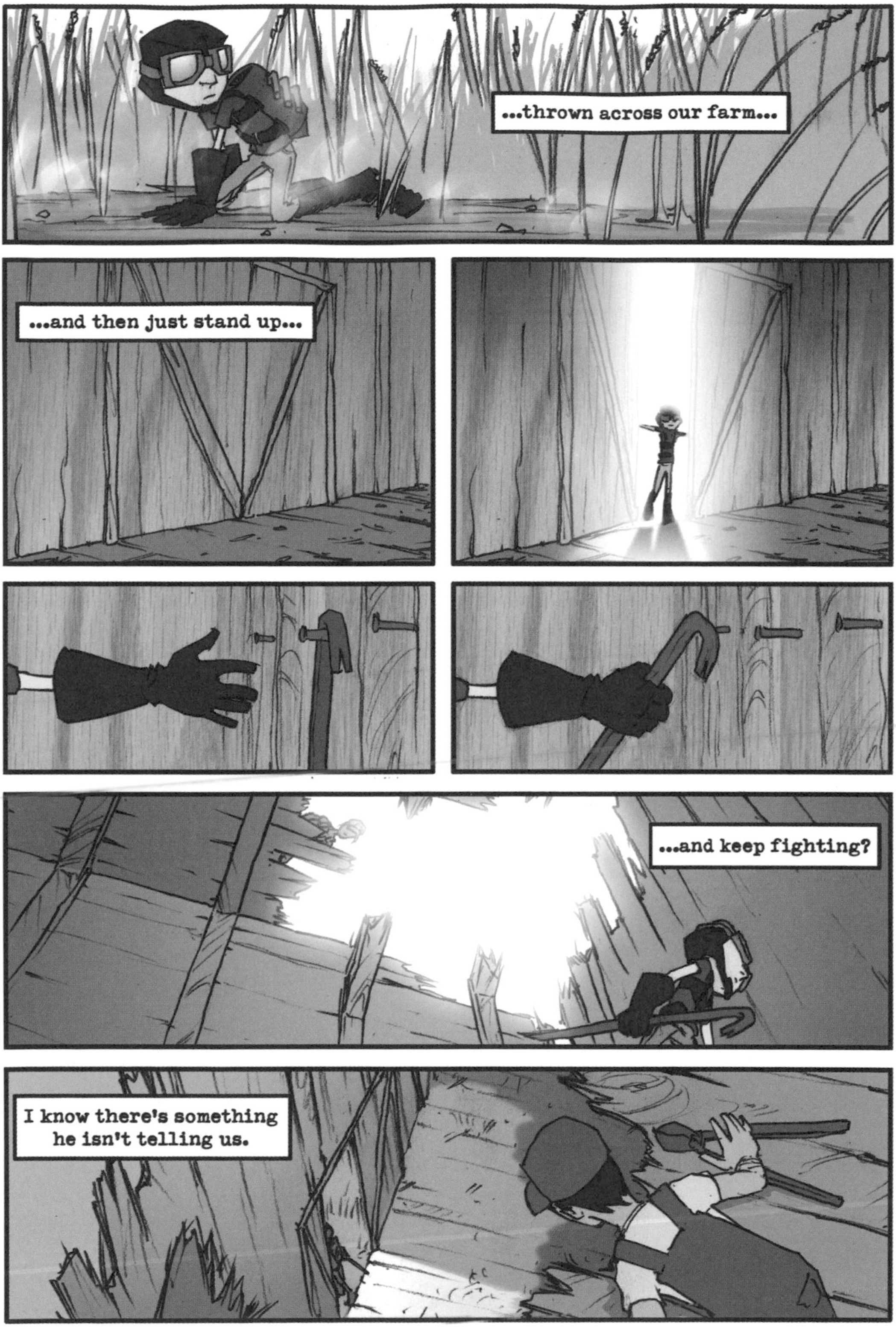
...thrown across our farm...
...and then just stand up...
...and keep fighting?
I know there's something he isn't telling us.

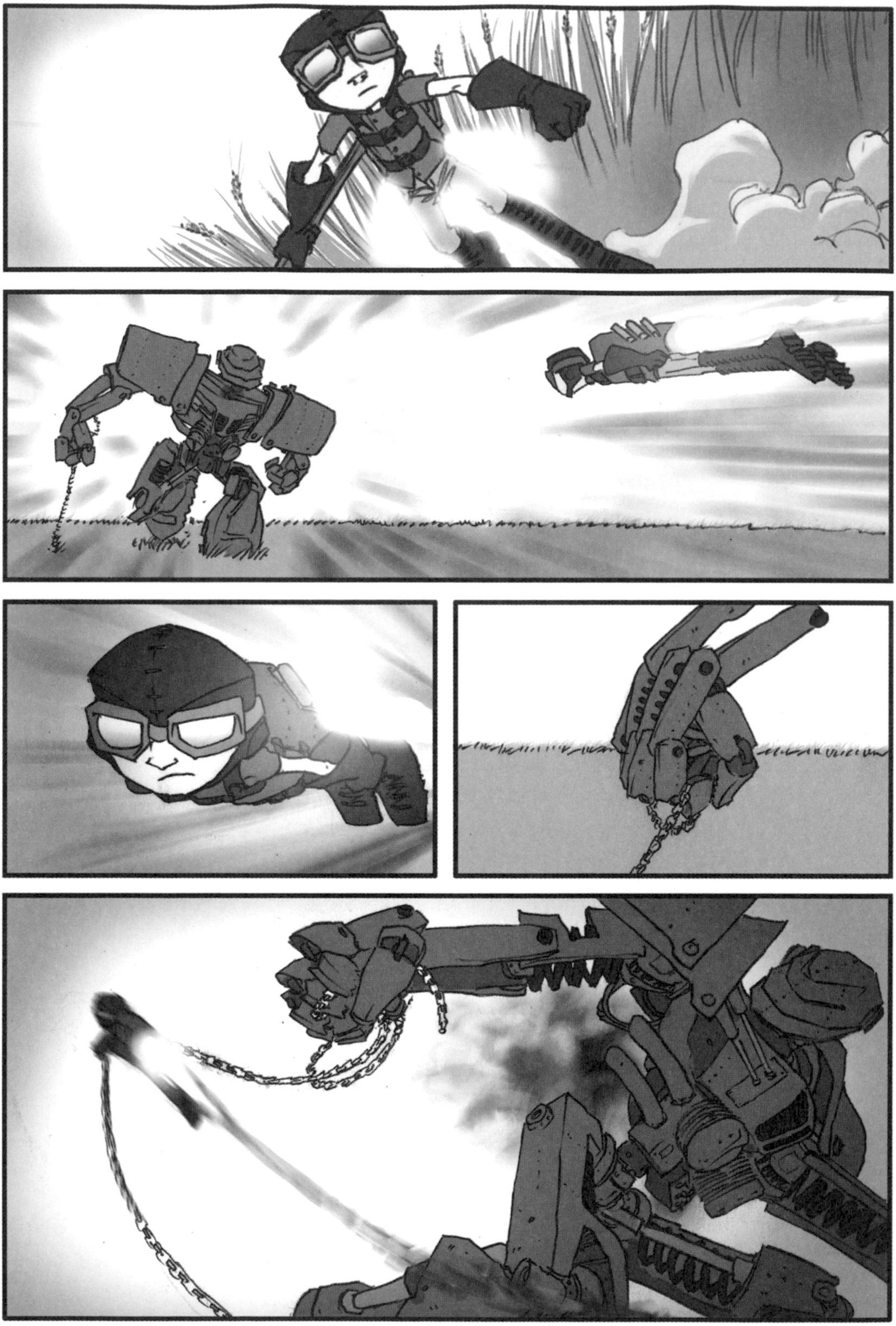

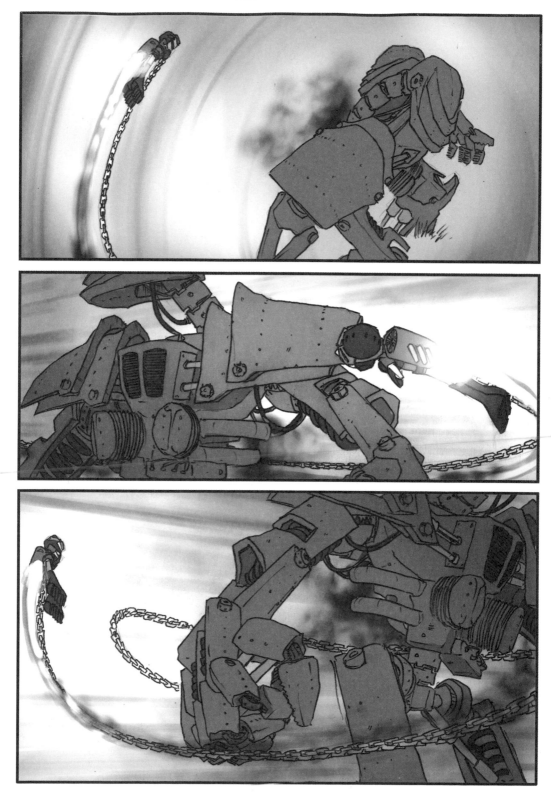

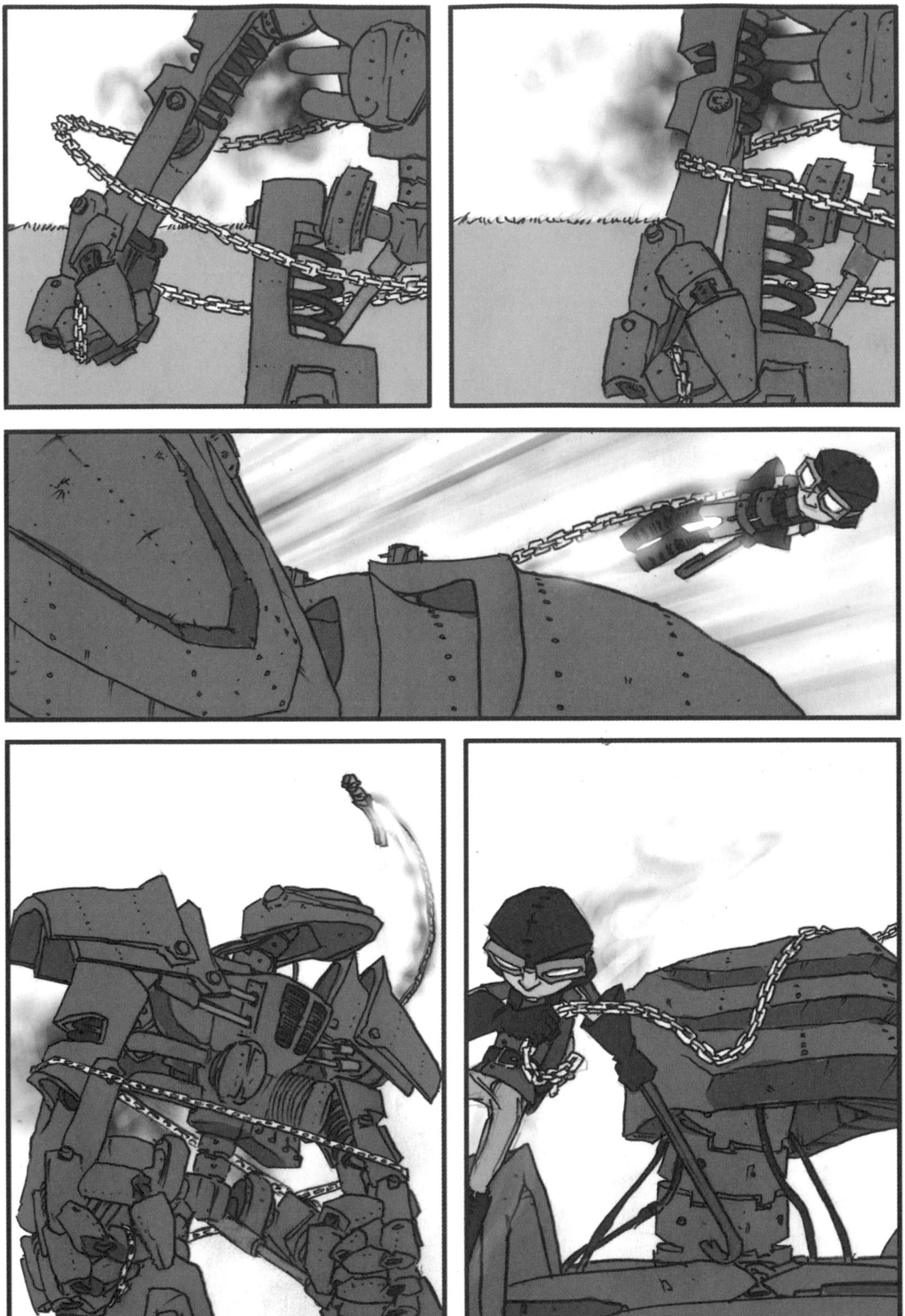

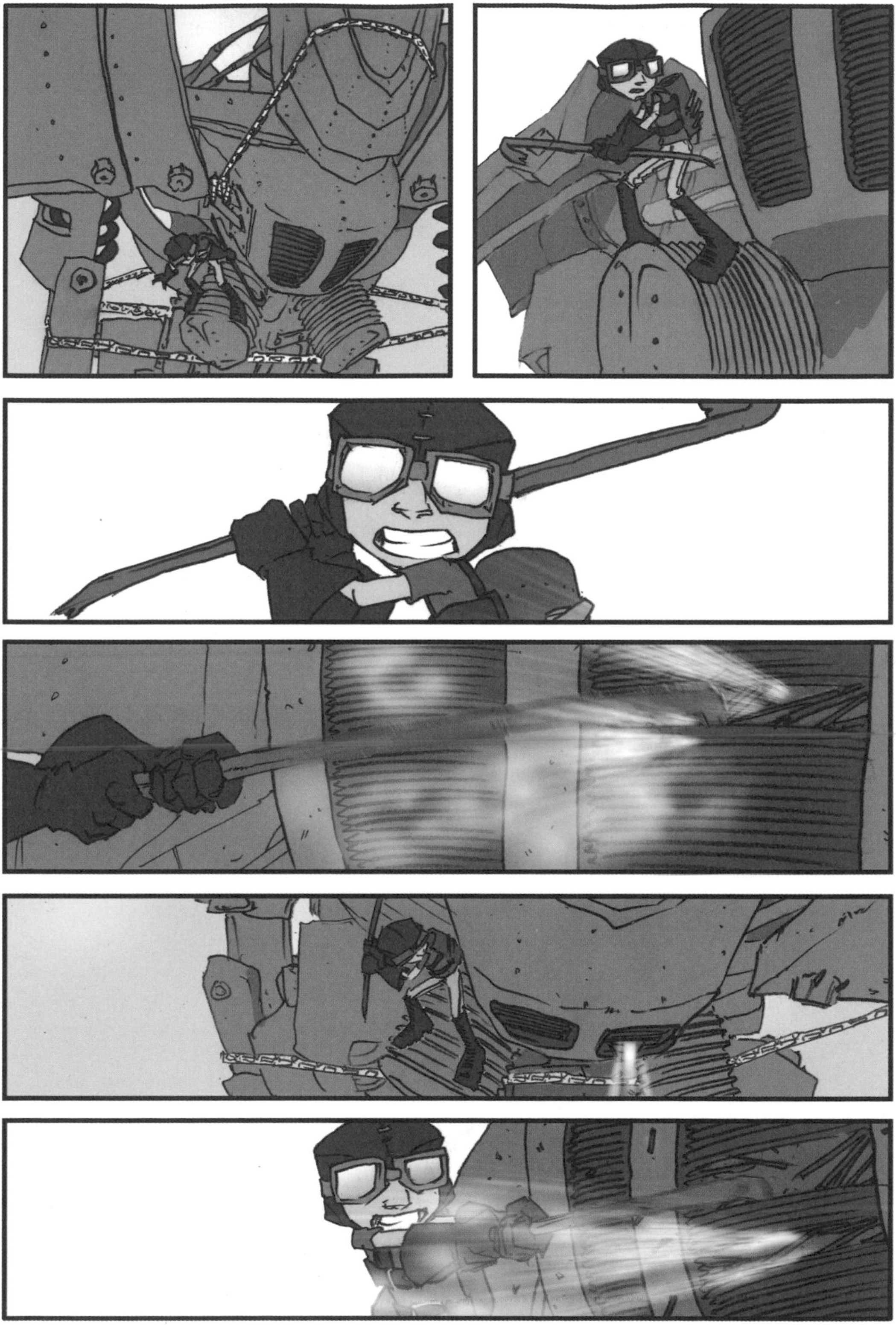

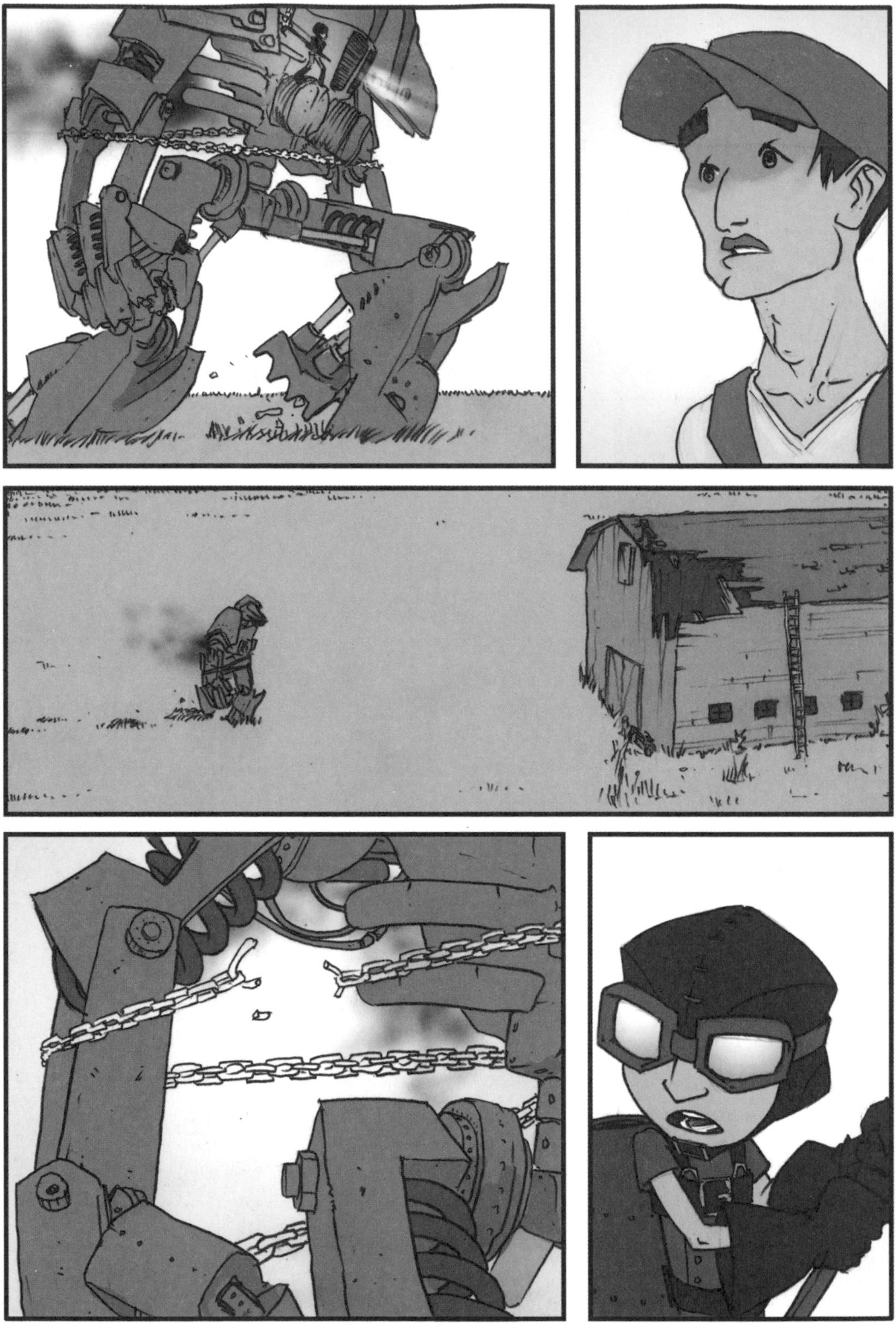

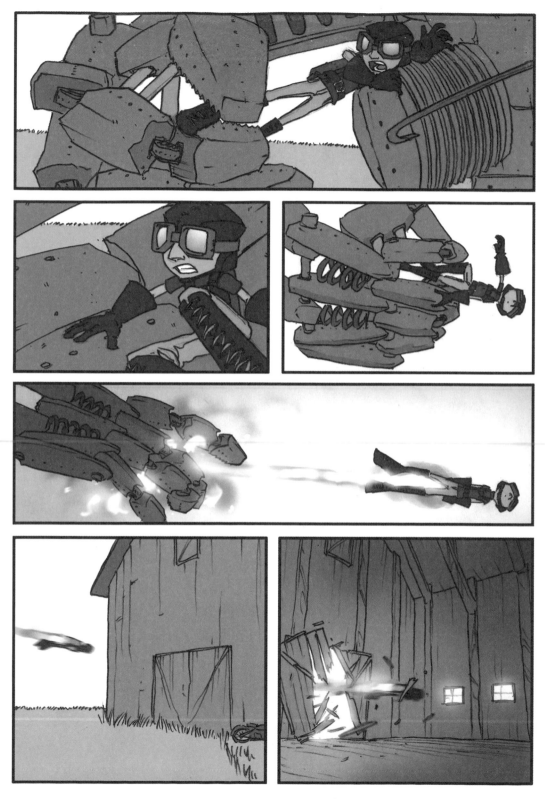

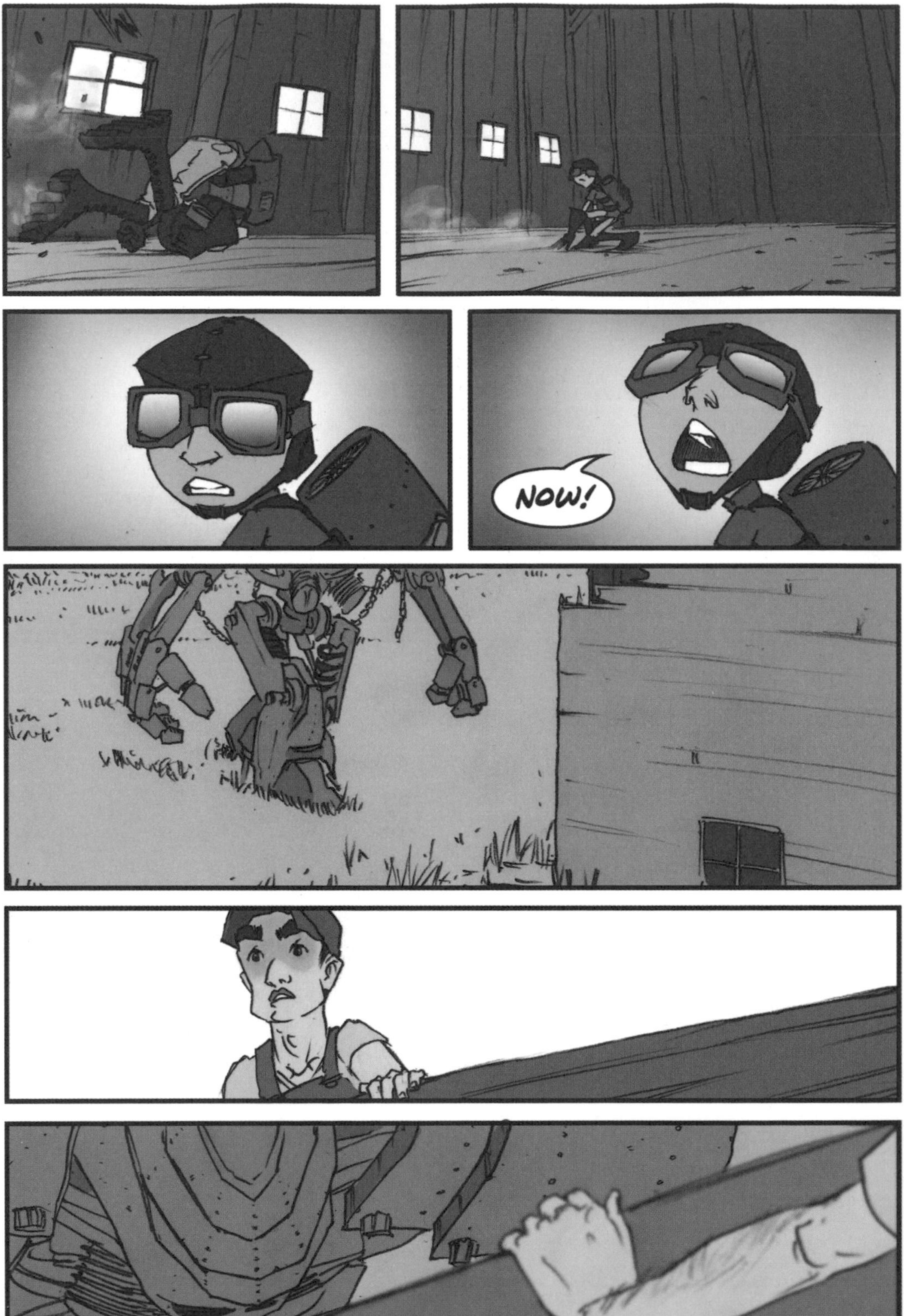
NOW!

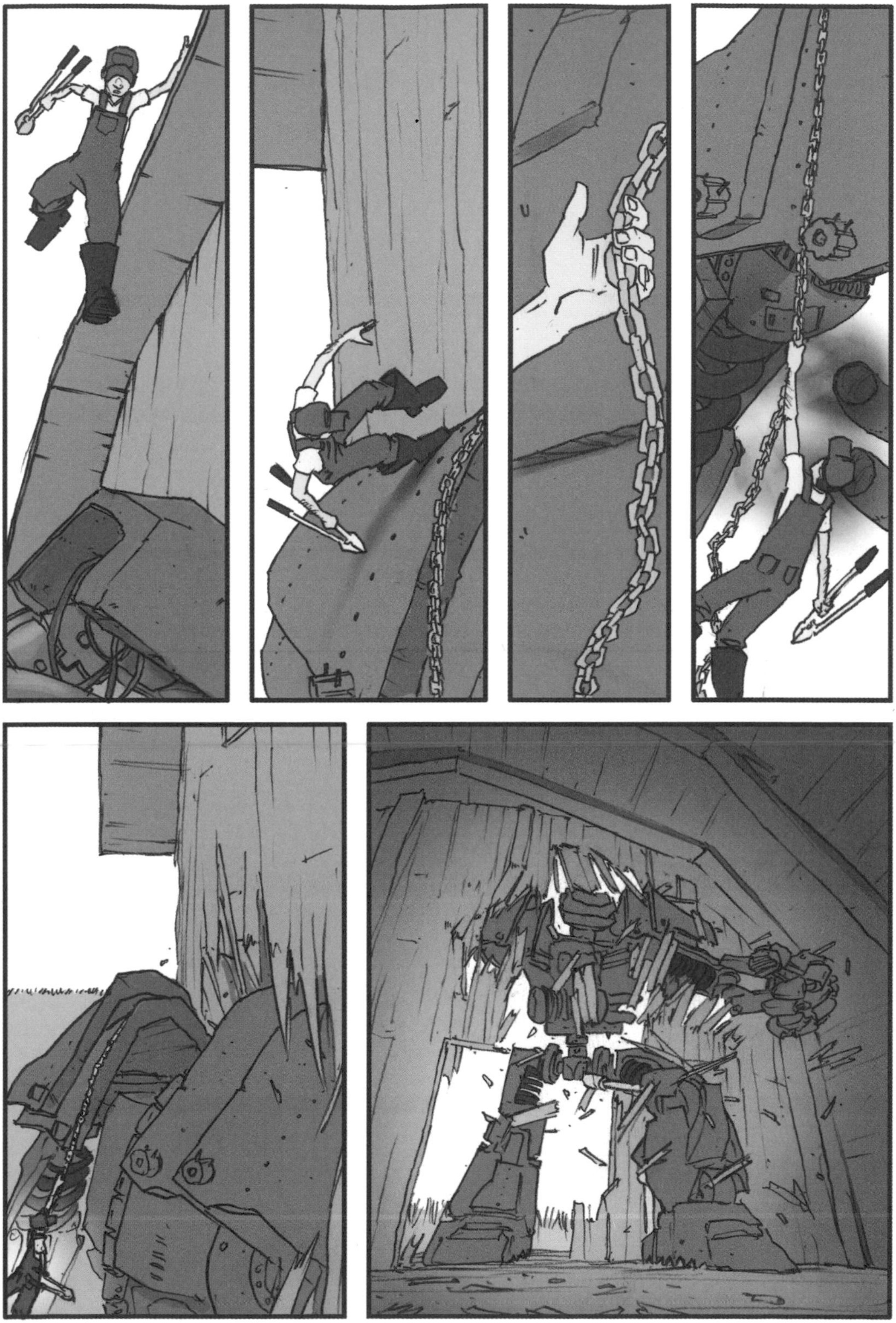

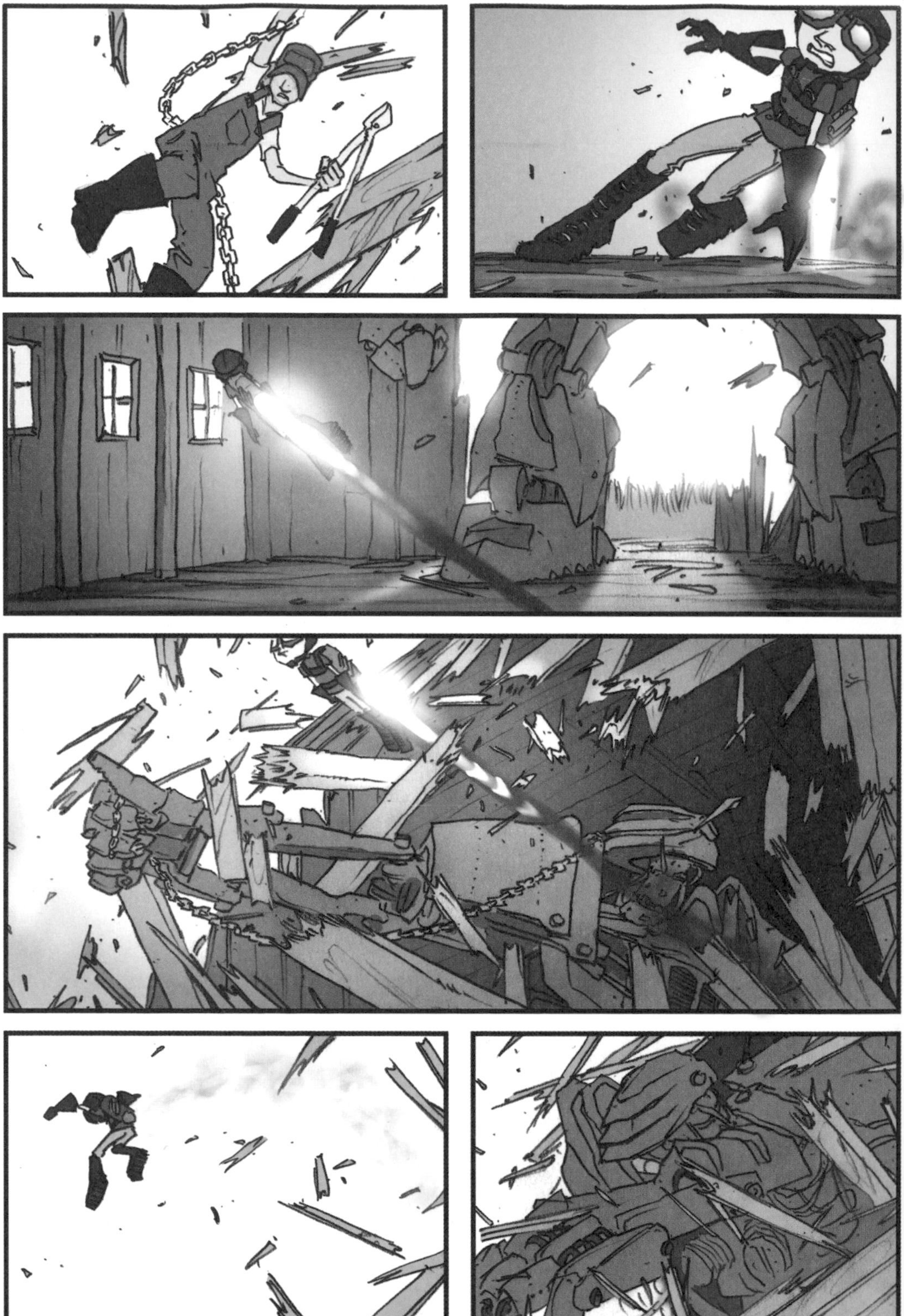

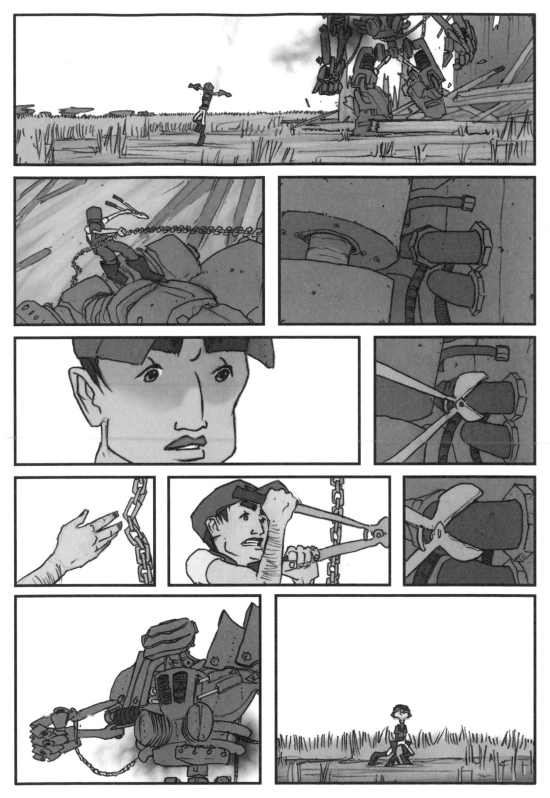

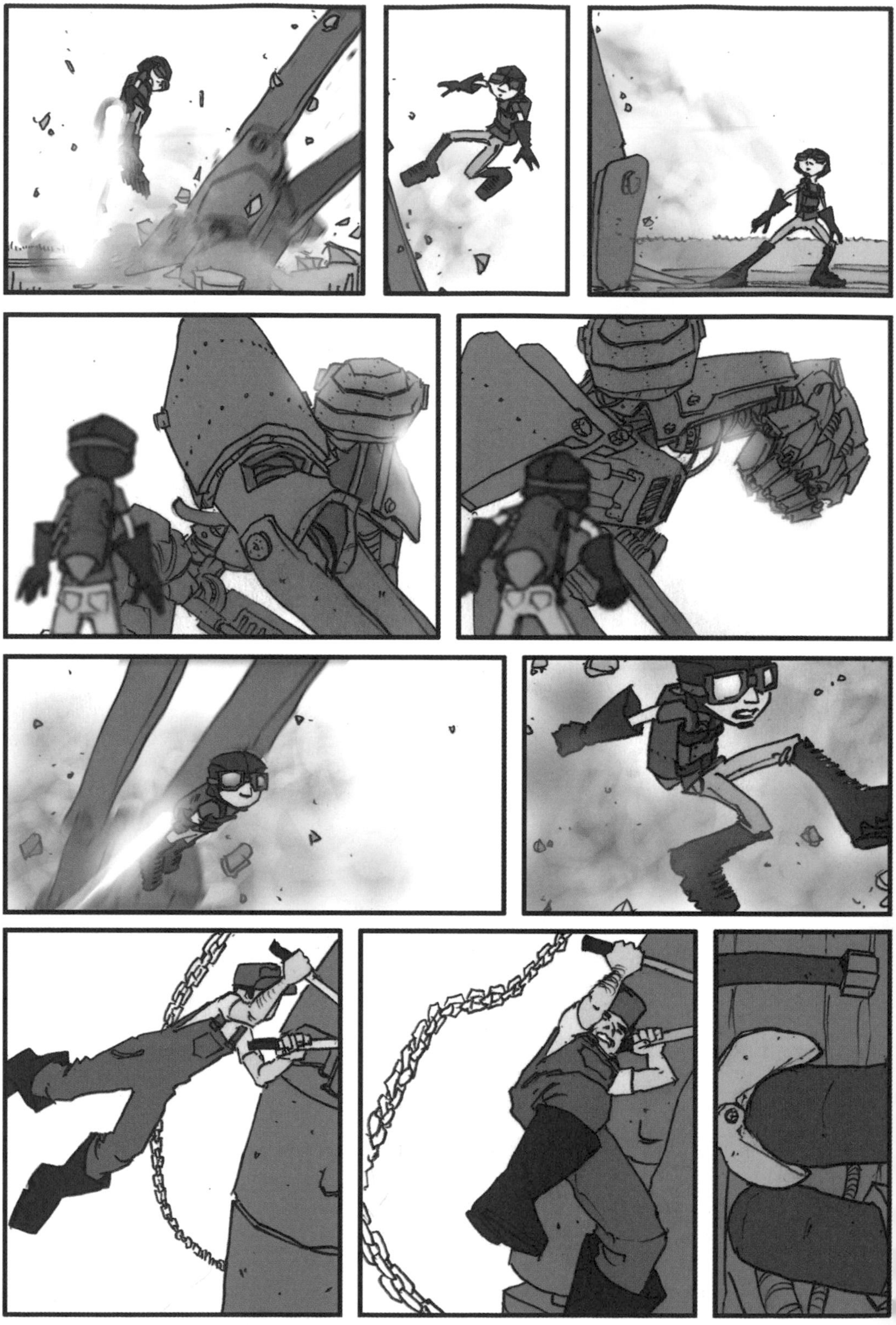

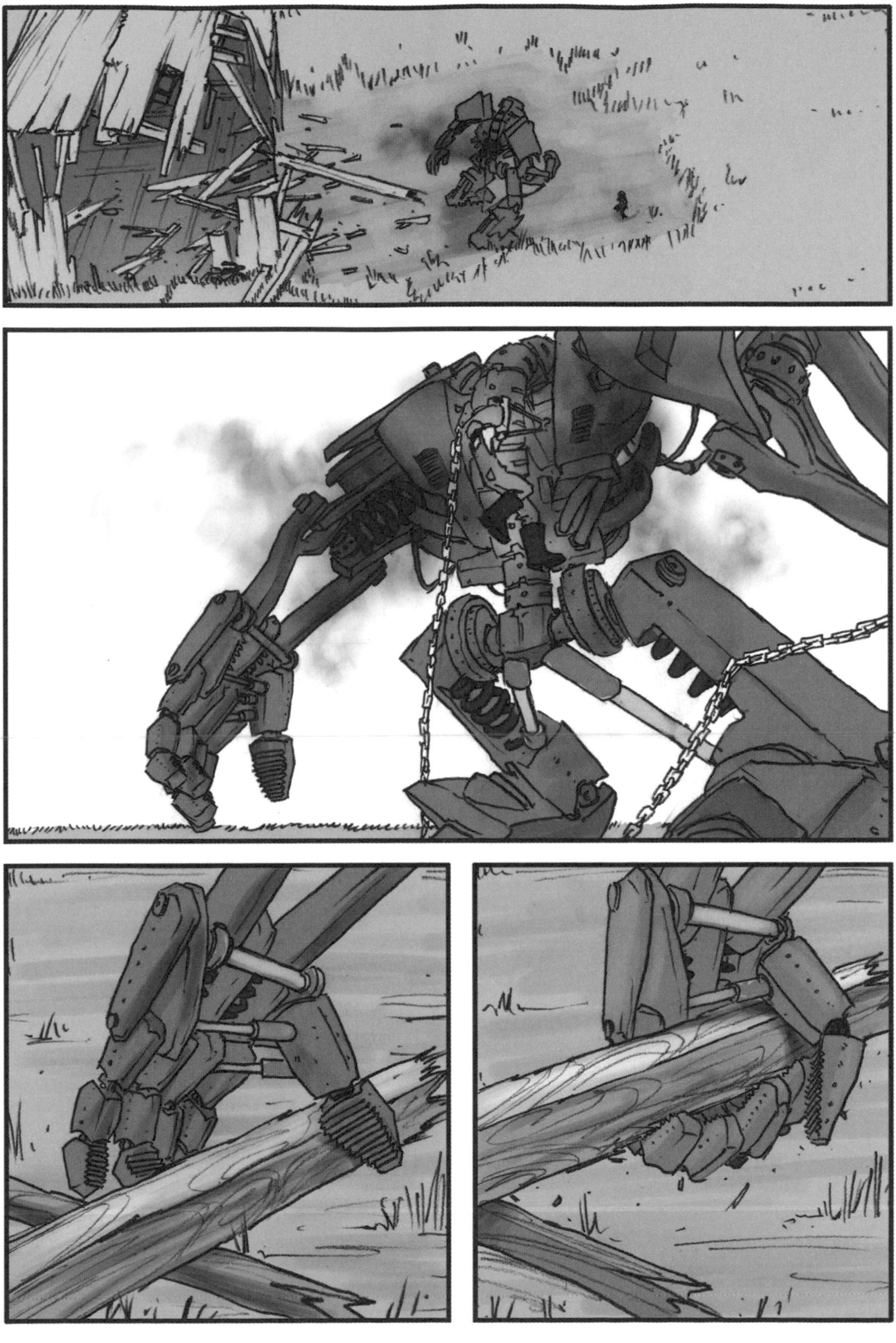

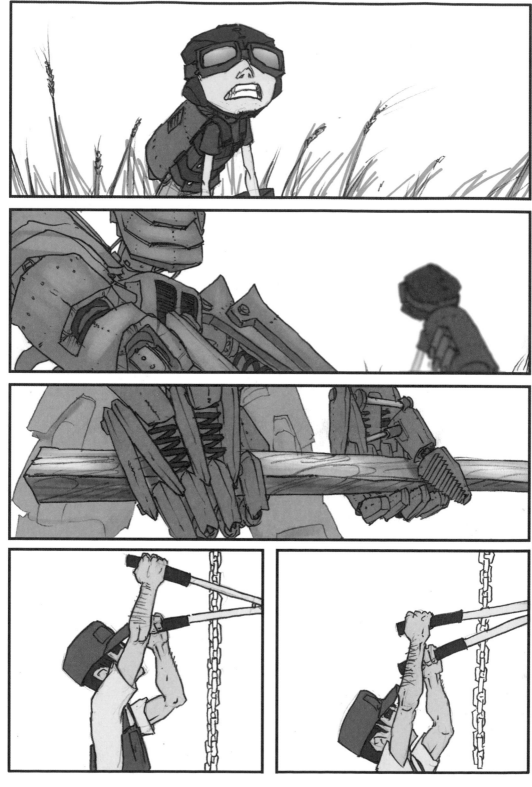

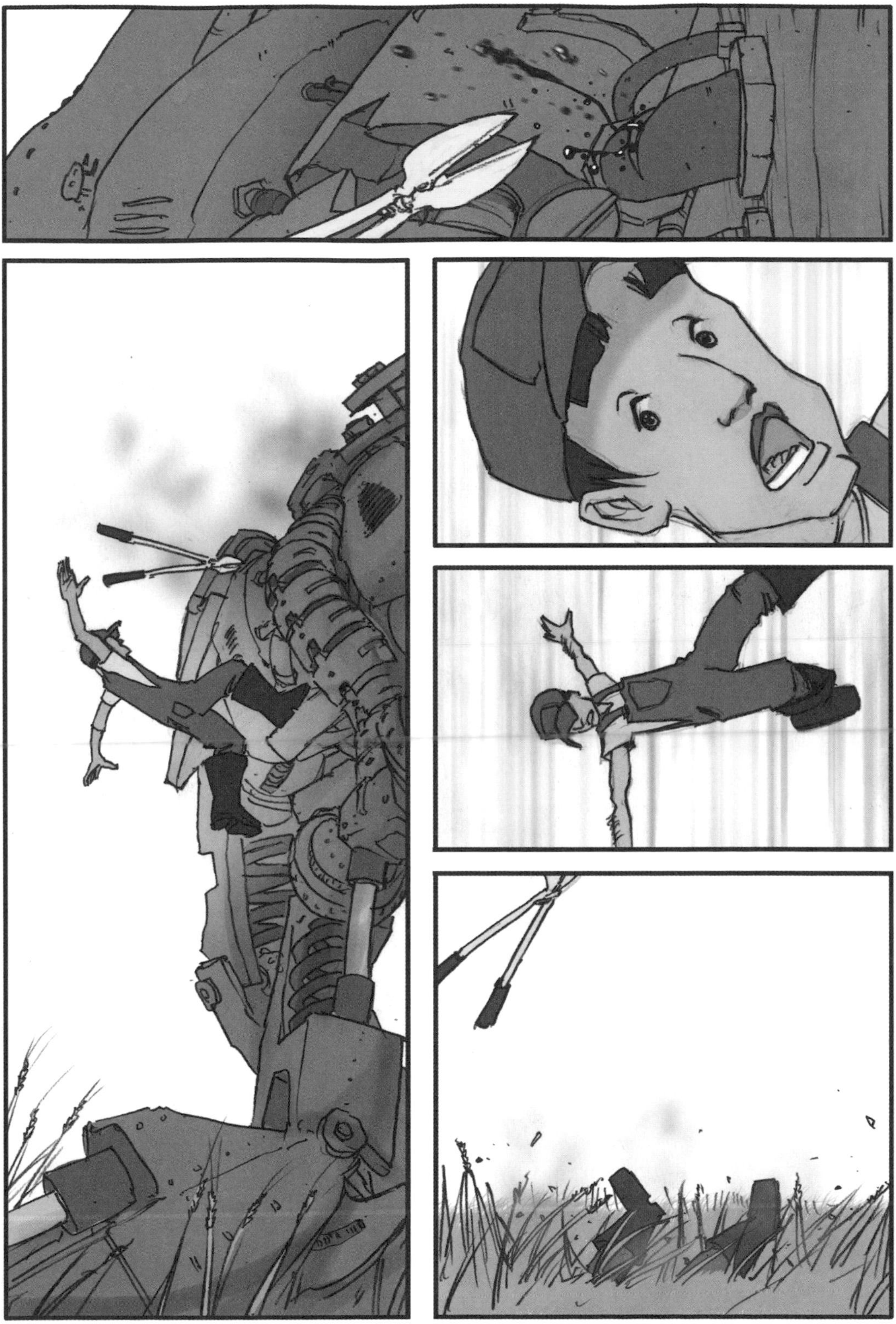

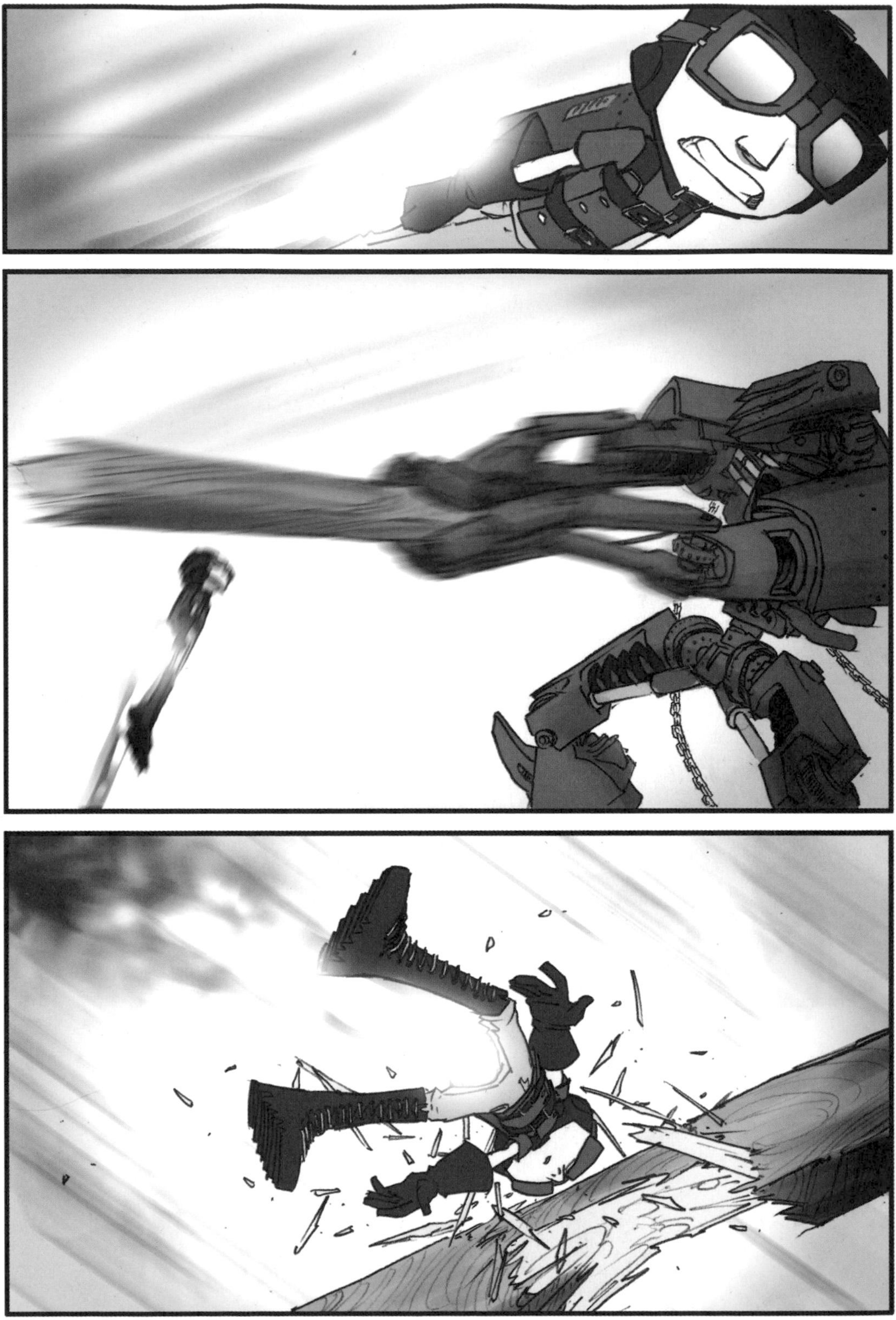

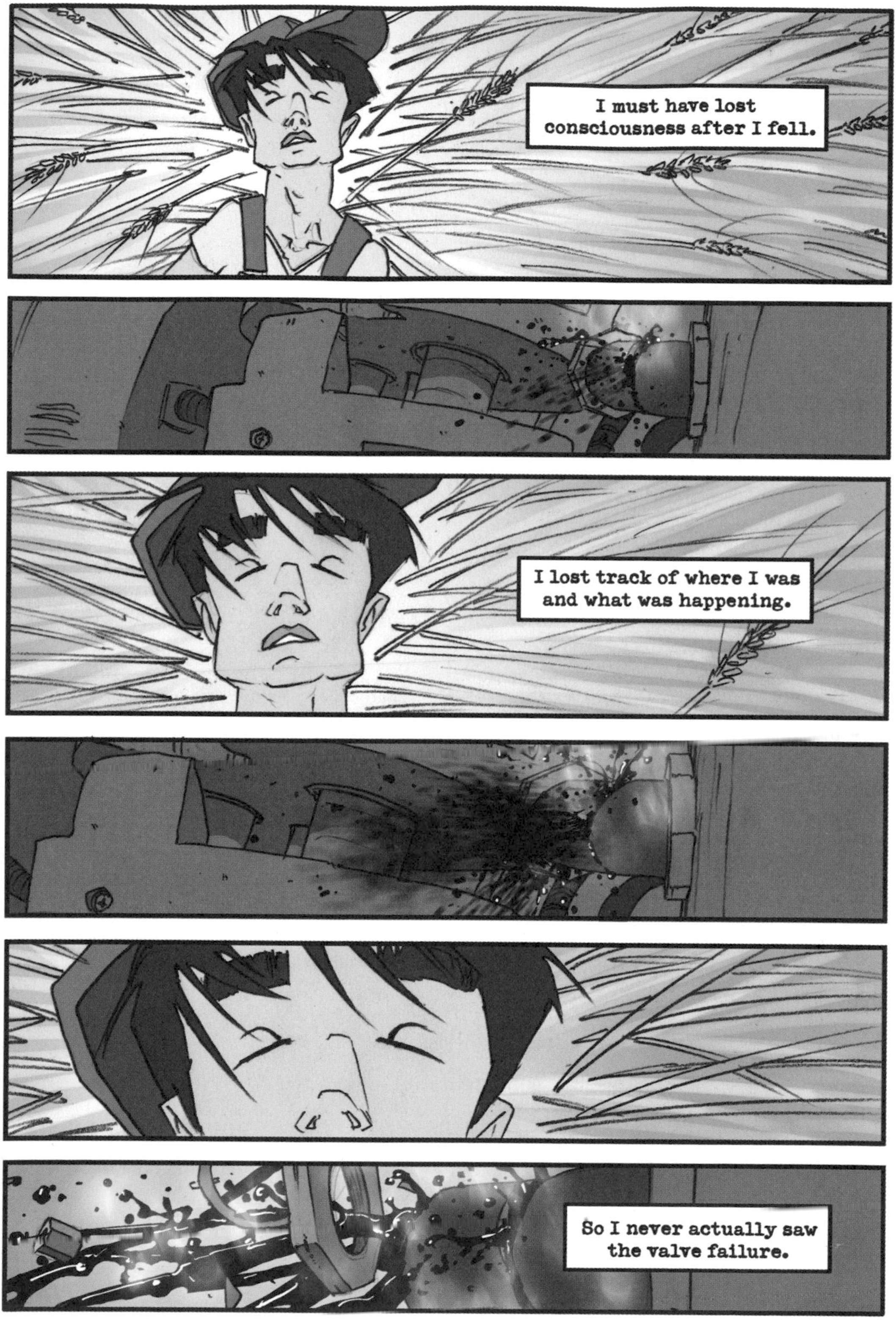
I must have lost consciousness after I fell.
I lost track of where I was and what was happening.
So I never actually saw the valve failure.

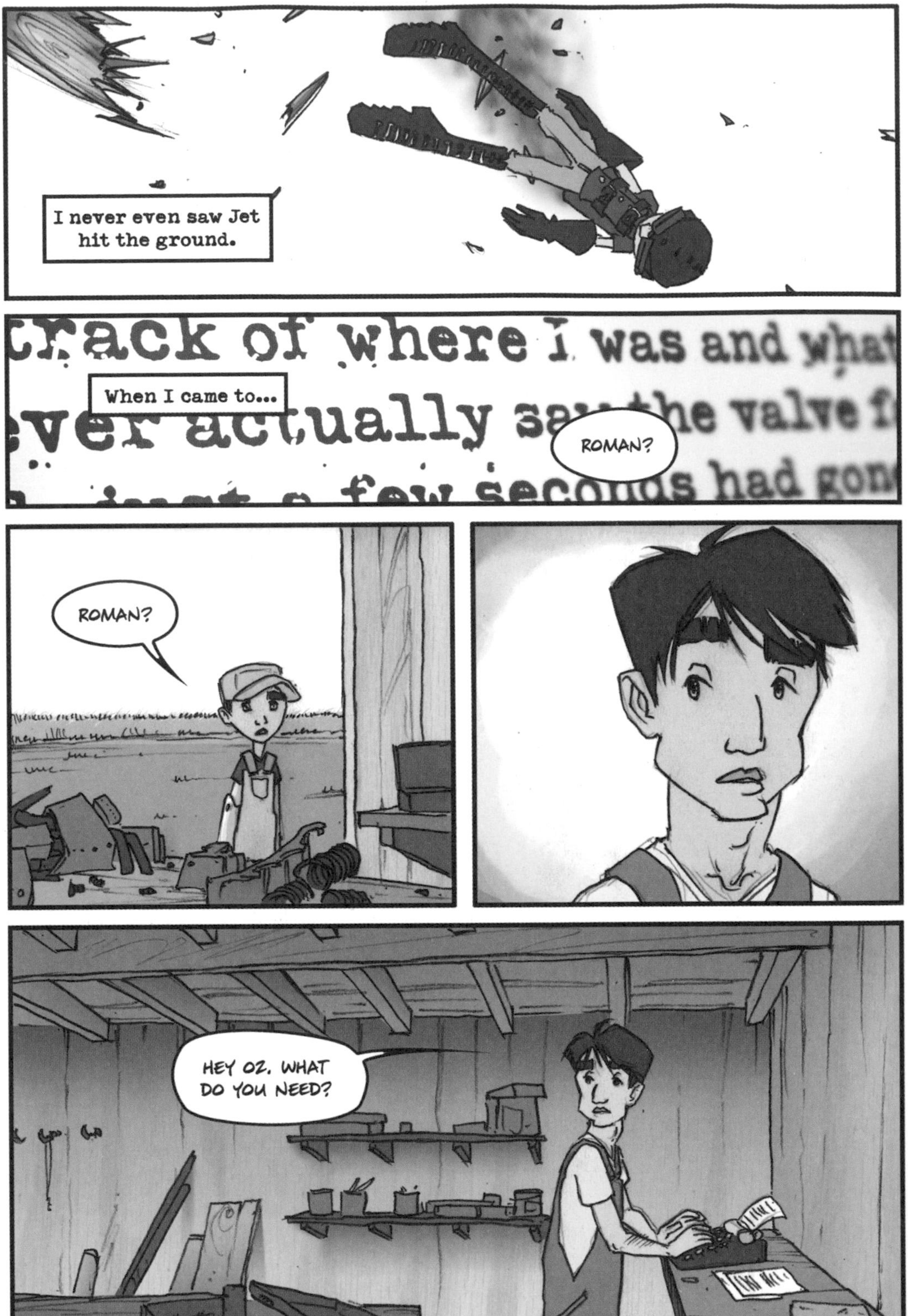
I never even saw Jet hit the ground.
When I came to...
ROMAN?
ROMAN?
HEY OZ. WHAT DO YOU NEED?

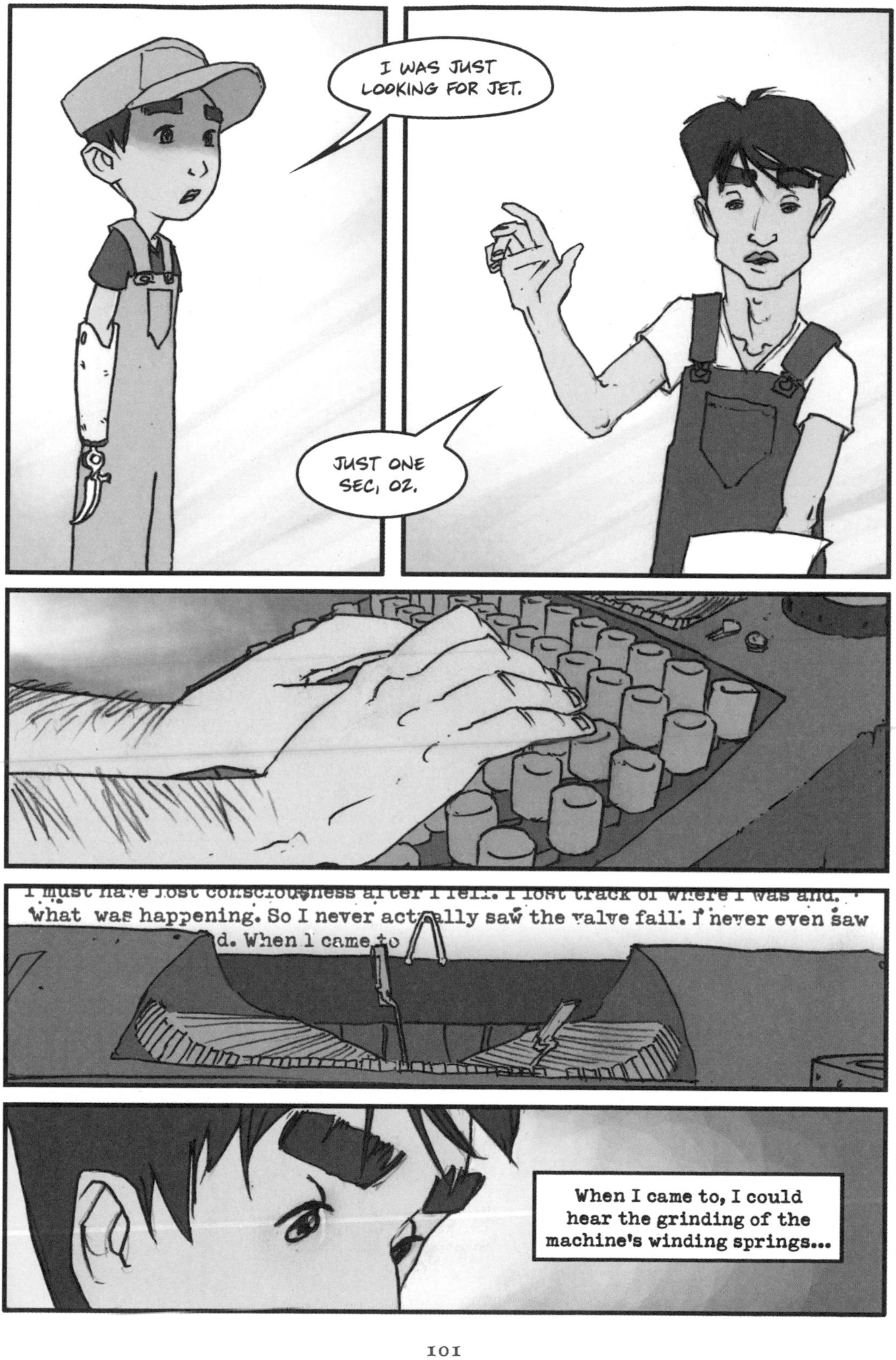
I WAS JUST LOOKING FOR JET.
JUST ONE SEC, OZ.
I must have lost consciousness after I fell. I lost track of where I was and
what was happening. So I never actually saw the valve fail. I never even saw
d. When I came to
When I came to, I could hear the grinding of the machine's winding springs...

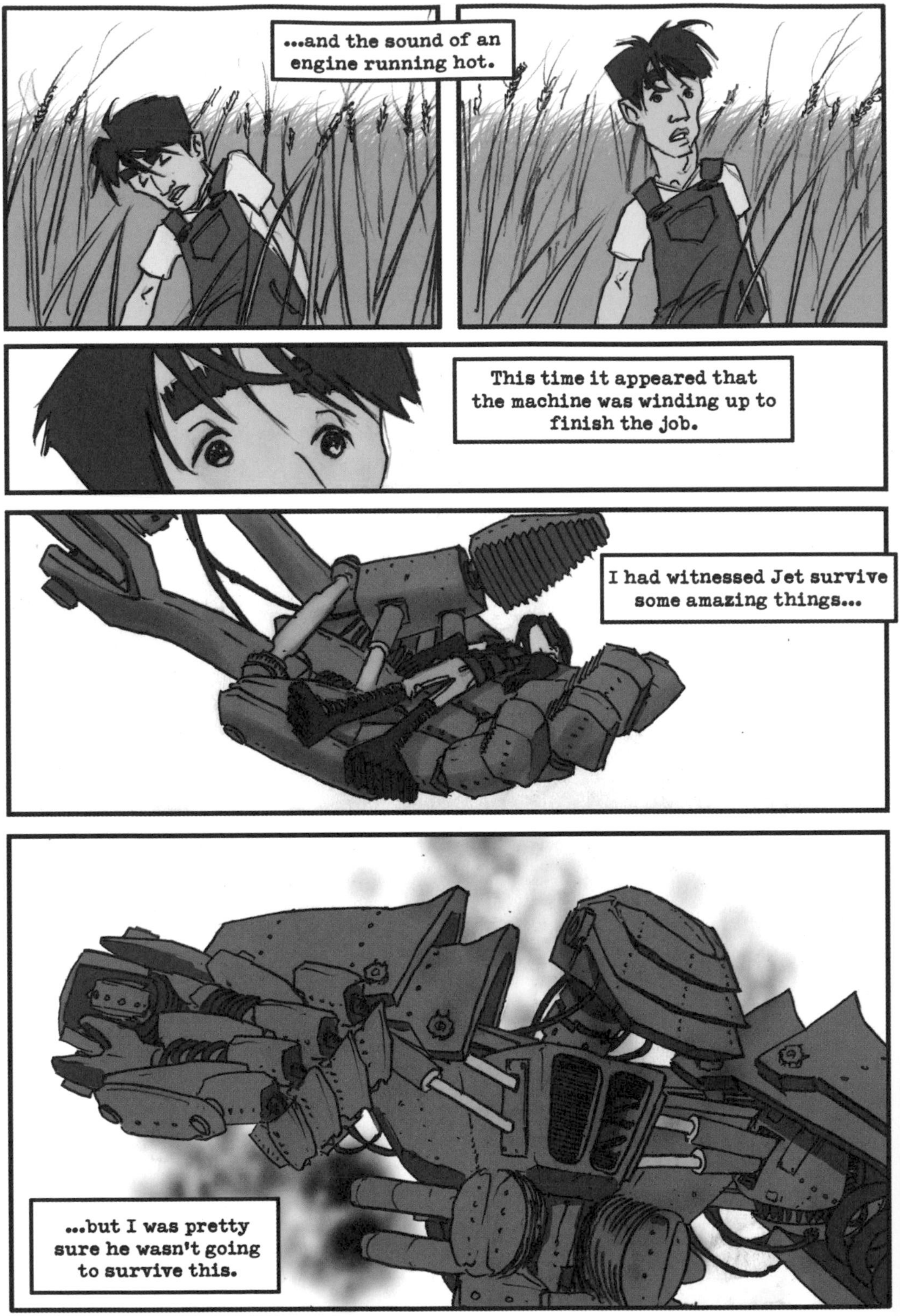
...and the sound of an engine running hot.
This time it appeared that the machine was winding up to finish the job.
I had witnessed Jet survive some amazing things...
...but I was pretty sure he wasn't going to survive this.

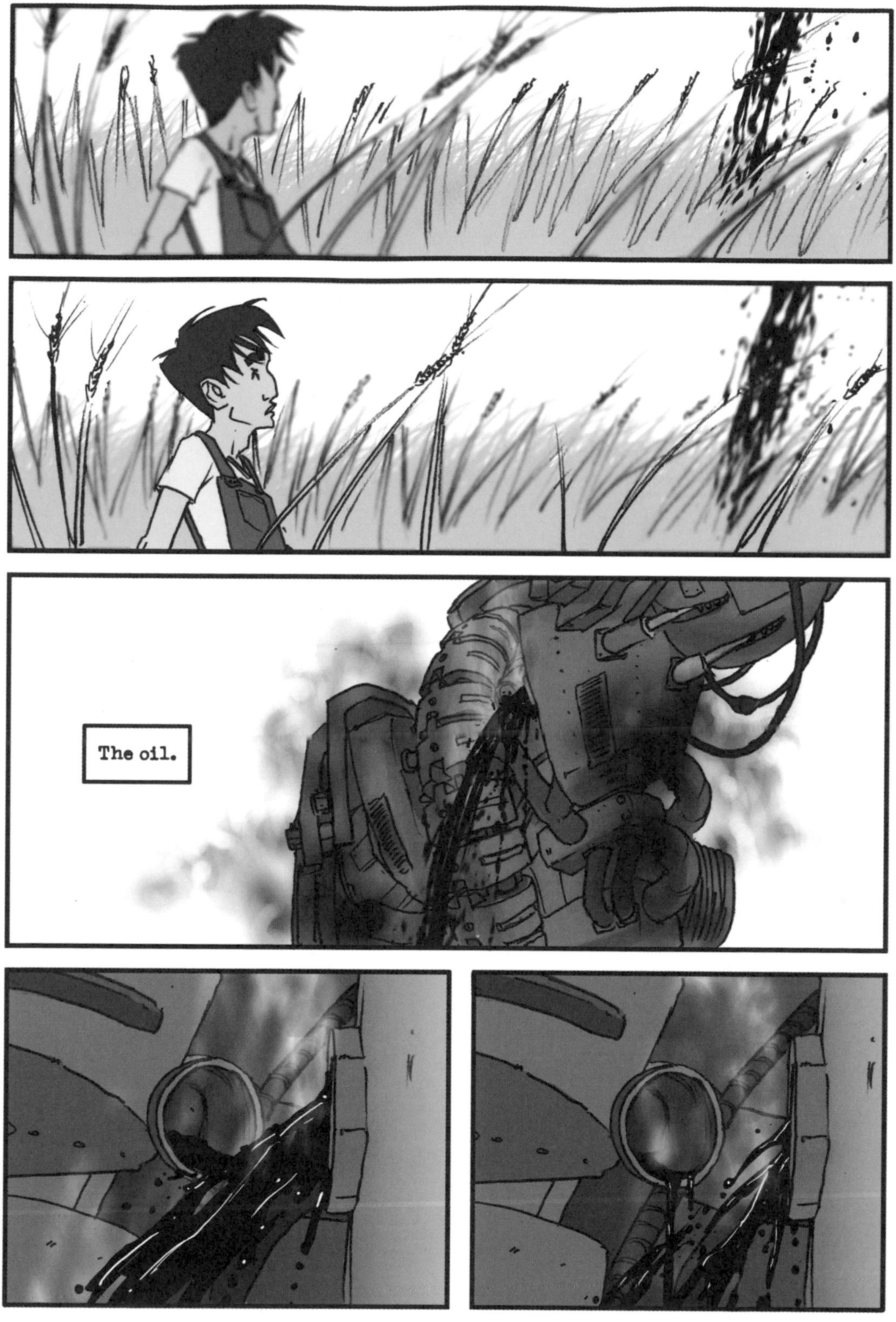
The oil.

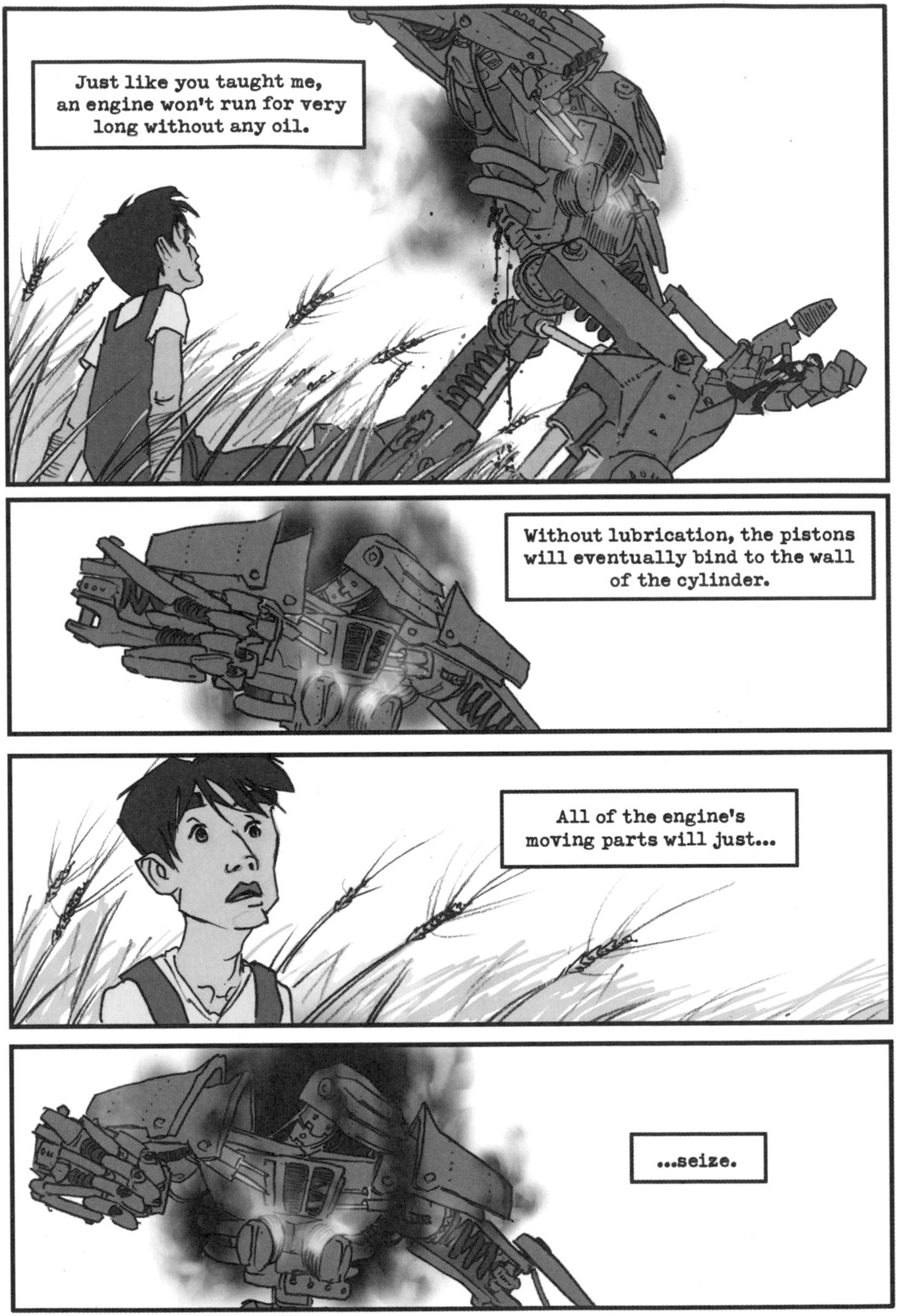
Just like you taught me, an engine won't run for very long without any oil.
Without lubrication, the pistons will eventually bind to the wall of the cylinder.
All of the engine's moving parts will just...
...seize.

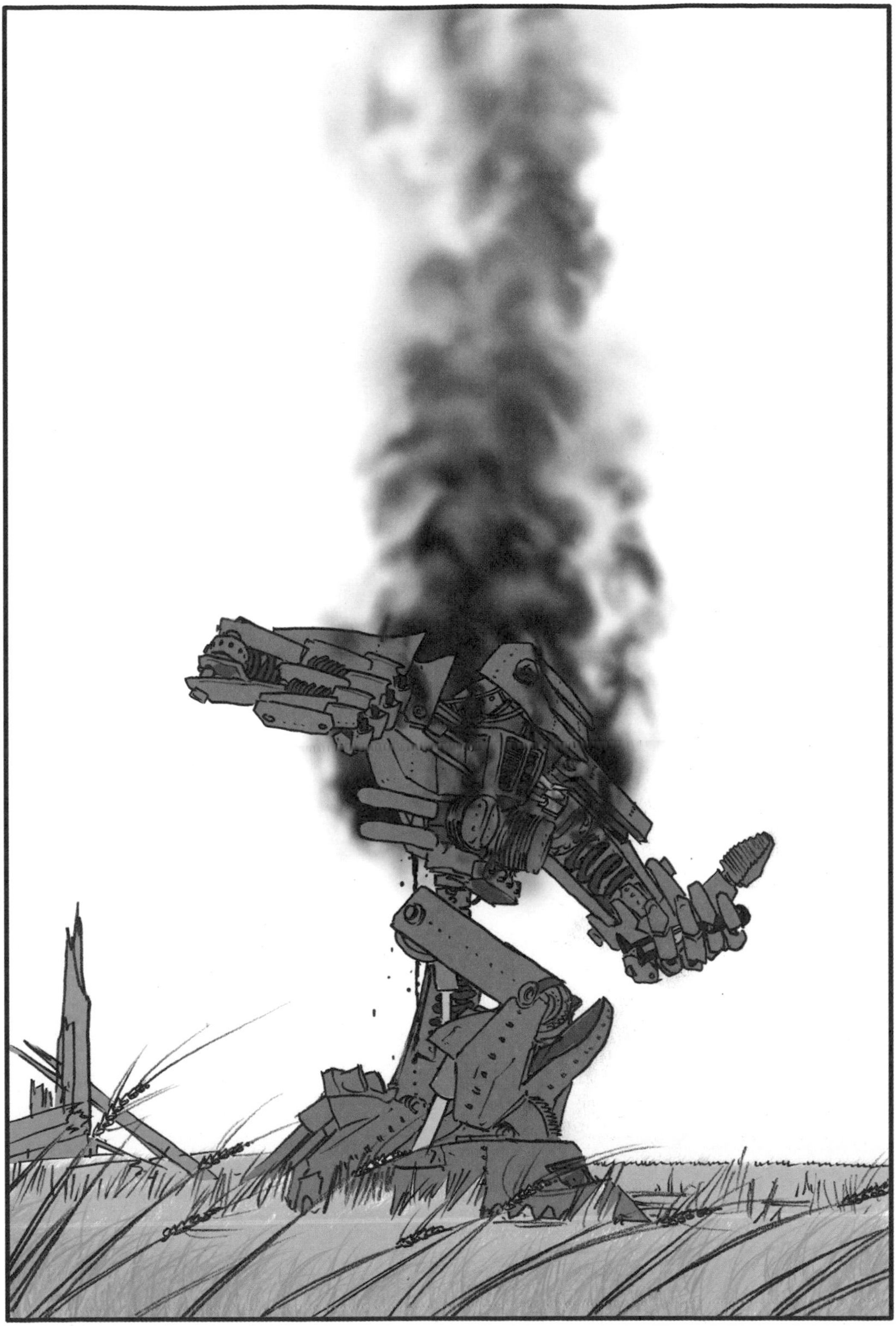

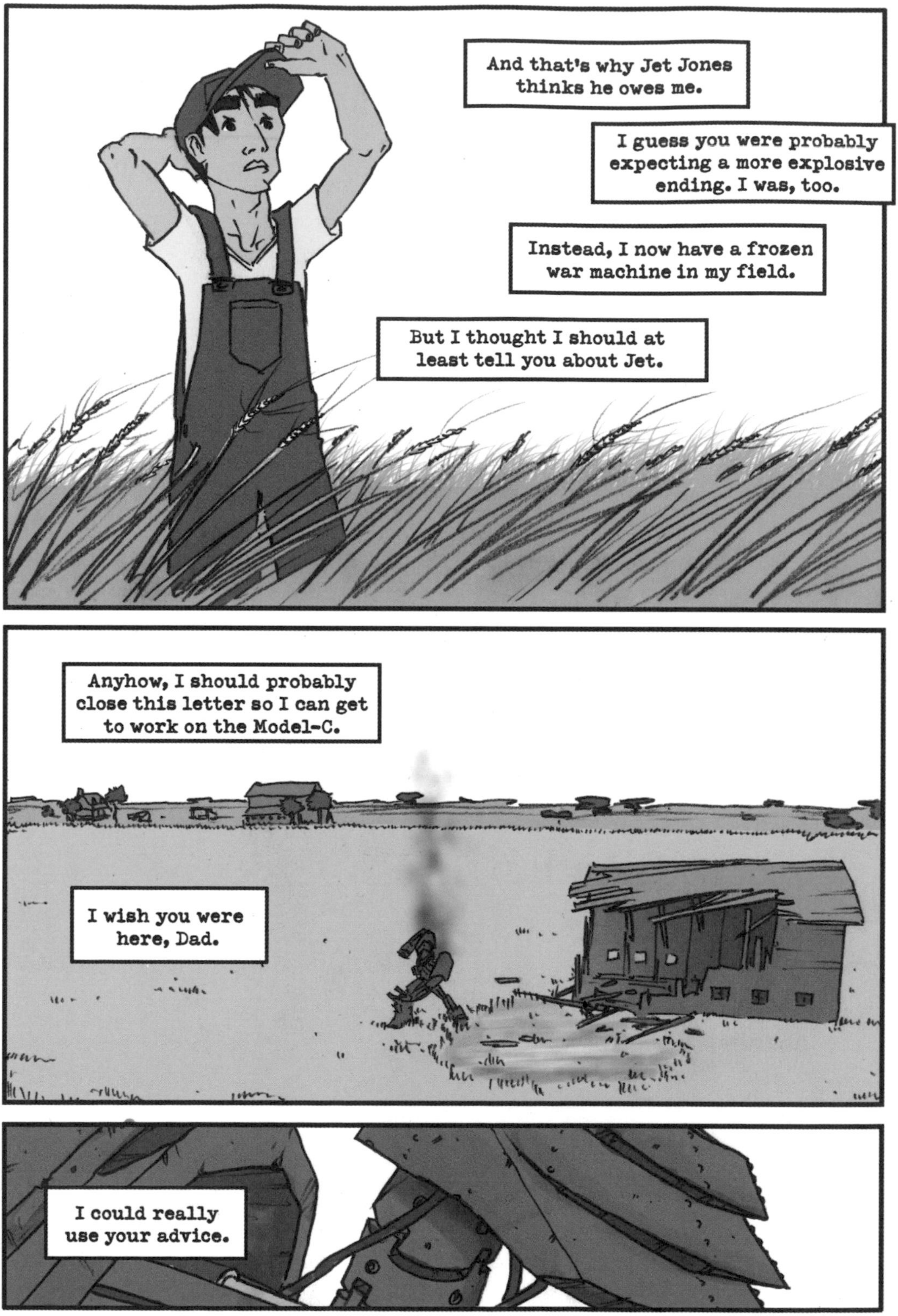
And that's why Jet Jones thinks he owes me.
I guess you were probably expecting a more explosive ending. I was, too.
Instead, I now have a frozen war machine in my field.
But I thought I should at least tell you about Jet.
Anyhow, I should probably close this letter so I can get to work on the Model-C.
I wish you were here, Dad.
I could really use your advice.

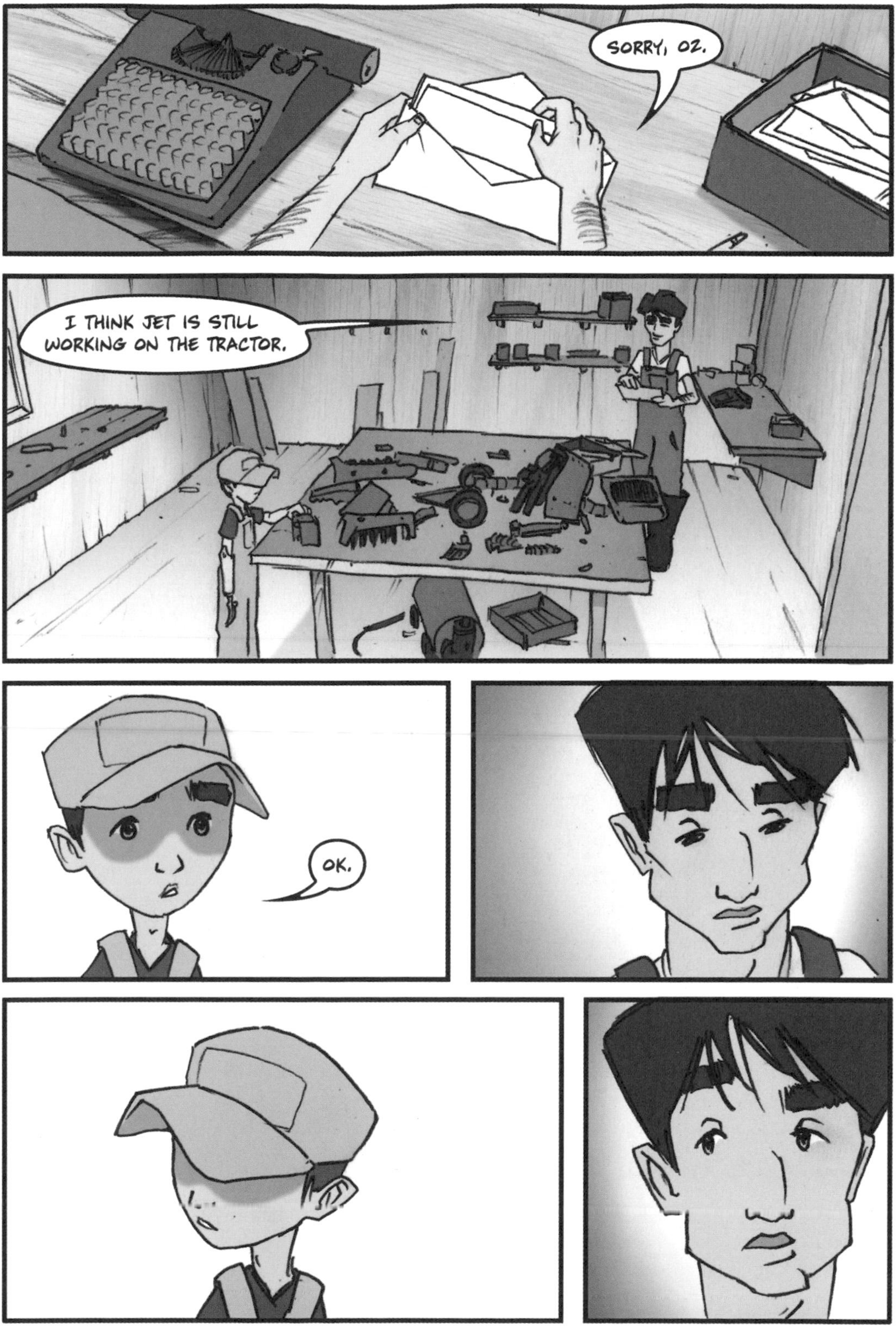
SORRY, OZ.
I THINK JET IS STILL WORKING ON THE TRACTOR.
OK.

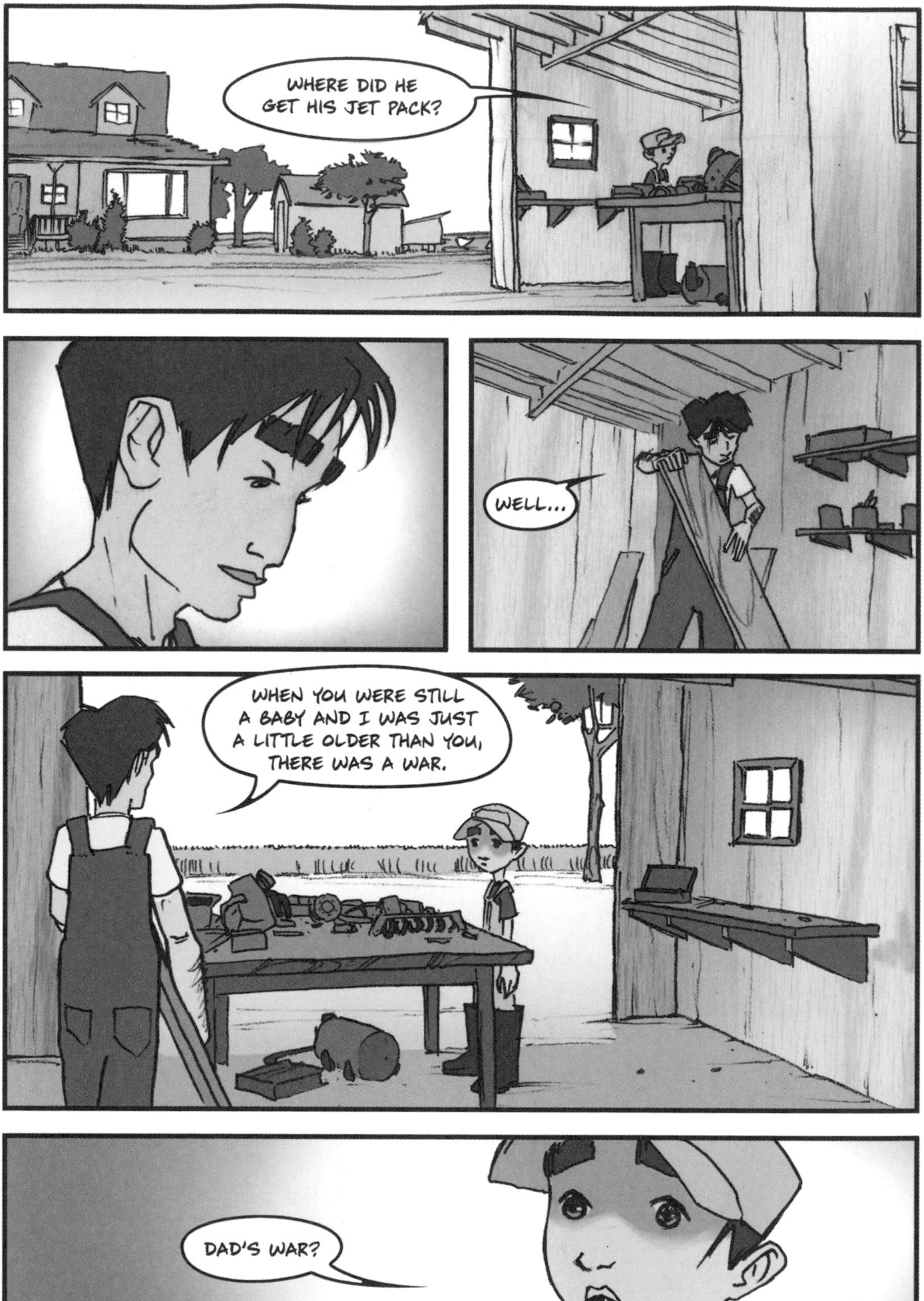
WHERE DID HE GET HIS JET PACK?
WELL...
WHEN YOU WERE STILL A BABY AND I WAS JUST A LITTLE OLDER THAN YOU, THERE WAS A WAR.
DAD'S WAR?

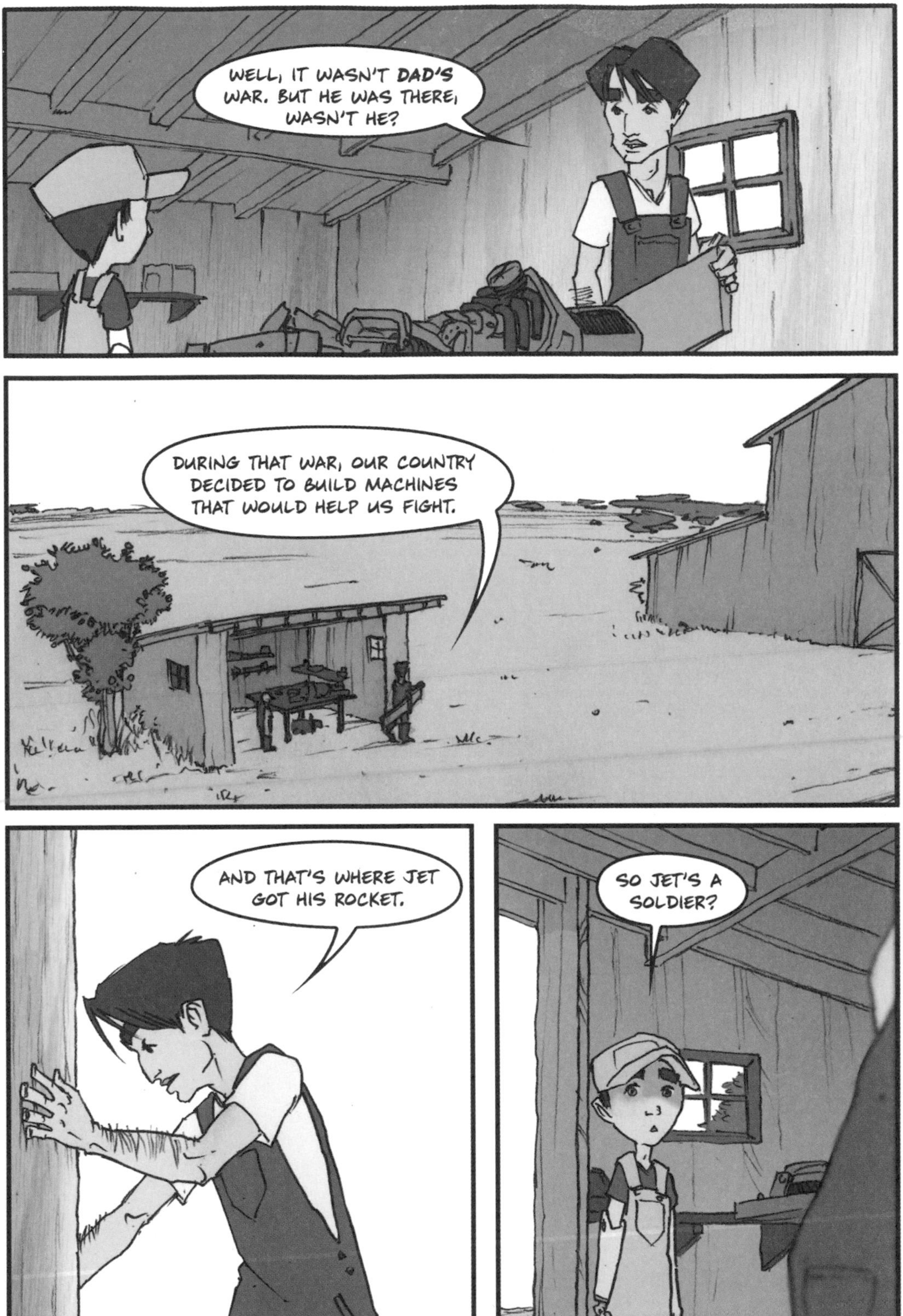
WELL, IT WASN'T **DAD'S** WAR. BUT HE WAS THERE, WASN'T HE?
DURING THAT WAR, OUR COUNTRY DECIDED TO BUILD MACHINES THAT WOULD HELP US FIGHT.
AND THAT'S WHERE JET GOT HIS ROCKET.
SO JET'S A SOLDIER?

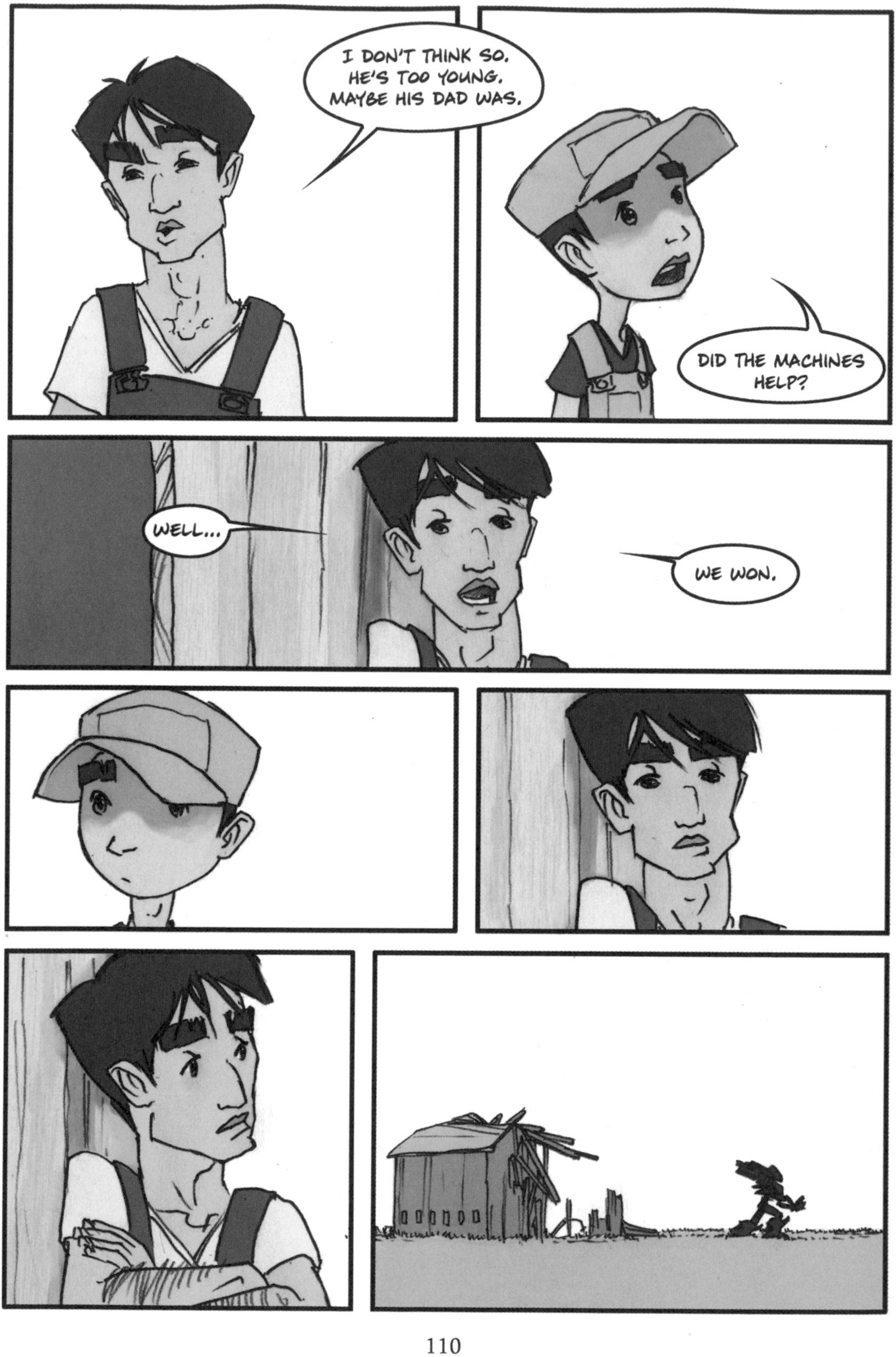
I DON'T THINK SO. HE'S TOO YOUNG. MAYBE HIS DAD WAS.
DID THE MACHINES HELP?
WELL...
WE WON.

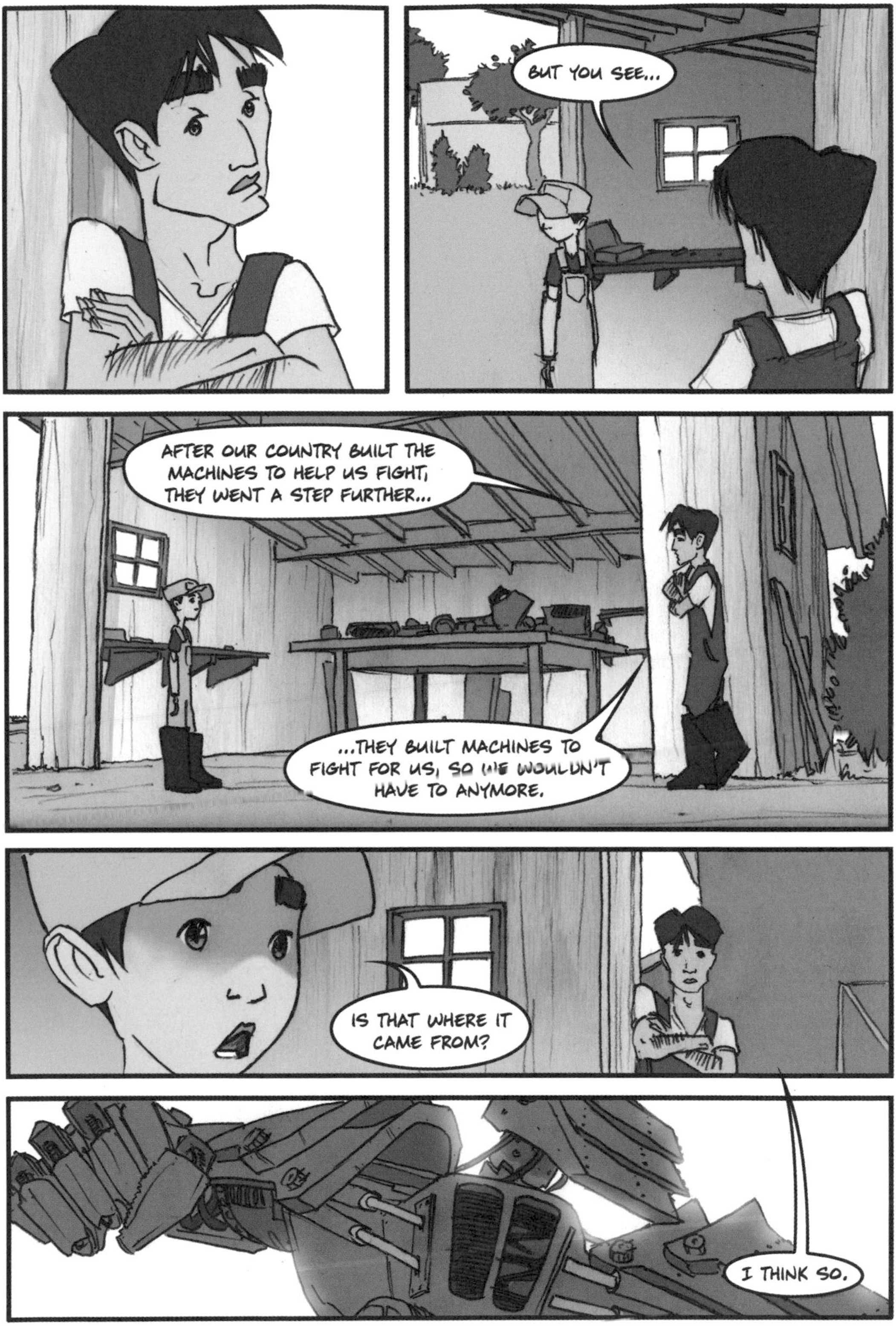
BUT YOU SEE...
AFTER OUR COUNTRY BUILT THE MACHINES TO HELP US FIGHT, THEY WENT A STEP FURTHER...
...THEY BUILT MACHINES TO FIGHT FOR US, SO WE WOULDN'T HAVE TO ANYMORE.
IS THAT WHERE IT CAME FROM?
I THINK SO.

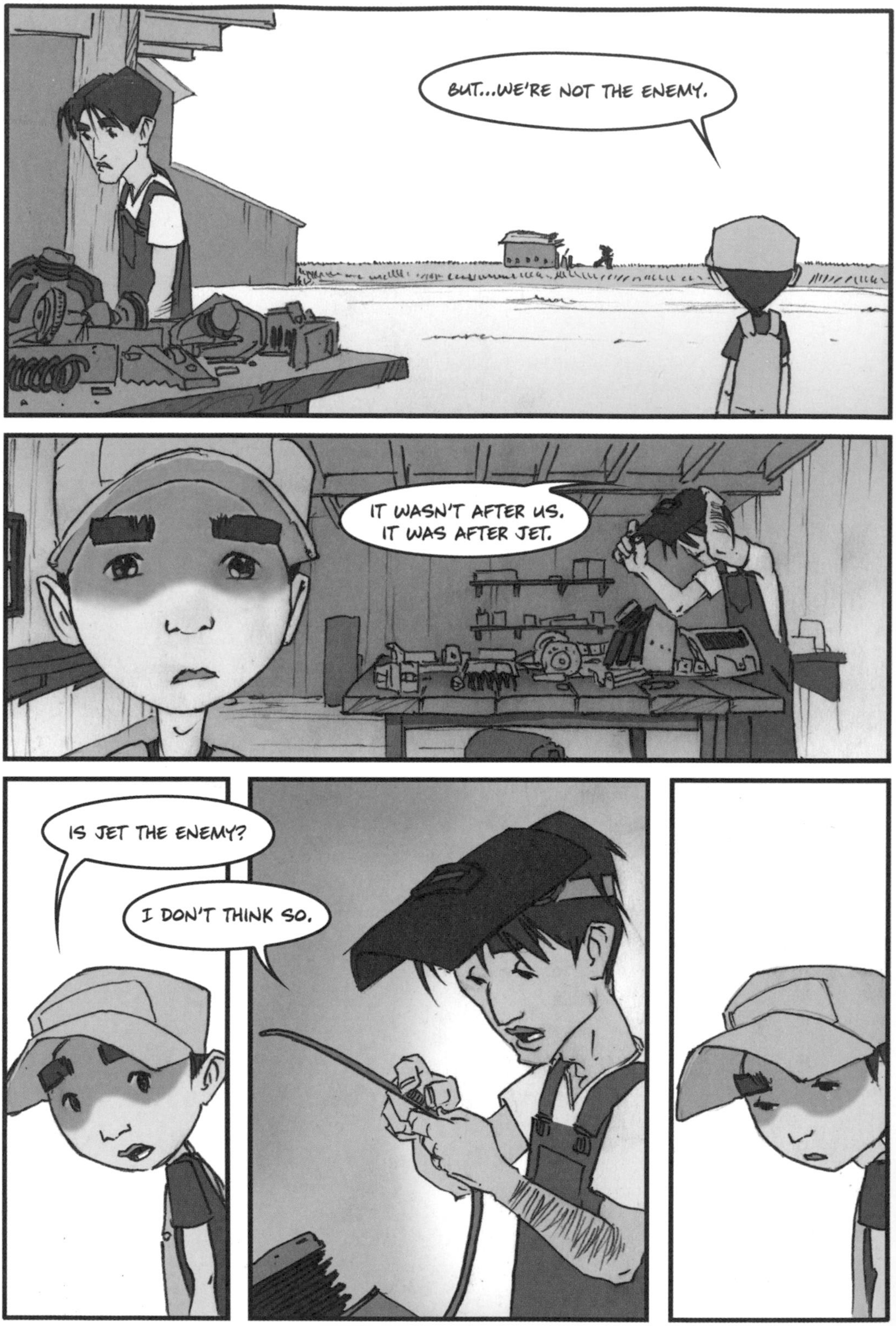
BUT...WE'RE NOT THE ENEMY.
IT WASN'T AFTER US. IT WAS AFTER JET.
IS JET THE ENEMY?
I DON'T THINK SO.

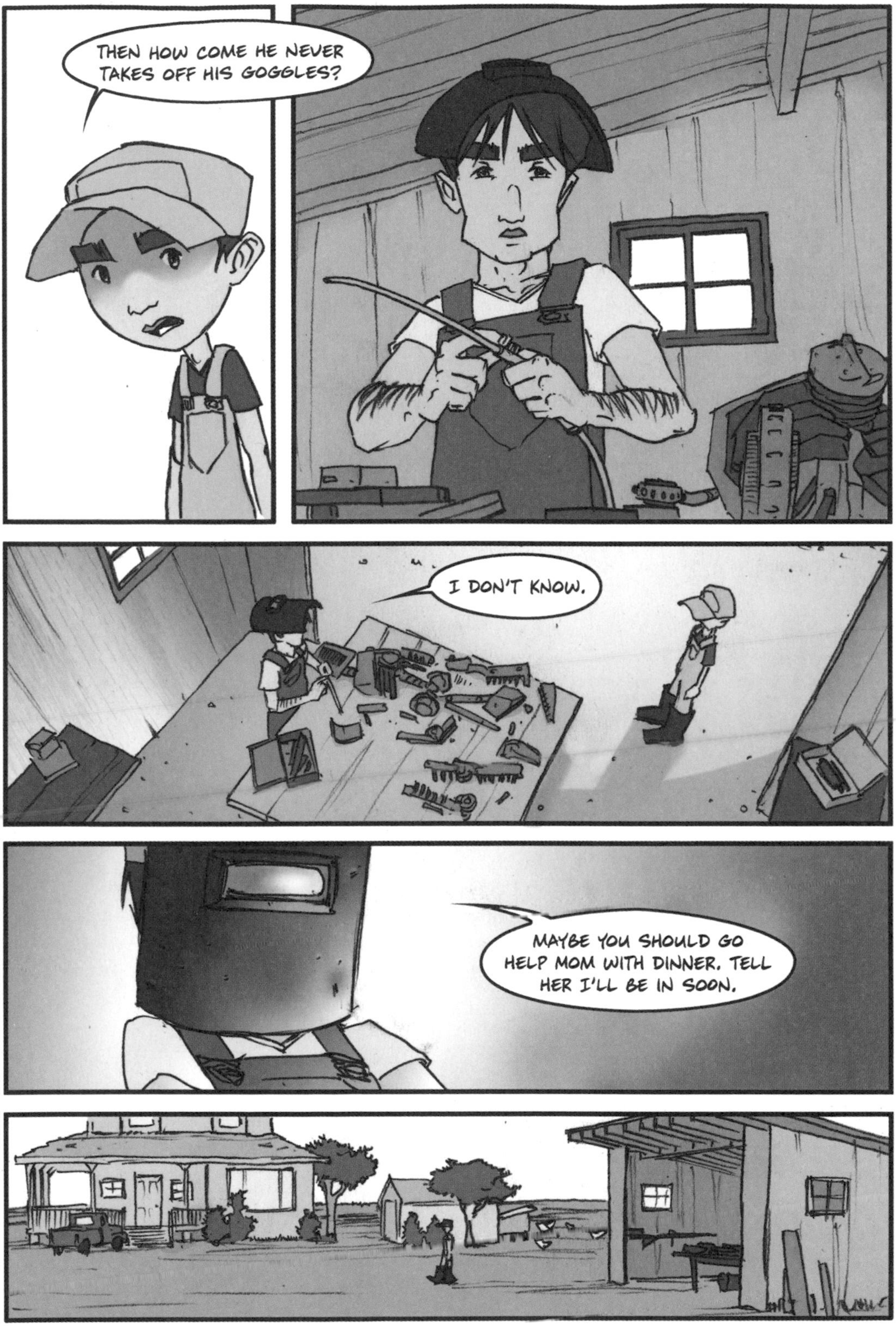
THEN HOW COME HE NEVER TAKES OFF HIS GOGGLES?
I DON'T KNOW.
MAYBE YOU SHOULD GO HELP MOM WITH DINNER. TELL HER I'LL BE IN SOON.

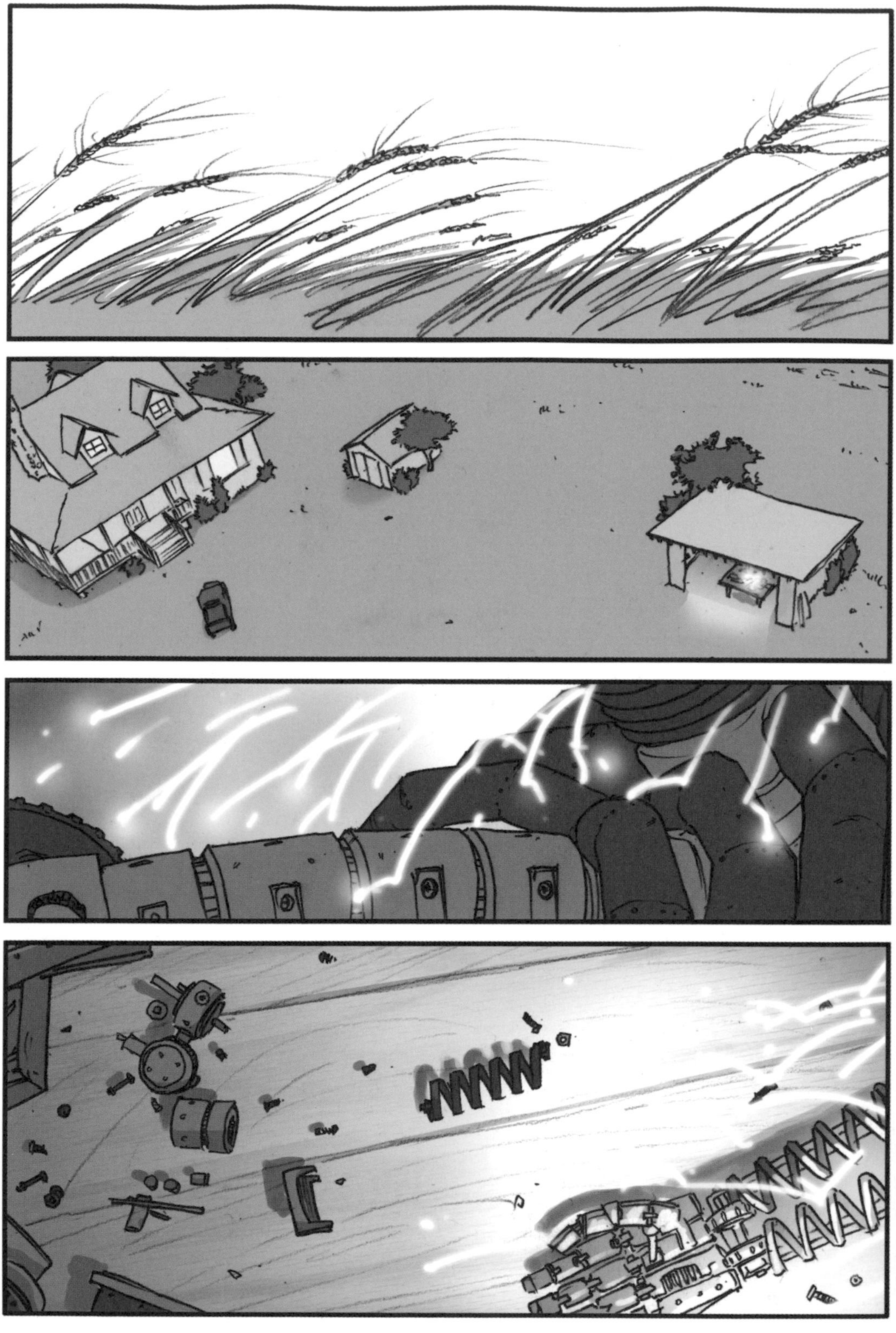

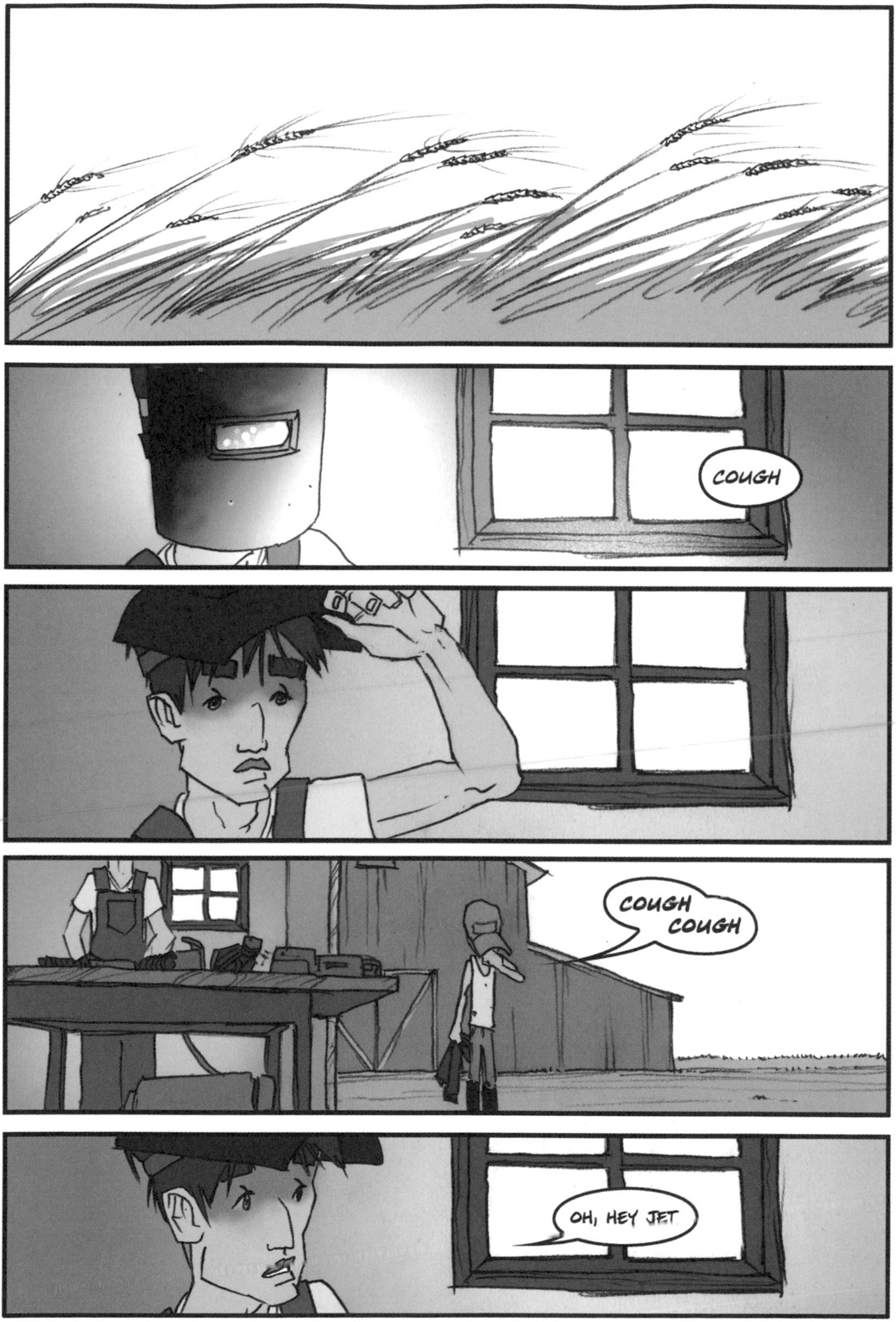
COUGH
COUGH
COUGH
OH, HEY JET

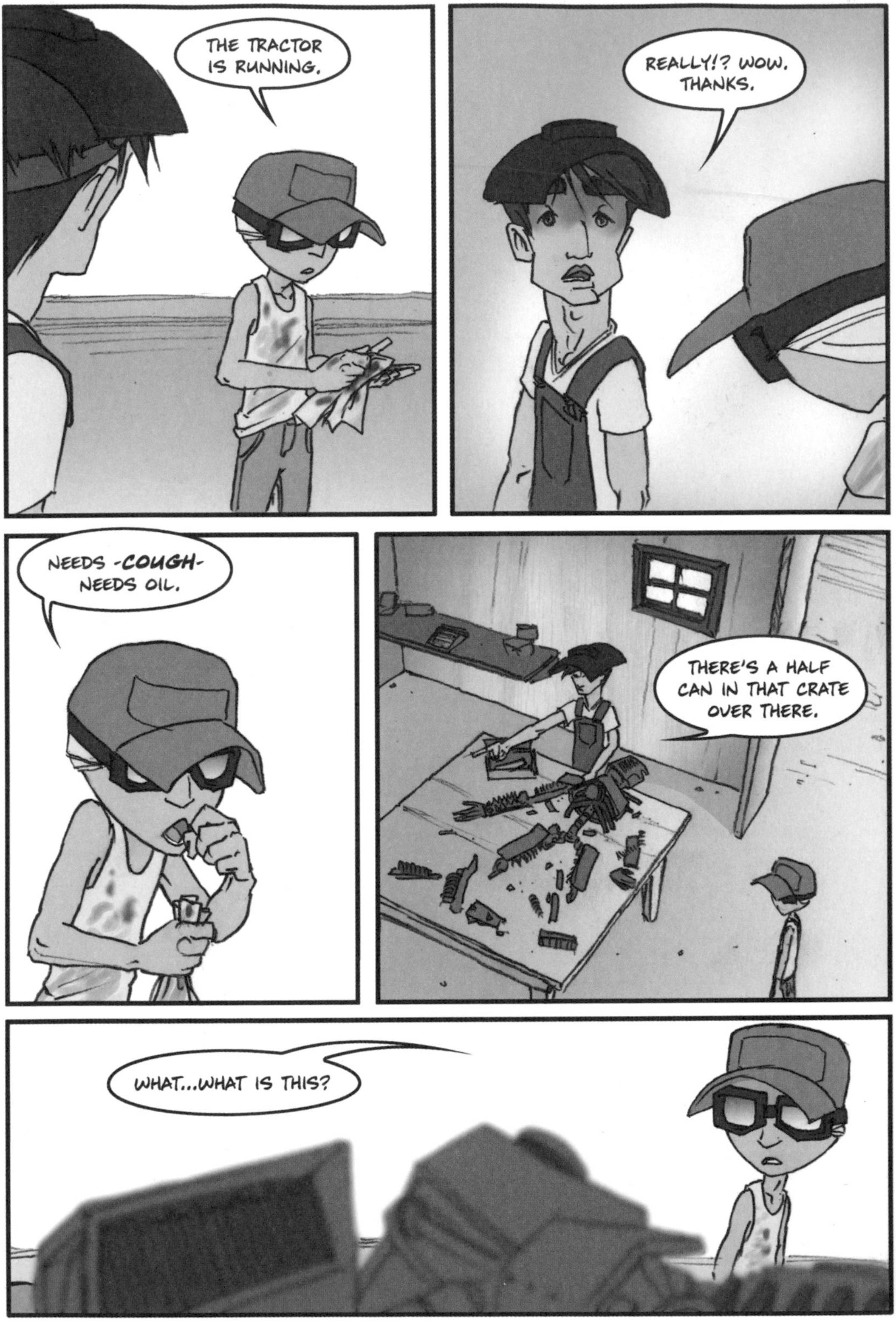
THE TRACTOR IS RUNNING.
REALLY!? WOW. THANKS.
NEEDS -COUGH- NEEDS OIL.
THERE'S A HALF CAN IN THAT CRATE OVER THERE.
WHAT...WHAT IS THIS?

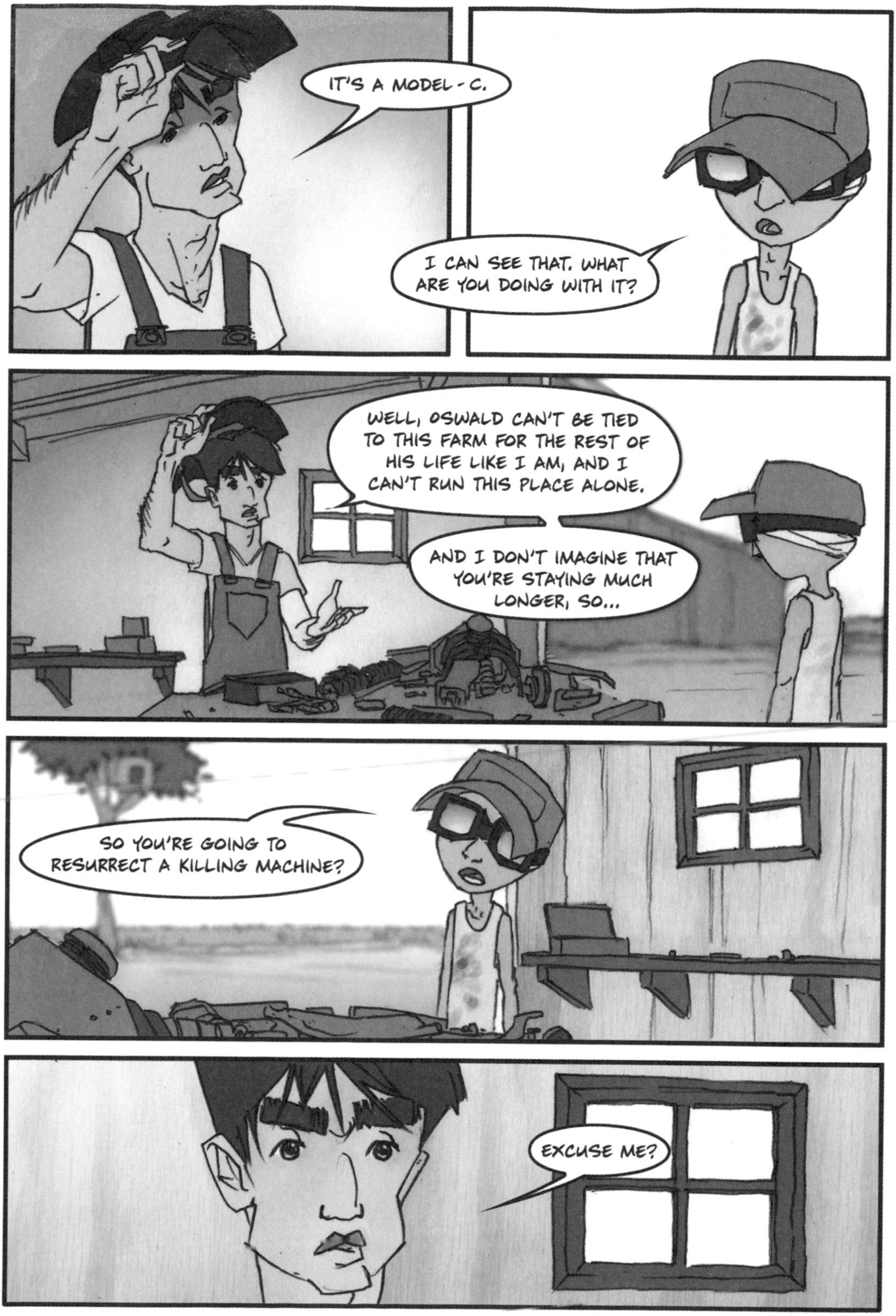
IT'S A MODEL - C.
I CAN SEE THAT. WHAT ARE YOU DOING WITH IT?
WELL, OSWALD CAN'T BE TIED TO THIS FARM FOR THE REST OF HIS LIFE LIKE I AM, AND I CAN'T RUN THIS PLACE ALONE.
AND I DON'T IMAGINE THAT YOU'RE STAYING MUCH LONGER, SO...
SO YOU'RE GOING TO RESURRECT A KILLING MACHINE?
EXCUSE ME?

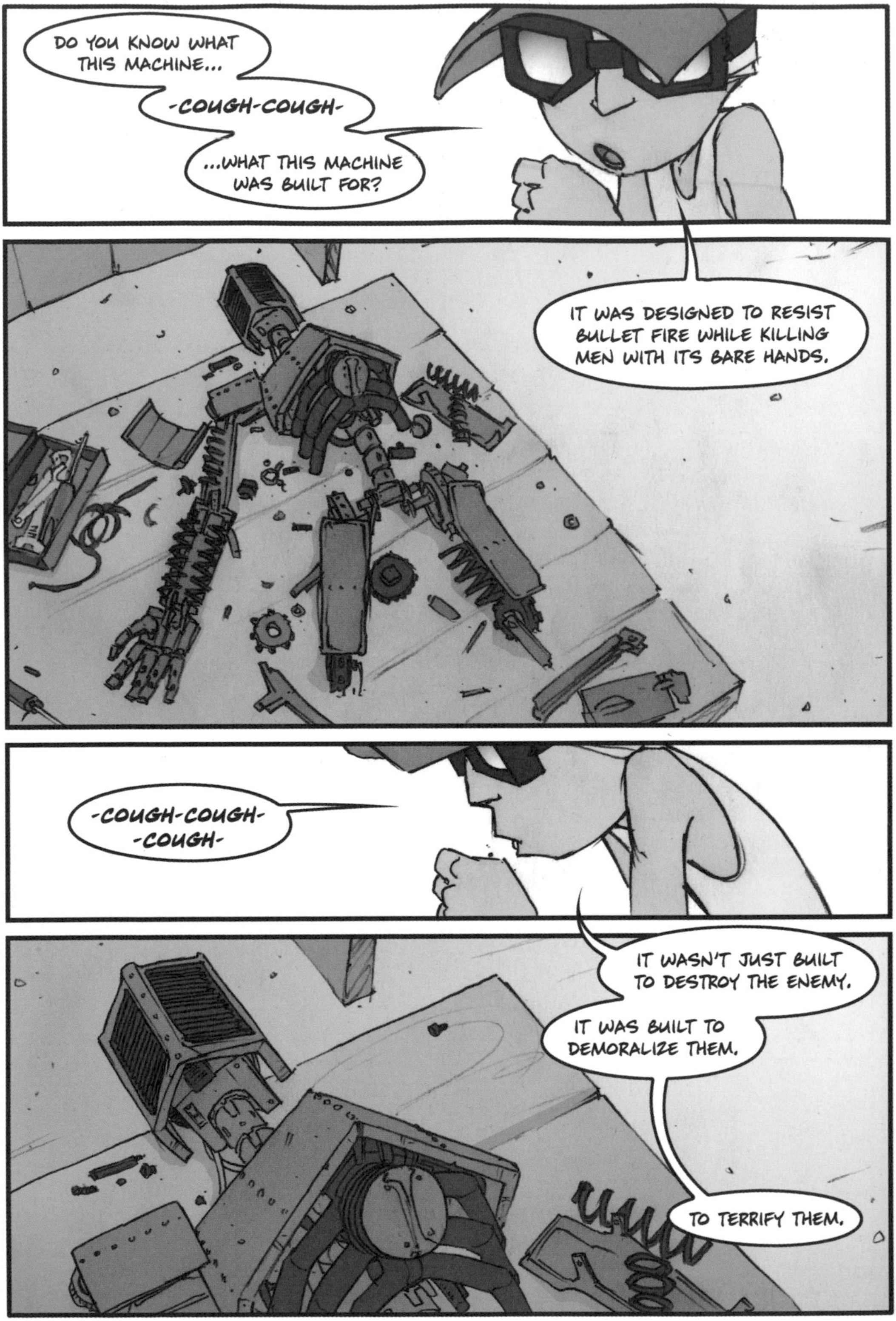
DO YOU KNOW WHAT THIS MACHINE...
-COUGH-COUGH-
...WHAT THIS MACHINE WAS BUILT FOR?
IT WAS DESIGNED TO RESIST BULLET FIRE WHILE KILLING MEN WITH ITS BARE HANDS.
-COUGH-COUGH- -COUGH-
IT WASN'T JUST BUILT TO DESTROY THE ENEMY.
IT WAS BUILT TO DEMORALIZE THEM.
TO TERRIFY THEM.

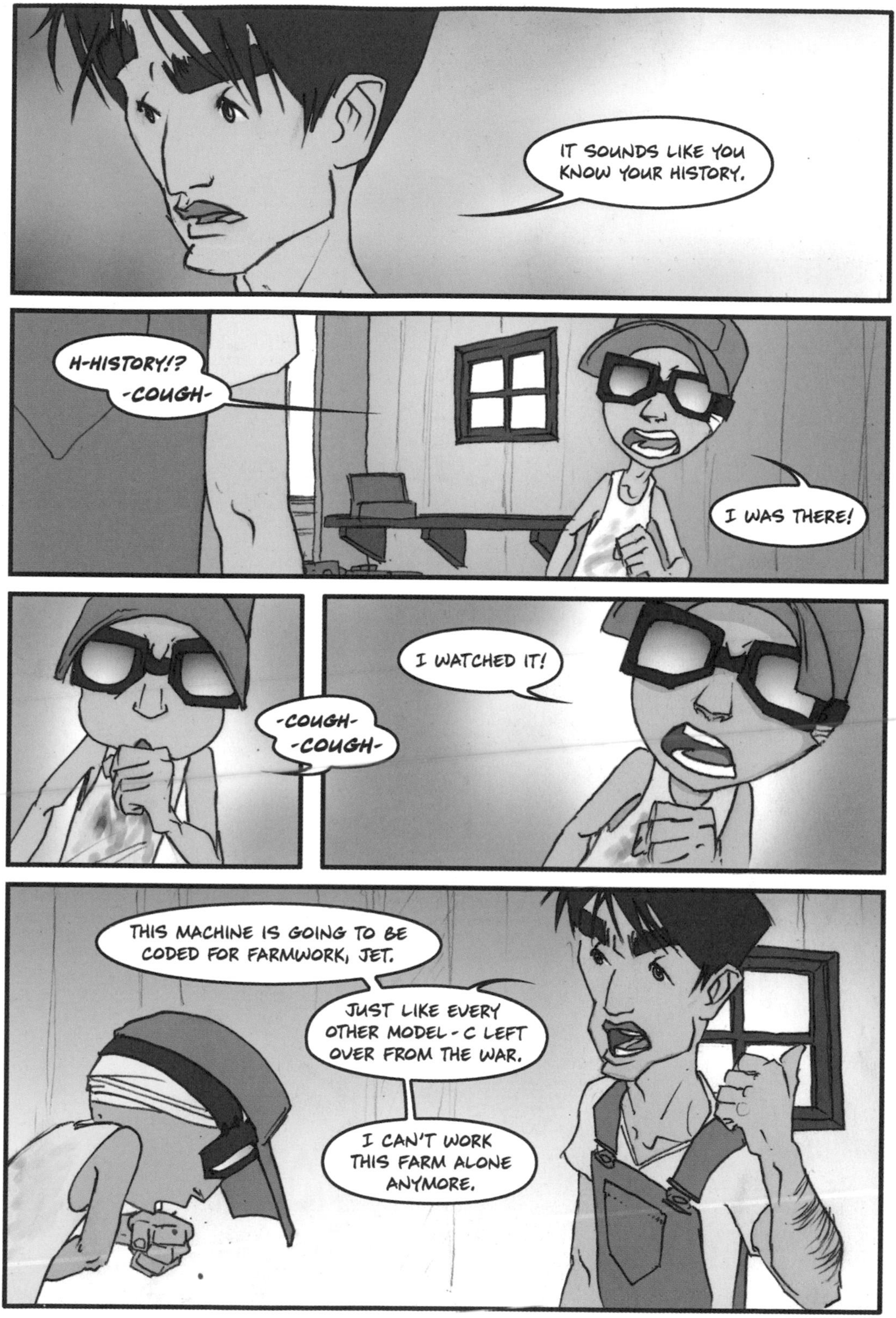
IT SOUNDS LIKE YOU KNOW YOUR HISTORY.
H-HISTORY!? -COUGH-
I WAS THERE!
-COUGH- -COUGH-
I WATCHED IT!
THIS MACHINE IS GOING TO BE CODED FOR FARMWORK, JET.
JUST LIKE EVERY OTHER MODEL - C LEFT OVER FROM THE WAR.
I CAN'T WORK THIS FARM ALONE ANYMORE.

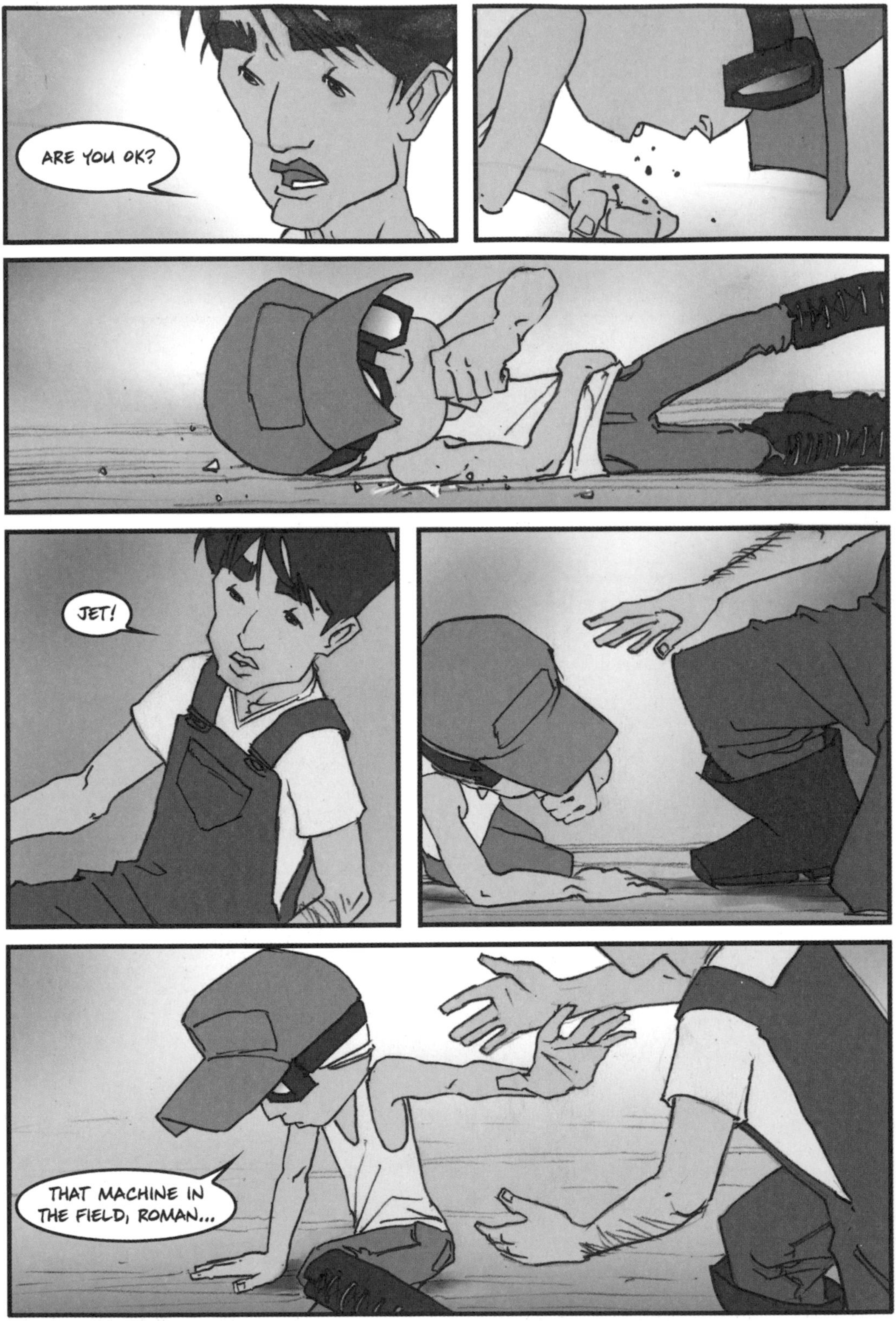
ARE YOU OK?
JET!
THAT MACHINE IN THE FIELD, ROMAN...

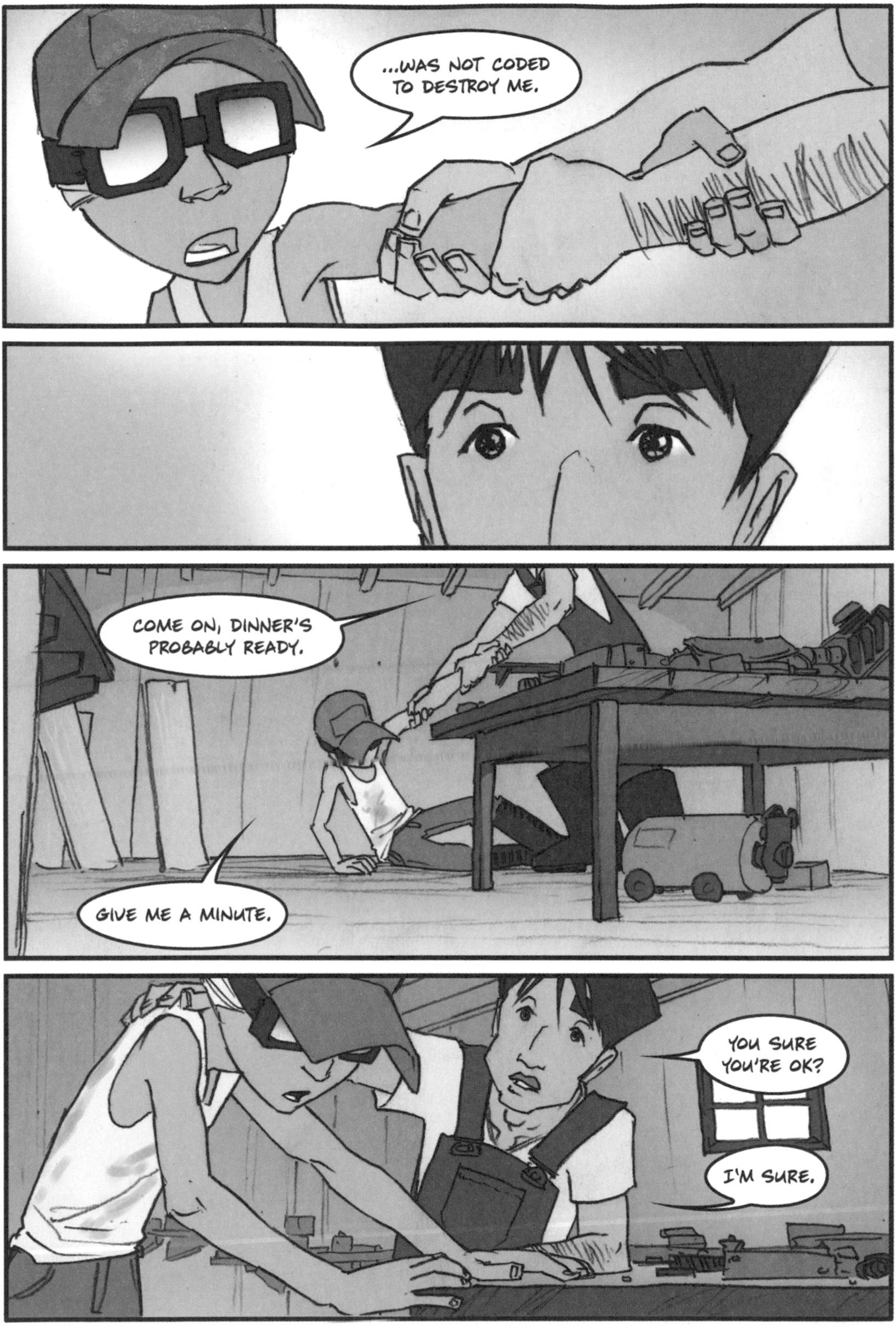
...WAS NOT CODED TO DESTROY ME.
COME ON, DINNER'S PROBABLY READY.
GIVE ME A MINUTE.
YOU SURE YOU'RE OK?
I'M SURE.

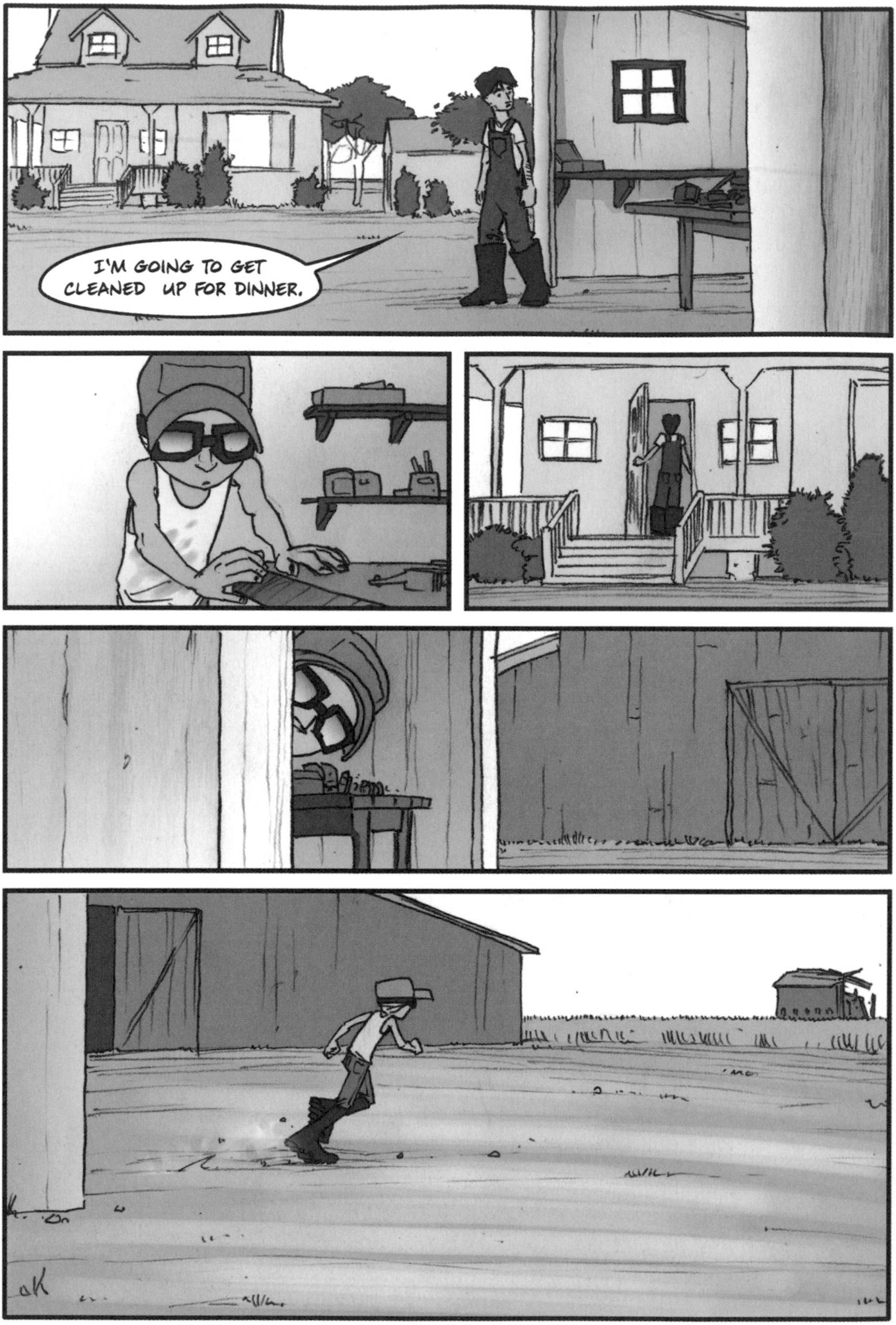
I'M GOING TO GET CLEANED UP FOR DINNER.

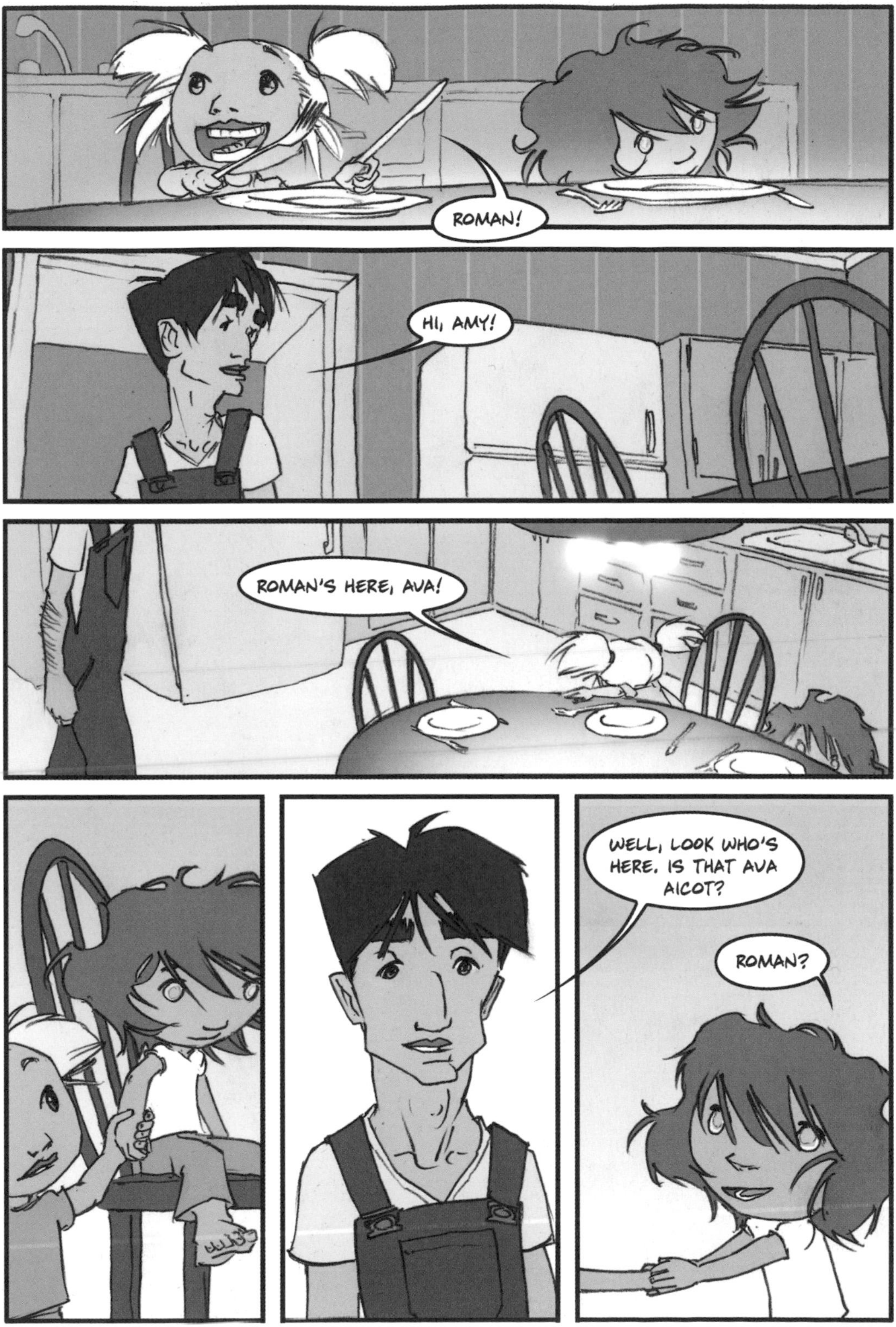
ROMAN!
HI, AMY!
ROMAN'S HERE, AVA!
WELL, LOOK WHO'S HERE. IS THAT AVA AICOT?
ROMAN?

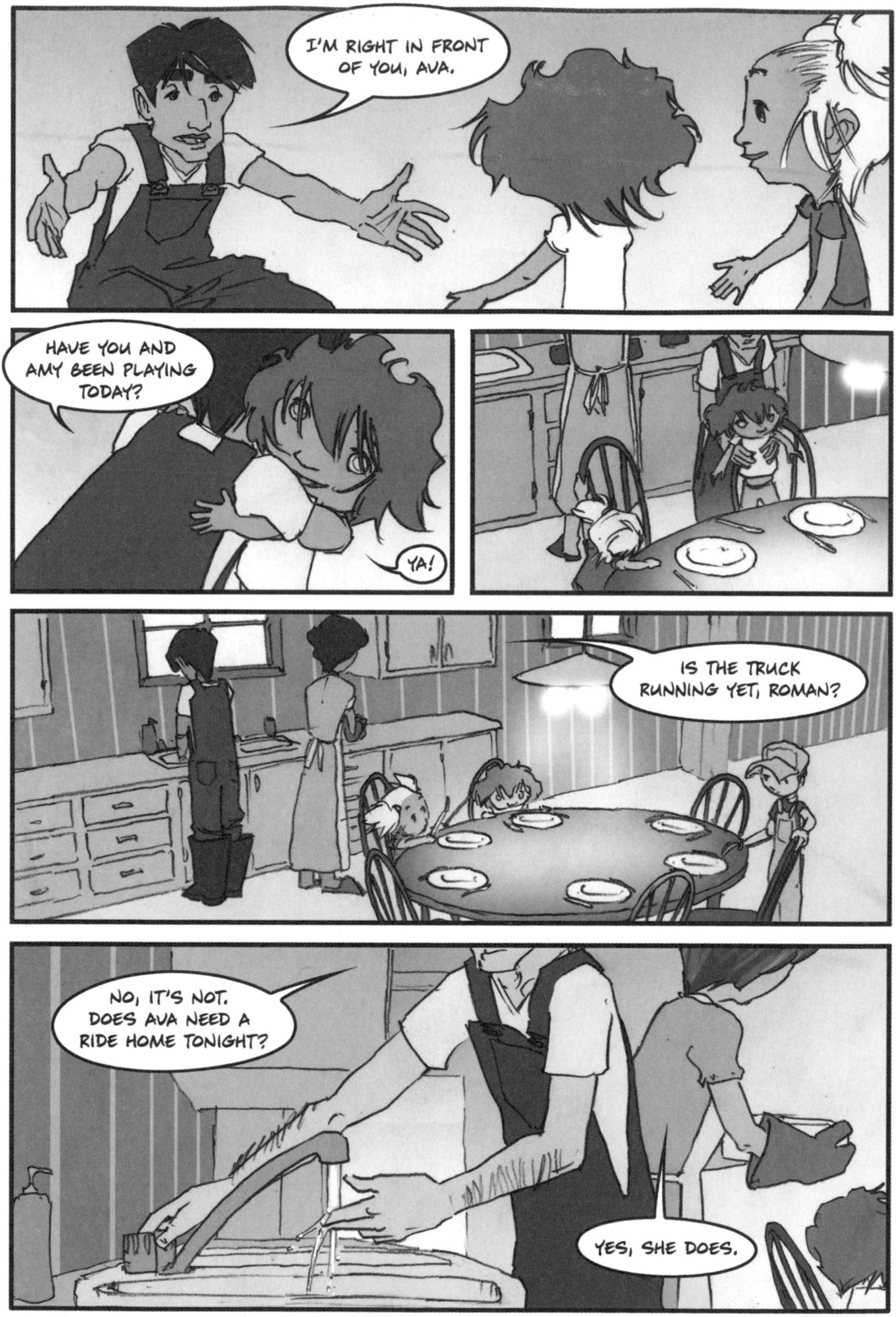
I'M RIGHT IN FRONT OF YOU, AVA.
HAVE YOU AND AMY BEEN PLAYING TODAY?
YA!
IS THE TRUCK RUNNING YET, ROMAN?
NO, IT'S NOT. DOES AVA NEED A RIDE HOME TONIGHT?
YES, SHE DOES.

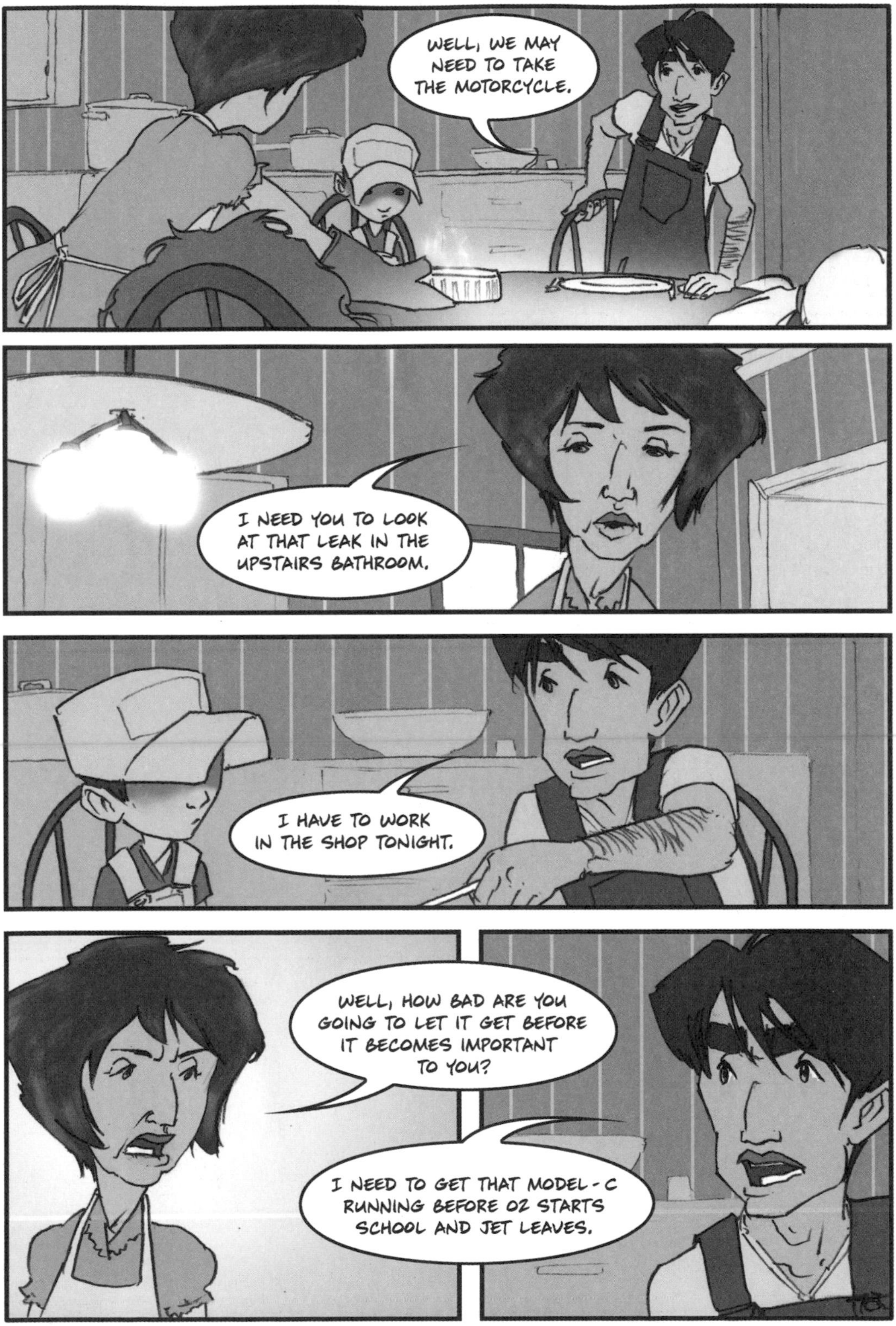
WELL, WE MAY NEED TO TAKE THE MOTORCYCLE.
I NEED YOU TO LOOK AT THAT LEAK IN THE UPSTAIRS BATHROOM.
I HAVE TO WORK IN THE SHOP TONIGHT.
WELL, HOW BAD ARE YOU GOING TO LET IT GET BEFORE IT BECOMES IMPORTANT TO YOU?
I NEED TO GET THAT MODEL-C RUNNING BEFORE OZ STARTS SCHOOL AND JET LEAVES.

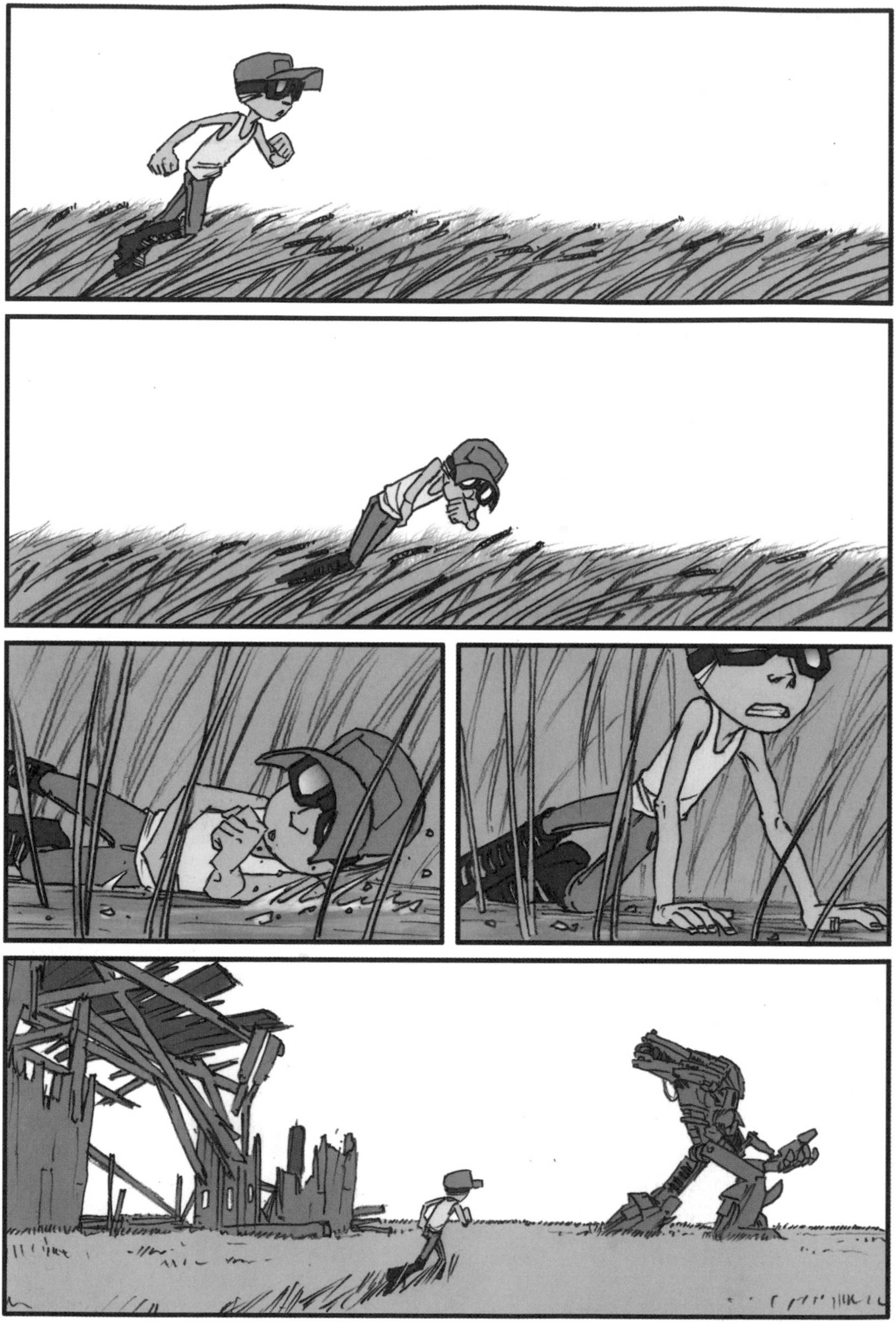

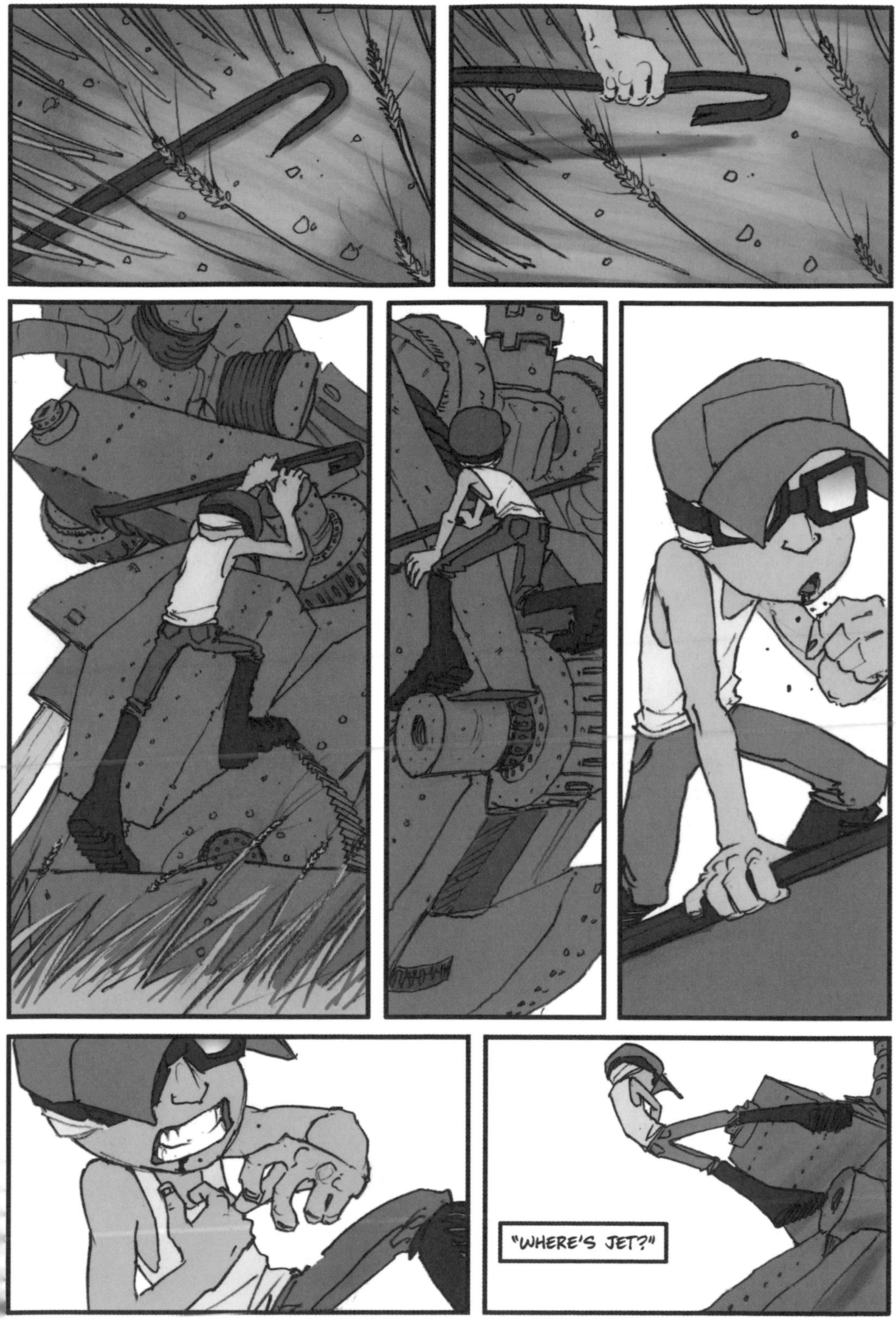
"WHERE'S JET?"

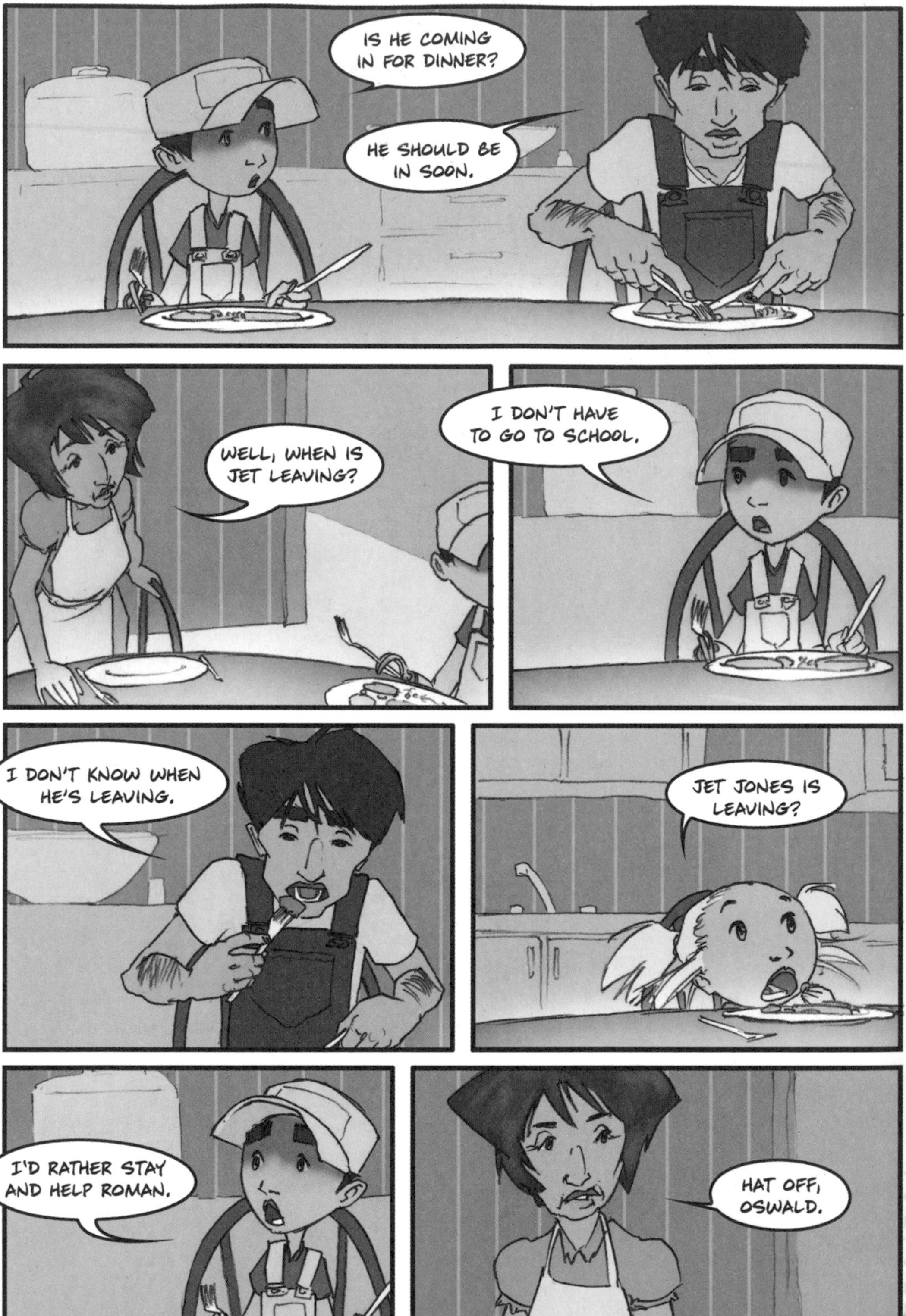
IS HE COMING IN FOR DINNER?
HE SHOULD BE IN SOON.
WELL, WHEN IS JET LEAVING?
I DON'T HAVE TO GO TO SCHOOL.
I DON'T KNOW WHEN HE'S LEAVING.
JET JONES IS LEAVING?
I'D RATHER STAY AND HELP ROMAN.
HAT OFF, OSWALD.

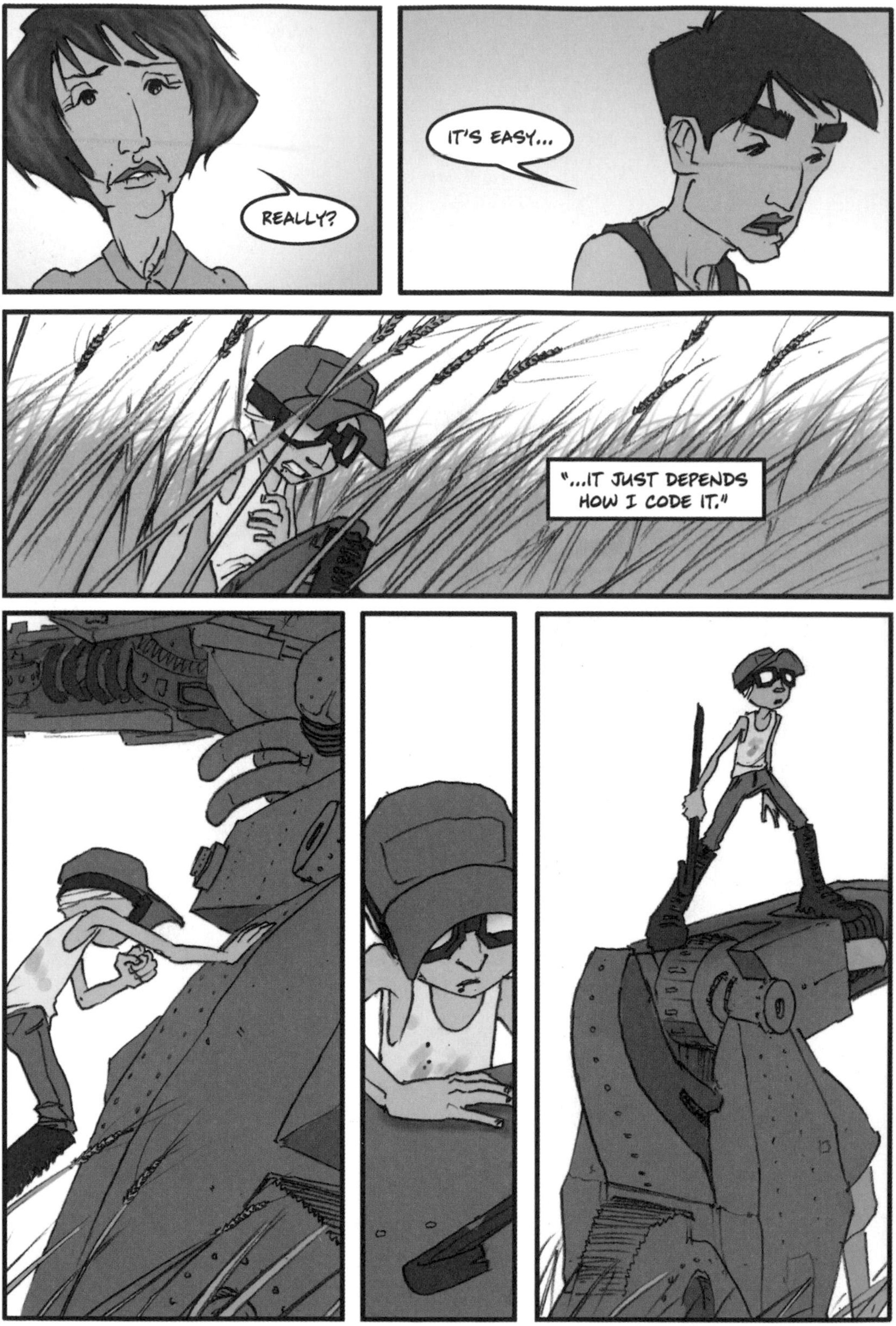
REALLY?
IT'S EASY...
"...IT JUST DEPENDS HOW I CODE IT."

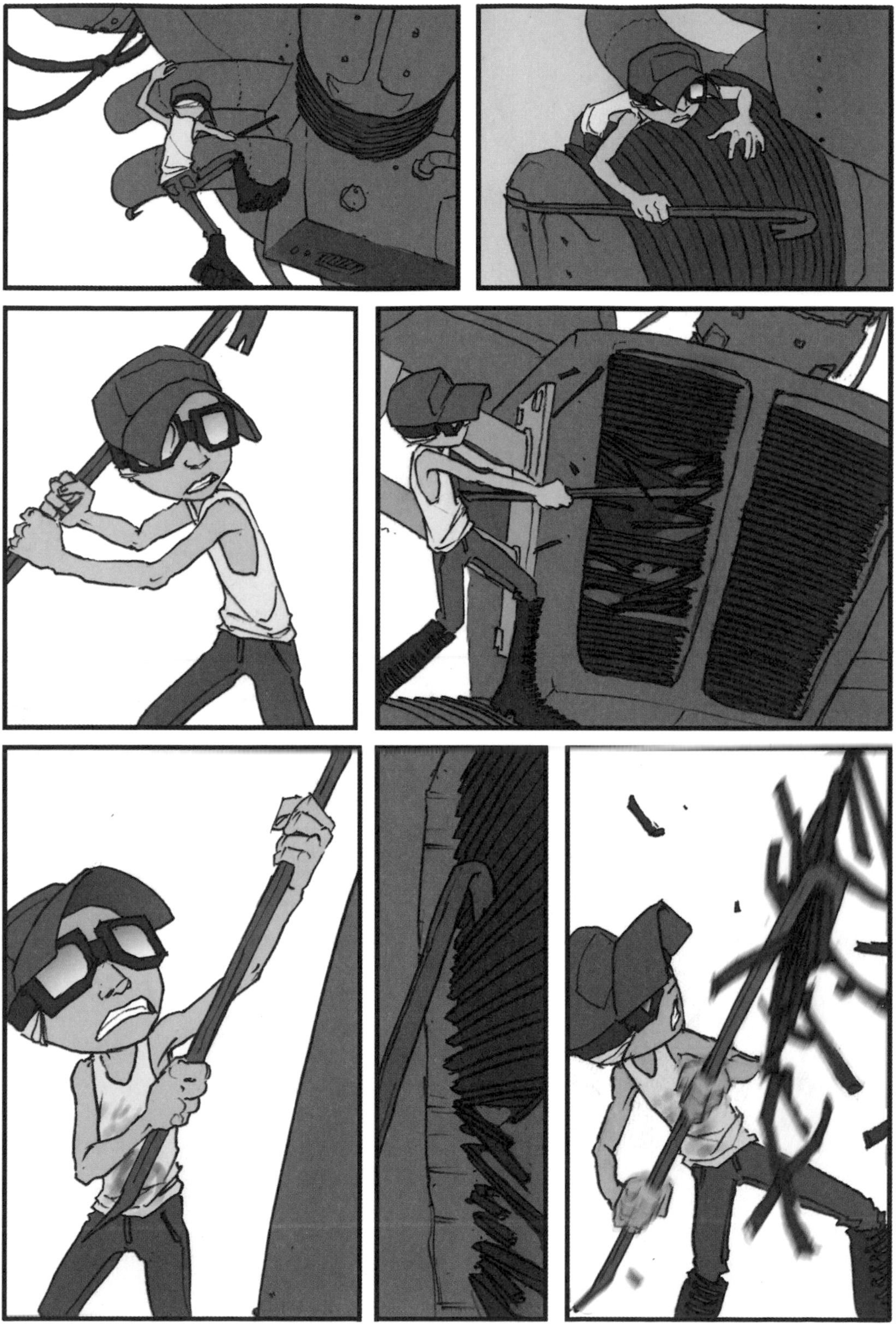

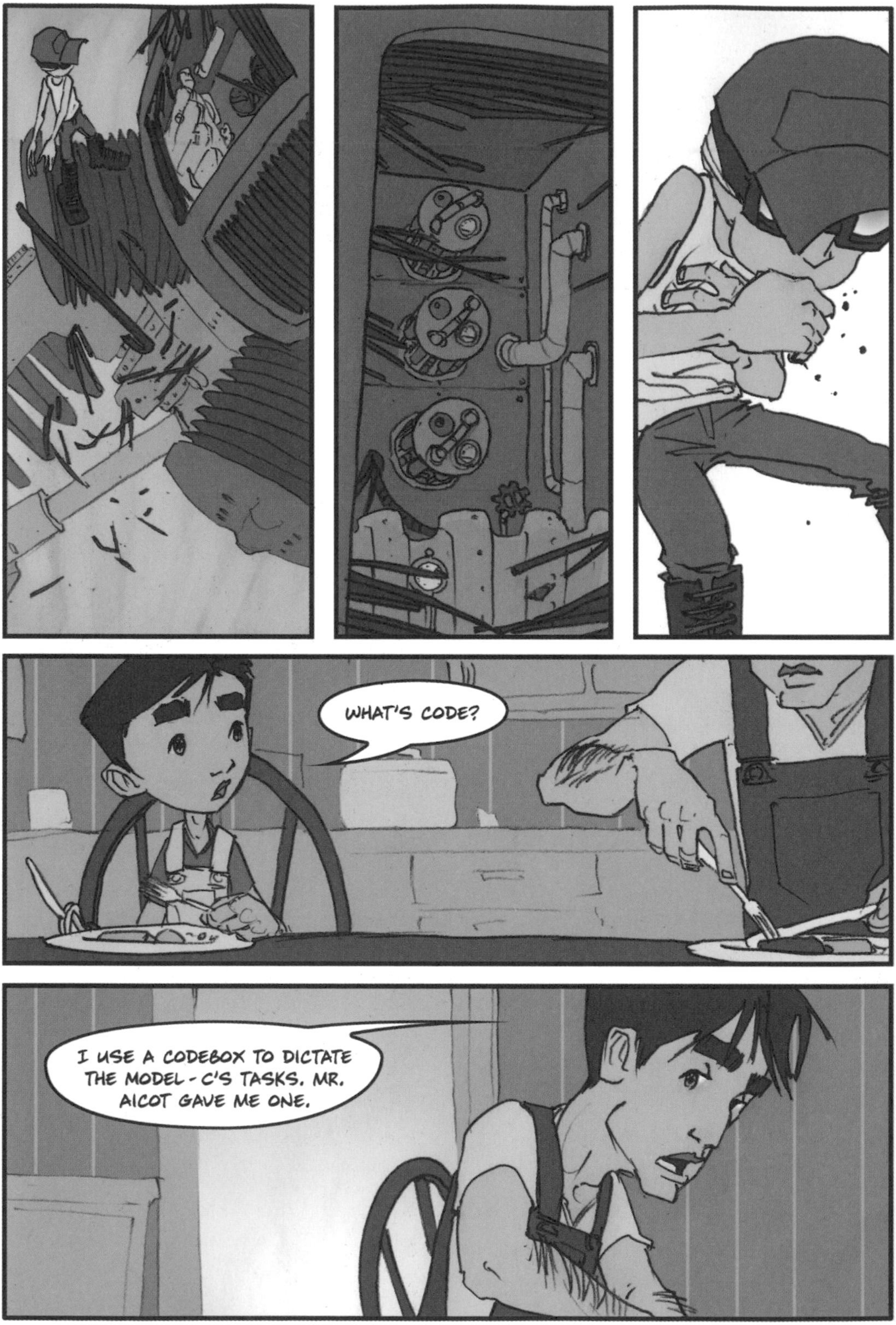
WHAT'S CODE?
I USE A CODEBOX TO DICTATE THE MODEL - C'S TASKS. MR. AICOT GAVE ME ONE.

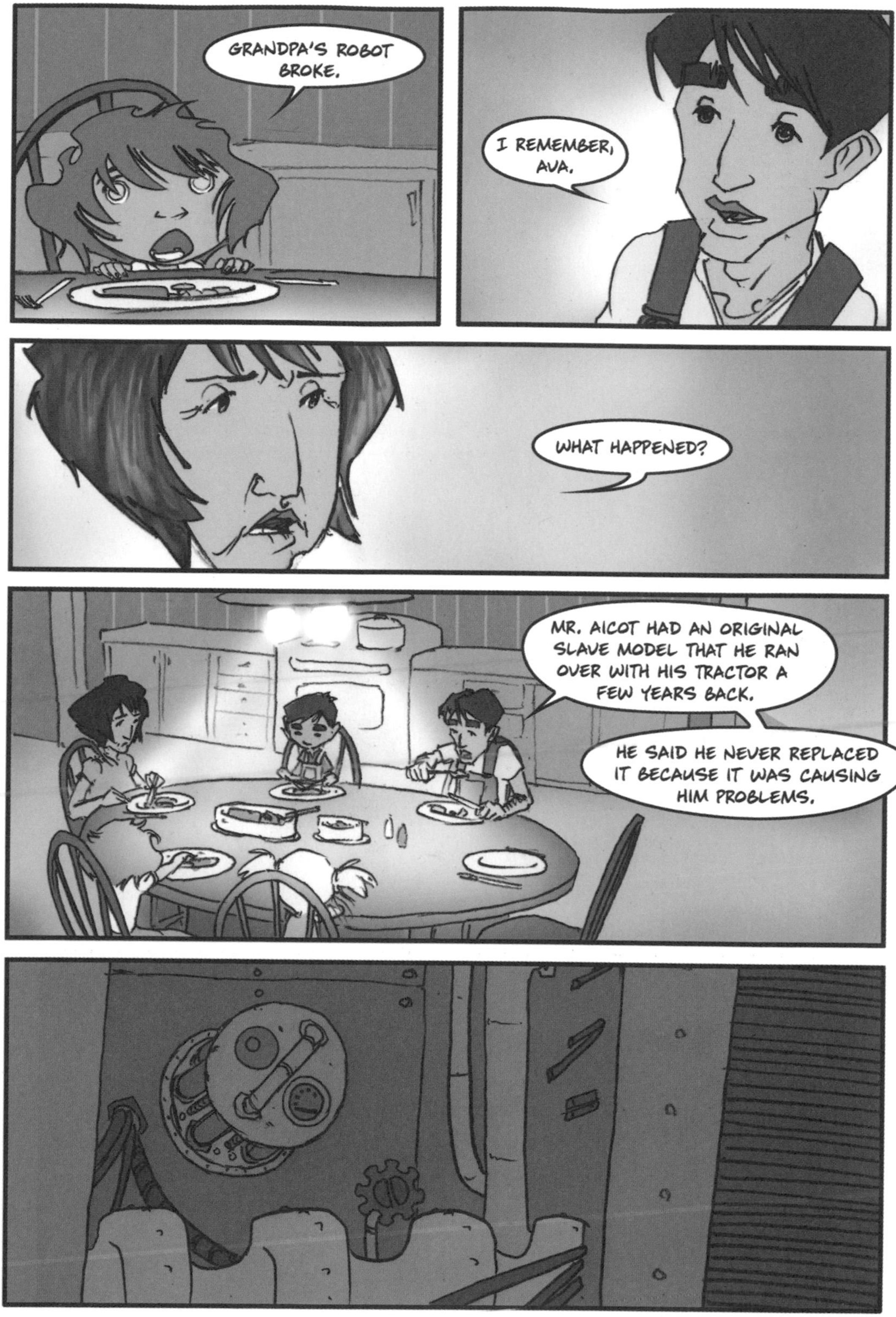
GRANDPA'S ROBOT BROKE.
I REMEMBER, AVA.
WHAT HAPPENED?
MR. AICOT HAD AN ORIGINAL SLAVE MODEL THAT HE RAN OVER WITH HIS TRACTOR A FEW YEARS BACK.
HE SAID HE NEVER REPLACED IT BECAUSE IT WAS CAUSING HIM PROBLEMS.

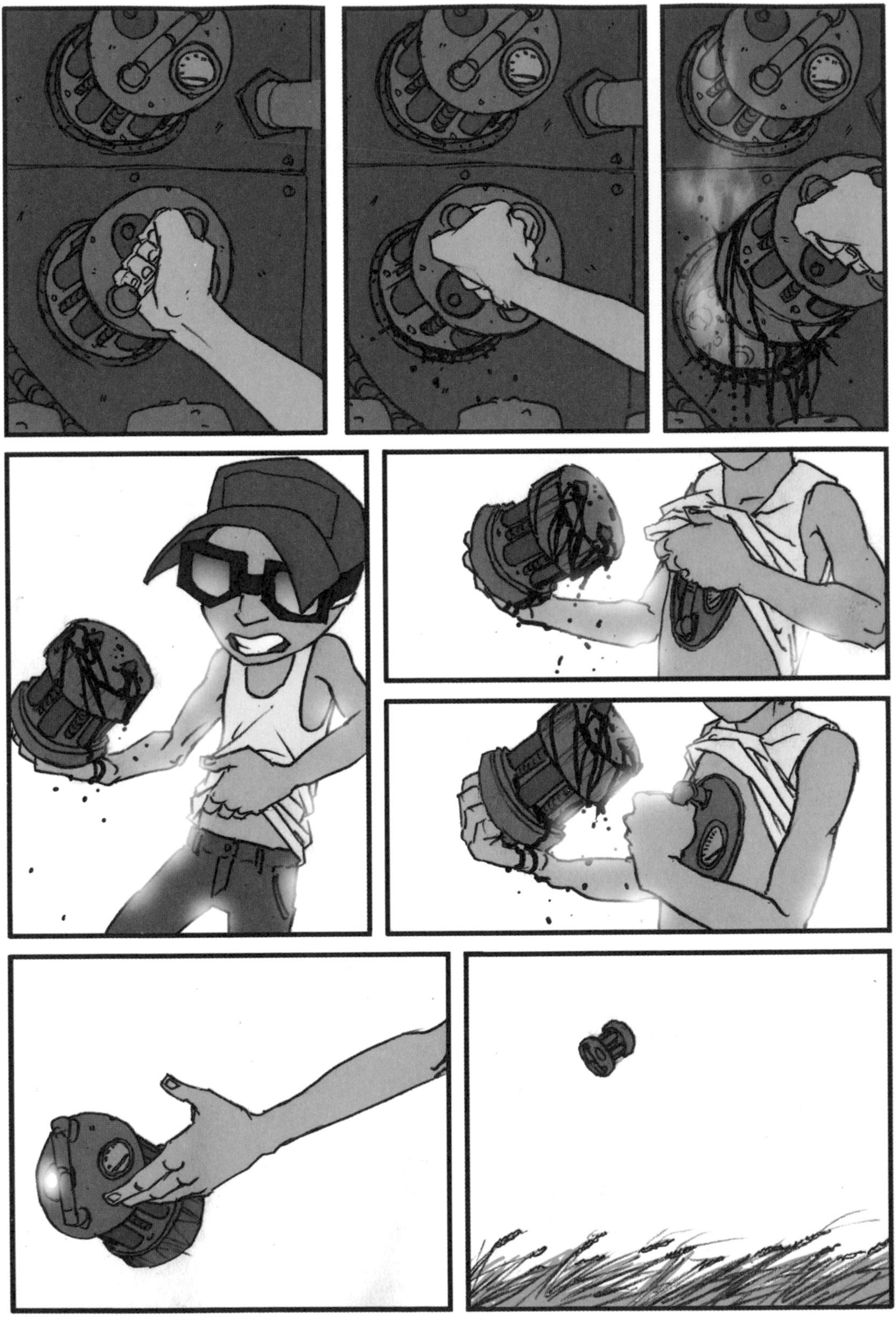

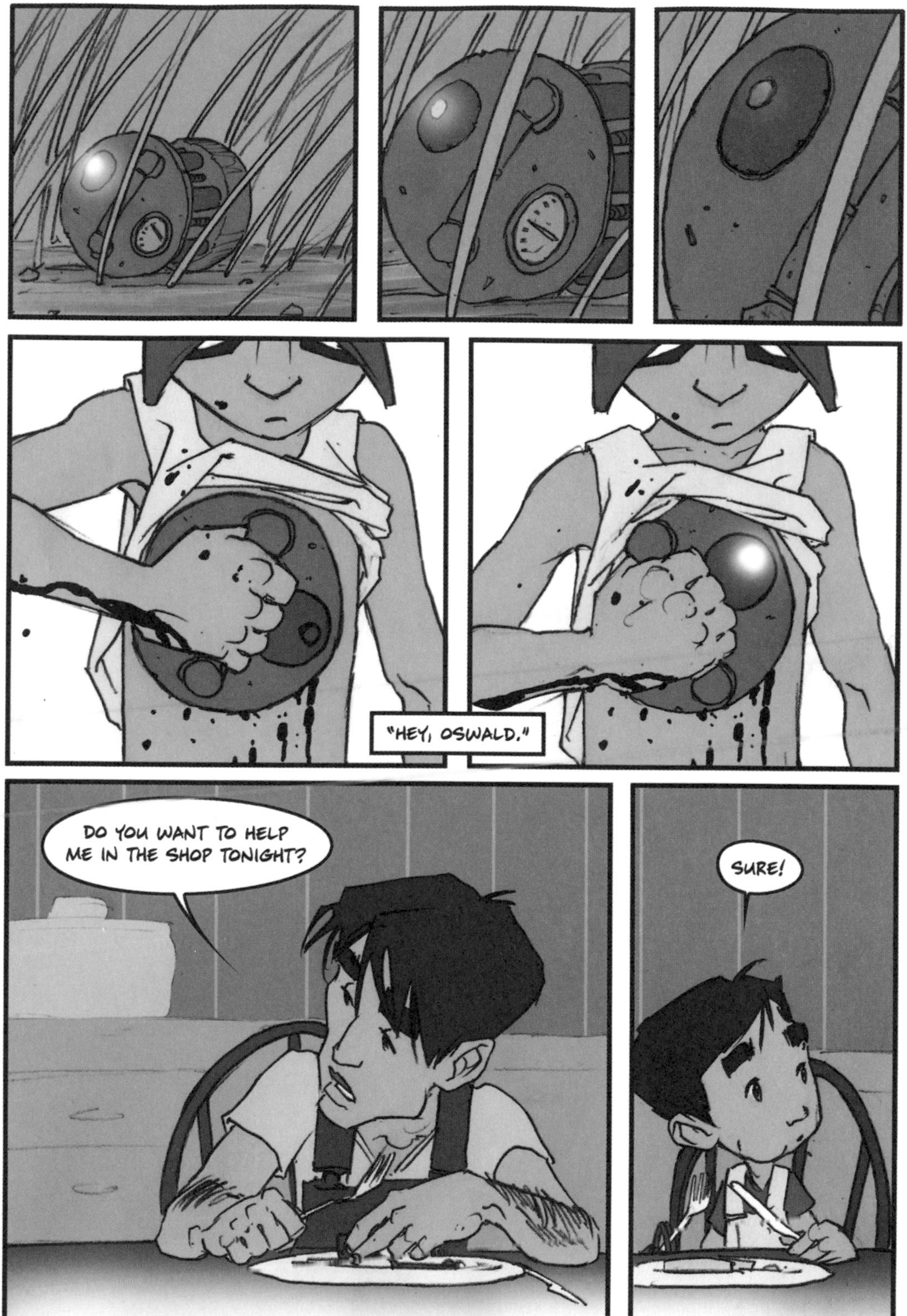
"HEY, OSWALD."
DO YOU WANT TO HELP ME IN THE SHOP TONIGHT?
SURE!

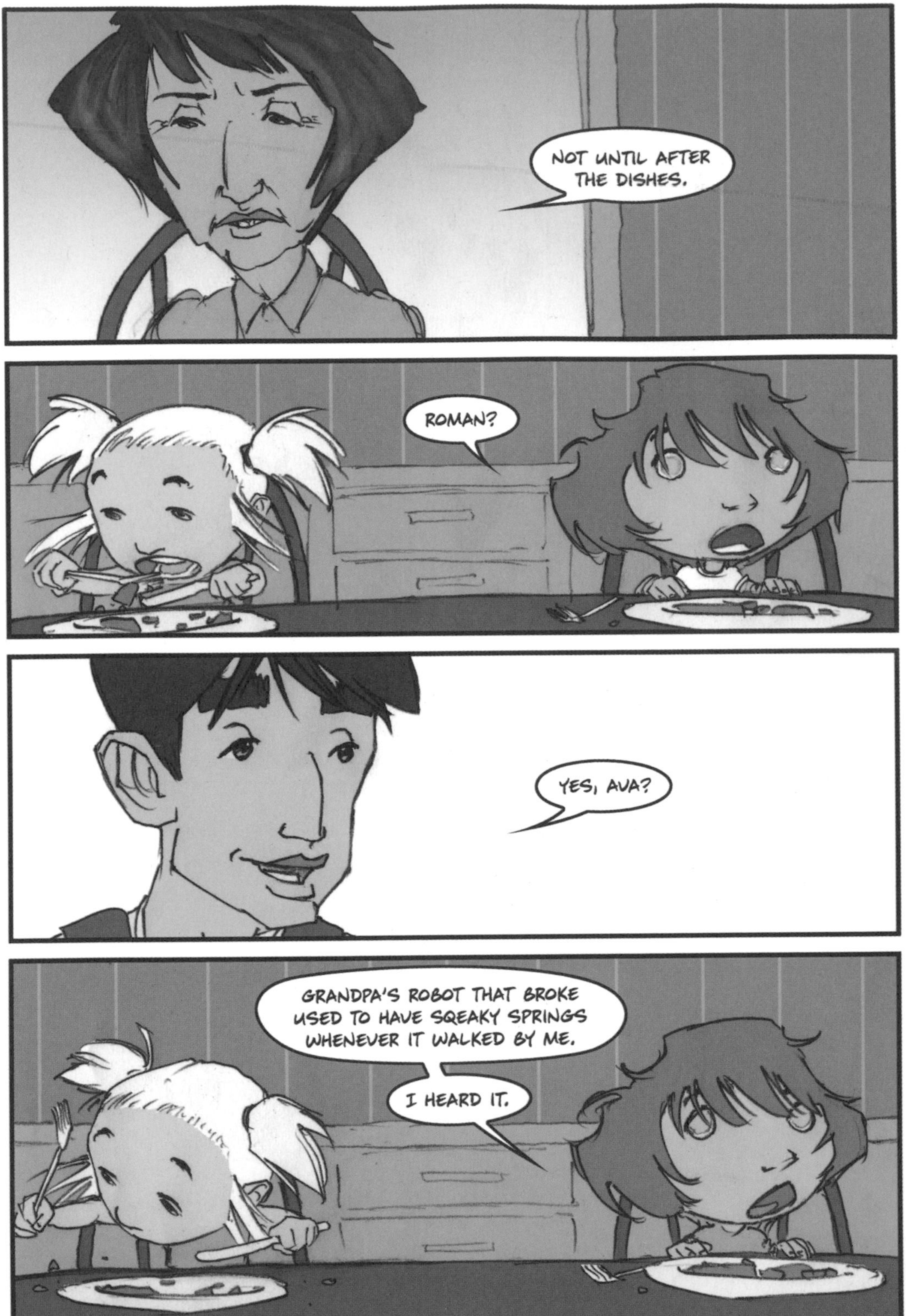
NOT UNTIL AFTER THE DISHES.
ROMAN?
YES, AVA?
GRANDPA'S ROBOT THAT BROKE USED TO HAVE SQEAKY SPRINGS WHENEVER IT WALKED BY ME.
I HEARD IT.

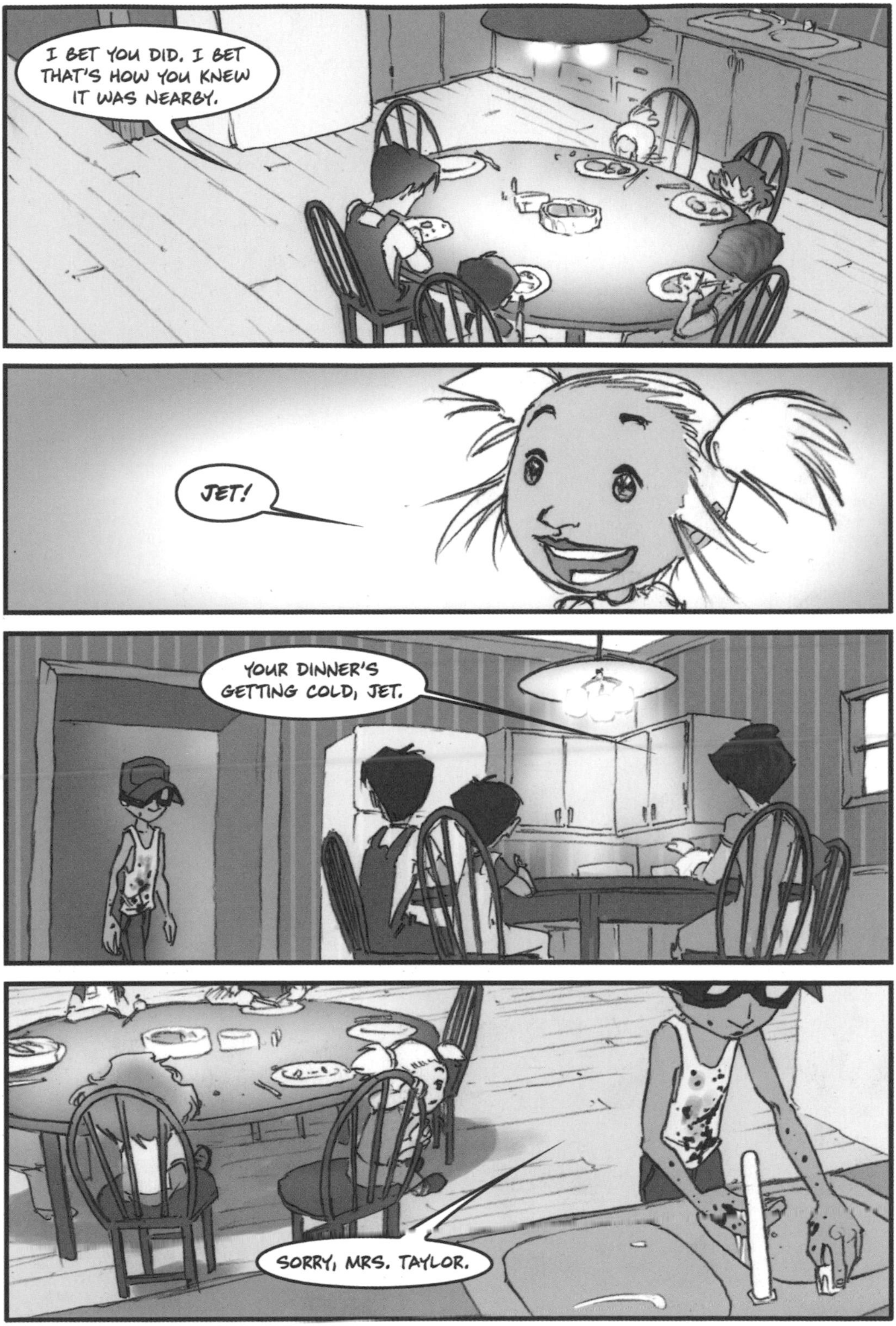
I BET YOU DID. I BET THAT'S HOW YOU KNEW IT WAS NEARBY.
JET!
YOUR DINNER'S GETTING COLD, JET.
SORRY, MRS. TAYLOR.

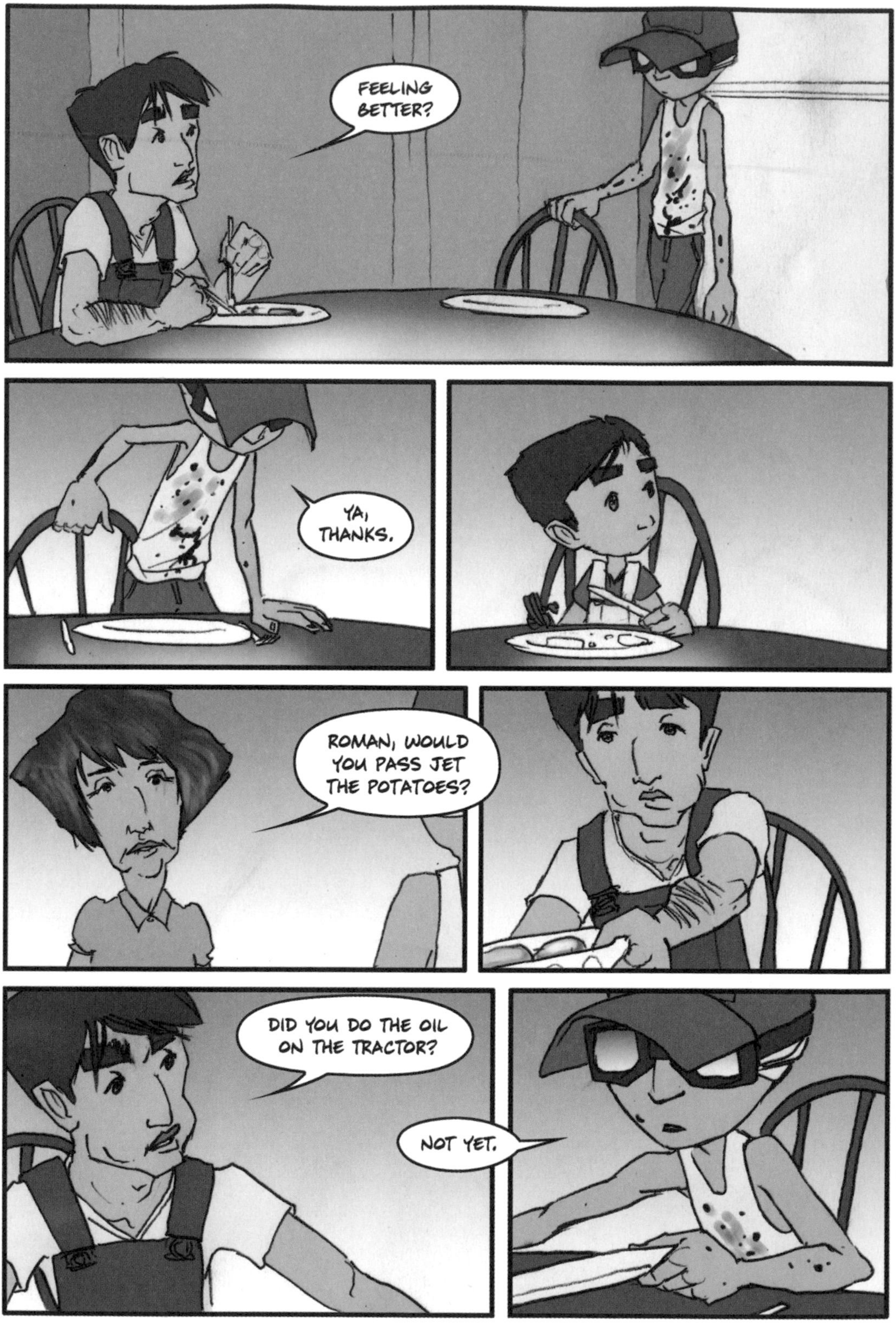
FEELING BETTER?
YA, THANKS.
ROMAN, WOULD YOU PASS JET THE POTATOES?
DID YOU DO THE OIL ON THE TRACTOR?
NOT YET.

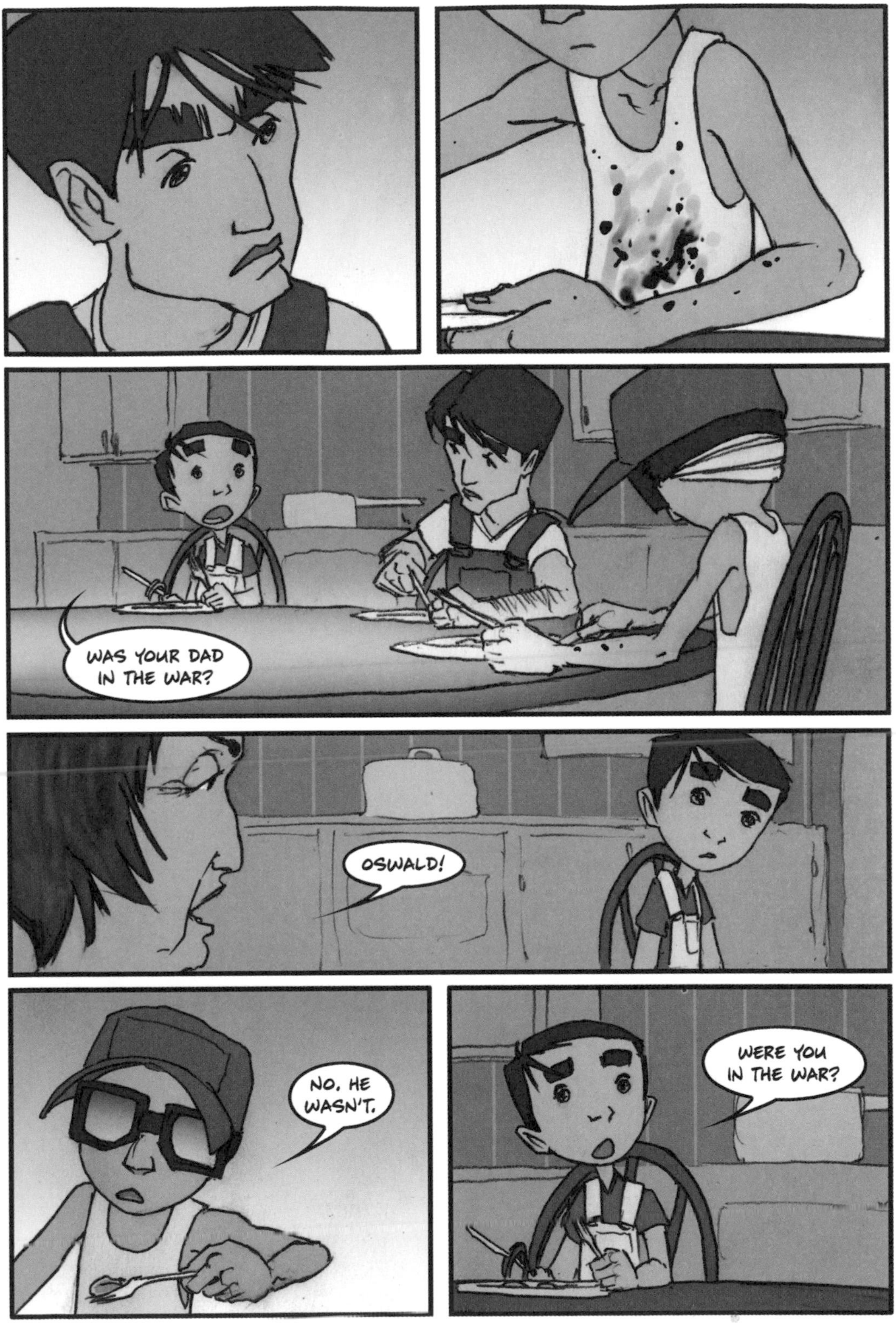
WAS YOUR DAD IN THE WAR?
OSWALD!
NO. HE WASN'T.
WERE YOU IN THE WAR?

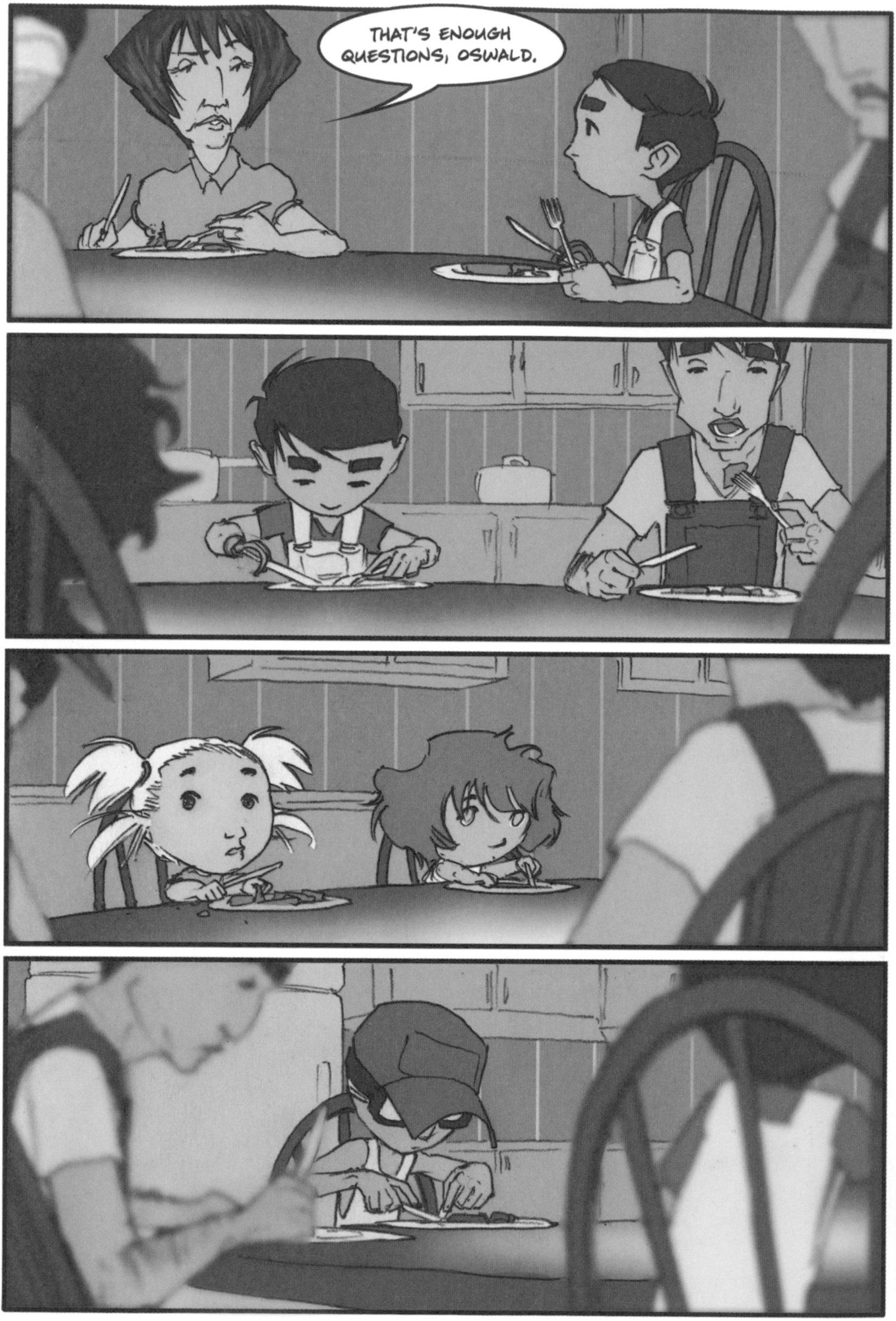
THAT'S ENOUGH QUESTIONS, OSWALD.

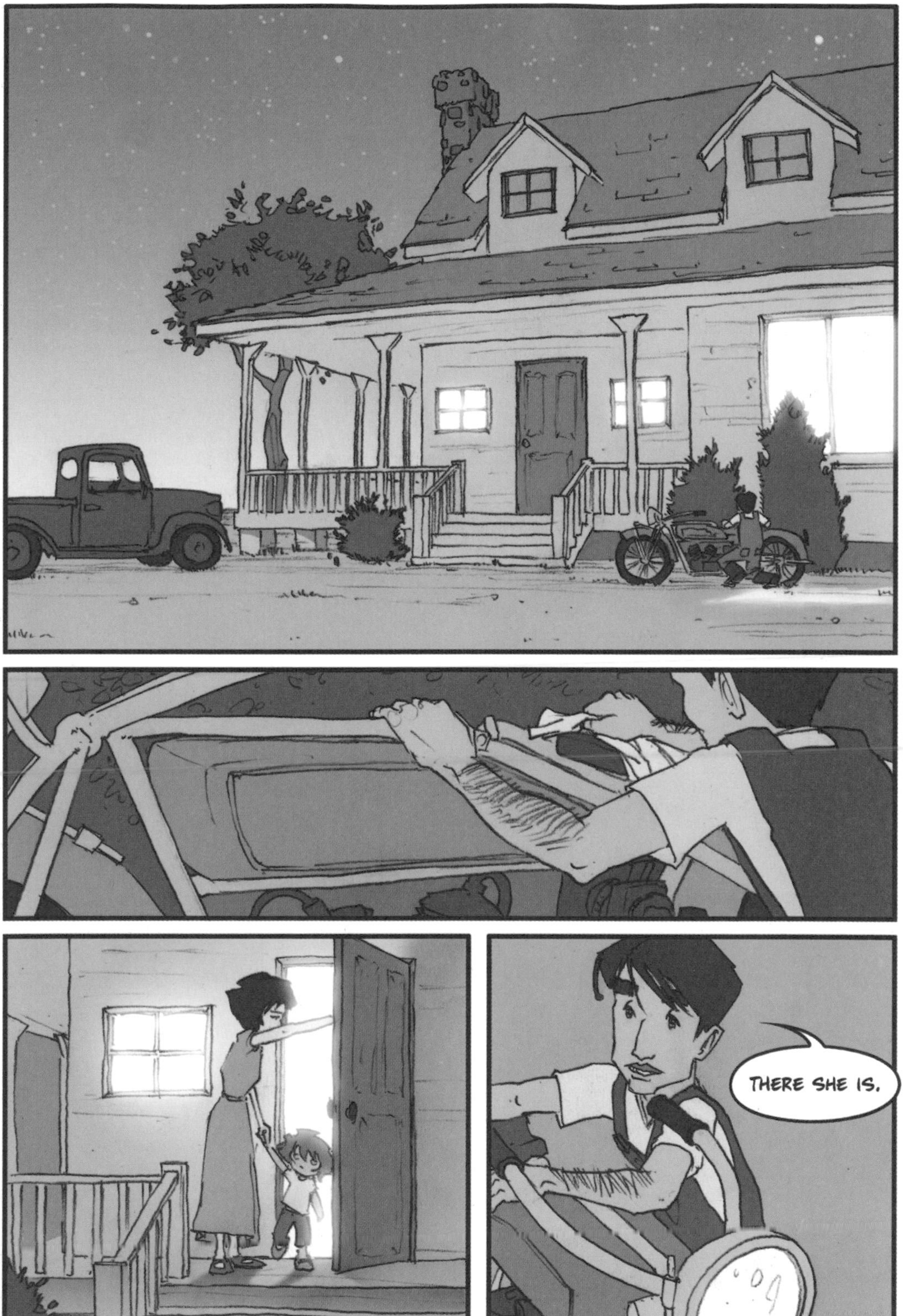
THERE SHE IS.

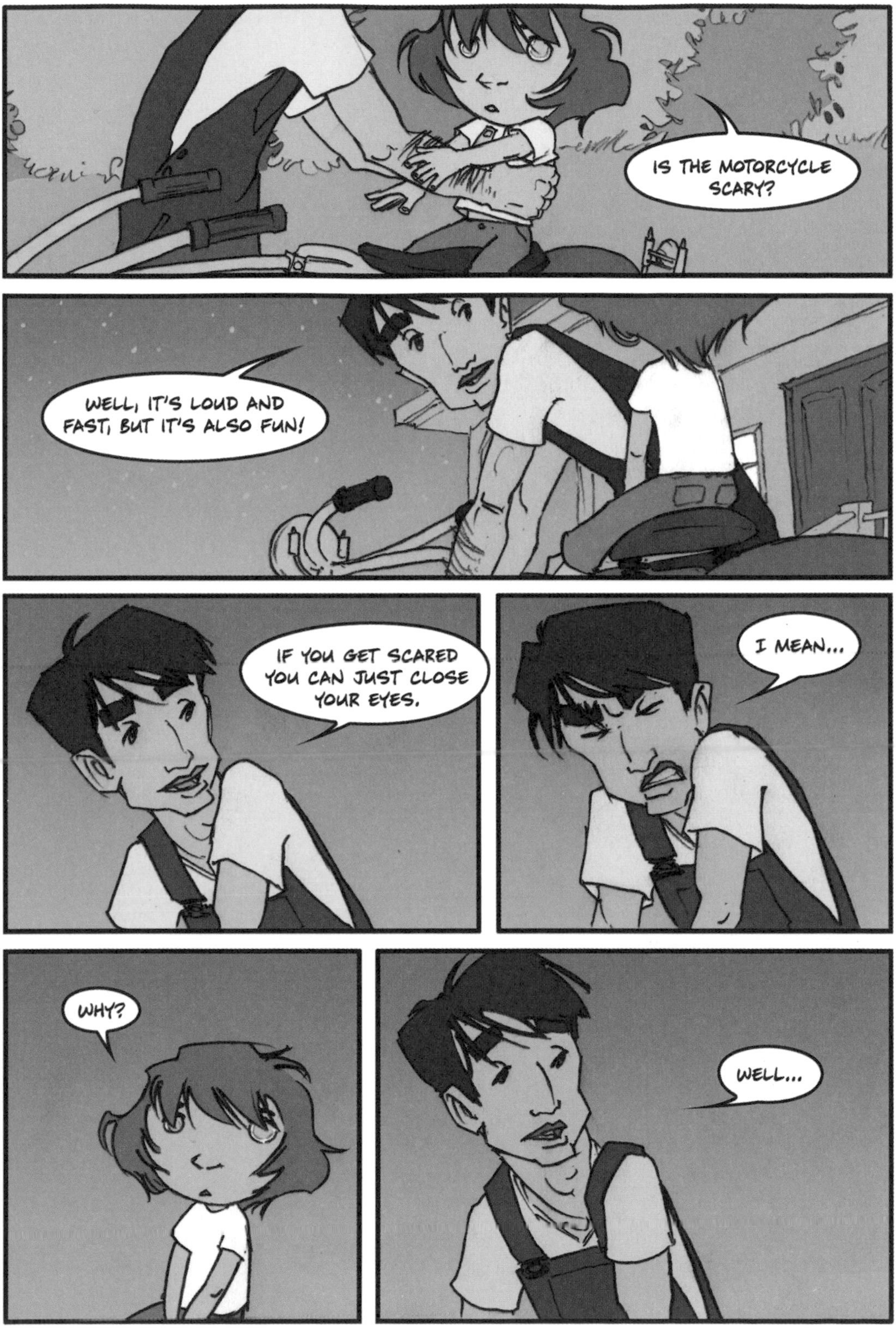
IS THE MOTORCYCLE SCARY?
WELL, IT'S LOUD AND FAST, BUT IT'S ALSO FUN!
IF YOU GET SCARED YOU CAN JUST CLOSE YOUR EYES.
I MEAN...
WHY?
WELL...

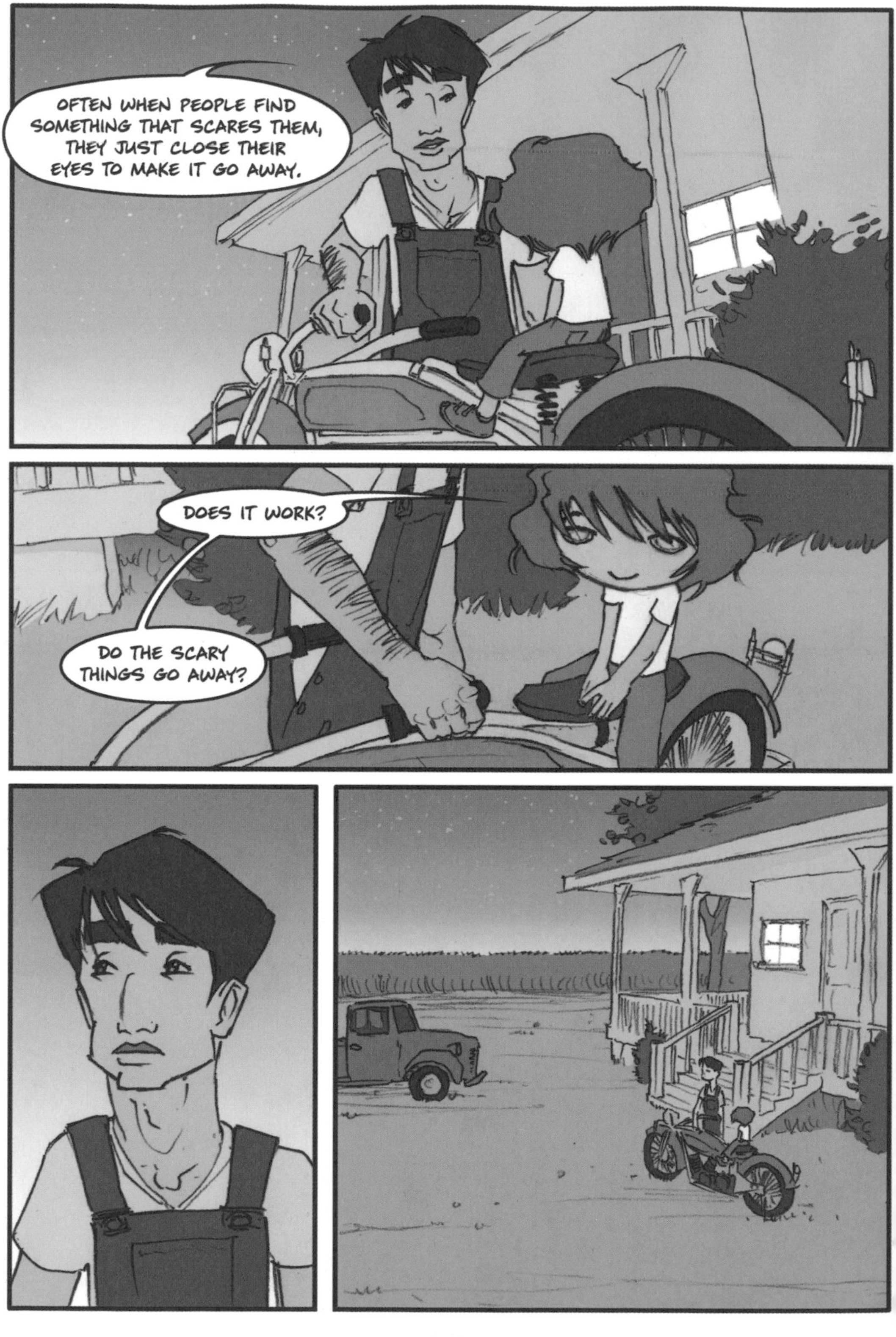
OFTEN WHEN PEOPLE FIND SOMETHING THAT SCARES THEM, THEY JUST CLOSE THEIR EYES TO MAKE IT GO AWAY.
DOES IT WORK?
DO THE SCARY THINGS GO AWAY?

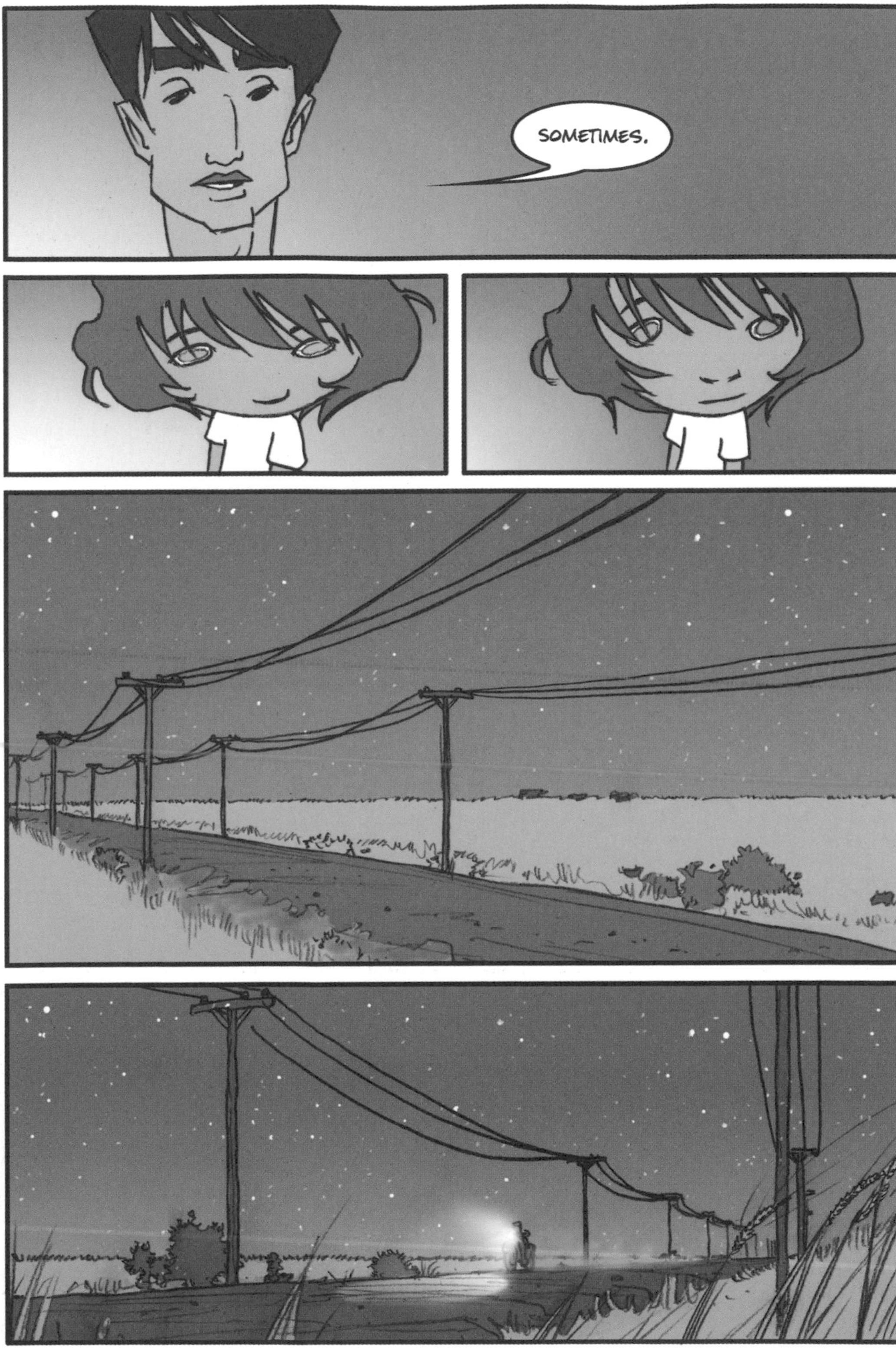
SOMETIMES.

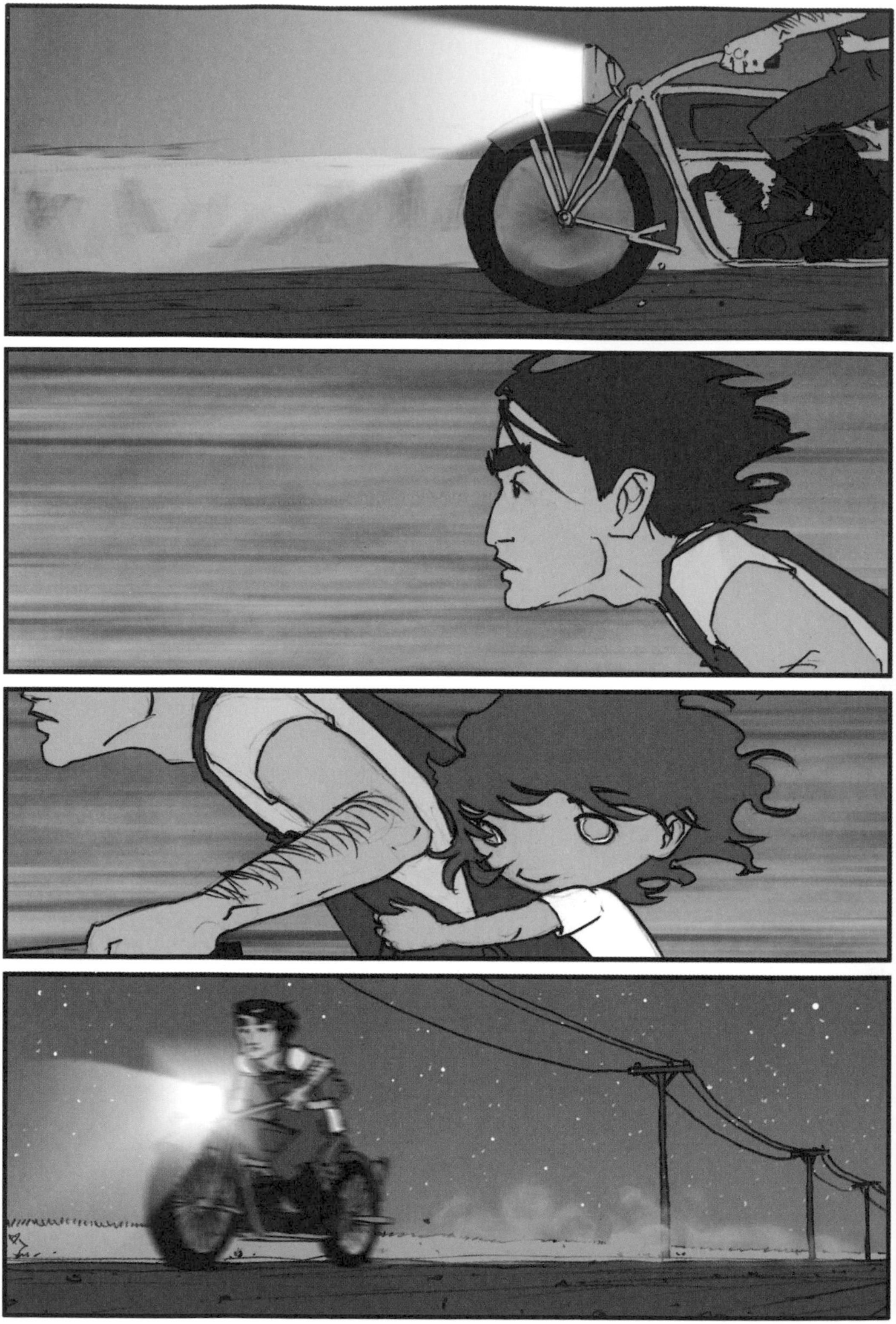

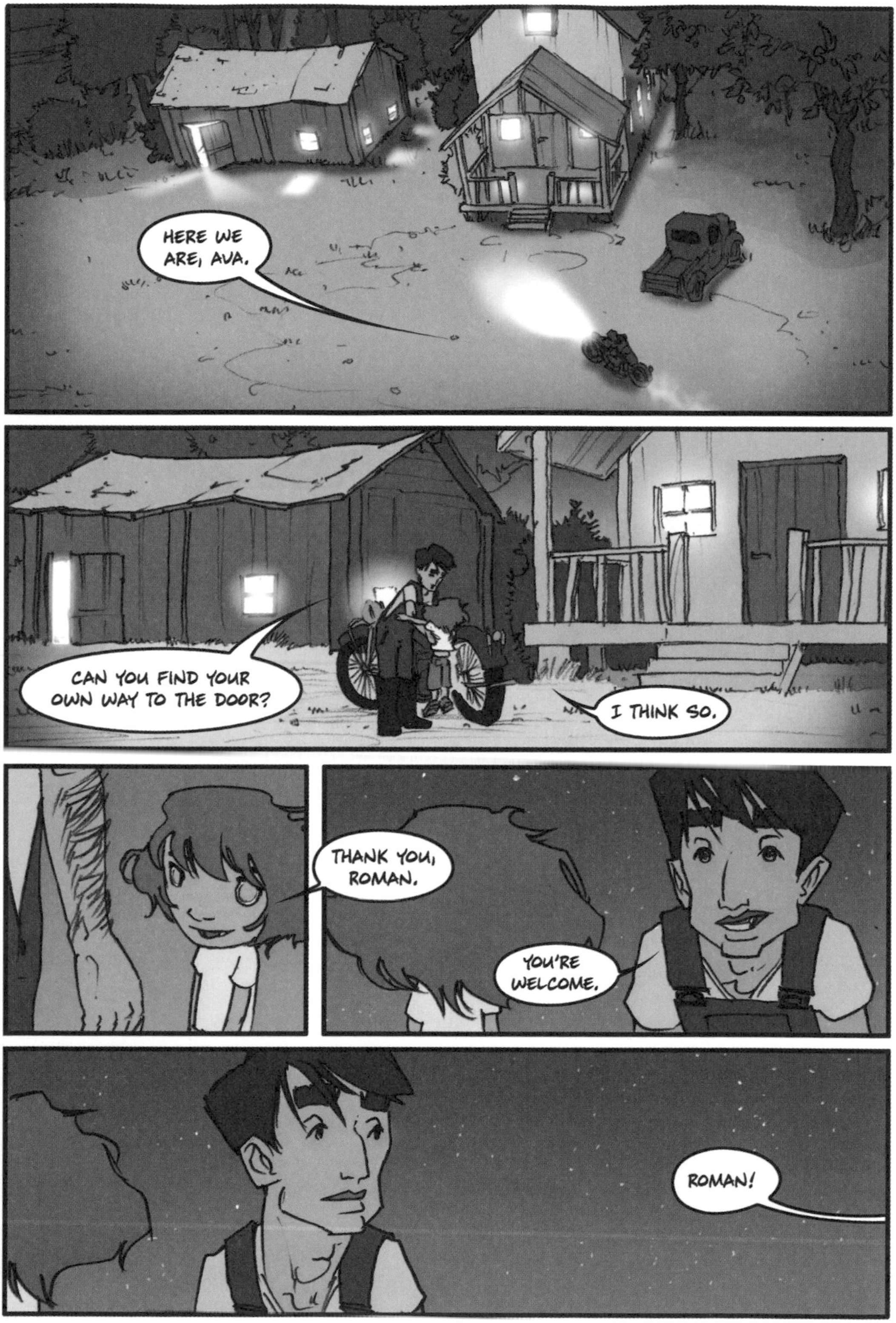
HERE WE ARE, AVA.
CAN YOU FIND YOUR OWN WAY TO THE DOOR?
I THINK SO.
THANK YOU, ROMAN.
YOU'RE WELCOME.
ROMAN!

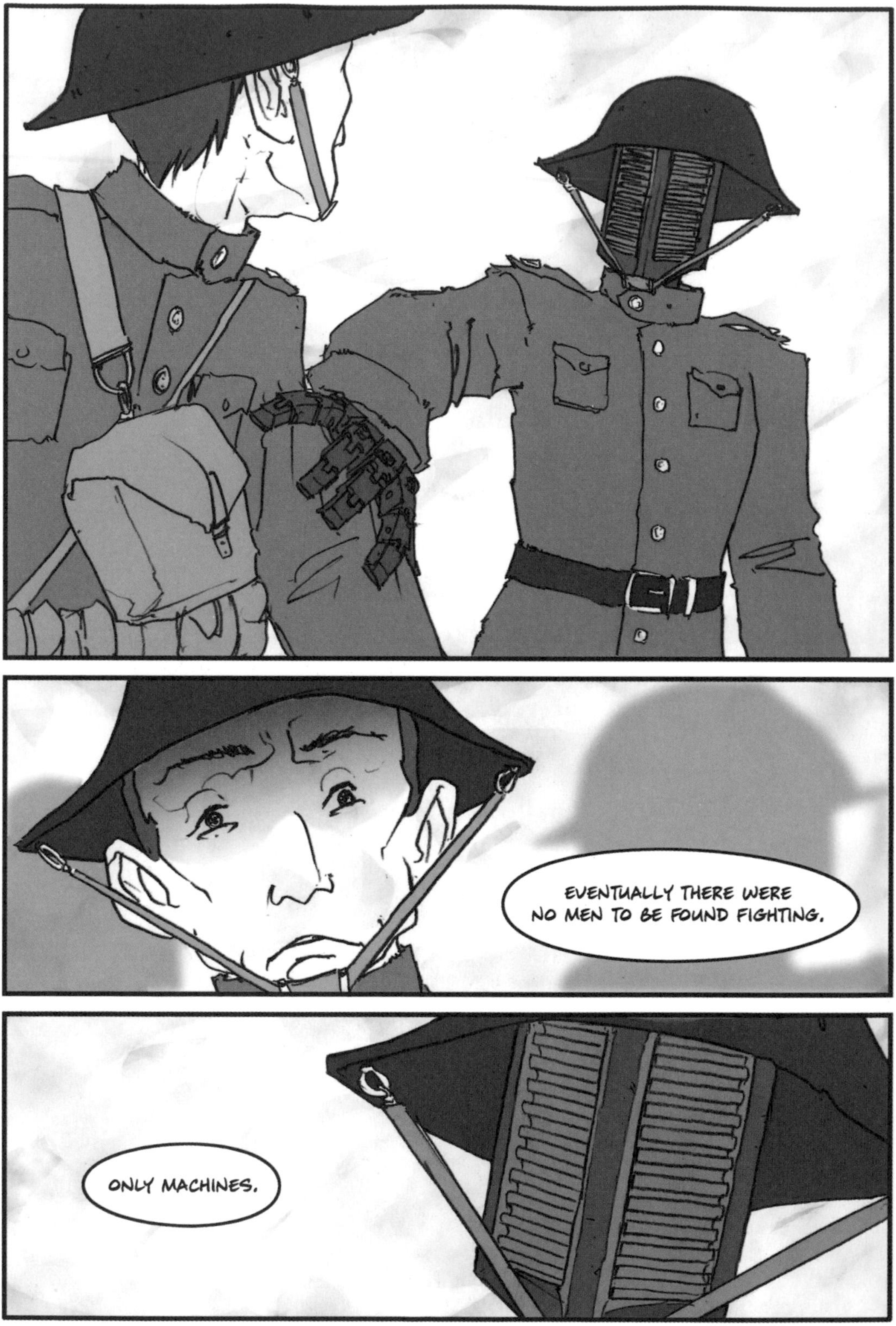
EVENTUALLY THERE WERE
NO MEN TO BE FOUND FIGHTING.
ONLY MACHINES.

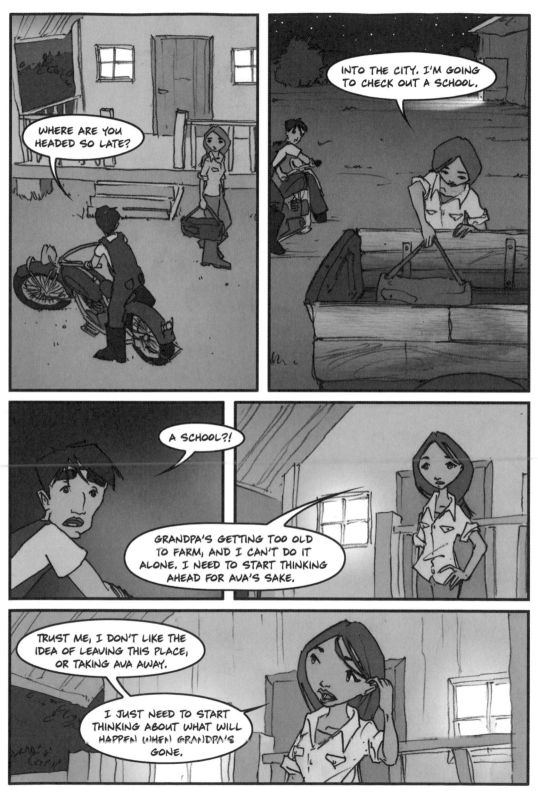

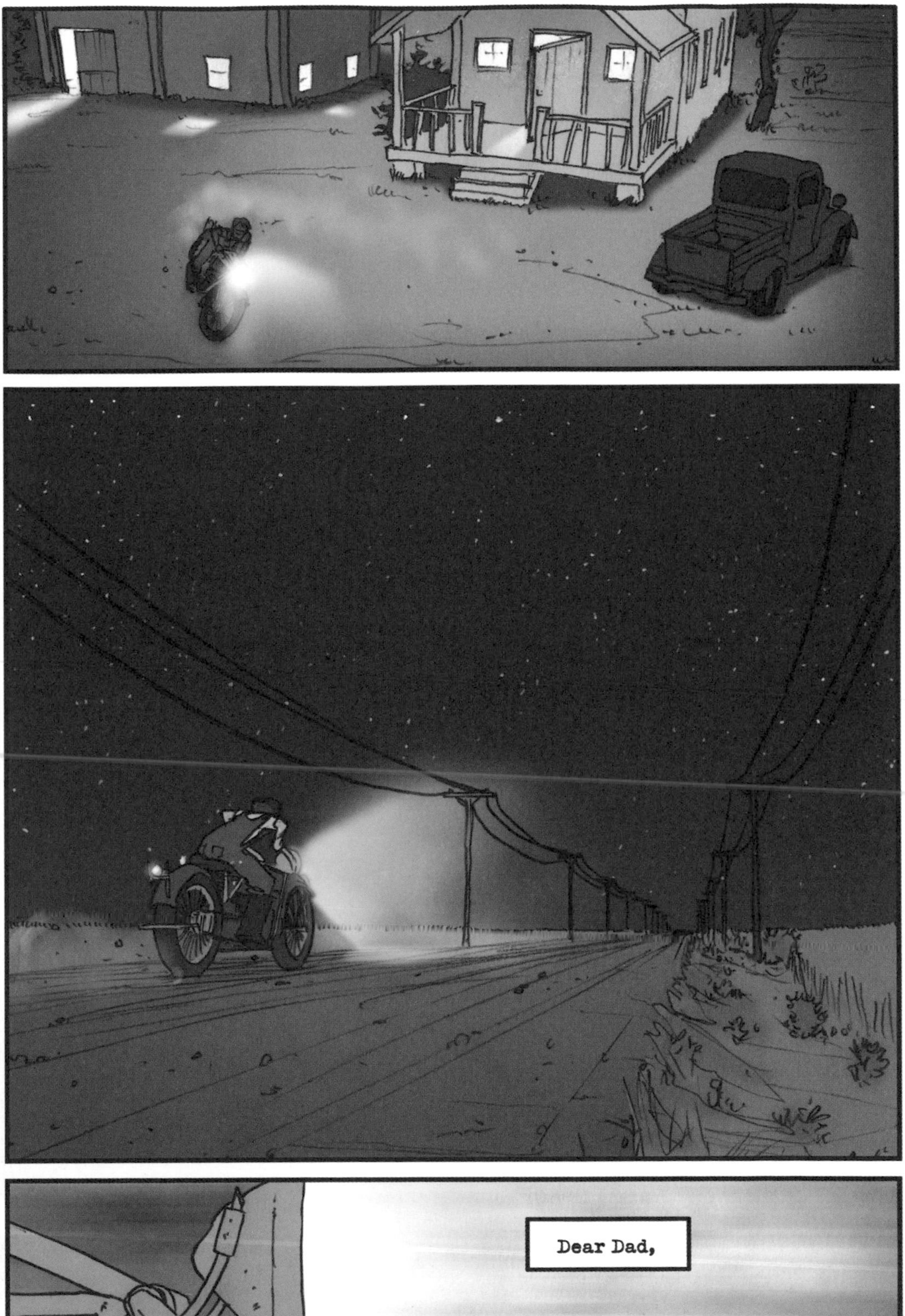
Dear Dad,

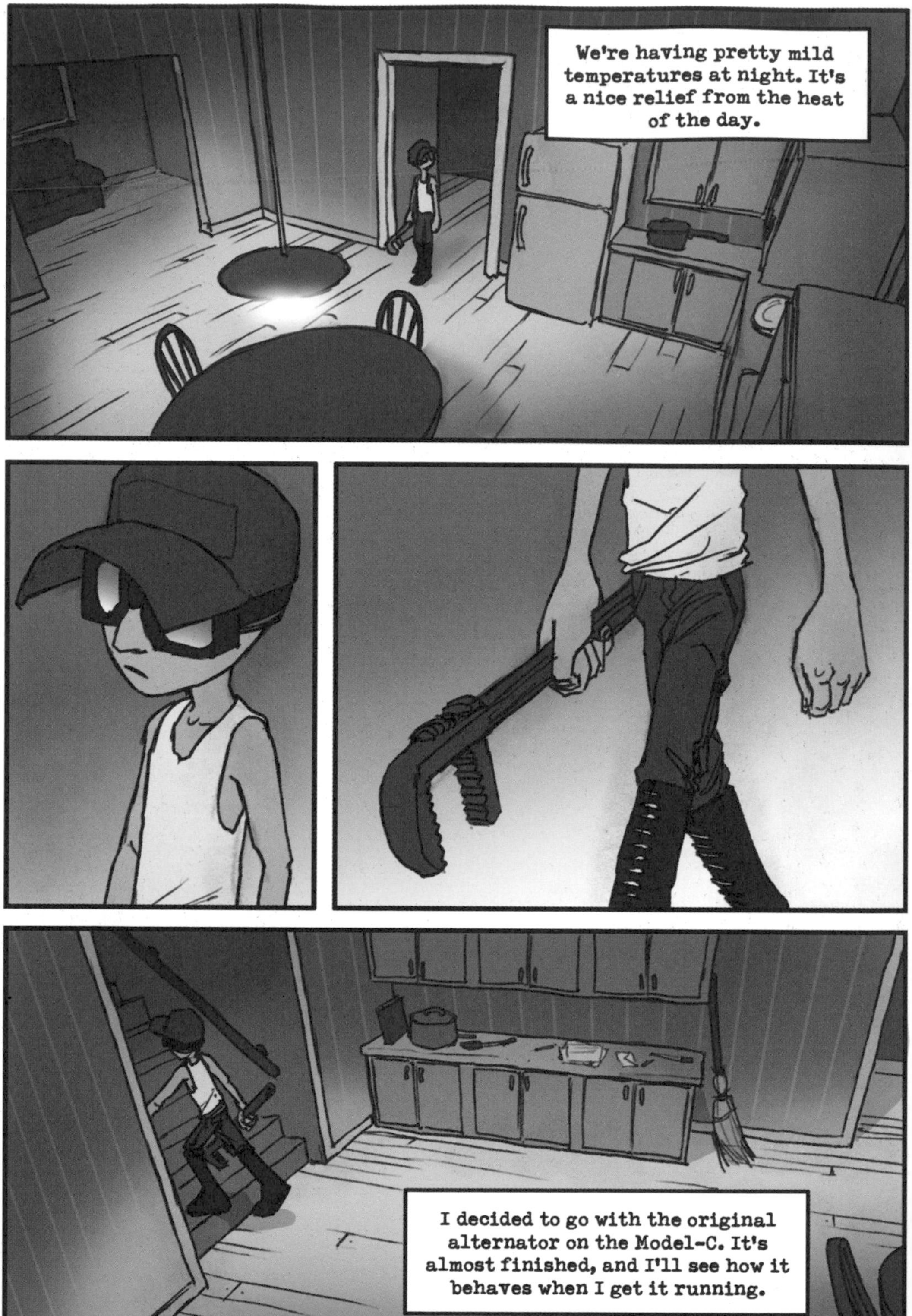
We're having pretty mild temperatures at night. It's a nice relief from the heat of the day.
I decided to go with the original alternator on the Model-C. It's almost finished, and I'll see how it behaves when I get it running.

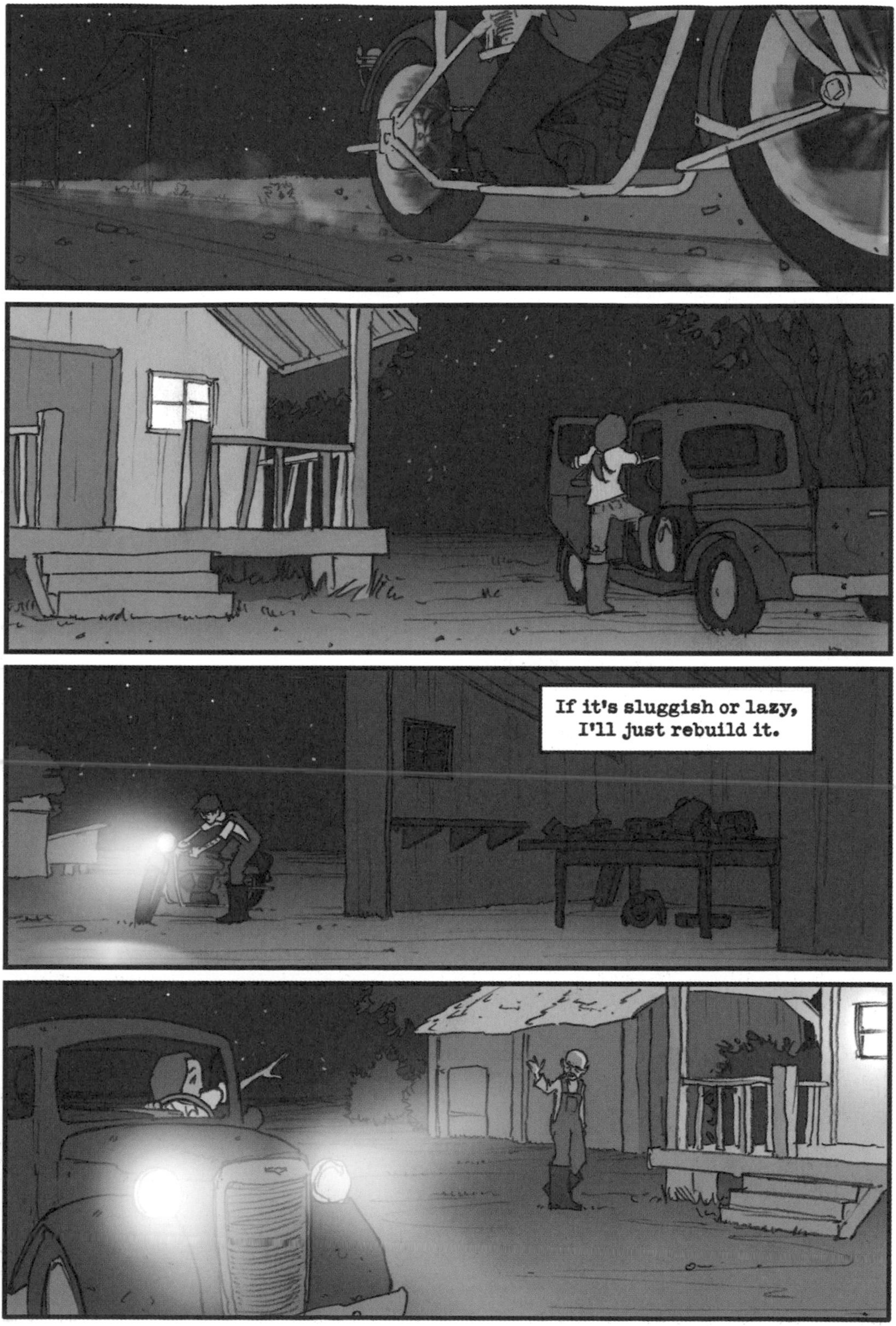
If it's sluggish or lazy,
I'll just rebuild it.

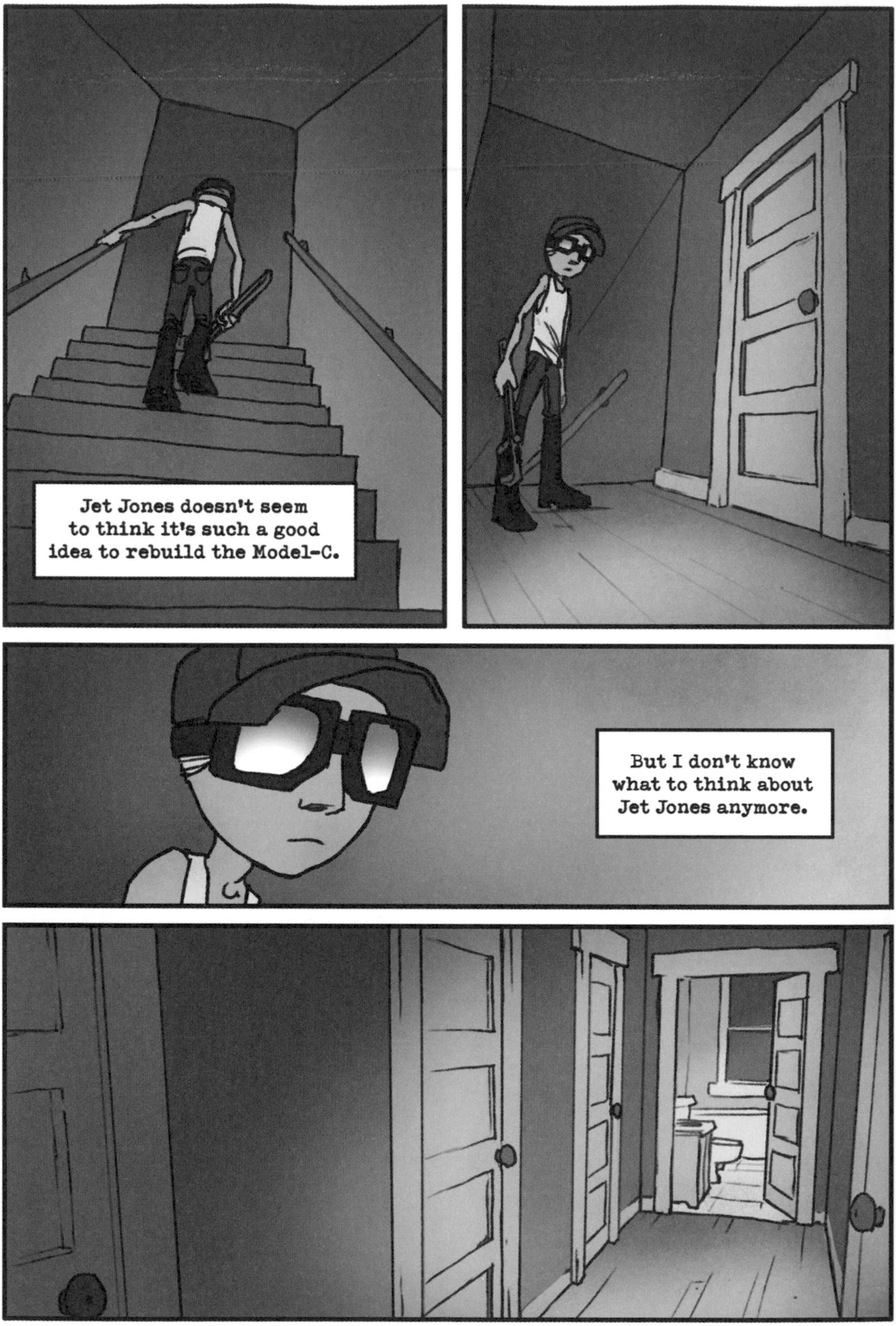
Jet Jones doesn't seem to think it's such a good idea to rebuild the Model-C.
But I don't know what to think about Jet Jones anymore.

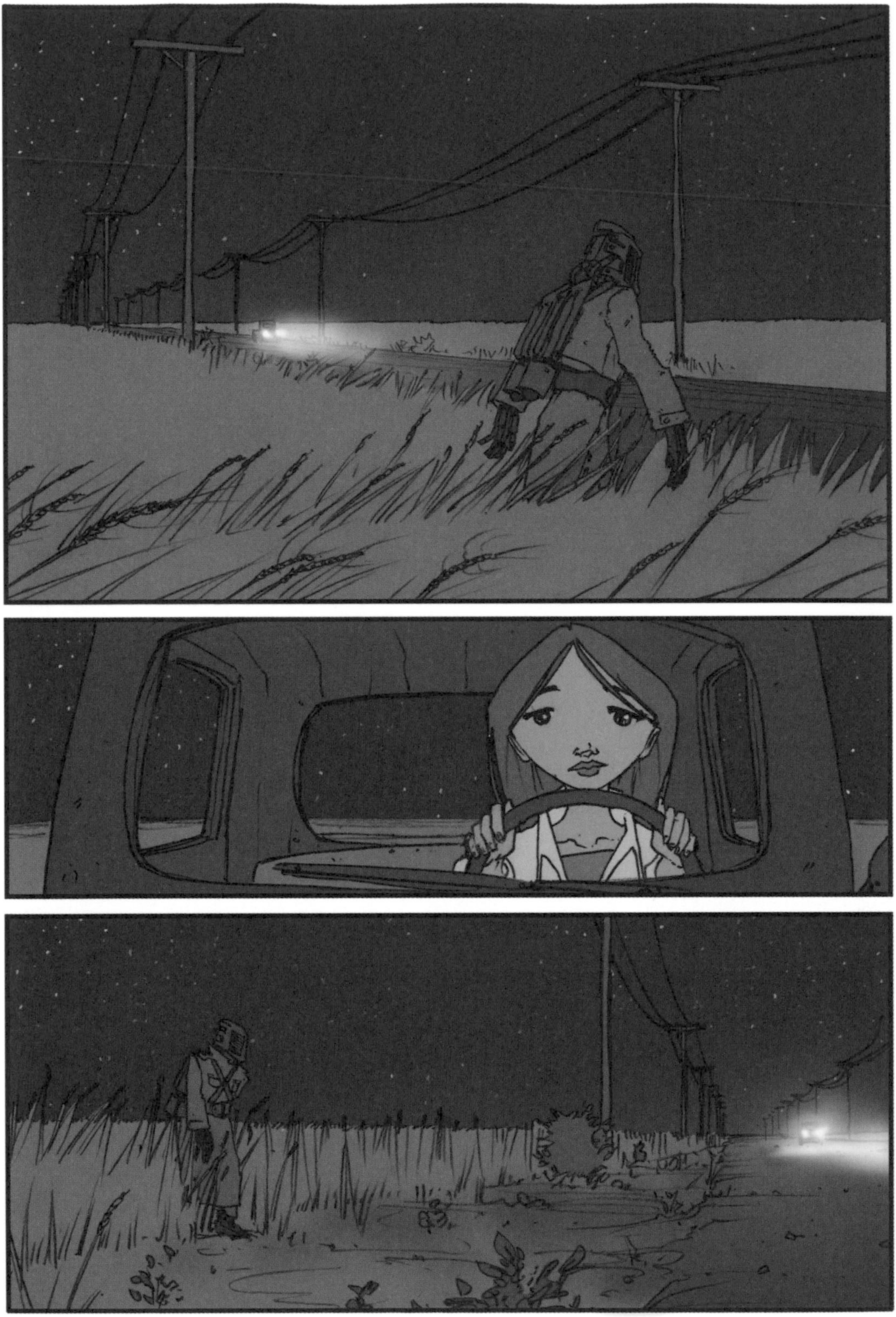

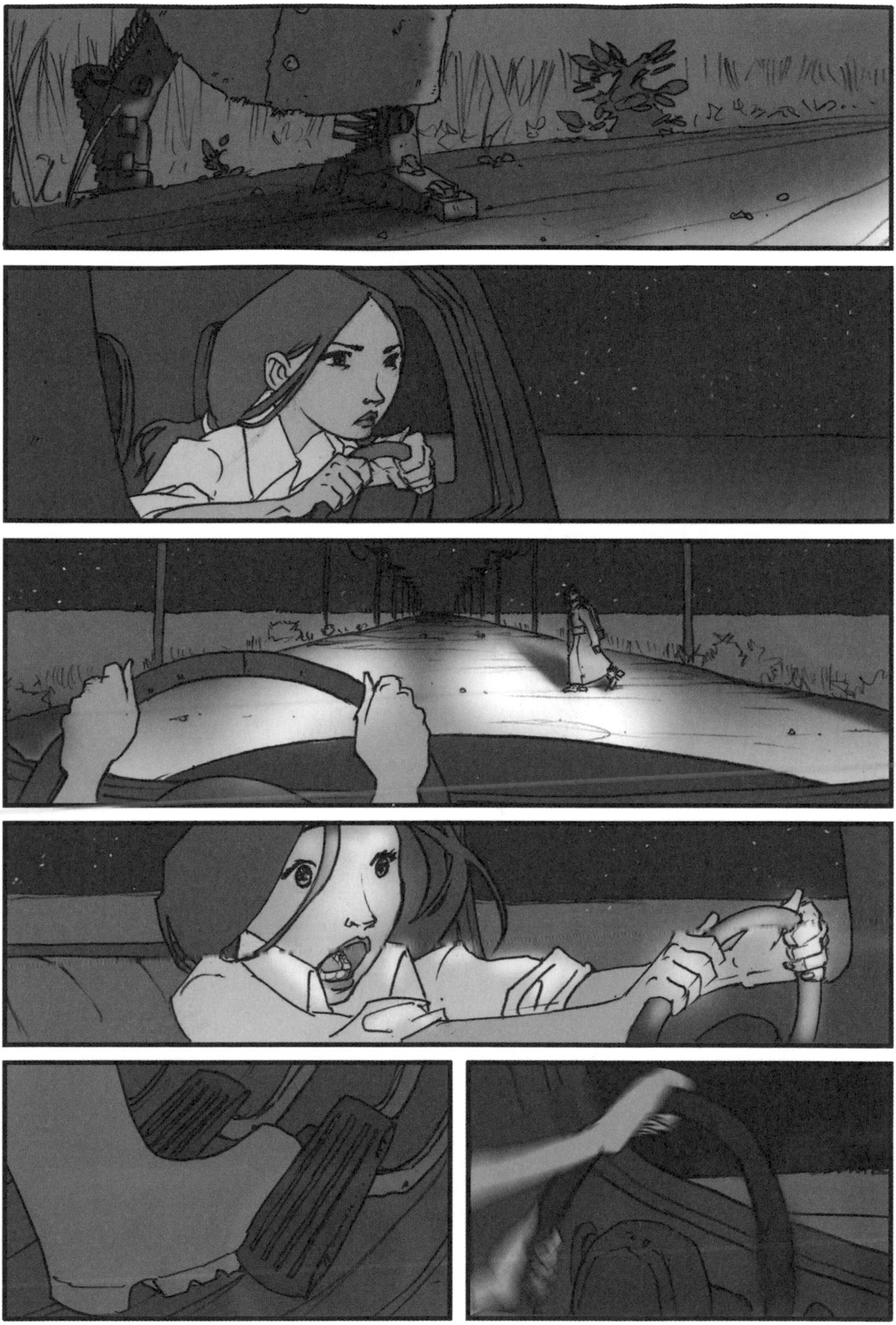

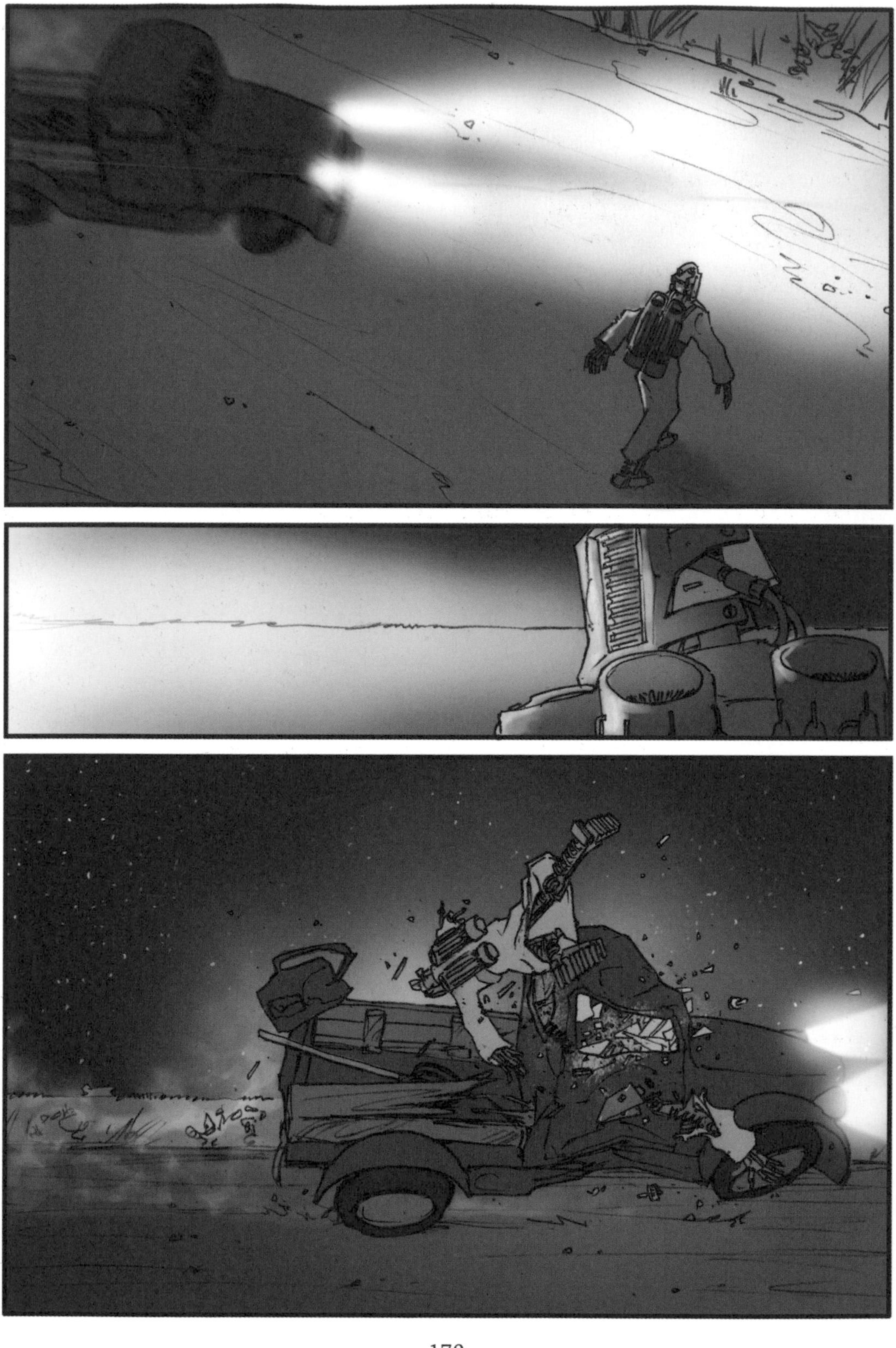

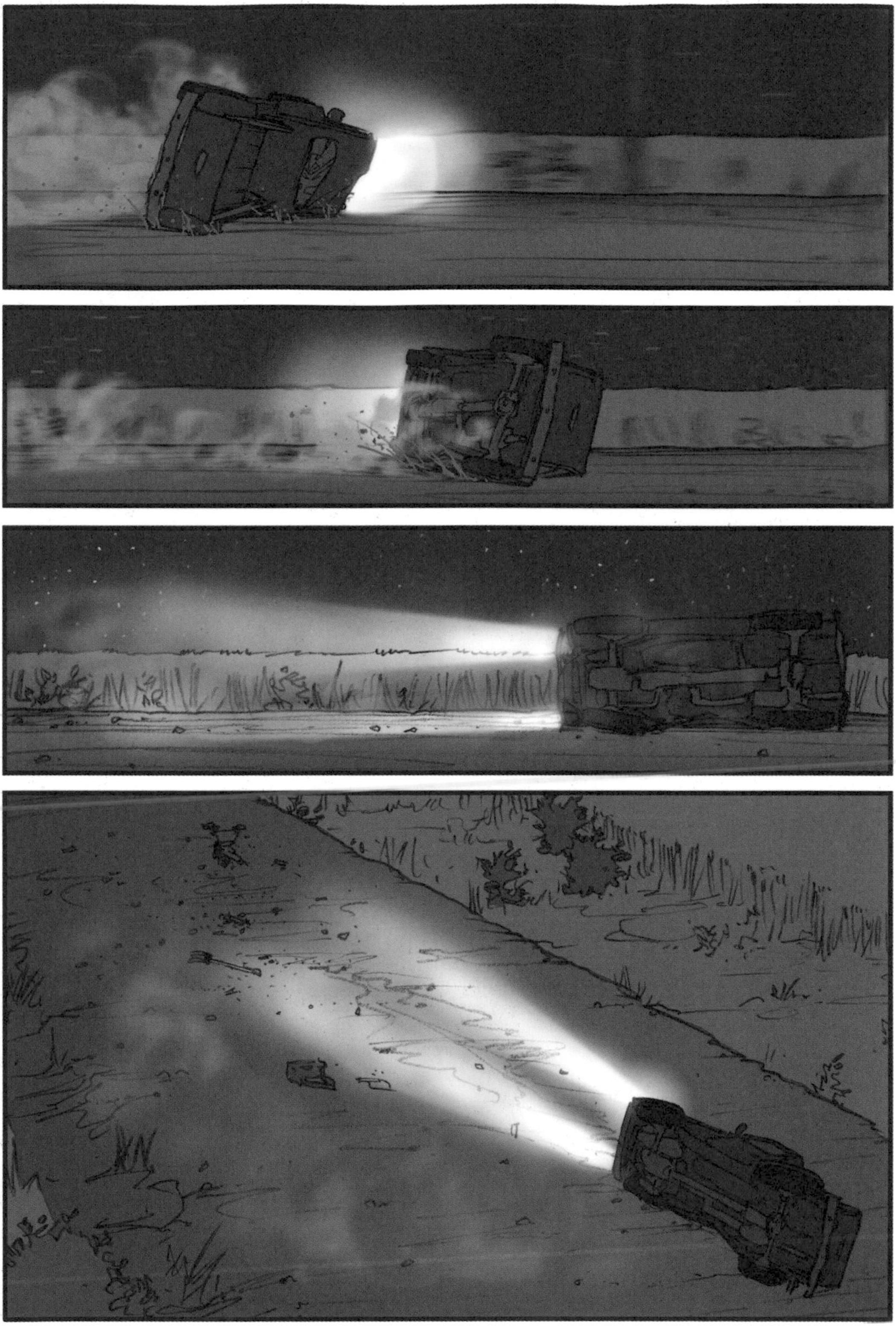

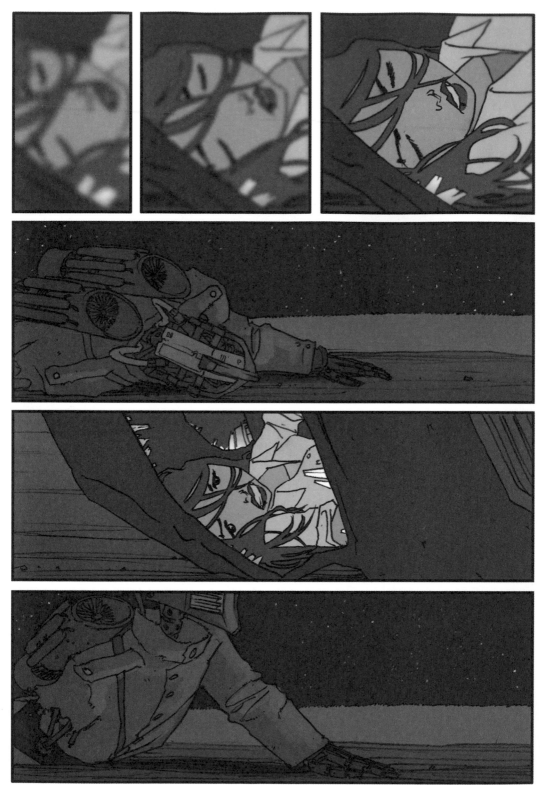

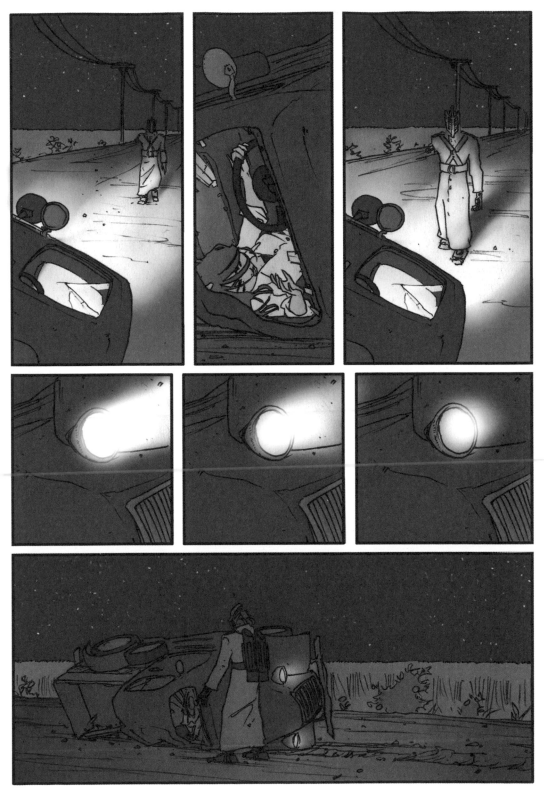

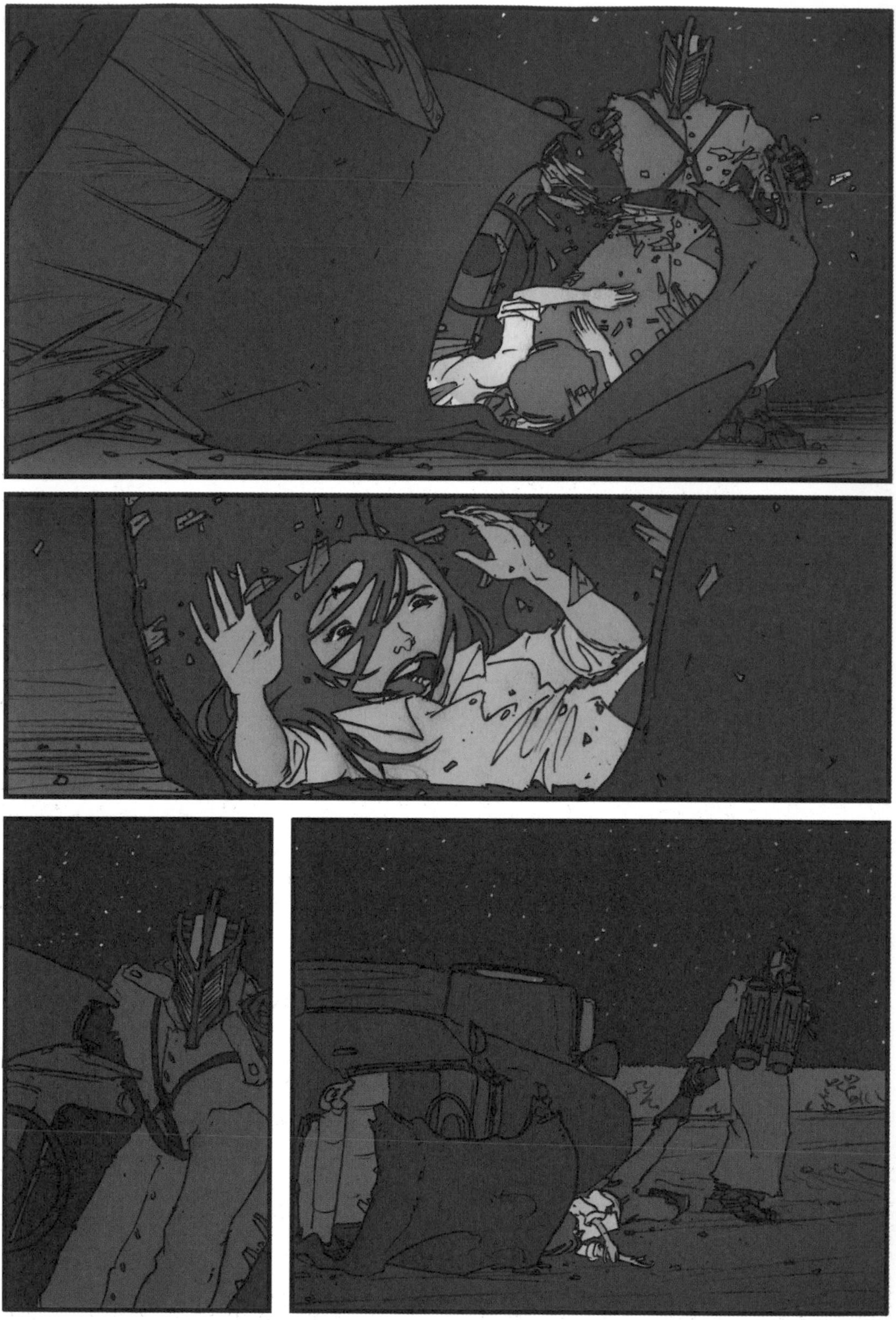

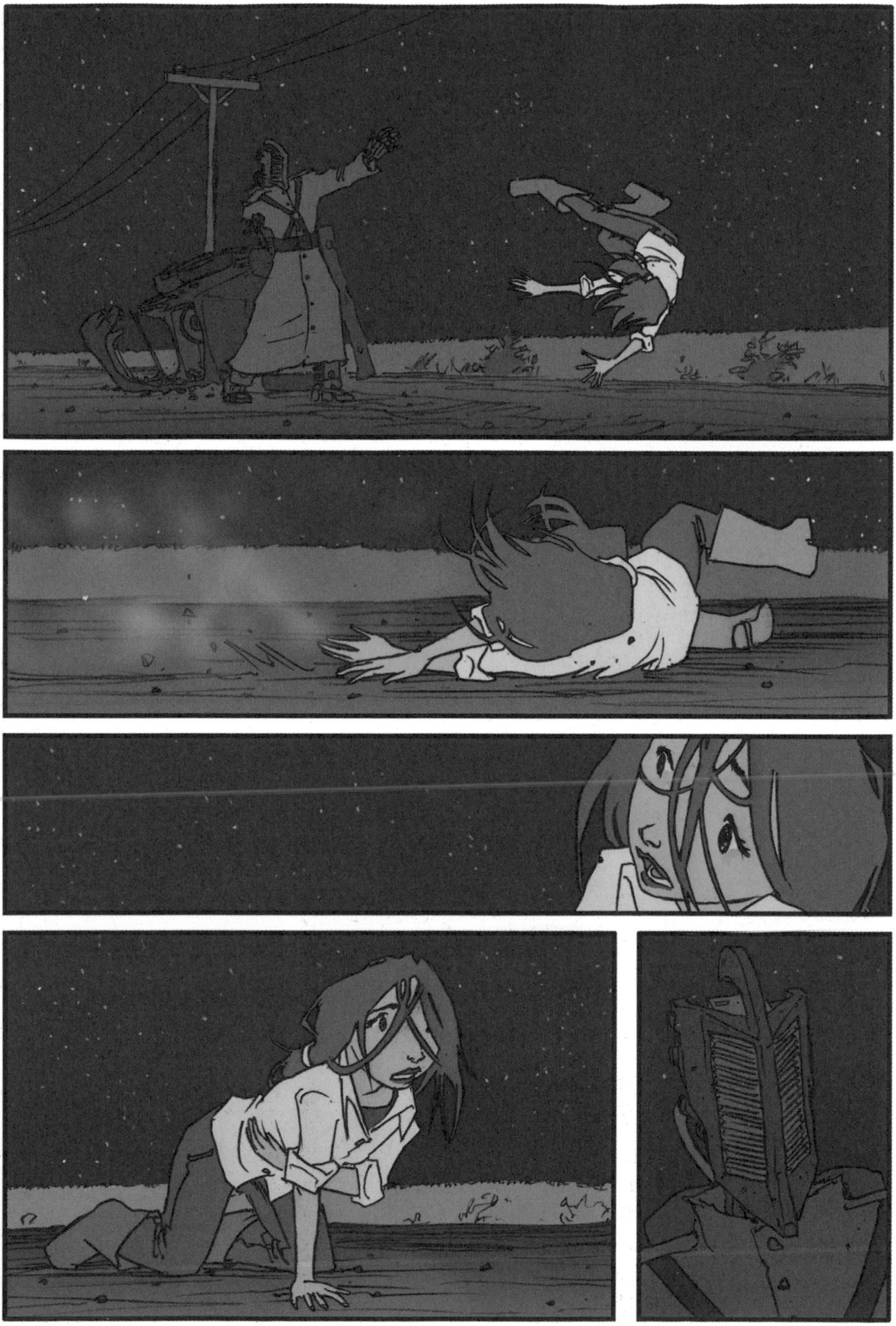

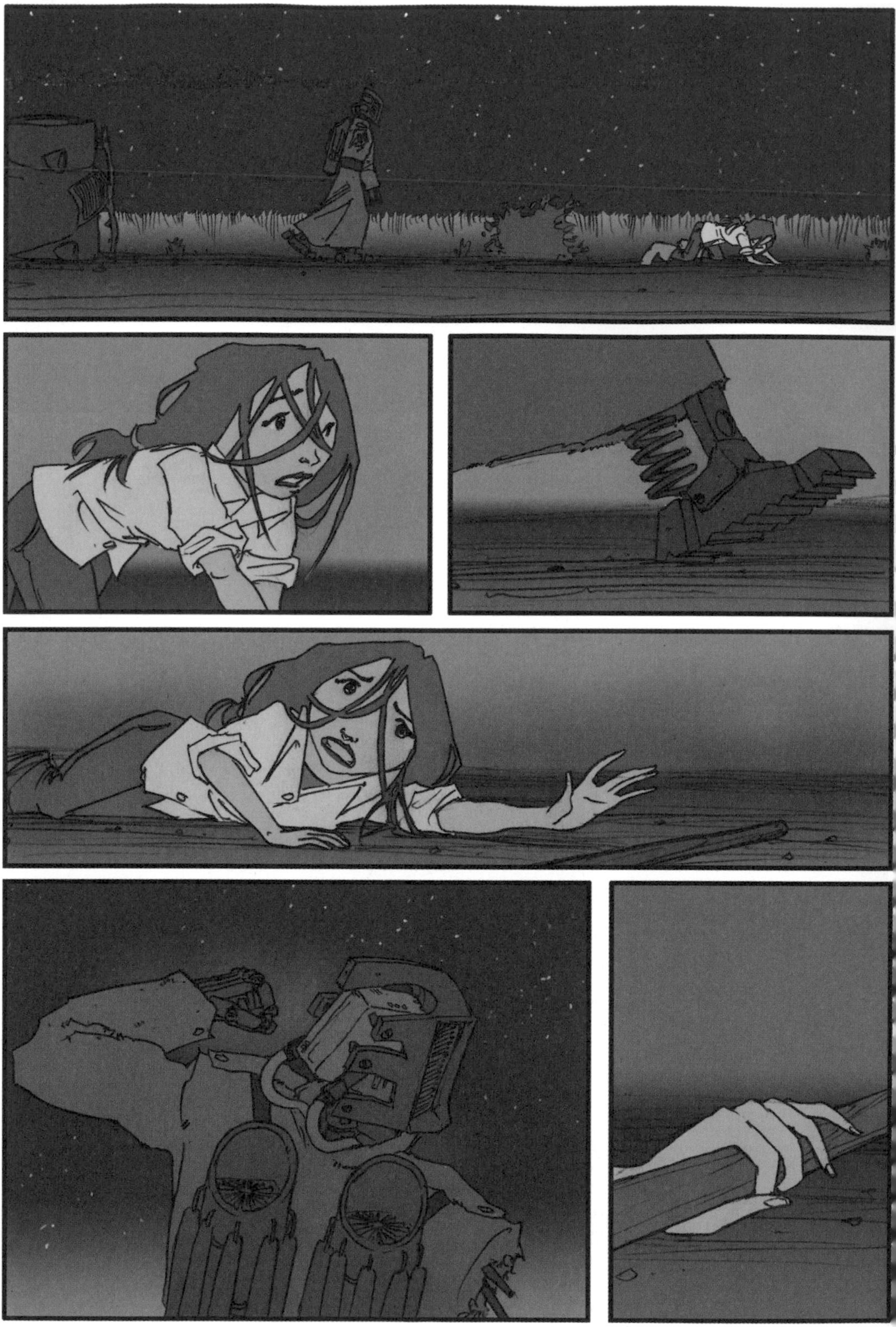

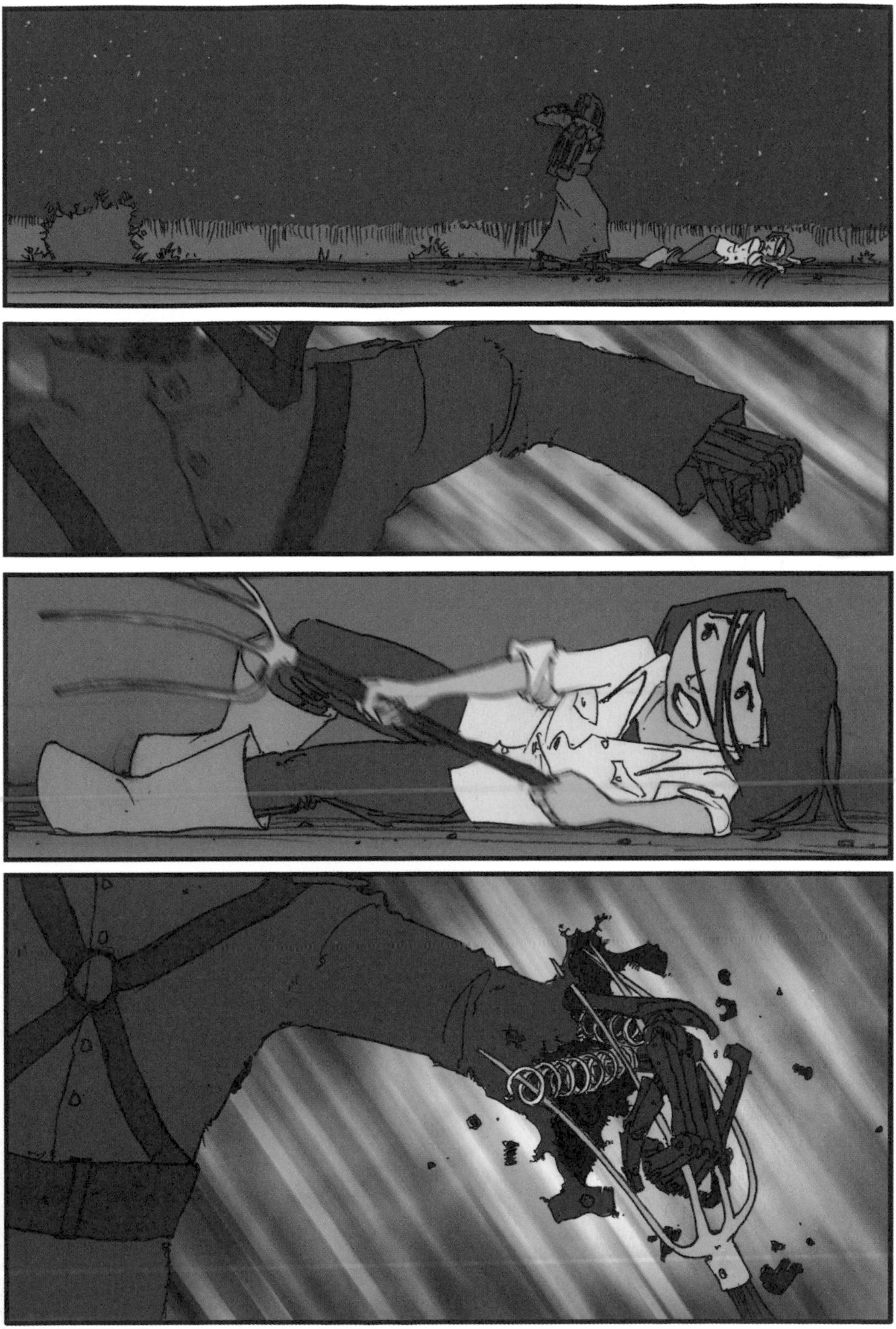

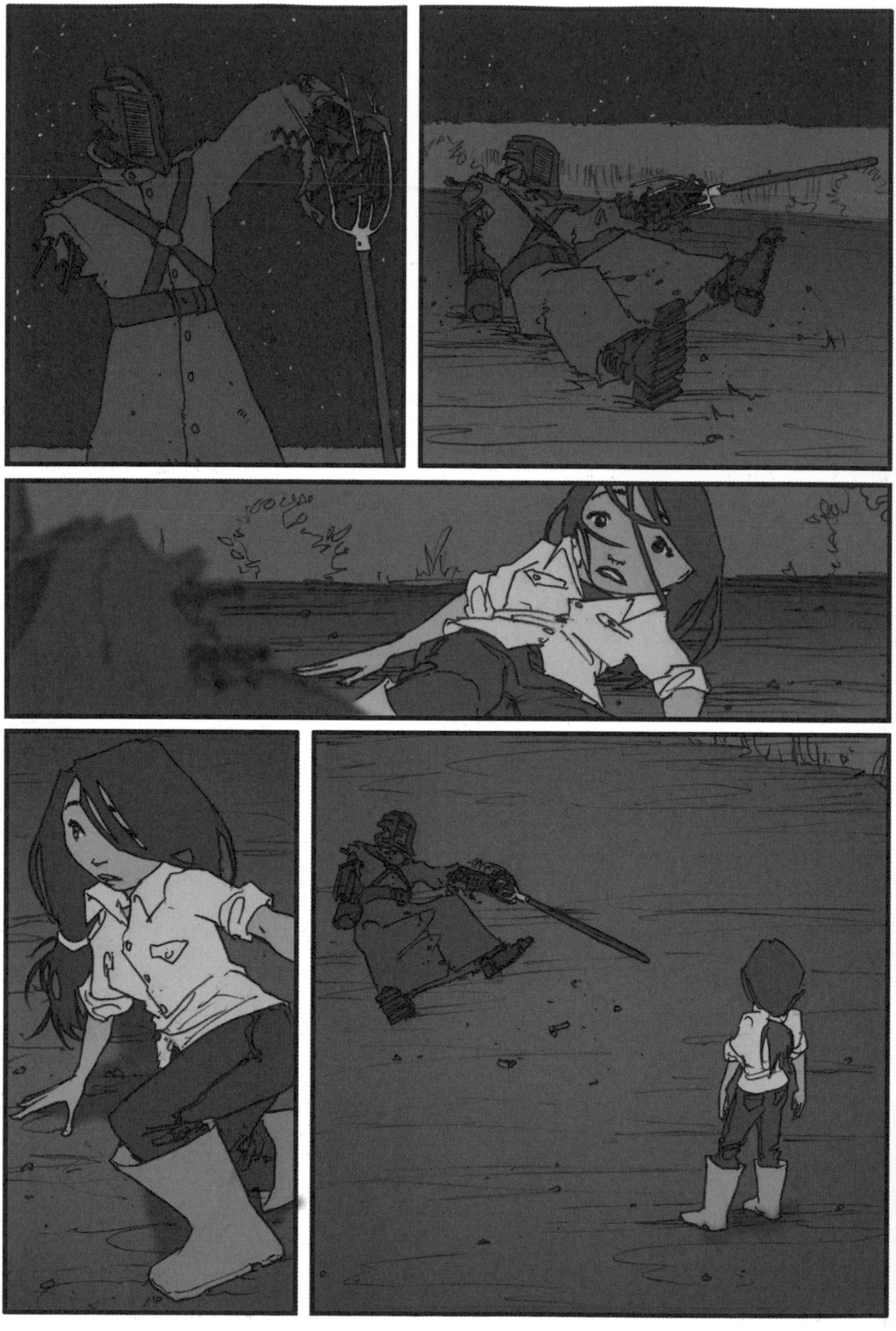

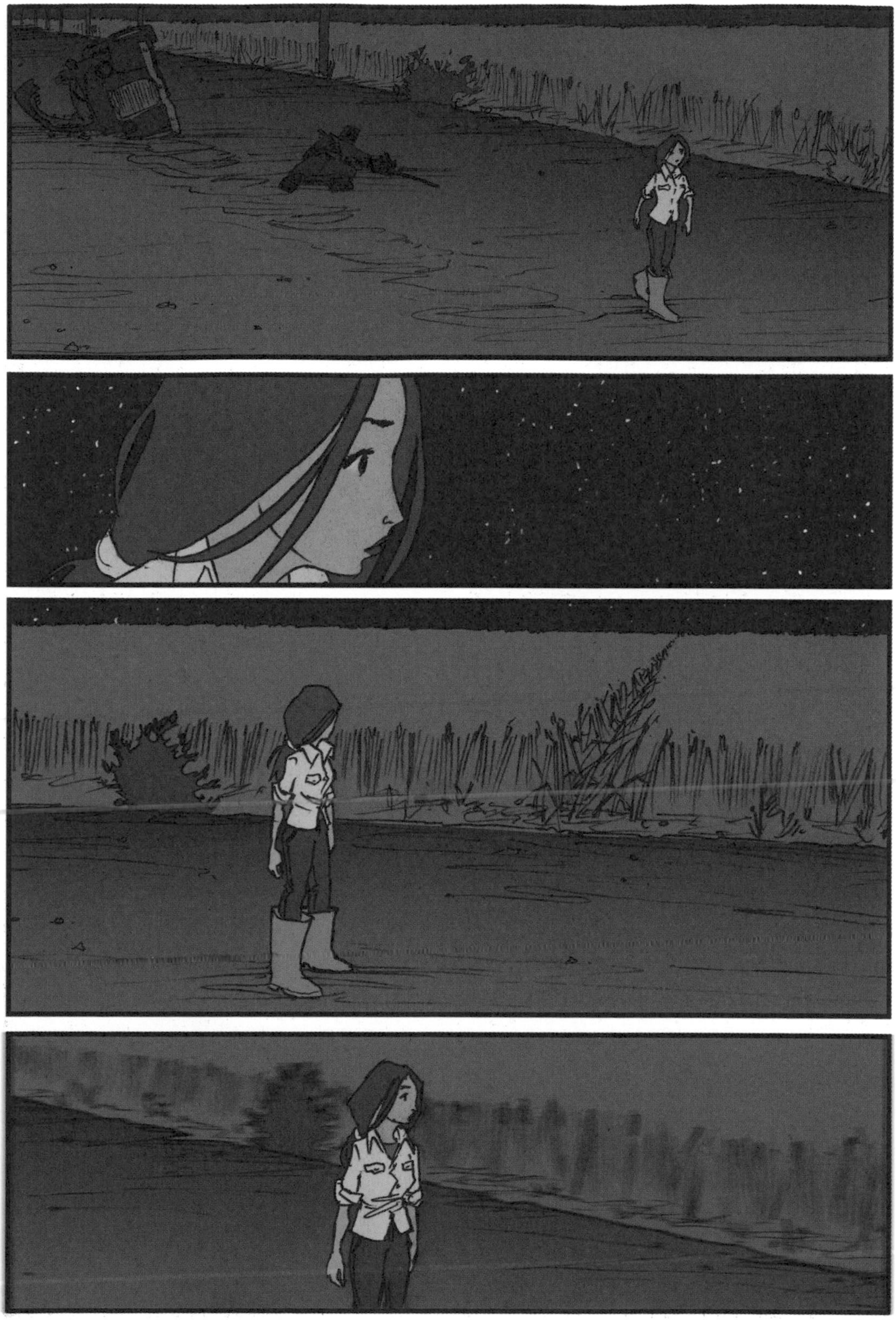

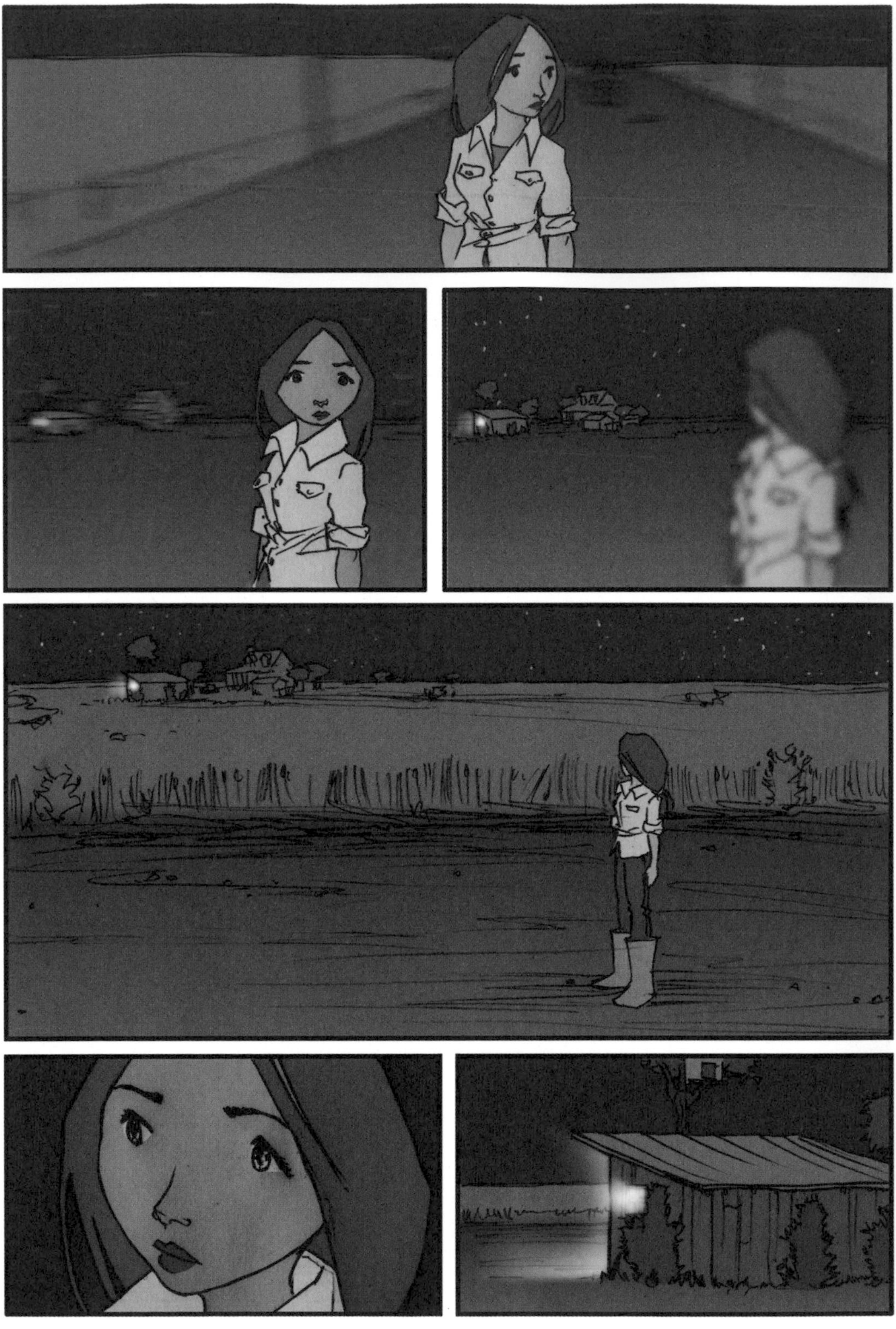

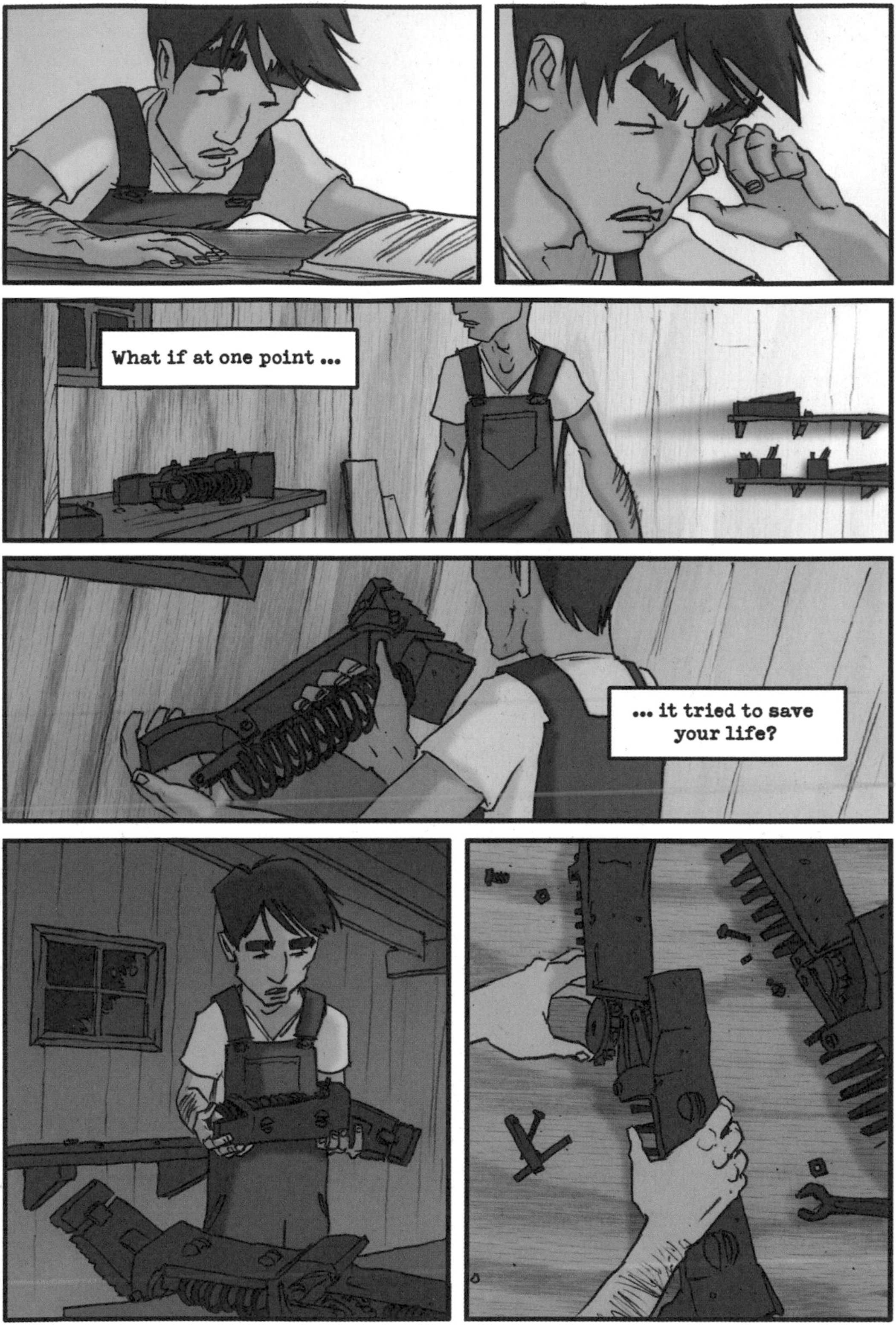
What if at one point ...
... it tried to save your life?

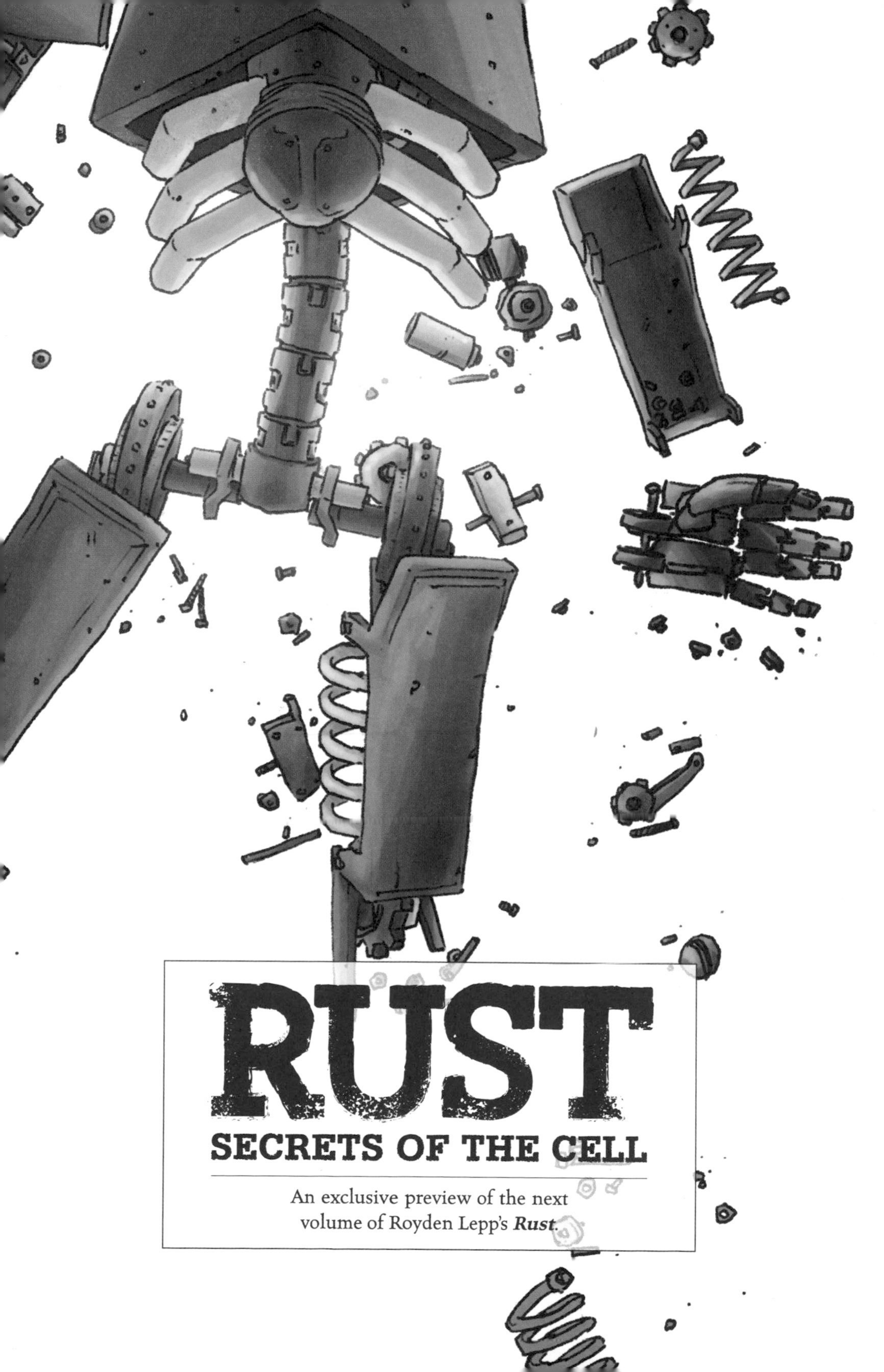

RUST

SECRETS OF THE CELL

An exclusive preview of the next volume of Royden Lepp's ***Rust***.

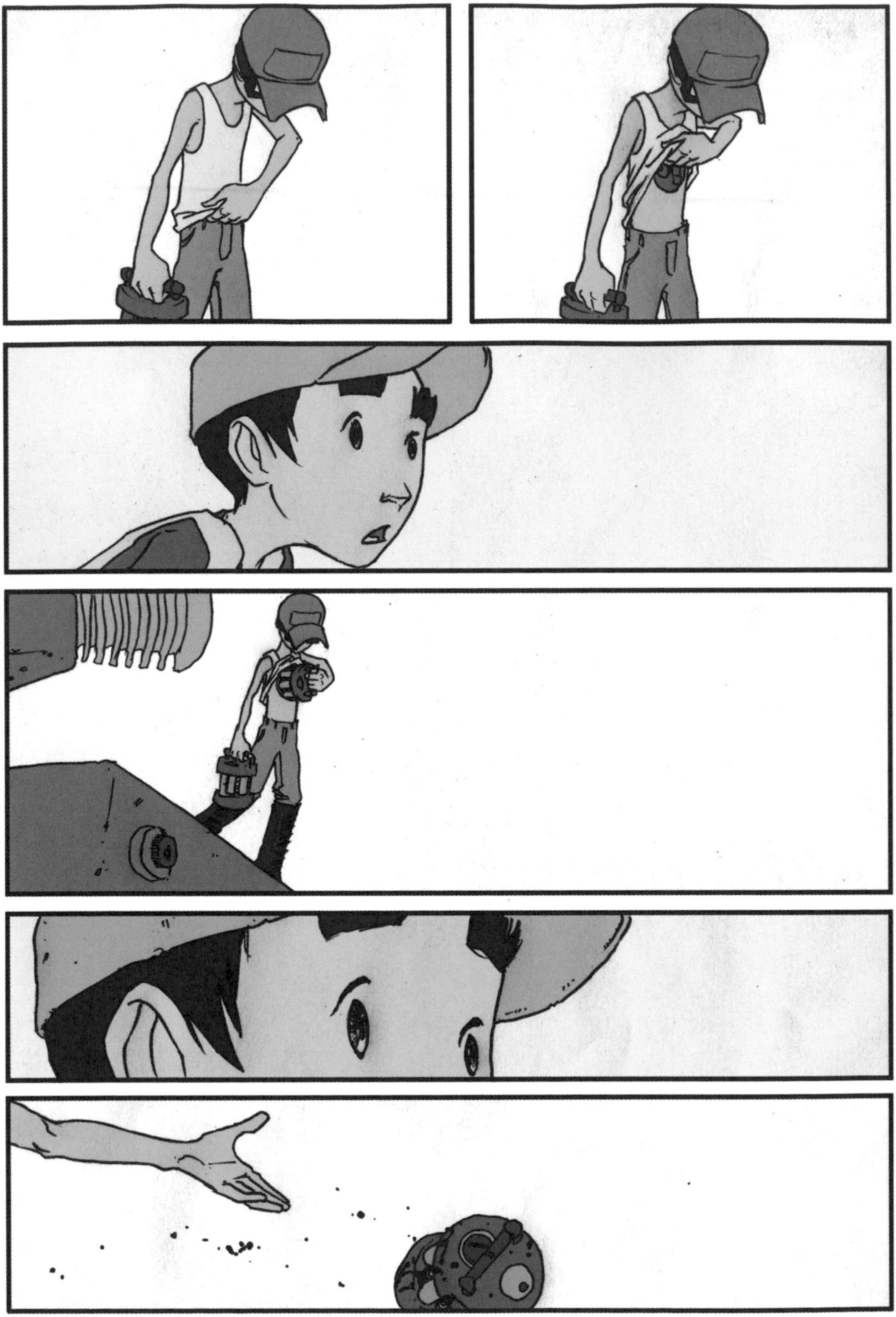

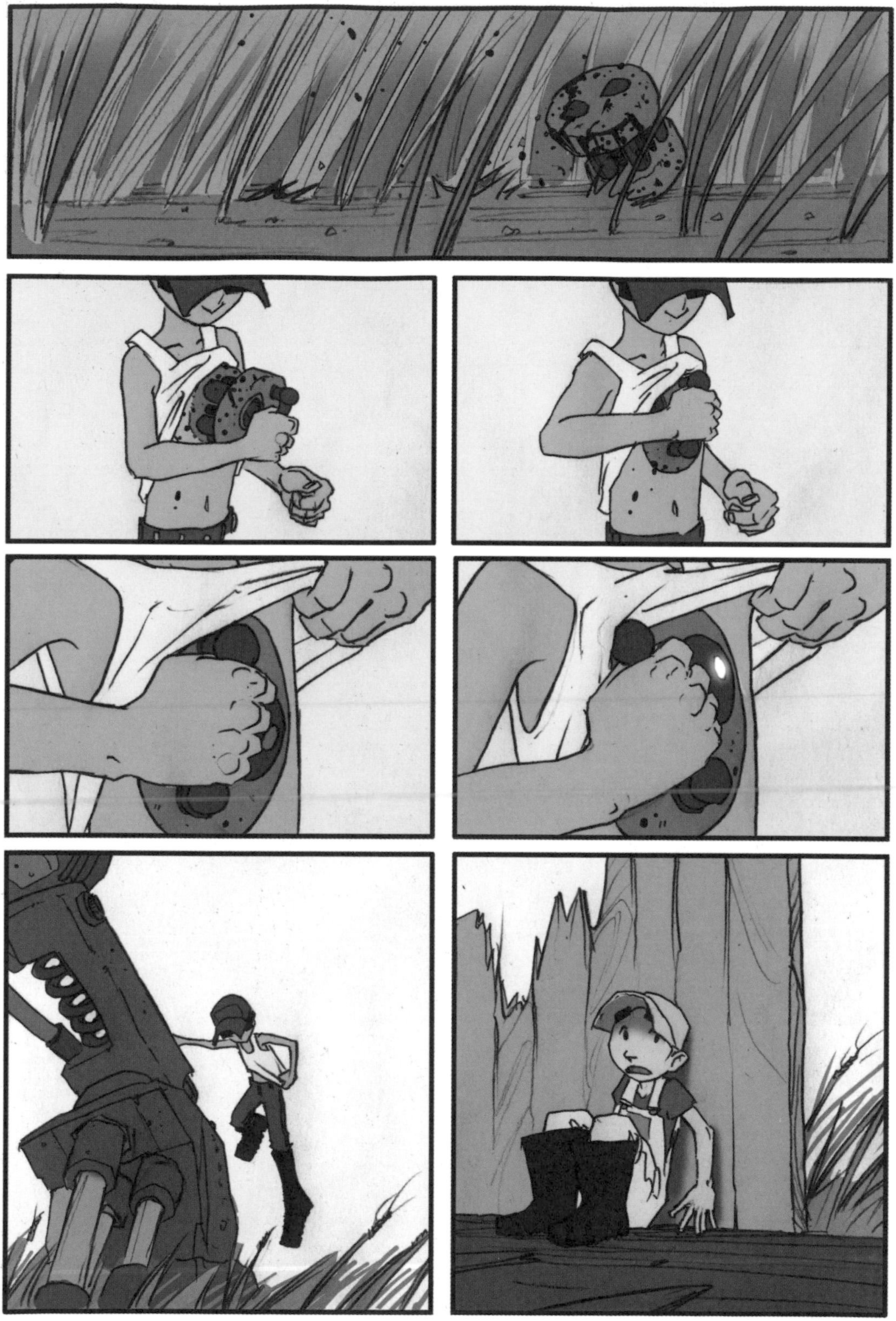

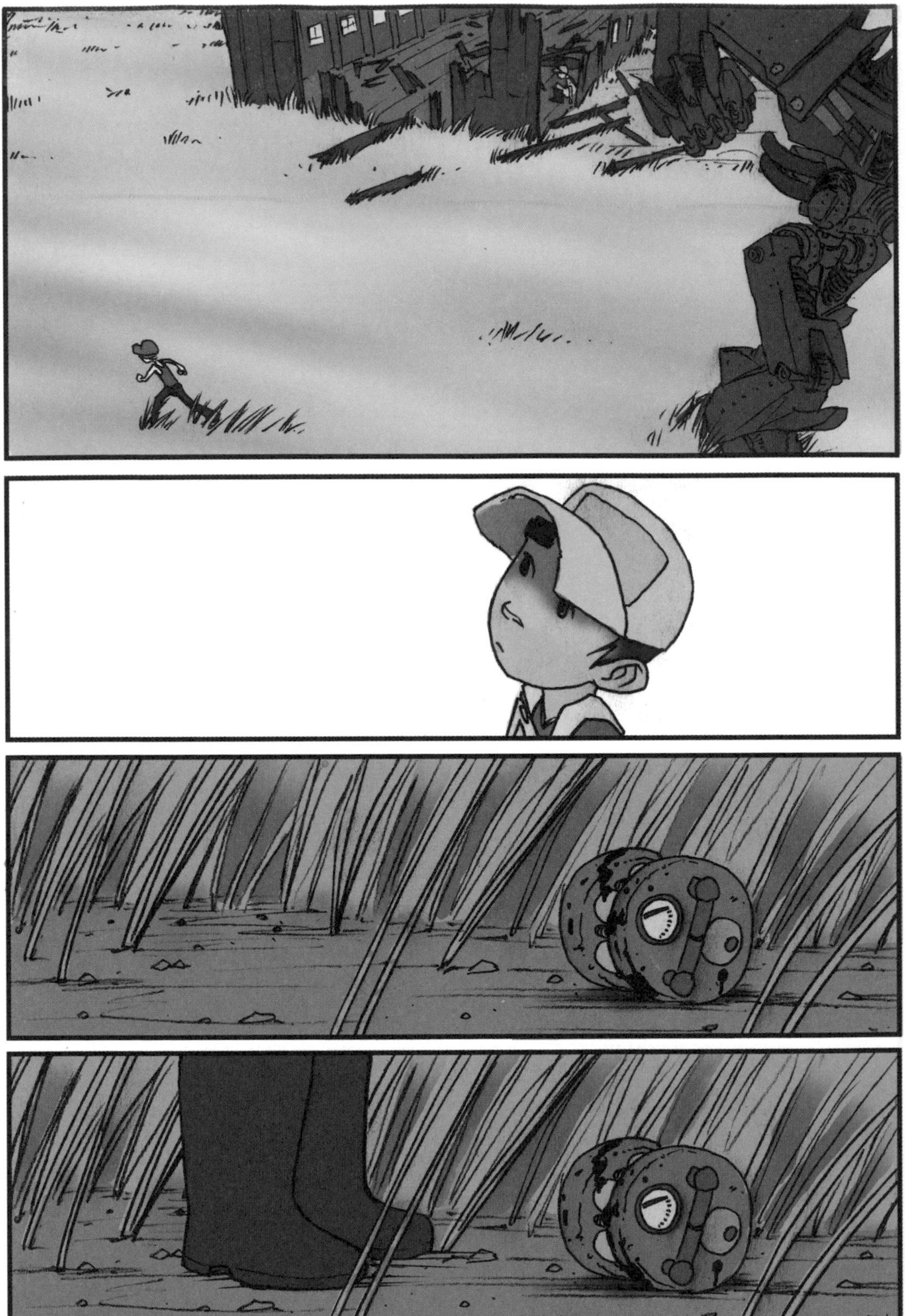

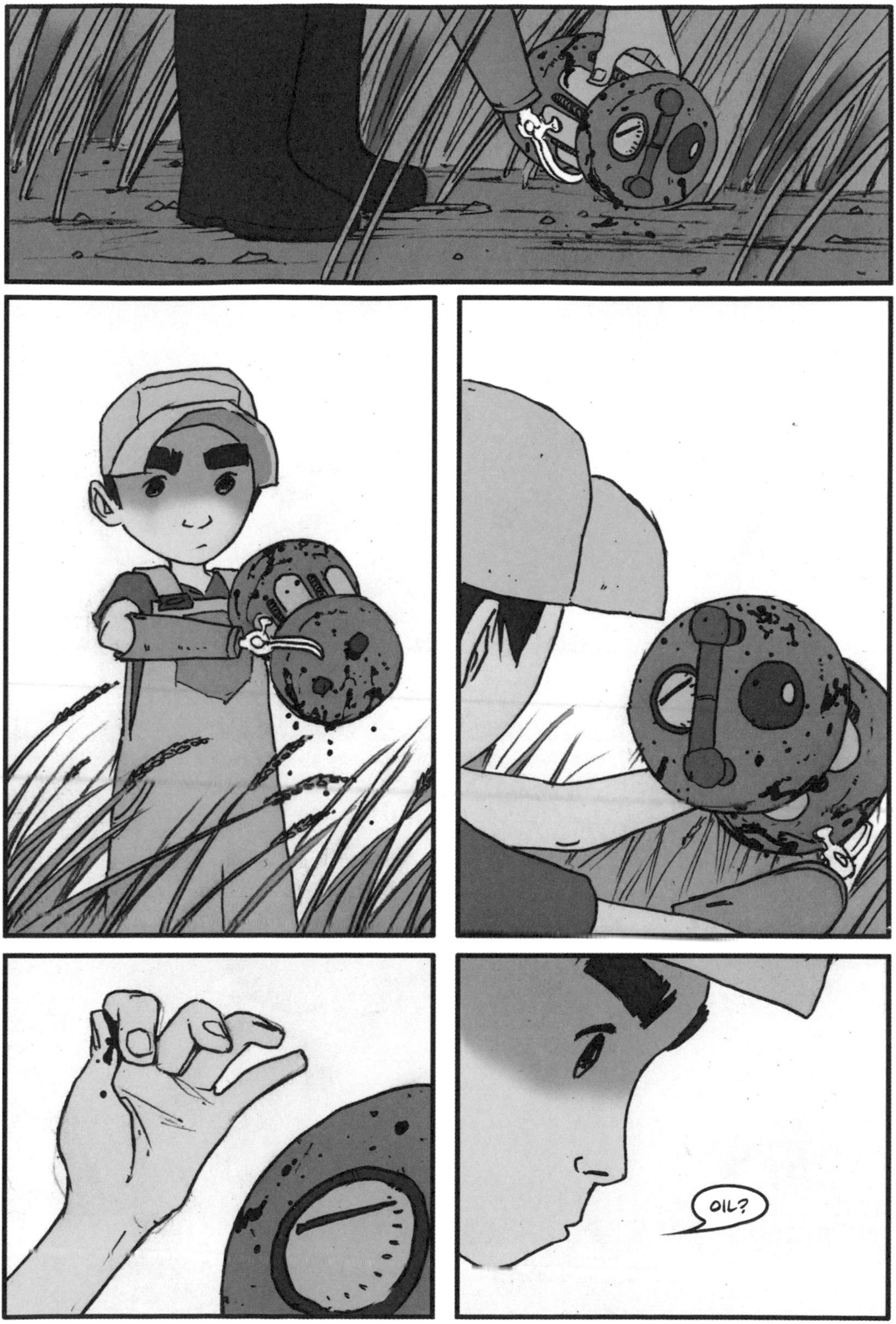
OIL?

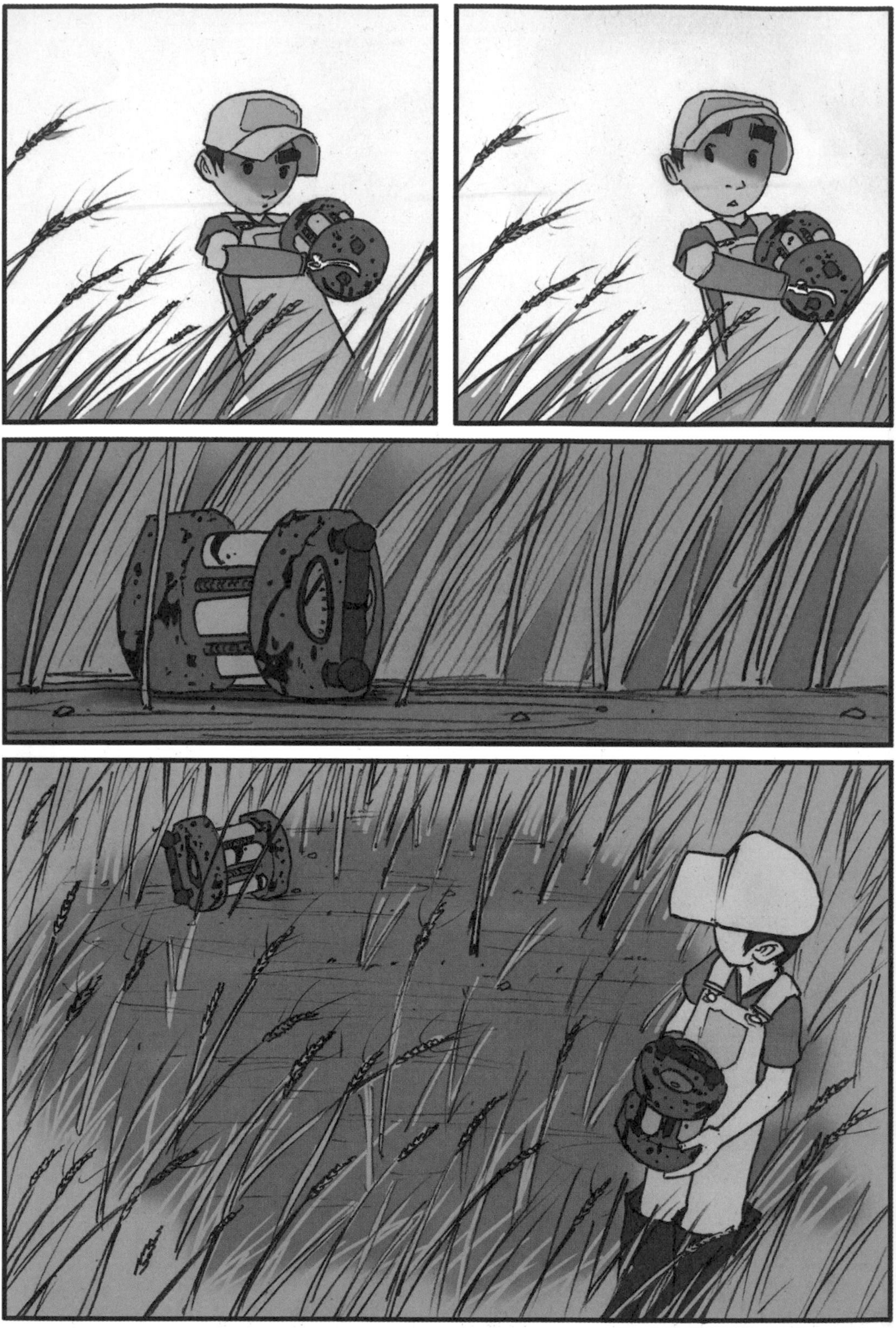

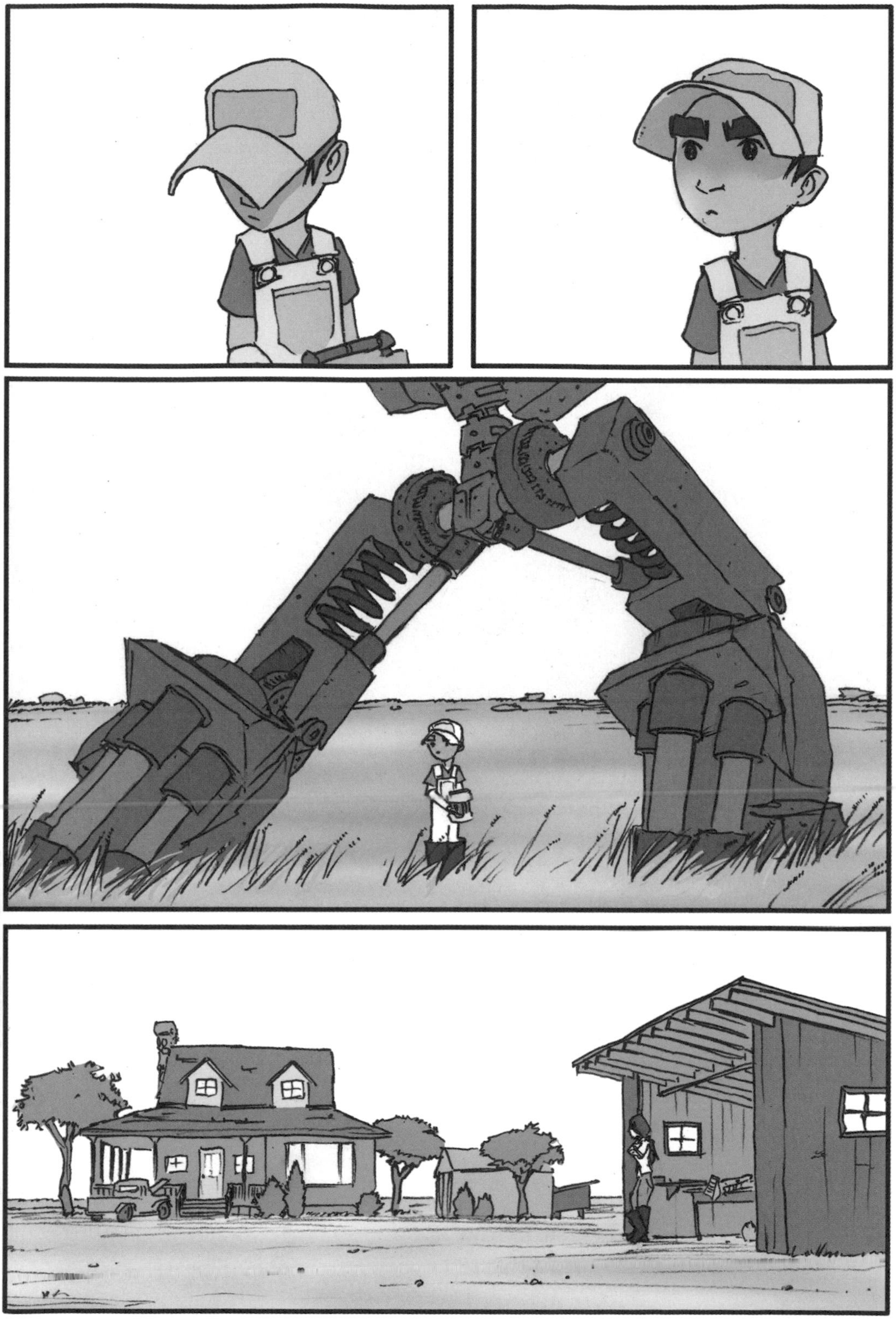

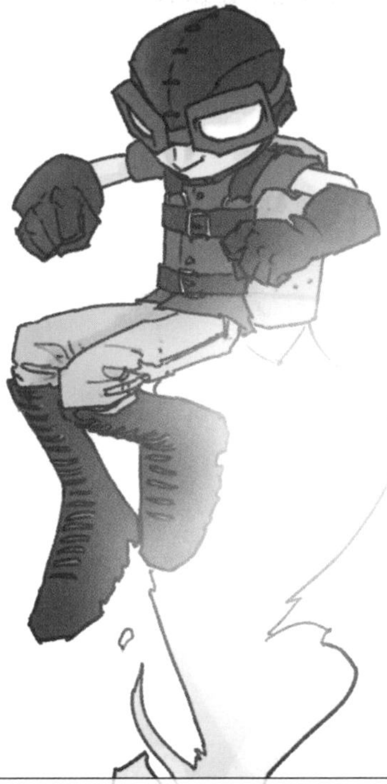

ABOUT THE AUTHOR

Royden Lepp was born and raised on the Canadian prairies. He was kicked out of math class for animating in the corner of a text book, and he failed art class for drawing comics instead of following the class curriculum. He now draws comics and works as an animator in the video game industry. Royden resides in the Seattle area with his wife, Ruth.

SPECIAL THANKS

Special thanks to my wife, Ruth, for all her patience;
Bruce Nuffer for believing in this project;
Seth Fishman, Bud Rogers, Kevin Hanna,
Vshane and Rebecca Taylor.

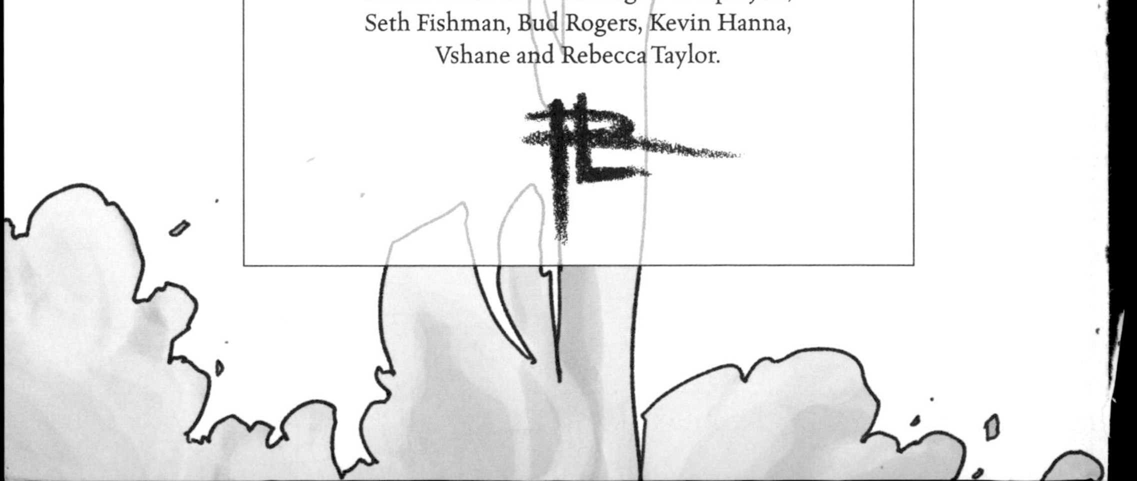

Rebecca Taylor, *Editor*
Scott Newman, *Production Manager*
Fawn Lau, *Logo Design*
VShane & Joanna Estep, *Flatters*

Archaia Entertainment LLC

PJ Bickett, *CEO*
Mark Smylie, *CCO*
Mike Kennedy, *Publisher*
Stephen Christy, *Editor-in-Chief*

Published by **Archaia**

Archaia Entertainment LLC
1680 Vine Street, Suite 912
Los Angeles, California, 90028, USA
www.archaia.com

ARCHAIA™
NEW STORIES. NEW WORLDS.

RUST: VISITOR IN THE FIELD. August 2011. FIRST PRINTING

10 9 8 7 6 5 4 3 2 1

ISBN: 1-936393-27-1

ISBN 13: 978-1-936393-27-5

RUST is TM and © 2011 by Royden Lepp. All Rights Reserved. Archaia™
and the Archaia Logo™ are TM 2011 Archaia Entertainment LLC. All Rights
Reserved. No unauthorized reproductions permitted, except for review
purposes. Any similarity to persons alive or dead is purely coincidental.

Printed in Korea.

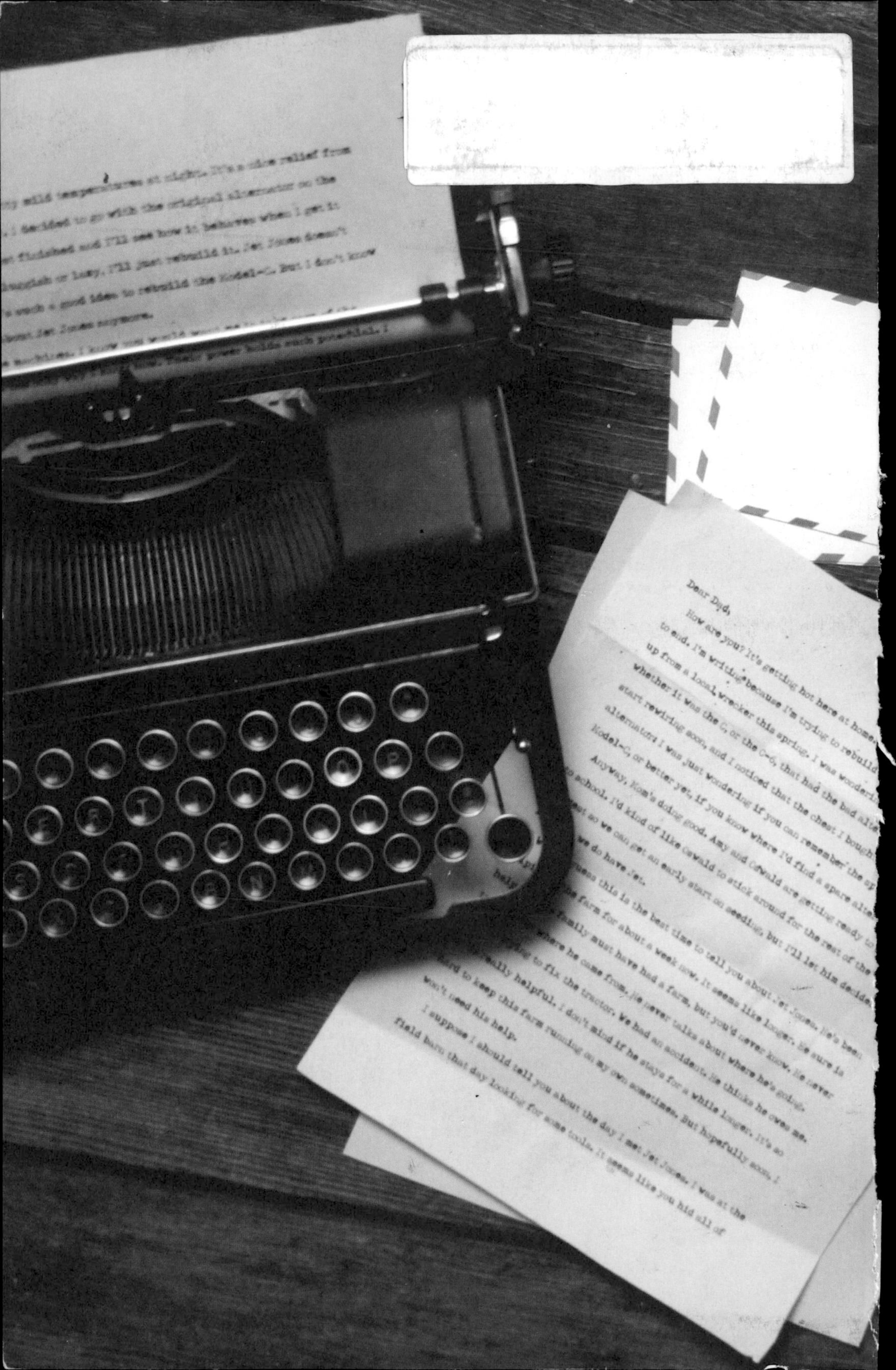
Dear Dad,
How are you? It's getting hot here at home.
I suppose I should tell you about the day I met Jet Jones. I was at the
field barn that day looking for some tools. It seems like you hid all of